"*Pand*

This time she obeyed. "I desire you."

He nodded and kissed her again, deeply, passionately, savoring the smell of her, the taste of her.

His strong hands roamed over, down her neck to the creamy swell of her breasts to her waist and down her thighs over the silk of her heavy skirts, then back up to her face. She sighed and trembled, both at once, hardly knowing whether to fear or urge on what was to come.

He plunged his hands into her hair, sending a shower of pins down to the ground and her hair tumbling across white shoulders.

"And to think I was never partial to blondes," he said.

Marianna staged a feeble protest to this.

One strong hand kept her pinned against the tree, while the other hand caught up her skirts and petticoats.

"It occurs to me belatedly. . ." he began.

She murmured something, too intoxicated with his prolonged touch to speak.

"It's your skirts," he breathed in her ear. "I want them off."

*　　　*　　　*

Also by Julie Tetel

For Love of Lord Roland
The Viking's Bride

Published by
POPULAR LIBRARY

Tangled Dreams

Julie Tetel

POPULAR LIBRARY

An Imprint of Warner Books, Inc.

A Warner Communications Company

POPULAR LIBRARY EDITION

Popular Library® and the fanciful P design are registered trademarks
of Warner Books, Inc.

Cover illustration by Max Ginsburg

Popular Library books are published by
Warner Books, Inc.
666 Fifth Avenue
New York, N.Y. 10103

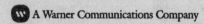 A Warner Communications Company

Printed in the United States of America

First Printing: February, 1989

10 9 8 7 6 5 4 3 2

I

An Unexpected Proposal

Marianna Lowth had been used to thinking of her life as an open book. The pace and plot of her days were set. Her modest role in her brother's household was well established. Her end, she had thought, was predictable from her beginning.

Now, she did not interpret these circumstances as tragic. She saw no use to complain, even less to bruise herself against the narrow limitations imposed by her genteel birth, her family's lack of fortune, and her sex. Certainly she was not the first woman on earth, nor would she be the last, to suffer such a fate.

So, Marianna accepted her lot. She accepted it, yet was not satisfied with it; and if she did not have it within her power to defeat the doom of the predictable, she was at least determined to ensure for herself, within her given confines, a measure of personal happiness.

But on the day that she sat with Anthony Maddox in the vicarage parlor, where the wan winter sun was slanting through the tall, narrow windows and the fire that roared on the hearth was holding at bay the cold desolation of a February day, she learned just how unpredictable life could be. A fine instinct cautioned her that many a foolish woman had traded known limitations for unknown freedoms. A deeper insight, dimly realized, warned her that future happiness might not depend on her will alone.

Although a guest in her home, Anthony Maddox was clearly in control of the proceedings from the very beginning. He stood at the sideboard. "Miss Lowth?" he asked, his hand poised over the small array of decanters on the sideboard.

"A sherry, if you please," Marianna replied in a cordial manner, adding belatedly, "my lord."

Maddox smiled faintly at that. "Yes, the title is new to me, as well," he said.

He poured out two glasses of sherry. A large, muscular man, he cramped the small room. Although he was not what the world would call handsome, Anthony Maddox, the new Lord Westleigh, was certainly worthy of a second look. In addition to his sheer size and powerful presence, his face made a striking landscape: strong nose, jutting jaw, and luminous deep-set eyes of gray-green. He approached the fire, where Marianna was standing, with an unhurried deliberation that had its own particular grace.

Handing her the glass, he invited her to sit down with a nod of his head. "A new title, a new position," he remarked. "It will take time to adjust." His voice, despite his build, was light, with hidden melodies.

"Oh, yes, for it happened so suddenly!" she said, disposing herself opposite him in a wing chair next to the fire. "Well, not so suddenly, as we all know," she amended. "But one is never entirely prepared when the end comes, even though it is expected." She drew a quick breath and offered her condolences without delay. "I . . . we . . . are in deepest sympathy with the Maddox family. Your Uncle Edward was much adored here and shall be sorely missed! But, of course, you gathered how well he was loved from the large gathering at his funeral and the outpouring of emotion."

"Yes, I noticed—which will only make it that much

harder for the village to accept me in Uncle Edward's role," Maddox commented. "Especially since I rarely visited Stanthorpe."

"Or," she countered, smiling easily, "your absence in the past might make it that much easier for everyone to accept you now as the new lord and master, since we do not know you well as Mr. Maddox. And, to tell you the truth, the villagers are so very devoted to the Maddox family that I am sure they will make every effort to help you feel immediately at home in your new role."

"Prettily said, Miss Lowth," Maddox replied with a slight bow of his head. "And is that why you granted me the indulgence of this private interview on such short notice?"

Marianna caught his faintly sardonic tone. She chose to ignore it and smiled again. "I can imagine that you have been horribly busy this week past with all the details of the succession, so please do not consider it an indulgence on my part to receive you at any moment you have to spare for me!"

"Obliging!" he said. "Then I need not excuse myself for the peremptoriness of my note this morning."

"I didn't regard it; I was only too happy that you wanted to speak with me! And, in any case, my lord, it would not be necessary for you to excuse yourself, since I know why you have come."

"Do you, Miss Lowth?" he said.

This time she could not ignore the strange, almost ominous note in his voice. She looked over at him directly and was disconcerted by what she saw in the depths of his eyes. She had had no qualms before his arrival at the vicarage only minutes ago, but she felt a nervous tremor now, one wholly alien to her character. She firmly suppressed it.

"I thought that you had come because of my relationship with your uncle," she replied. Upon seeing the quirk in his brow, she added hastily, "Have I misunderstood your intention? Since I was the last one to speak with Lord Edward, that is, since I suppose you know that I was with him

the afternoon of the day . . . the day his heart failed him, I
thought that you would naturally want . . ."

"You were with him on his last afternoon?"

"Why, yes," she replied, a little surprised. "I thought
you must have known that."

Maddox paused, apparently searching his memory.
Then, in a way that indicated he did not give the matter
much importance, he said, "Perhaps."

"Did you not request to see me in order to talk with the
last person to have spoken with your uncle?" she asked.
"Oh, I don't mean his retainers, or anyone like that, but the
last person to really talk with him; the one who would
know what was on your uncle's mind in his final hours."

"And for that I would require a private interview with
you?" he asked.

Marianna had indeed wondered, upon receiving Maddox's note, why he was making the request, but she had
not puzzled over the point at length. "Well, as to that—"

He interrupted her rudely with the blunt words, "I believe you were a kind of companion to my uncle."

She heard the question behind that statement and so was
not offended. It seemed that her first idea had been correct:
he had indeed come to discuss Lord Edward. Her smile
was warm once again. "Not a companion, exactly. Your
uncle and I were—if I may say so—great friends. I admired him enormously, you see, and we were able to discuss almost everything in the world . . ."

At mention of her friendship with Lord Edward, however, a lump formed in her throat. She took a sip from her
glass to ease the sudden ache and swallowed hard. She was
not going to spoil this interview with a maudlin display of
sentiment. She continued calmly, "On that last afternoon,
Lord Edward and I were speaking, in fact, of the turmoil in
France, as we often have done in the past year and a half
since the fall of the Bastille. He was touting Mirabeau's
chances for keeping Louis on the throne. I was arguing
exactly the opposite because of Robespierre's latest tricks,

you know," she explained with animation, "and although his heart had been failing him for some little time, Lord Edward was in rare good spirits that afternoon and made some excellent arguments!"

Marianna felt a slight rebuff when Anthony Maddox did not pursue the topic of Lord Edward's spirits or his political views. Instead he asked, "How long did you know my uncle?"

"Four years," she answered, then amended, "no, almost five years now." Her friendship with Lord Edward dated from her refusal of Timothy Goforth's proposal of marriage. The approaching end of winter would mark five years since she had taken her defiant little stand to determine her own life.

"And have you lived in Stanthorpe your entire life, Miss Lowth?"

She replied that she had lived in the village for only the last eight years. After an infinitesimal silence, she continued, a good bit less warmly than before. "I came to Stanthorpe to live with my brother and sister-in-law when my father died. My brother and his wife, Jeanne, have been here twelve years now." A perverse spirit prompted her to add, since he was so curious, the slightly irrelevant details. "They have two children. My sister-in-law arranges for all the raising of funds at the orphanage. In addition, she keeps the books as a charitable service. My brother spends his free time in improving conditions for the dock workers and fishermen, that is, when he is not ministering to the needs of the tenants on the estate or writing the week's message. I believe that Lord Edward found my brother's sermons unusually inspirational."

His lordship did not comment on this recital of good works. "What do you contribute to community service?"

"I write a monthly column entitled 'Notes from the Countryside' for the *Anglican Mirror*, which, as you may know, is published in Canterbury," she replied, deciding to let him make of that what he wanted.

He made very little of it. "Ah." Then, "Your brother is somewhat older than you."

"Yes, he is. We had different mothers," she explained.

"I see. How old are you, Miss Lowth?"

She had already decided not to simper or blush in his presence, but she had not anticipated a turn in conversation that would make her blanch. "I am three-and-twenty," she said, conscious that the blood was draining from her face.

The sudden change in his expression might have been surprise. He did not reply for a moment but merely regarded her steadily, which did nothing to restore the color to her cheeks. His gray-green eyes, as they rested on her, were unrevealing, and she could not determine the thoughts revolving behind them.

It was just as well, for these were anything but kind. Now, Maddox could see well enough the pleasing physical attributes of the young woman before him. She had blond hair with thick curls she could not quite control; pale, but not dazzling, white skin; eyes of speedwell blue that did not shine but glowed, as if candles were lit behind them; and a straight little nose.

He also could not help but notice her shapely figure. A kerchief of white tulle that fell softly on her shoulders with a flounce enhanced the effect of the neatly fitting bodice of her gown. It crossed in front, flattering her very pretty curves, and tucked at the waist into a full-length apron gathered over a skirt of dove gray. It was a simple country dress, not a London fashion, but she wore it well.

It was generally agreed in the village that what Marianna Lowth lacked in conventional beauty, she more than made up for in allure. Anthony Maddox's opinion of the woman before him was, by contrast, rather brutal. He thought that she had an uncommon measure of gall and more than enough guile to have thoroughly duped his Uncle Edward. In fact, all thoughts of Marianna Lowth this week past had inspired in Maddox an anger beyond reason, but he had come this day for a purpose.

He asked, harshly, "The ages of your brother's children?"

Marianna was taken aback, but she rarely lost her poise, and it did not desert her now. "They are thirteen and nine," she answered evenly. "Two boys. However, I assume that your flattering interest in my family is more than idle curiosity or . . . or the need of a new lord to acquaint himself with his dependents. I am most happy to answer your questions, but you might have asked all this of my brother."

Anthony Maddox stood up and walked to the window. It was fringed outside with thin fingers of ice hanging from the eaves, shining hard and slick in the sun. Marianna's eyes remained on the man while he stood in the pale light and gazed out over the barren wastes of the February landscape.

She approved of his unpowdered brown hair, which was tied back at the nape with a black ribband. His mourning dress was utilitarian rather than elegant. A coat of black superfine stretched across his magnificent shoulders, and his powerful legs showed to advantage in black knee-breeches and white silk stockings. He wore a froth of Lunardi lace at throat and wrist, but his dress was otherwise devoid of the usual accessories of a gentleman's costume: the fob, the cane, the snuffbox in hand.

Marianna wondered if his eyes could twinkle with laughter, but when he turned again to look at her, amusement was not apparent. To her puzzlement, she saw his regard harden with resolve.

"Forgive me, Miss Lowth," he said, with a slight bow and a certain rough charm, but for all of that, there was ice in his manner and in his voice that Marianna did not think had anything to do with the temperature outside. "Indeed I might have asked your brother the very same questions. I shall have to attend to the estate and my dependents before next week, but today I am on a rather different sort of errand."

"On behalf of your uncle, then," she said quickly, and with a kind of premature relief. "I had hoped that he might have left me something, that you had come to carry out some request of his." His penetrating look prompted her to explain herself. "That is, it was rumored that his will was read after the burial last week, and I had thought . . . I had hoped that perhaps he had bequeathed me a favorite book of his, or the brass paperweight on his desk, or some other memento that he desired you to give me . . . ?"

"Modest wishes," he observed.

"I had no claim on your uncle," she replied simply.

The hard look in his eye made her nerves tingle. He did not move away from the window, but held her eyes steady with his.

Then, without further preamble, he announced, "I need a wife. It is true that we hardly know each other, but you are well known and well connected in the neighborhood. While these are not absolute requirements for the future mistress of the Hall, they are a decided advantage in this case. I am here today to extend to you a proposal of marriage."

Stunned surprise held Marianna motionless. She experienced a strange moment, as round and full as the drop of water she saw clinging to the end of a long icicle just outside the window, which, she imagined, held a miniature world mirrored in its minute curve of distortion. So it was, in that brief moment, that her mind caught and held all the images around her. The fire mulled on the hearth. The clock ticked, once, on the mantelpiece. The pale sun slanted down, just so, on the stark, masculine figure at the window. She glanced down at the goblet in her hand. The light from the fire blazed and broke in its crystal facets and caught the gleam of the amber splash. The moment passed, and the drop fell from the tip of the icicle to be absorbed in the puddle below.

"When I first met you at the door today," he was continuing, "I thought you somewhat younger, thus making my errand a possibly useless one. My initial impression was that my thirty-three years would make a poor match for your eighteen. I am satisfied, however, with only ten years between us, that age need not be a bar."

Marianna looked over at him, her composed features

hiding entirely her speechless astonishment. She would have been rather more astonished, astounded even, had she known how Anthony Maddox interpreted her outward calm. However, he did not wear his thoughts on his face any more than did Marianna, and so she could not guess what was in his mind.

After a pause, he added, "It may interest you to know that I admired Doctor Lowth's writings."

"You knew my father?" she asked, finding her voice.

"Only his essays."

Which was, she supposed, his way of saying that her birth and background were good enough. To another man under different circumstances, Marianna would have made a light, teasing remark to the effect that acquaintance with Doctor Lowth's writings saved even the most well-dressed gentleman from frippery. For the moment, all raillery was swept aside.

She asked, forthrightly, "Why do you need a wife?"

"A ward, a young girl, has recently come into my charge," he answered without hesitation. "As a bachelor, I am not capable of properly seeing to her protection or to her introduction to Society."

"How old is she?" Marianna asked.

"Seventeen," he replied.

"What is she like?"

"Like any other girl of seventeen, I suppose."

"Is she well dowered?" Marianna asked, seeking rather more information.

"Modestly. I intend, of course, to provide her with something."

"Then your need for a wife," she said slowly, "is most probably for the short term, is it not? You might well marry her off before the summer is over. By next year at the latest, I would think. Can you not as easily hire a companion for her, as find a wife for yourself?"

He paused. The hard, inscrutable look in his eyes set her nerves to tingling again. "As you have said, one is never entirely prepared for change, even when it is not unexpected. Maddox Hall is a large estate, one which needs more time and attention than I have to give it. I find myself unprepared at present to undertake the new responsibilities alone."

A slight frown puckered Marianna's brow. "Shall your wife be required to reside at Maddox Hall?"

"Required?" he repeated with an inflection of distaste. "No. Her place of residence shall be as she desires. My own estate is inland, in Northampton. I also keep a house on Cavendish Square."

He evidently did not care where his wife resided. She looked up at him. "Since you knew of my father, you might also know that I grew up on the Continent, first in Munich and then in Milan, where my father died." This was naturally not the moment to disclose that when Dr. Lowth had left this world for the next, he had hardly enough money to cover his daughter's passage back to England. "Although I was very young at the time and did not circulate in Society," she went on, "I am more accustomed to city life than country life. I have not been unhappy in Stanthorpe, but if I had a choice, I would prefer London."

"As you wish," he said with a bow. "And with your background, I am sure that you would do well in a style of social interaction that must be very different from the ways of the village."

His words were polite, but Marianna suspected him of sarcasm. She said the first thing that came to mind. "That is taking quite a lot on faith, is it not, my lord?"

"I also put great faith in my uncle's opinion of you. You would not have had the social relationship you did with him if you had not had something to recommend yourself."

His tone did not suggest that he was paying her a compliment. Before she could check herself, she replied, "Just as I am to accept your proposal on the strength of your family relationship to Lord Edward?"

Green glints flashed in Anthony Maddox's eyes, but

since he had shifted his gaze out the window just then, Marianna did not catch them. When he turned toward her, his face was impassive. "Am I to plead my case, then? Very well," he said, with another bow, but this one held a hint of mockery. "I do not wish to give you pain, Miss Lowth, but your position as a dependent in a household with children cannot be comfortable. I imagine that you have been, over the years, an unpaid nurse and governess."

"I am very devoted to my nephews," Marianna said with dignity. "They treat me with respect and a good deal of affection. I do not complain for having their care."

"Your feelings do you credit," he said. "However, boys of their ages will soon be entirely in the care of tutors, in which case, you may become something of a convenient maid."

Marianna flushed at the accuracy of his assessment. Her heightened color was very becoming, but Anthony Maddox was in no mood to appreciate the effects of her particular beauty.

"I can offer you a position of the first consequence," he said. "You would be at no one's beck and call. You would be your own mistress. You would reside where you please and form the attachments you wish."

These statements were so dispassionately delivered that the stray thought crossed her mind that he would surely not object strongly if she were to decline his offer. Under different circumstances, she would have declined at once. However, with Lord Edward's death, her world had suddenly changed and become unstable. She felt as though she were poised, very delicately, on a precipice. She did not know whether firm ground lay behind her in Stanthorpe, or ahead of her as Anthony Maddox's wife.

He continued, "And you would have a husband, I promise you, who would make no unreasonable demands of you."

Surprised, she asked involuntarily, "None?"

His gray-green eyes appraised her. "That depends on how you interpret 'unreasonable,'" he said.

Marianna hesitated.

"Or, perhaps, it depends on what you desire from the marriage," he added after a moment.

The implication was plain enough—or was it? Marianna was suddenly embarrassed. She was instantly pink, as though she were a shrimp dipped in boiling water, and she silently cursed her fair skin for so betraying her. Did she gather correctly that he was leaving the question of their marital intimacy up to her? Did it indeed rest on her interpretation, on her desire? But how was she to decide, when she hardly knew the man? To cover her embarrassment, she put the question back to him. "Did you, perhaps, have in mind a marriage of convenience, after the French fashion?"

She could not, in truth, read the expression that crossed his strong features. "A marriage of independence, rather," he replied. "I will be extremely busy in the coming months, and will have little time to devote to your comfort."

She nodded, half relieved, thinking she had understood. "And what shall I do for you, in addition to chaperoning your ward?"

"You shall see to the responsibilities of running my houses. Not the estate in Northampton, only the house on Cavendish Square and now, of course, Maddox Hall here in Stanthorpe."

When she stood up, he moved toward her, his presence looming large. She chose her words carefully. "You do me a great honor, my lord, but you have taken me by surprise. Do you think that I may have some time to consider your offer?"

"That, Miss Lowth," he replied, "is the one thing that I do not have to give you."

Marianna understood that the offer could be withdrawn as suddenly as it had been delivered. She would have liked to defer the decision, but the moment was all, and the choice was clear. She dared to look straight into his face. It was all planes and crags, with a distinct, compelling character entirely its own.

"In that case, then, my answer is yes."

His response was restrained. "Very well. I will return

tomorrow evening to discuss the particulars with your brother."

Marianna agreed to that. They made the usual parting remarks, then he bowed briefly and left. With his departure, the room regained its normal proportions.

Marianna stared down into the depths of the crackling fire. It cast its reflection, like wayward flames, across floor and wall alike, giving the planks and paneling a deeper glow. She felt the heat on her face and, as if suddenly scorched, she stepped away from the hearth.

In the vicarage entry, she heard muffled voices bidding Anthony Maddox farewell. She hoped for a few moments alone to collect her thoughts, but she was not granted the time for that either.

Only seconds later, her brother and sister-in-law burst into the room, a dozen questions on their lips. However, the jingle of the bridle, the crack of the whip, and the sound of carriage wheels crunching furiously over the frost-rimed drive penetrated the parlor.

"Well, well, now! Of all things!" the Reverend Jonathan Lowth said, diverted from the topic uppermost in his mind. He crossed the room to peer out the window. "His lordship certainly seems in a hurry!"

"Yes," Marianna agreed quickly. "He tells me that he has been very pressed this week past and has many things to attend to." She did not, just yet, wish to speak of the purpose of Anthony Maddox's visit.

"But such reckless driving in this weather!" The reverend persisted, frowning his disapproval. "With all the hazards of the snow and ice! I think it argues an unsteady character, don't you, Mrs. Lowth?" he said, referring the question to his wife.

Jeanne Lowth, a nervous woman, was looking over her husband's shoulder through the window at the fast-departing coach. She, too, was concerned about the character of the man who now paid her husband's salary. "Oh, yes, yes, Mr. Lowth! Very unsteady!" she agreed.

"A hothead, I fear, the new Lord Westleigh," the reverend pronounced heavily.

"Yes, a hothead!" Jeanne repeated obediently, and added, "It's just as Mrs. Wynchley said. According to Mrs. Wynchley, his lordship—the new one—left Stanthorpe last week very abruptly, just a few hours after Lord Edward's burial. Immediately after the reading of the will, it must have been. Mrs. Wynchley saw him drive his coach out of the village late that afternoon. She said that he drove like a man with the devil at his heels! And that was *exactly* how she phrased it, Mr. Lowth. Although *I* would never have described it like that, *she* said that the man had the devil at his heels!"

"An unsteady character," Jonathan Lowth repeated darkly.

"Oh, indeed, most unsteady. And, added to that, when his lordship left Stanthorpe like that, he did so without a word to anyone." Jeanne added, "Mrs. Wynchley thought it most improper!"

Marianna suddenly found herself on firm ground again in this conversation. She cocked a brow at her sister-in-law. "And what do *you* think, Jeanne?" she asked.

"Now, Marianna!" her brother reproved her. "Do not change the subject. And do not attempt to pressure Mrs. Lowth into taking an unbecoming opinion. I know you! You will say something nonsensical—"

"That his lordship is free to come and go as he pleases?" Marianna suggested.

The reverend majestically ignored his sister's comment and continued without pausing for breath. "—and wear poor Mrs. Lowth down until she agrees with whatever wild idea you put forward. Why, just this morning you were advancing the most unladylike ideas on the trouble in France and wishing everyone to agree with you!"

"The trouble in France, as you call it," Marianna pointed out, "is nothing short of a revolution—"

"Ah!" Jonathan said with deep satisfaction. "But His Majesty King Louis XVI still sits on his throne."

"A precarious one—admit it, Jonathan."

"I will not!" Jonathan Lowth replied, his face suffusing with a dull red. "And Lord Edward was inclined to agree with me on that point, I think."

"At least he had some reasons for thinking so," Marianna retorted. "Then, too, he was aware of the grave dangers of the Revolution. He also said that we'd have the French swarming on our back doorstep before too long—both refugees and revolutionaries—which is more than you're willing to see. But, just at the moment," she said, waving this away, "none of this seems to be very pertinent."

"You are right—it is most impertinent," Jonathan Lowth concurred, for once agreeing with his sister. "What is more, these opinions of yours, Marianna, are thoroughly improper. And speaking of improprieties, I must say that the new Lord Westleigh seems to have no sense of the proprieties himself. And an unsteady character to go along with it! Now, what did he need to speak to you about that was so private?"

Marianna had composed herself. "It was exactly what I suspected when I received his lordship's message this morning. He wanted to speak with me about Lord Edward's last afternoon."

"Hrumph! And for that he needed to be alone with you?" the reverend said, unconsciously echoing Maddox's words. "Just as I thought," he snorted. "An unsteady character and no sense of the proprieties!"

II

A Mysterious Box

*F*ar into the night Marianna lay awake, listening to the wild gusts of wind blowing against the narrow windows of her chamber. She lay on her side, watching the darkness from beneath her mound of woolen blankets and forgetting to move for so long that her arm began to ache. When she turned at last, her arm prickled and then cramped. She stretched it up behind her head and caught her breath sharply when she grasped a cold iron bar of the bedstead.

Never one to turn away from unflattering truths, she decided the reason she felt such apprehension at the prospect of marriage to Anthony Maddox was that she had grown too comfortable in her predictable little world. She did not regret having accepted his offer. Still, she would have liked time to weigh the decision before giving her answer, rather than afterward.

She sighed in perplexity. Her request for time had not been prompted solely by surprise and suspicion. Her pride had desired the delay as well, for Mr. Maddox had offended her with his brusque manner. Yet, insult or no, the proposal had been plain. She knew what she could expect, and she was neither so craven nor so foolish as to deny herself a life of ease and independence on Mr. Maddox's terms.

She could imagine several reasons why a man like Anthony Maddox would make this impersonal selection of a wife, none of them flattering to the woman he might choose. However, since Mr. Maddox did not know her personally, Marianna decided not to take to heart his reasons for choosing her. No, his almost random choice of wife was not the source of her misgivings. Rather, she had sensed something amiss in the manner of his proposal, something contradictory that, under different circumstances, she should have been able to identify. But she could not, and it teased her, like the answer to a conundrum that dances around the edges of one's memory and will not be pinned down. At length, she gave up and concluded that the true state of Mr. Maddox's mind was known only to the man himself, and he, independent husband-to-be, was not likely to share it with her.

As she stared up at the rafters, images of a winter's day not more than a year or so ago came to mind, a day when the fire soughed on the hearth of Lord Edward's library and the wind battered with angry futility at the trefoil windows. Marianna remembered how happy she had been that Lord Edward had recovered so well from his heart attack. She remembered seeing leather-bound books crammed into mahogany shelves, and tarnished brass and pewter so old and black-streaked that it resembled the leaden skies outside. She had pulled her knees up to her chin and had laid her head across her arms as she sat at the feet of her dear old friend. They were warmed by the fire and cheered by friendship and strong tea, and did not think it beyond their powers to solve the world's problems between them.

They had had a spirited discussion of merchants and kings, and prices on the Stock Exchange, when Lord Edward said, in a rare allusion to his nephew and heir, "Have I never told you that Anthony fancies himself a good

Whig, my dear? Liberalism, he calls it! International relations, he calls it! The future, he calls it! I call it money, London money! Whigs have money and trade with foreigners and should be put in their rightful place."

"And where is that, if not in London?" Marianna had replied. "Mr. Maddox lives in London, after all, does he not? What quarrel do you have with his politics?"

"Aye, he lives in London for most of the year, but he does not know where his real interests lie," his lordship had grumbled. "He owns a rich enough estate in Northampton, I'll have you know. Money is Whig and land is Tory, my dear. Land and the king! That is all there is to bet on when times are bad."

Marianna had opened her mouth to speak, but her friend had come to know well the workings of her mind.

He wagged his finger. "And if you quote Jonathan Swift to me, O well-read Miss Lowth, I shall hurl this cup at your head!"

Marianna laughed, delighted, and accepted the challenge. "Oh, was it Swift who said something about the power which used to follow land having gone over to money?" she ventured innocently, as she twisted her head around to slant a sly look up at him. "Throw the cup if you will," she invited. "I'll take it as a compliment, since it's from my favorite Rockingham service of yours, but it's a pitiful waste of your nephew's inheritance—whatever his politics."

Lord Edward scowled but was very pleased with her response, for all of that.

Marianna asked, suddenly curious, "You could always assign another heir, could you not, if you think Mr. Maddox unworthy of the title and estate?"

"I could," his lordship admitted. "There's a cousin or two who'd be happy to fill my shoes, and I've a legal right to change the name of my heir, if it suits me, for the estate is not entailed. But, no. It's only Anthony's politics I don't like!"

"Well, then," she laughed, "you could always make your will to read that he pledge to the Tory cause before he inherits."

Lord Edward's eyes rested a moment on Marianna while she gazed into the fire. "Oh, a condition can always be added," he replied after a moment. "I could stipulate all I want, Miss Lowth, but the truth is that my nephew doesn't particularly need Maddox Hall, when all is said, and he's a strong-willed man. He'll make his own choices in life."

A strange enough choice he made this afternoon, she thought now as she lay in her bed. Stranger still was the realization that she had always loved Maddox Hall but had never coveted it. Now she was to be the mistress of its graceful furniture suites, its ogee mantelpieces, and its gothic mirrors, of which Lord Edward had been so proud.

A faint shivering broke out along Marianna's bare arm. She quickly tucked it in again under the bedclothes. Lying there in the darkness, she thought her way down one path that went across the vicarage yard, sloping down over a rocky, wind-swept hillside, past brambled hedges, past open seams of loamy turf, and past the rivulets that would find their way, a few miles farther, out to the open sea. The path ran for a mile or more, from the backyard of the vicarage to the steps of the stone Hall, its back side stark and exposed to the rigors of the sea winds that traveled, unchecked, the few miles inland.

The way was familiar to her in all its seasons, with blackberry tangles heavy with fruit in the summer, and thick yellow gorse in the autumn. On lazy days, when she was happy with her own company and the sun shone on the Kentish countryside, she took the long way to the Hall. At the first turning, a secondary path plunged down the hillside to the silver tail of a miniature harbor leading out to the Channel. Shadows would sweep across the green-tufted flanks of the hills and across the fall of granite hanging precariously above the steel-blue water. If she chose to follow the serpentine path in its entirety, she crossed to a biscuit lip of sandy beach with shady caverns and moss-covered stones, twisted thorn trees, and smudges of summer wildflowers.

One day, nearly five years before, Marianna had taken this as-yet-unexplored turning in the path and had come across an older man, stumping about with a stick. She recognized him immediately as the Lord of Maddox Hall, and it seemed that he had recognized her as well.

"You're the Reverend Lowth's sister, are you not?" Lord Edward had asked of the young girl in her plain dress and straw hat, carrying a rush basket filled with berries and flowers.

"I am Marianna Lowth, my lord."

"I've heard of you from my housekeeper," he said.

Marianna bobbed in acknowledgment and submitted to his scrutiny with no great loss of composure.

"My housekeeper also tells me, among other things, that you have had the unheard-of temerity to refuse a proposal of marriage. Who was the fellow? His name escapes me now."

"Timothy Goforth, my lord," Marianna replied, certain of his reaction.

His lordship nodded. "That's it: Goforth! You did right to refuse him, Miss Lowth," he said approvingly. "A coxcomb, that boy! An impudent puppy!"

Marianna's eyes widened with surprise. "You are the first person in the village to have said so, my lord."

"Or to have thought so, I warrant!"

"That is because Mr. Goforth is held in such esteem in Stanthorpe. He is considered to be a man of sense, my lord," Marianna explained.

"A silly jackanapes, that Goforth, puffed up with his own conceit!" Lord Edward exclaimed. His brow lowered. "Is that why you refused him?"

That was exactly why she had refused him. "It would be unbecoming to contradict your lordship," Marianna replied gravely, but a twinkle lit her eye.

"Hah! If you had the courage to turn down the offer of the village paragon, then I doubt you'd stop at gainsaying an old man like me! And don't refer to me as 'my lud this, my lud that'! I like you, gel, and your courage!"

Marianna smiled and spoke her mind. "It wasn't courage, but rather my lack of it that prevented me from accepting his very gratifying offer."

"How's that? You look as though you think for yourself, and where there's a brain, there's courage."

Marianna regarded him frankly. "For a man, perhaps," she said. "But for a woman, it is different, I think. Oh, I've a mind of my own, but it's rather more of a nuisance at times than a blessing. In any case, I could not imagine having the courage to defend Mr. Goforth's views to my friends and neighbors for the rest of my life. His opinions of the world differ so strongly from mine own, you see. In the end, I had not the courage to face a lifetime of loyalty to his opinions."

"Is that what marriage to him would have meant?"

Marianna replied that Mr. Goforth had made quite clear the signal honor he was according her with his proposal. "And he was careful to explain how I, as his wife, would receive the respect and admiration of the community. In other words, I was to assume the role of prop for all his virtues and mouthpiece for all his opinions, as the price of accepting the honor of his name and worldly goods."

"Courageous, good instincts, and forthright to boot!" his lordship commented, admiringly.

"My brother says that my forthrightness will never win me a husband," was Marianna's demure reply.

Lord Edward barked a laugh. "Probably not! But tell me: did you refuse his offer so forthrightly?"

Marianna's lips curved into a smile that his lordship would come to know well. "Will it spoil your opinion of me if I tell you that I seriously considered Mr. Goforth's proposal during the course of an entire day?"

This admission had not, apparently, affected Lord Ed-

ward's opinion, and he had enjoyed their five years of
friendship as much as she had, she knew.

Friendship. Marianna had made other friends in Stanthorpe in the eight years she had lived in her brother's
household. She was on excellent terms with most of the
village matrons including, improbably, the shy young woman
whom Timothy Goforth had eventually taken to wife. She
also found satisfaction in her bond with her nephews and in
watching them grow up, she had learned to discern and
appreciate her sister-in-law's qualities, and she was even able
to avoid most of the unpleasant friction with her brother.

But Lord Edward's friendship had given Marianna
something more, and it was only now that he was gone and
she lay in bed that she realized how she had depended on
his presence in Stanthorpe to give her a sense of well-being
and expectation. On the days that she had been to visit
him, she had felt like a happy child waking with the
knowledge that the day of a promised treat had dawned. It
had given her a contentment to know that there was something to wake up for, that the waking was an excitement,
and it would flood her whole being, making her happy to
be alive. Lord Edward's friendship had given her a fresh
feeling so that she could greet every new day as one with
new promise, and she would rise with an inner happiness.

The long, sleepless night passed. Marianna rose slowly
from the bed the next morning after a sleepless night and
went to the window, her bare feet bitten by the cold of the
hard planked floor. She rustled the curtains aside and un-
latched the shutters to see the sun squinting over the horizon. It was a dreary, dismal sight. She stood there for a
long while, wrestling with depression and trying to find the
equilibrium that had been part of Lord Edward's gift to her
but which, with his death, seemed to have died in her, too.

There was something depressing and hostile about the
onset of a February day, she decided, after the splendor of
a white dawn in deep winter and before the sweetness of a
spring morning. February was a dingy, lackluster month,

when all the shortcomings of the world stood exposed to
view: graceless, naked branches; a stern, hard earth lying
exposed, lacking veils of snow or grass; sullen clouds that
mustered their dirty battalions along the horizon; a gray,
impersonal sky, collapsed against the curve of the earth, as
if too weary, when drained of color, to maintain its arc
overhead.

If ever there was a reason for accepting Anthony Maddox's proposal, she thought, it was that nothing was left for
her in Stanthorpe.

She was seized by a strong, wholly unaccustomed impulse to go out into the dawn, to be free of her room and
the house and her family. As she cast aside her night rail
and stood shivering in the morning chill, she knew that she
must visit Lord Edward's grave for the first time since the
burial, in order to make her peace with him. She donned
her most serviceable dress, rolled thick stockings up to her
knees, and laced stout walking shoes. She pulled her old
merino cloak from the clothespress and threw it over her
shoulders, tied the hood around her unbound, uncombed
curls, and crept down the back stairs.

She felt a strange relief in the out-of-doors. The wind
caught at her hood and hair with robust fingers; it slapped
her face and brought quick tears to her eyes. The night had
brought counsel, and she was resolved this morning to reveal to her brother the purpose of Mr. Maddox's visit. Yesterday afternoon she had been in no mood to withstand the
exclamations and inquiries that would have undoubtedly
followed her disclosure.

The path was so brittle with frost that it crunched underfoot. In the indistinct light of the dawn she imagined that
the mounds of earth at each side of the path formed human
shapes, as if they were shoulders hunching against the
cold.

Marianna shrugged and turned her thoughts to her life
ahead. She felt a rush of excitement at the prospect of
entering the world of the beau and the wit, the belle and the

blue-stocking, then a wave of sadness that Lord Edward
would not be there to share it with her. These feelings were
followed immediately by a wash of pure fear. Had she truly
grown so staid and sober after all these years in Stanthorpe? Why, when faced with living a life she had avidly
read about but never hoped to experience firsthand, should
her strongest response be one of cowardice?

Lord Edward had once asserted that the end of reading
was not more reading, but more life.

Marianna had taken up the topic with zest. "How can
you say so," she argued, "when you have read more than
any other human being I know—except perhaps my father
—but have not left Stanthorpe anytime these past ten years
to see the world beyond? I would think that, in your case,
reading is a recommendation for more reading, for you are
content to stay in your library."

"Ah, but I am an old man," he countered.

"That is not an argument," she objected with a frown of
dissatisfaction.

Lord Edward laughed at her expression. "Should I add
that my health is uncertain?" He shook his head. "Then
take your father as the better example. He was brilliant and
learned and did not stay in his library. He went out to see
the world and took you with him."

"And, for all his brilliance, he died friendless and left
his only daughter with two liabilities," she answered
glumly, "no dowry and a head stuffed with reading."

"Inconsistent, my dear!" Lord Edward responded with
mild triumph. "I thought you objected to the fact that
women were taught to sew, rather than read, and to form
no opinions of their own!"

"But that *is* my point," Marianna argued. "Women who
are being groomed to echo only the opinions of their husbands are educated accordingly. My father educated me to
think for myself, but neglected the small matter of provid-
ing me with independent support. An unpleasant bind, I
assure you!"

"Has your reading done you any harm?"

Finding herself backed into a corner, she took recourse in humor. "Well," she said with a laugh, "Jonathan says that all my reading will not win me a husband."

"You turned down your best offer in order to remain independent in your ideas," Lord Edward pointed out. "You did have a choice to make, and you made it. Do you tell me now that you regret it?"

"Unfair!" she protested, laughing again. "How dare you use my own decisions against me! Especially when Mr. Goforth fell so very short of my ideal!"

"Which is . . . ?" Lord Edward prompted.

"I don't know, really!" Marianna admitted. "The father of my children. A man to talk with and laugh with. One who shares my tastes and my views. One who likes what I like and wishes to do what I wish to."

"A masculine version of yourself, I collect," Lord Edward commented.

Marianna merely laughed at that, then said seriously, "I don't regret having turned down Mr. Goforth's offer, but allow me to amend my original statement. A man has a hundred choices to make every day and then comes home to a wife who manages his household and cares for his children. I am not against that! But I have been educated to make choices, and it's just that sometimes . . . sometimes I have the feeling that I was to be offered but one choice to make in my life, and that it has already come and gone!"

"Do you? But you are young and cannot foresee whether life will present you with any further choices," he had said.

As she trod the frozen path to the cemetery, Marianna was so lost in considering the relevance of Lord Edward's remark that she did not immediately perceive the lone figure on the horizon. When she had all but emerged from behind a small wall of thorn bushes that marked the village boundary proper, her feet stopped of their own accord.

Then her mind registered an unexpected presence in the cemetery that lay just beyond the bushes.

There, not fifty feet in front of her, was a man she had never seen before. She found it extremely peculiar, to say the least, that he should be in the cemetery at this odd hour of the day.

Marianna stole behind the bushes and studied him. She could not see his face, but his figure was distinctive. He was tall and gaunt, almost cadaverous, and with the wind whipping his black cloak around his spare frame and the uncertain light of the early morning winter sun playing tricks with her eyes, Marianna fancied that here was a dark spirit risen from the ground.

She saw that the man had paused momentarily in his labors, for he was leaning, heavily, against the long handle of a shovel. Her eyes were drawn to the curious box at his feet. It was not large, less than two feet long and not more than a foot wide, and fashioned as a treasure chest or strongbox. The curved top of the box was adorned with an insignia that resembled a bee, and the latch was chained and padlocked.

When the man began to dig, Marianna let out the breath that she had been holding unaware. He struck at the unyielding ground with single-minded intensity. He had already begun a hole, she saw, right next to Lord Edward's new grave, where he apparently intended to bury the box.

She decided to confront him and to demand an explanation, but she quickly discarded this brave resolve. She was alone with no means of defending herself, and she had no right, in any case, to intervene or demand an explanation of anyone. As far as she knew, there was no law against burying a box in a village cemetery, and perhaps (although it seemed singularly unlikely) the man had been authorized to do so. It did occur to Marianna that his choice of this site for the box served two purposes. First, since the ground had been newly turned, the fresh evidence of digging would not be noticeable, and secondly, since Lord

Edward's grave was well marked, the box would be easily retrieved.

Marianna had become thoroughly chilled in her immobility. When she felt a sneeze welling up inside of her, she decided to quit her vigil. The man was completely absorbed in his labors, and if she crept away now, he would never know that he had been observed. She felt that someone should be notified of this man's activities and decided, for lack of a better idea, to discuss the incident with her brother.

As the sun was scattering the last of the stubborn shadows, Marianna turned and hurried home. Soon she saw the plume of smoke rising from the vicarage chimney, signaling that the household had risen, and when she arrived at the back doorstep, she felt distinct relief. She entered, pushed the hood back from her tumble of gold curls, and warmed herself a minute or two at the hearth before seeking out her brother.

The reverend was seated in the parlor with a heavy frown on his face. In his hands was a letter. It was too early for the mail, and so when she asked him how he had come by a letter at this hour, he looked up briefly and grumbled something about the dratted daily girl having misplaced this most important missive nearly a week ago and his having just found it under the tea tin in the kitchen when he went to make his own tea this morning. He held up the sheets so that Marianna could see an offending stain in the middle of one page.

"It's from Arnold Lawrence," he informed her tersely. "Oh, he tells me that your last installment of 'Notes from the Countryside' is very amusing and that the column is improving the *Mirror*'s circulation," he added absently. "He wants the next one as soon as possible."

"Thank him kindly for me and tell him that I have not felt like writing in the past ten days . . . but, Jonathan, I must tell you something."

The reverend was not attending. The rest of the news

contained in the letter was not at all pleasant. Arnold
Lawrence, it seemed, had been named to a very nice position at Canterbury, one that the reverend himself had hoped
to receive.

"Jonathan," Marianna tried again, "I have just seen the
strangest thing in the cemetery. Now, you may wonder why
I was at the cemetery this morning."

The reverend only half heard what she said. "I do not
wonder at anything you do, Marianna," he replied curtly.

"No, really, Jonathan, you must listen."

"I am listening," he said, but gave no evidence thereof.

Marianna saw his preoccupation. Nevertheless, she explained what she had seen, feeling sure that she would
capture his attention. She told of the man and the small box
at his feet, and of his evident intention to bury it.

"A box, you say?"

"Yes. Jonathan, have you not been listening?"

"Of course I have been listening," he said without looking up. "You have told me of a box, and I should like to
know why you think it could be of any importance."

"But a man was burying this box in the cemetery."

"It is the custom to bury things in cemeteries," he replied repressively.

"But a small box, rather more like a treasure chest?"

"Hm. What do you think is in it?" he asked, absently.

Marianna had lost her patience. "Why, an elephant, of
course," she said dryly. "What else but an elephant should
be in a small box that a strange man has buried in our
village cemetery at this hour of the morning?"

This observation penetrated the thick shrubbery of the
reverend's cogitations. "Your levity will never win you a
husband, Marianna," he commented severely, glancing up,
"and neither will your extremely disheveled appearance."

The opportunity was golden, and Marianna succeeded at
last in securing her brother's undivided attention. When
she told him of the purpose of Anthony Maddox's visit to
her the day before, the reverend's reaction was all that she

could have hoped. He mumbled and grumbled and expressed surprise, denial, and wonder at so extraordinary a turn. He blustered and expostulated, completely forgot about the new Lord Westleigh's unsteady character, and pronounced him a capital fellow. He derived a keen pleasure, when it dawned on him, that he, the Reverend Jonathan Lowth, would naturally perform the ceremony. After several minutes happily contemplating the prospect of basking in his sister's reflected glory, the reverend looked down at the letter in his hands and decided that Arnold Lawrence should be congratulated on his new post at Canterbury without delay. A postscript containing news of his sister's impending marriage would, naturally, not be inappropriate.

Anthony Maddox's visit to Jonathan Lowth that evening set into swift motion a series of events that gave Marianna no pause to think of anything other than her own radically altered life. She became Lady Westleigh a few days later on the twentieth of February, 1791, at a quiet family ceremony in the old Norman church at Stanthorpe. Before the predicted snow came to make the roads impassable, Lord and Lady Westleigh retired to the Maddox estate in Northampton in order to honeymoon in seclusion before removing to London.

And so began Marianna's marriage of independence. Judging by the amount of time that Maddox chose to spend in her company during the honeymoon, Marianna saw that it was going to be a very independent marriage indeed. However, since she had expected him to be preoccupied with his work, she neither demanded her husband's attention nor needed it. They tacitly agreed, it seemed, on the ground rules of this marriage of independence, except for one crucial point: Maddox had expected he would exercise normal marriage rights, Marianna had not. Thus, when he came to her chambers on their wedding night, Marianna was surprised, confused, and a little indignant that they had

so misunderstood one another. Maddox withdrew and did
not seek out her company again at night.

Suffice it to say, then, that enough had happened for
Marianna to have forgotten the man with the box in the
cemetery. It was not until she had been in Town a good two
months or more that a small occurrence in the streets of
London would cause her to think of that strange, cadaverous man again.

III

My Lady
Marianna Westleigh

Marianna arose early the morning after the new-
lyweds' arrival at Maddox House on Cavendish
Square. Since she had enjoyed her new status as
Lady Westleigh less than two weeks, she still preferred to
dress without aid, although she was learning to like her
ladies' maid, Rachel. She descended, unaccompanied, the
gracious Palladian split staircase and made her way, by trial
and error, to the nobly proportioned and sun-filled dining
room.

There she checked herself on the threshold. In the center
of the room stood her husband, in full riding dress with a
cape tied carelessly around his broad shoulders. One hand
was resting negligently on the ladder back of a chair at the
table, while the other hand held a sheaf of papers. On the
table beside him were a plate bearing the remains of a
sirloin, a silver coffee pot, a Chelsea cup, the London
Times, his crumpled linen, and a scattering of documents.

The figure he cut was not without effect. Marianna felt
a slight jolt at sight of him, but she dismissed it as surprise
that he should be up and about. She had half a mind to
withdraw from the room.

It was too late. He glanced up from the page he was reading and bowed slightly. He crossed to her side with another slight bow and inquired, civilly, after the first night she had spent in her new home.

She assured him that she had spent an excellent night after the long journey and added that she had not expected him to be up at this hour. "I thought to have the dining room to myself," she continued. "I had no idea you were such an early riser, my lord, but here you are already finished . . . and on the point of departure, I see?"

"Yes, I am having the carriage brought around now," he acknowledged. He gestured to his empty plate and cup. "I breakfasted without you. Pray, excuse me."

She waved away the perfunctory apology with a bland reply. "Not at all! I am not very sociable first thing in the morning." After ten days of marriage, she had learned to respond in kind to his polite but palpable indifference. It certainly had not dampened her love of laughter and lively conversation, but she had no desire to waste her wit or warmth on him.

"Now that you are here," he said, "I will give to you personally some of the instructions that I have written out for you and left with Browne."

A footman hovering in ghostly attendance led her to the chair that stood opposite her husband's and seated her formally. A fresh cup of coffee and a coddled egg materialized at her right hand.

"Browne?" she repeated. "Oh, yes, Mrs. Browne, the housekeeper," she remembered aloud.

"You can review anything you don't understand with her."

"And the instructions?" she inquired, a little puzzled.

"There is quite a bit to cover, so I've written down all the names and addresses you'll be needing in the next few weeks," he said.

"The next few weeks?" she asked, surprised.

"I'll be gone a month at the most, three weeks at the least, I should think," he replied.

She took a sip of coffee, and pondered the information that he had planned an absence from London beginning the day after their arrival. She betrayed no surprise at this and, indeed, felt none. She wondered if she was allowed to ask him where he was going, but decided against it.

"I see," she said, placidly. "Pray, do not let me detain you. I am sure that Browne can repeat whatever I do not understand in the written instructions."

"She'll have to," he said, "for once the carriage arrives, I must be off. In the meantime, I might mention that, if you are looking for distraction, you are to contact the Marchioness of Ainsworth. She is a distant cousin of mine. As you know, the Maddox clan is sparse, and I have no close relatives to keep you company in my absence. But the Marchioness is well connected and will be sure to sponsor your entrance in Society, if you desire it."

"How kind. Yes, of course," Marianna replied and repeated obediently, "the Marchioness of Ainsworth."

"And on Bond Street, the dressmakers you will want to patronize are Clairette's and DeLey's," he went on, businesslike. "Which reminds me: I have given an envelope to Browne with a bank draft for your first quarter's allowance. I have had no time to deposit it myself or to open an account for you, so you will simply have to take care of that with my man of affairs, Charles Duguid. I've written down his name and address for you, too. You have only to write him a note and he will come here and take matters in hand for you. Your signature will be required on a few documents."

He looked out the window. The faint sound of carriage wheels clattering over the cobbles drifted into the room. "That will have to be all for now. Any questions, my lady?"

"None, my lord," she said.

"Don't forget: the Marchioness of Ainsworth, and

Clairette's or Deley's. But first contact my man of affairs
to set your bank account aright." He came around to her
side of the table and bent his head to her hand, but he did
not touch it with his lips.

This time she could not attribute the slight shock she felt
to anything other than his touch. Unaccountably, she
blushed, still the new bride. She wondered why it was that
she should lose the ability to breathe normally in his presence. "I won't forget!" she said to him. "Godspeed, my
lord."

A minute later the carriage was rumbling down the
street, by which time Marianna had requested her husband's newspaper and was reading it. While one part of her
mind scanned the fascinating account of "Three Notorious
Pickpockets picked up by Two Stout Men appointed by the
Ward of Cheap," another part was busy sifting through the
events of the past week and a half. Anthony Maddox's
initial distance had become, over the days, more like a
civil indifference, but there was always something else
again lurking just below the surface that she could not put a
name to. In their ten days of marriage, they had engaged in
a minimum of conversation. He had taken no real initia-
tives to get to know her, except in the biblical sense, but
since the memory of her wedding night caused her deep
chagrin, she tried not to dwell on it. This morning, however, her long-felt desire for children jostled violently
against the girlish dream she hardly knew she held of the
man she would choose as their father: that ideal, loving
man, husband and friend, who would cherish her above all
else in the world. Clearly, Anthony Maddox was not that
man.

Marianna had wasted little effort imagining why he had
offered for her. He certainly did not crave her companion-
ship, nor did he, apparently, strongly desire heirs, for the
issue of marital intimacy seemed to have been firmly
closed. Marianna had no intention of altering the terms of
the marriage that had been established since the wedding

night. She had even decided to accept those terms with calm and dignity.

Her admirable equanimity suffered a severe setback an hour later when she opened the envelope containing the bank draft that was her allowance. The sum staggered her. She struggled with a jumble of emotions that she did not understand and that became further entangled when she realized that the amount represented but a quarter of the annual figure. The total struck her forcibly as a kind of contemptuous generosity. Calmer reflection suggested that she had misinterpreted the gesture, that her husband was merely making what he thought a reasonable allowance for the woman who was his wife. Even so, something inside her was violently offended. In this marriage of independence, she was suddenly aware of a weighty imbalance: she was intolerably dependent on her husband's purse strings.

However, with her husband out of sight, she pushed him out of mind. She set her mind instead to adapting to her new life as Lady Marianna Westleigh. This was an entirely pleasant task. Over the next few days, she explored the many silk-hung rooms filled with Sheraton furniture and Aubusson carpets, acquainted herself with the running of the large household, and established an agreeable relationship with Mrs. Browne. She luxuriated in a freedom she had not enjoyed in years and wrote a final essay, "Farewell from the Countryside," for the *Anglican Mirror*. She reveled in the excellent library, where she spent several quiet hours every day reading and musing on what Lord Edward would say if he could see her now.

For the very first time in her adult life, she was free to make choices. In assuming the life of Lady Westleigh, it was as if she had been handed a magic lamp and had only to rub it to release the magic within. Or, better yet, it was as if she was the genie and had been suddenly released from all the strictures imposed on her in the past eight years. The power of choice ran through her veins like an elixir. She alone decided when she would rise, when she would dress, when she would eat, when she would read: it was glorious! Although she thoroughly enjoyed her first few weeks of splendid solitude, Marianna desired to enter Society. With that decision came more wonderful choices to make. First came the practical matter of her wardrobe and, of course, she had absolutely no intention of patronizing either Clairette's or Deley's. She proceeded with great resource to discover the talents of the vivacious Fanny Lane, who had a sharp mind and an eye for fashion, and had just opened for business.

Miss Lane gave Marianna the name of a Signor Luigi, a *parruchiere* who was not currently employed. When, as custom dictated, he was summoned to her chambers for an interview, the slim Italian hairdresser, a vision in mauve from his coat embroidered in faux-gold to his impossibly tight knee-breeches, clapped a hand over his heart upon seeing her masses of blond curls and sighed, "*Magnifico!*" He pirouetted about her, touched her cloud of curls, and shook his own bewigged head emphatically. "You have possibilities, signora. You are not beautiful. No. You are near beauty. You are my challenge. I, Luigi, shall make you radiant!"

Marianna engaged him on the spot.

Satisfied with her choice of dressmaker and hairdresser, Marianna also decided to choose her own her social circle. She elected not to visit the Marchioness of Ainsworth. Instead, she sought out a woman whom she remembered as having been an acquaintance of her father's over twenty years before. She addressed her first envelope, bearing her new name and style, to a Lady Louisa Hester.

Marianna was in luck. Mrs. Hester, in the intervening years, had become a well-known hostess, and she was more than happy to include on her guest list the amusing Dr. Lowth's daughter, who had recently become the Lady Westleigh. Marianna was invited to Mrs. Hester's very next *conversazione*, which was held near the end of March.

She chose for the occasion a gown of delicious peach silk with a modest neckline and tight sleeves with small stitched cuffs to show off her pretty, rounded arms. The skirt was of glazed cotton patterned by spiny stems in green, depicting pine trees complete with roots and cones, lilacs, and daisy trails. It gathered at the waist and was left open to expose the front panel of a handsome petticoat of cream silk. Signor Luigi's work was (in his own estimation) inspired, and she swept off to the evening's diversions in a well-sprung coach, attended by no less than three footmen and two linkboys.

Marianna had entertained some fears about Society's attitude toward the oddity of such a very new bride going visiting unescorted. They vanished within minutes of her arrival.

Mrs. Hester resided with her husband in a charming villa in Chiswick, only a short ride from Cavendish Square. In the summer, Mrs. Hester's guests might stroll amongst the high hedges and noble statues of her gardens, but in March they remained indoors in the gracious saloons.

Mrs. Hester was universally considered to be the kind of woman who was ugly in an attractive way, what the French called *une jolie laide*, but she was English to the core; and because she held so few illusions about herself, she had cultivated that ugly attractiveness with a good deal of finesse. She was also an ardent advocate of the Rights of Woman and so accepted without demur the fact that a bride of a mere month would circulate in Society without her husband. She tossed off Maddox's absence with the light words, "Tony is one of my favorites, my dear Lady Westleigh, but quite my despair. I'm rarely able to catch him for one of my parties. He's not much of a talker at social occasions such as this, as I am sure you must know! But here you are, and I am delighted you did not stay away because your husband could not accompany you! I do hope you'll enjoy yourself!"

Lady Hester led Marianna first into a brightly lit dining room abuzz with the animated conversation of small groups clustered around the tables spread for light dining with squabs fricassee, capons *enfans*, salmon, cold artichokes and asparagus, gooseberry pies, and currant tarts. The hostess made a point of introducing Marianna to a number of her guests, but apart from the bland comment from one young man who had seen the announcement of the Maddox wedding in the *Times* a few weeks previous, no one evinced the least curiosity about the circumstances surrounding her marriage or the present whereabouts of her husband.

Marianna soon discovered, however, that this discretion did not mean that the fashionable of London did not gossip.

Marianna fell into conversation with Mrs. Eliza Parrish, a dark, vivid beauty, powdered and patched, whose husband Marianna would later learn was years older than his wife and lived exclusively in the countryside. The Viscount Stoke, handsome, polished, with no pretensions to wit, and an apparent *habitué* of Mrs. Hester's house, joined their discussion. When her companions had exhausted the topic of the thinness of the company this time of year, they promised Marianna, as a newcomer, that the real treats were in store for her, with supper boxes and fireworks at Vauxhall and Ranelagh, and balls and routs and ridottos.

"But Louisa manages to assemble the few interesting creatures among us that languish in Town at this time of year," Viscount Stoke remarked, "and without the Hester hospitality, we would no doubt be bored to extinction. Why, there is an unexpected presence. Is that not Lady Marsh, Eliza?" he asked Mrs. Parrish, directing her attention to the door as he raised his eyeglass to peer across the room. "Yes, it is Susannah Marsh," he explained to Marianna. "She is not usually in Town in the off-season. A beautiful woman, and rather nice, but keeps to herself."

Eliza Parrish sniffed audibly, and her face looked suddenly pinched.

Marianna looked at the woman who stood for a moment, framed, perhaps deliberately, by the arch. She was exceptionally beautiful, taller than average, exquisitely proportioned, with golden hair and heavenly blue eyes. Her features were classic, her skin flawless, and her dress was an ingenious creation of gold-shot silk with a draping shawl pleated and stitched to shape the simple lines of the gown.

"Very true, Richard," Eliza Parrish answered and turned back to Marianna. "Susannah does rather keep to herself, Lady Westleigh. Not one close friend that I know of, even after all the years she has been in Town."

"Years?" Marianna echoed, disbelieving.

Lady Marsh moved away then from the arch and into the room, heading toward her hostess. She looked no older than the freshest bud, yet her looks, her toilette, the way she moved was all of a piece and had a rhythm to it that did not belong to a debutante. She had a womanliness that left no room for one to think that a folded petal remained or a latent dewdrop still clung to this perfectly developed rose. Still, she hardly looked a day over twenty, and Marianna said as much.

"Add ten," Mrs. Parrish replied with a feline smile, "and we'll call it even. Of course, she is the loveliest thing in London. In England, as well, no doubt! It's rumored that the Duke of Kensington is *épris*—"

"Mad about her," Viscount Stoke interjected knowledgeably, "*éperduement amoureux*. It's an open secret."

"—but, then, so are half of the men she meets," Mrs. Parrish finished.

"She isn't married?" Marianna asked.

"Widow," Mrs. Parrish replied. "She married a childhood sweetheart of hers from the petty nobility in France. Her mother was half French, from the Crécy family in Anjou, where Susannah was mostly raised. She and this

Sire Somebody-or-other had been married only two or
three years at the time of his death, so the story goes. Some
say her husband died in a hunting accident. Others say he
was killed in a duel over her honor. It's not really known.
His name isn't known either, if it comes to that, for she had
no issue, poor thing, and so she dropped his surname after
her arrival in England . . . five years ago already. She
always maintained that she preferred the English sound of
Marsh! Anyway, it was whispered then that she was never
really married. She returned to England immediately after
her husband's death and stayed in widow's weeds only six
months. Well, since she recovered her spirits so quickly
and began to be seen absolutely everywhere, it was said
that she was never widowed at all . . . never married at all,
in fact, but left France because she had been disappointed
in a love affair."

Marianna felt that she had heard quite a bit more than
she should about a woman who was standing not twenty
feet away. Nevertheless, some response to these disclosures seemed required, and so Marianna asked, in her
straightforward fashion, "Is that not a contradiction?"

Mrs. Parrish raised her pretty brows in inquiry.

"I mean," Marianna explained, "that the rapid recovery
of her spirits does not argue one way or another about her
having been married or her having been disappointed in
love. Does one recover quicker from an unhappy love affair than from the death of a husband?"

The Viscount Stoke laughed. Mrs. Parrish made a pretty
moue, and Marianna wondered if she had misstepped.

"She was just covering up!" Mrs. Parrish replied, not
bothering, or simply unable, to clarify which state of affairs Lady Marsh was supposed to be hiding in the recovery of her spirits. Then, after a pause, Mrs. Parrish said,
"Let me drop a word into your ear, Lady Westleigh. Since
you are new in Town, you should know that the first rule in
Louisa's house is never to take one up too literally on what
is said!"

Marianna nodded her thanks for the advice. Then, hoping to close the subject of Lady Marsh with the kind of response expected of her, Marianna remarked that Lady Marsh's past certainly sounded very mysterious.

There was, apparently, no pleasing Mrs. Parrish. "Not at all! There is no mystery to it. No one pays the least attention to one's past, and Susannah has been around so long now that no one knows any longer and no one cares!"

Mrs. Parrish had overplayed the point of Lady Marsh's age, Marianna thought, and she found the blithe, uncaring repetition of someone's personal history to a virtual stranger in the worst possible taste. She did not consider the matter at length, however, for Lady Hester was coming toward them with Lady Marsh beside her. Marianna watched the golden woman approach. There was, indeed, an aura of mystery that hung about Lady Marsh, as if she was aware of the stories that accompanied her entrance, and she wore the mystery, Marianna thought, as surely as the shawl so elegantly disposed across her elbows.

"I want you to meet my newest find, Susannah," Mrs. Hester said and introduced Marianna to Lady Marsh. Marianna touched her hand and looked into the celestial blue eyes. Suddenly rueful, Marianna realized that speaking with Mrs. Parrish and the Viscount Stoke were one thing, but Lady Marsh was certainly another. She felt that one should say something terribly witty, but she managed only the conventional, "It is a pleasure to meet you, Lady Marsh."

"A pleasure for me, as well," Lady Marsh replied, equally conventional, but her voice was husky, with a break in it, as attractive and rhythmic as the rest of her, and she made it seem, to Marianna, as if something quite extraordinary had been said.

Before Lady Marsh could properly greet the rest of the group, Mrs. Parrish said, with a cagey look, "We were just instructing Lady Westleigh on the conventions of Louisa's *conversaziones*. I was saying that it was not polite to take

one up too closely on what is said. Lady Westleigh has, I
fear, a literal turn of mind."

"How refreshing," Lady Marsh said. She slipped her
arm through Marianna's, and the gesture was oddly reas-
suring. Lady Marsh nodded to the Viscount Stoke and
smiled at Mrs. Parrish without liking. She said, "You're in
looks this evening, Eliza."

"Oh, Susannah, my dear," Mrs. Parrish said, making a
play with her fan, "what in the world have you done to
your eyebrows? They made you look so . . . surprised."

"I am," Lady Marsh admitted, amused. "I cannot imagine your giving anyone instructions in polite conversation."

Mrs. Parrish's sly expression soured. "But Lady Westleigh is a newcomer, by her own admission. Oh, Richard,
there is Diana Matherby." She looked across the room, crit-
ically. She said, "Did I not tell you earlier that I had been
dying to see her this evening?"

If she had, the Viscount Stoke had forgotten it. To his
lack of confirmation, Mrs. Parrish continued chattily, "For
I mean to tell her the latest *on-dit* about Caroline Larch,
who was rivaling her for the affections of the man who is
rumored to be the future prime minister. But now Caroline
is said to have fallen under the protection of the Marquess
of Adenborough . . . the old goat! And I am perishing for a
drink. Can you get one for me, Richard? Oh, never mind,"
she said, moving away from the group, "I will get it myself. Are you coming, Richard? I've always thought it a
wretched shame that the Hesters do not countenance cards
at their gatherings! I'm in the mood for a hand or two
tonight!"

The Viscount moved obediently behind her and said,
"The next prime minister? Who is it, and who is your
source?"

Mrs. Parrish replied waggishly, over her shoulder, "That
would be telling!"

"The soul of discretion, Eliza Parrish," Lady Marsh remarked, smiling at Marianna. Then her face changed, and

she said seriously, "I am not sure that there are any rules for Louisa's parties. Perhaps the rule is to break them. Does it trouble you?"

"Not really, but I admit to being new to this." Marianna paused, wondering how much to divulge. Then, "This is my very first evening out."

"Is it?" Lady Marsh smiled again, warmly. "How nice! And I don't think you need any advice on how to go on, except to mention that you should not pay the least heed to what Eliza says. What did she mean by your literal turn of mind?"

Marianna did not think that Lady Marsh was trying to uncover the subject of her conversation with Mrs. Parrish. Lady Marsh must have known that she herself had been the topic of discussion. "Mrs. Parrish proposed an idea that I asserted was contradictory, and I asked her to explain it," Marianna explained.

"Lady Hester would thoroughly approve," Lady Marsh replied. "The object of her parties is, after all, Good Talk."

"So I should suppose, since the evenings are called *conversazioni*," Marianna replied.

Lady Marsh paused. "Do you know Italian?"

"Why, yes," Marianna answered with some surprise. "I grew up more or less in Milan. Why do you ask?"

"Something in your pronunciation just now made me wonder, especially since you claim to be new to this." A small sweep of her hand encompassed the room. After a moment, "But, then, somehow, you do not seem at all out of place. Do you know, by chance, the Italian ambassador and his wife, Marcello and Cipriana Montenegro? No? They are a lovely couple, and I am sure that they would love to meet you. Well informed and articulate. I shall introduce you!"

Marianna said that she would be delighted to meet Signor and Signora Montenegro and looked forward to sharing Good Talk with them in Italian.

"But we must find you some here in English before the

evening is over," Susannah Marsh said with a wink, implying that Marianna had not found any with Eliza Parrish.

Lady Marsh led Marianna to a group, introduced her, and then left her. An elderly gentleman refilled Marianna's glass and supplied her with a plate of food. She was content to consume her refreshments and to listen. It was stimulating discussion that ranged over literature and politics and newsworthy people, and she found that, for the most part, she had her own opinions on most of the issues. Since she was not pressed to offer them, she kept them to herself.

After a while, a particularly elegant man entered the group. He was tall and willowy and undeniably handsome in his fashionable Catogan wig and magnificent coat of light blue satin foaming with lace.

The elderly gentleman performed the introduction. "Allow me to present to you, Lady Westleigh, one of your husband's very dear friends . . . and London's most fashionable fribble. Lady Westleigh, Mr. Peter Everly."

"You flatter me, dear boy!" Mr. Everly said, and made an elegant leg to Marianna, who curtsied in turn. "So, Tony's wife!" he commented with evident appreciation.

Before Marianna could reply, Everly continued inconsequently, "I have always admired your husband, Lady Westleigh! He is one of the few men of birth in London with the courage to wear his own hair. I have often told him how right he is to adopt the merchants' fashions. Wigs are devilishly hot . . . and they itch! Shall we follow Maddox's lead and dare to cast ours aside too, sirs?" he asked, addressing the group.

The topic was seized upon, and the conversation ran merrily over the relative merits and demerits of wigs. From there the evening passed quickly and successfully.

Over the next few weeks, Marianna did not suffer from having too much of her own company. She met the men and women of title and estate who orbited in the charmed circles of ease and privilege. She had many occasions to encounter that polished specimen of Town life, Peter

Everly, and she found that she could converse with him as comfortably as she had done with Lord Edward. Once she had been approved by Lady Hester's set and taken under Lady Susannah Marsh's wing, invitations inscribed with her name began to flow into Maddox House on Cavendish Square.

Marianna was enchanted by her new life. At first, she merely watched and listened to the nuances of these new forms of social discourse, waiting until she was ready to make her mark. She learned that the object was to keep the ball of conversational banter in the air, to toss it back as deftly as it was thrown. She discovered, as well, that all her reading had not gone to waste and that her literal turn of mind could be an asset rather than a liability. She was delighted to find in herself a vein of flirtatious banter, which she had never before tapped and which Peter Everly mined with finesse. She still had much to learn, but she felt her feet ever firmer on the ground in this new world.

Thus it was that Anthony Maddox returned to London to find a slight, but discernible, change in his bride.

At an unseasonably early hour one morning in mid-April, Anthony Maddox strode unannounced into his home on Cavendish Square. He shed his light cloak into the arms of a surprised footman and purposefully crossed the black-and-white tiled hall in the direction of the dining saloon, bringing in his wake a number of sleepy servants roused to instant life.

Maddox had driven the night through. The long coat of mulberry velvet he wore did not betray signs of the strenuous journey; however, the shirt sparingly frilled with needle lace did not look fresh. His lordship's hair was longer than when he had left but still tied back neatly. His complexion was swarthier, suggesting that he had recently spent a deal of time out-of-doors. The lines of his face were harsher, too, from lack of sleep and preoccupation, emphasizing his natural roughness that silk and velvet could not hide; but his gray-green eyes were fully alive.

He was in no good mood. A man of temper with a passion for his work, he chafed at the critical loss of time this month past. He did not specialize in wild goose chases! He wondered how badly support for his economic reforms had eroded during his absence; and as he opened the doors to the dining room himself (no servant having been alert enough to perform the office for him), he reviewed in his mind the full day of meetings he had planned in the House of Lords.

Seated to the right of his place at the table, Maddox was agreeably surprised to see his first appointment of the day apparently awaiting him, head buried in the newspaper.

Swiftly crossing the room, Maddox said, "Good that you are come, Johnston! You got my note, then? I had not expected to see you here, man, and now you have saved me the damnable trouble of making myself presentable and appearing in Parliament at ten o'clock. You cannot imagine the night I have just spent on the road! Excuse me in all my dirt but, good God, I'm ravenous!"

The newspaper lowered to reveal the face of a woman. Maddox's expression changed, almost imperceptibly. Then he bowed low.

Marianna was as surprised as he, but since she had had the slight advantage in this unexpected encounter, she had been able to catch the swift, blank look that crossed her husband's face. The month before, she might have been disconcerted that he had not immediately recognized her. This morning she was amused, and rather intrigued by the glimpse of fire and intensity in her husband that he had always kept hidden from her.

"My lady," he intoned, setting his mask of civility firmly into place. "I trust I find you well."

"My lord," she returned, with a composed smile. "You find me just where you left me. At the breakfast table."

Had he been less prejudiced against his wife (whom he had all but banished from his thoughts since the fiasco of their wedding night), he might have admired her aplomb and her early morning freshness. Instead, he seated himself at his place, making a great effort to suppress all the ill will he harbored against his wife-in-name-only. "A symmetry, I perceive," he remarked.

"Almost!" Marianna replied. She felt some explanation necessary for her new seating arrangement. "You may well wonder why I am not occupying the ladyship's place at the other end of the table. In order to take best advantage of the reading light of the morning sun, you see, I have moved to this end of the table. Had I known you were returning—"

"You are free to choose the place that suits you best, my lady," her husband interrupted with punctilious courtesy, placing his napkin in his lap and signing for food and drink.

Such flattering consideration! Marianna bit back the retort that hovered on her lips. She saw that he must be very weary and that no good purpose was served in provoking him. Instead, she calmly volunteered the information (for future reference) that she had established the habit of breakfasting at eight-thirty and offered him the opportunity to excuse her from the room. "Since you see that I have already finished my meal this morning, my lord, I hope that you will not take it amiss if I leave you now, so that you may get on with your business for the day."

He considered her briefly. "Don't go yet," he said, as she rose from her chair. "I'm to spend the day and, no doubt, most of the evening at my offices. If you don't bring me up to date on household matters now, we might have to postpone this same discussion until tomorrow evening."

Marianna was used, by now, to his peremptory commands, and she shrewdly guessed his desire to get this— surely the least important of his interviews—out of the way. In that moment she abandoned all the distant formality he seemed determined to impose on her. She decided to have a little fun.

She sat back down and agreed gaily, "Very true! Besides which, I myself am engaged to go to the theater this evening . . . and tomorrow night a *soirée musicale*. Tonight, it's Mr. Kemble in *Macbeth* . . . my first visit to Covent Garden. Naturally I am very much looking forward to it!" She pursued cheerfully, in the face of her husband's evident lack of interest, "And I go in very amusing company, too! Mr. Everly, Mr. Peter Everly . . . he is a friend of yours, is he not . . . ?"

She had the satisfaction of seeing Maddox's fork hesitate, ever so slightly, over his plate.

" . . . Yes, well, Mr. Everly has invited me along with Lady Marsh and Julia Thrale and the Earl of Ware and his brother, the Baron Childe, you know, and Lord and Lady Hester, who are friends of yours, too, I believe . . . ?"

"Good friends," Maddox said with a nod. "Amusing and very fashionable company." After a slight pause, he asked, "And how does the marchioness go on these days?"

"The marchioness?"

"Of Ainsworth."

"I don't know," she disclaimed, and met his eye directly when his appraisal of her suddenly became more measuring and penetrating. She added, guilelessly, "I had not heard that she was doing poorly, so I don't think that there is any cause for concern, if that is what you mean. Should you like me to write to her to inquire after the state of her health?"

Maddox, although preoccupied this morning, was still quite sharp. He replied that he did not think that would be necessary and began to focus his entire attention on the woman at his side. He ran his eyes over her as if for the first time, and asked, evidently referring to her gown, "Clairette's? Or Deley's?"

Marianna was wearing a charming morning dress of robin's egg blue shantung that set her coloring off to perfection. She shook her head and said, "Fanny Lane," with

an assured air that suggested she had engaged the best cou-
turiere in Town.

Maddox cocked a mobile brow. "Ah!" was all he said to
this, but he was acute enough. Without referring to the
other instructions he had given her upon his departure all
those weeks ago, he asked, "But tell me: you did manage
to see my man of affairs, did you not?"

"Oh, yes, I did see *him*!" Marianna assured her husband
in a light, provocative tone.

Just then the doors to the dining room opened. Through
them came the butler ceremoniously bearing the first delivery of the daily mail on a heavy silver salver.

Marianna suddenly remembered that she was expecting
to receive this morning a crucially important letter. She had
erred to have so capriciously drawn her husband's attention
to herself while he was seated not two feet away, within
easy view of all her personal correspondence.

IV

A Question of Finances

M̲addox cast a quick glance over the stack of letters that had been placed at his left hand by the butler. When this worthy withdrew from the room a moment later, his lordship's gaze returned to Marianna.

"Two newspapers?" he inquired, nodding first at his copy of the *Times* folded neatly under his bundle of envelopes and then at Marianna's, which she had been reading upon his entry. "You have your own subscription?"

"Why, yes, I enjoy reading the paper first thing in the morning," Marianna replied. To his look of mild inquiry, she explained, as she casually sorted through her correspondence, "Your Uncle Edward introduced me to the habit. He regularly sent his day-old *Times* every morning to the vicarage. He taught me to stay abreast of the outside world." Her heart leapt at sight of the letter she had been expecting from Mr. Morgan Vaughan, but she shuffled it calmly to the bottom of her stack. "He said it was good for me, but what he really wanted, I suspect, was someone who could discuss the news with him." She continued smoothly, raising her eyes to meet Maddox's. "And since I am an early riser, I wanted my own copy so that I would not have to wait upon anyone else to read it, you see."

Maddox lifted a brow. "Myself, for instance."

Marianna laughed involuntarily. "Actually, I was thinking of my brother. Jonathan was adamant in his claim that Lord Edward intended the newspaper for him! Women weren't supposed to fill their minds with such important matters. But Lord Edward found my brother's grasp of world affairs hopeless, and it always irritated me the way Jonathan would dither over the paper in the morning, making me wait, folding it this way and that. And so, I indulged myself in my own subscription."

Maddox merely nodded to all of this and reverted to the original topic by asking his wife about the domestic details and difficulties the new Lady Westleigh had encountered in the past six weeks.

While her husband finished his meal, Marianna obliged him by recounting, as briefly as possible, those items most pertinent to the running of Maddox House; and she assured him that she had encountered no difficulties whatsoever in establishing herself as the new mistress, finding Browne and the rest of the staff cooperative and most pleasant.

Maddox listened, asked a few pertinent questions which Marianna was able to answer easily, and pronounced himself satisfied with the report. Then, the conversation having come to its natural conclusion, he invited her to peruse her mail. He pointedly picked up his copy of the paper and began to read.

Marianna felt a mixture of relief and irritation. She was relieved to be able, at last, to open that most important letter; she was irritated that she had not been excused from the room.

She suddenly found her husband's proximity uncomfortable. Although he was ostensibly engrossed in reading the front page of the newspaper, Marianna was subtly aware that half of his attention remained on her. She judged it unwise to open Mr. Vaughan's letter, the letter that was most evidently not of a social nature. She suddenly found the intimacy of their seating arrangement most inconvenient. Too late she perceived the advantages of having the length of the table separating her from him. She could hardly change her seat now without arousing suspicion, and so she made a small show of opening her many invitations while sliding, unobtrusively, Mr. Vaughan's letter into the pocket of the skirt of her morning dress.

She was satisfied that her little maneuver had escaped her husband's notice, but she was soon to wonder whether he might not have seen it, after all.

Presently, having lingered over her mail the correct amount of time, she excused herself and stood up. Maddox surprised her by rising with her and politely escorting her to the door.

"One last thing, my lady," he said, almost as a lazy afterthought. "You did tell me that you contacted my man of business as I had instructed, did you not?"

Marianna looked up at him. She was aware of the easy set of his muscled shoulders beneath the velvet coat, the deepened expression lines of his face and the thick, dark curves of his unpowdered hair. It was not any one thing that set him apart from other men, she had noted before, but rather the inseparability of the whole, the general impression he made of rough force and vast wealth. He had never smiled at her yet, but a slight lift to his brow and another at the corner of his mouth made her wonder if his smile would be as disarming as she supposed it might.

"Yes, my lord," she replied, directly. "I wrote Mr. Duguid a note shortly after you left, and he was prompt in coming to the house. I signed all the necessary papers." She smiled prettily. "I followed your instructions exactly."

"Indeed?" he said with a trace of amused irony at this avowal of obedience. "And do you find your allowance sufficient?"

"Why, yes, most sufficient," she replied.

"Your account is in order and all your expenses covered?" he inquired, in a most husbandly fashion.

"Yes, of course, my account is in order," she answered, a little surprised at the question. "I am quite sure of it."

"No uncomfortable bills that might fall overdue before the next quarter?" he pursued. "Miss...er...Lane does not charge unreasonably for creating such charming fashions?"

She thought of Mr. Vaughan's letter. If, out of the corner of his eye, her husband had seen her slide it into her pocket, he might easily have mistaken it for a creditor's reckoning. "No, no outstanding bills, my lord. Miss Lane is very reasonable," she said, and offered by way of explanation, "in fact, she is considerably less expensive than Deley's and Clairette's."

"I was not aware that my wife would have need to economize on her dressmaker," he replied smoothly.

A faint flush crept up Marianna's cheeks. She had evidently not pleased him with the information that Fanny Lane came at bargain rates. "No, of course not," she said with admirable aplomb, "but I do like to consider my entire budget with every purchase. For instance, there is the newspaper..."

"At four pence daily, the subscription," her husband interpolated.

"Well, yes, it *is* cheap, isn't it?" Marianna countered swiftly, "and not likely to break my account. Then, too, there is Signor Luigi for my hair and Rachel...I should not forget her...and...and, well, a host of other expenses—trifles! not worth the telling!...but I am sure that I am still in the black for being so early in the quarter." Then she added, in a wifely spirit, "Shall I balance my account this morning and show it to you to make your mind easy?"

"My mind is not uneasy over your bank account," he replied. "It is just that...sometimes, not always...when one is new to Town, one might tend to underestimate the expense of leading a fashionable life. And you have already told me what fashionable company you keep."

Marianna was both stunned and offended. Did he truly imagine that she had run through the enormous sum of her first quarter's allowance in so short a time? Before she had a chance to reply to this incredible suggestion, Maddox was continuing, "And it occurs to me, somewhat belatedly, that it was not, perhaps, the best idea to have left you so entirely on your own in the early days. I put all good faith in Browne and Duguid, but I doubt whether they were able to instruct you to find the services you wanted at the established prices. Miss Lane might have offered you an initial economy, but others might have strained your budget in unexpected ways. Your coiffeur, for instance."

"Signor Luigi, my *parruchiere*?" she corrected coolly.

"My Italian is not, I fear, what it should be," he murmured.

She waved this away with an impatient gesture and asked him—the chill in her voice pronounced now—whether he would care to know the precise figure she paid for Signor Luigi's services.

He declined this offer with the damping words, "No, I do not intend to be an interfering husband, my lady. You have assured me that your bank account is in no serious trouble, and I am satisfied."

With this, Marianna left the room, and Maddox returned to the table and to his rather large pile of correspondence. He was not, as he had said, truly worried about the state of his wife's finances, for there was only so much damage that could be done in the space of a mere six weeks. He did, on the other hand, believe the letter he had seen her slide into her pocket was most likely a politely worded and exceedingly unpleasant reminder of some extravagant bill or another. He was willing (for reasons best known to himself) to allow her to sink very deep into the River Tick before he would fish her out, and the deeper she sank, the grimmer would be his satisfaction.

However, he wanted no surprises on that score and decided to contact his man of business so that Duguid could keep him informed of any serious irregularities in his wife's account. Maddox had no intention of violating the terms of this marriage of independence by interfering with his wife's extravagances, but having Duguid keep a close watch on her account was another matter entirely. Registering a mental note to stop by Duguid's offices on his way to Parliament later that morning, Maddox mentally dismissed his wife and her financial affairs and turned to more pressing matters.

Marianna did not so easily banish this question of finances from her mind. She repaired to her chambers rather vexed. Instead of showing her husband that she was not a spineless doll (or whatever manner of creature he thought he had married), she had rather raised doubts in his mind about her ability to stay within an extravagant allowance. How dare he imply such a thing? How dare he threaten her with it? For threaten her he had! And it maddened her all the more to know that whatever else might be the case about the state of her finances, she was most definitely *not* overdrawn.

Maddox was correct in thinking that the letter from Mr. Vaughan burning now in her pocket had to do with her bank account. However, it concerned not the money she owed, but rather the money she was making.

Several weeks earlier, an acquaintance of Marianna's had passed her the business card of a Mr. Morgan Vaughan of "Number 7 Finch Lane, Cornhill," who described himself as "Hatter, Hosier, and Stock Broker." It was whispered in feminine circles that Mr. Vaughan specialized in "unusual investors." He was, for instance, most helpful to ladies experiencing financial difficulty. His delicate understanding, his exquisite discretion, and his reputation for speculative prowess all combined to make him an ideal source of potential ready cash to any number of fashionable women who, at times, were faced with unexpected and embarrassing expenses.

Mr. Vaughan's methods were simple. He would advance his client a sum of money that he would invest on the Stock Exchange. If, at the end of the short term, a profit was to be had, Mr. Vaughan would take it, and for this service, he would expect a mere twenty-five percent of the profit. If there were losses, the client would cover them, of course. His terms for repayment in the case of losses were obliging, even generous; and since his investments were most consistently profitable (and on occasion brilliantly so), he was quite a favorite among the most dashing, and therefore most impecunious, women in Town.

Marianna had not, at first, paid any attention to Mr. Vaughan's card. She had accepted it more as a token of acceptance into the select company of fashionable women than as a hedge against future financial embarrassment. But then a dazzling idea sprang to life in her brain and, without further reflection, she had made her first appointment in the respectable but rather dowdy suburb of Cornhill.

Mr. Vaughan had happily received Lady Westleigh in the front room of Number 7 Finch Lane. He listened with great interest to her request. Never before had Mr. Vaughan met a woman with any understanding of 'Change; never before had he met a woman who had made such a suggestion. Now, Mr. Vaughan admired Lady Westleigh's foresight. He was even charmed by it. He was accustomed to doing business with rather ignorant ladies of fashion and estate only *after* they had ruined themselves. Although he could not quite fathom why the wealthy Lady Westleigh craved additional financial security, he stood in all readiness to advise her in what she so enchantingly referred to as the building of her nest egg. Her ladyship could begin with a short-term purchase of the conservative Four per Cents. Accrued interest therefrom could be more aggressively reinvested later on. Lady Westleigh was sure to be well pleased, even in the short term of a few weeks, if all went according to plan.

In the privacy of her chambers this morning, Marianna ripped open the letter from Mr. Vaughan. She was assured by the first paragraph that all was, indeed, going to plan. The Four per Cents were doing nicely. He recommended that she leave her money there for the next little while, and if she desired to increase her modest investment, he could certainly purchase several more shares of these very good Consols for her with no difficulty.

The second paragraph explored new territory. Mr. Vaughan wrote that rumors of scandal and fraud were spreading through the Threadneedle Stock Exchange (though not, he hastened to add, touching such reliable open-market funds as the Four per Cent Consols). It was a sad affair, in Mr. Vaughan's opinion, but not one that came as a great surprise to him. Such were the vagaries of stocks and bonds and banks and dishonest men. Yes, it was a decidedly bear market, the mood skittish. However, it had been Mr. Vaughan's experience, contrary to the conventional wisdom in the wake of such a scandal, that now was the time for Lady Westleigh to make several shrewd acquisitions. The scandal affected India Bonds and Old Annuities and had drastically lowered their current selling price. A large purchase of these two stocks could prove highly profitable to the investor so adventuresome as to acquire them now. Lady Westleigh might contact him in the next day or two, but after a week or more the advantage of buying these stocks at unnaturally depressed prices would be lost. "For what was speculation, after all," ran the spidery scrawl, "but intelligent scrutiny, sight reinforced by mind, perception joined to conception?" This rather lengthy, gently persuasive passage closed with the purely rhetorical question, "In short, my dear Lady Westleigh, is there any reward without risk?"

Marianna smiled at Mr. Vaughan's flourishing periods, and she did not, in truth, know the relationship between risk and reward, for it was clear to her that Mr. Vaughan reaped quite a reward at no real risk to himself. She shook her head at his idea of buying scandal-tainted stock, as much as she perceived the potential wisdom in doing so. No, she was not so adventuresome, when all was said, nor was it her object to amass a fortune on 'Change. However, when she paused a moment to determine what her object was, she found that she could not quite define it. Her allowance already provided her with more money than she could spend. So it did not make sense, even to herself, to acquire more. Perhaps she had been too poor and too dependent for too long to believe that she could truly be taken care of for the rest of her life. Or, perhaps the money she was making had symbolic value, a kind of private moral victory over her husband, a concrete measure of personal worth in this strange marriage of independence. Whatever the reason, there it was: she had an irrepressible desire to make money of her own—but only a little.

She shook her head again over Mr. Vaughan's letter. No, she would continue as she had begun, with the safe and modest investment. She was not a speculator at heart, and would leave the buying of the India Bonds and Old Annuities to those who craved the thrill of money making.

In all events, Mr. Vaughan's letter could not go unanswered, and she determined that her first errand of the morning should be a quick visit to Finch Lane. She needed to discuss with Mr. Vaughan the further purchase of the Four per Cent Consols and, more importantly, to let him know that she could no longer receive any correspondence with him in the morning mail, now that her husband had returned. All letters would have to be hand delivered, by linkboy, in the late afternoon.

An hour later, Marianna stepped out of Maddox House, accompanied by Rachel, to proceed on foot to the suburb of Cornhill. Since Marianna was country bred, she had chosen to walk the streets to Finch Lane; and since the day was very fine, the walk was sure to be diverting. Cavendish Square was civilized enough, of course. The unbroken cobbled stones of the pavement presented no hazard to ladies with their dainty shoes. A serene fountain played idly in the center of this rather large square, which was filled with shrubbery and several gas lamps, and the whole was surrounded by a decorative iron railing. Once they were out of the immediate neighborhood, however, the scene took on rather more color and a good deal more noise.

Marianna was not yet jaded by the hurly-burly of London life. She wove through the streets that connected what was referred to as the City of London but which, in reality, comprised a maze of pathways linking one major borough and forty-six ancient villages. Heading north to Tyburn Road, Marianna crossed the lively suburbs of Bunhill Row, Portpool, and Saffron-Hill. Here the streets were lined with projecting fronts, bulk-shops with bright shingles, casement windows, and moss-covered churches. The houses were placed in a line. The windows were high and provided with sashes, and in front of the houses in the better streets the pavement was laid with flat stones. Posts at short intervals protected the unwary from reckless drivers.

At any given time a chariot-and-four proceeded majestically along the street, several men rode on horse back, and one-horse carts added to the congestion. These vehicles competed with pushcarts, barrows, and donkeys and the never-ending procession of pedestrians. The apple woman with a tin pan of live charcoal on her head on which to roast her apples was followed by the bandbox man, who carried a pole over his shoulder loaded with bandboxes neatly covered with colored papers. The bellows mender carried his bag of tools over his shoulder as well, and did his mending on the curb or on the doorstep. An old soldier with a wooden leg sold slippers. The sounds of a barrel organ, the cry of "Milk" or "Early peas" or "Hot loaves" competed with a distant German band and the strident invitations to "Buy! Buy! Buy!" Everybody complained about the noise, but nobody did anything to stop it. One daring Englishman who had crossed the ocean to America had returned to write an angry letter to the newspaper, likening the combined effect of the constant quarreling, cursing, and hawking in the streets to the thunderous roar of the Niagara afar off.

All through the city, Marianna crossed pleasure grounds and gardens, where the people resorted in spring and summer and on Sundays to drink punch or chocolate, to order a syllabub, or to take a peaceful pipe of tobacco.

At last she arrived at the village of Cornhill, a quieter neighborhood where the goodwives sat with open doors, running in and out, gossiping over their work, pleasing their babies in the morning sun. When Marianna turned on to Finch Lane, these women recognized at first glance one of Mr. Vaughan's clients. They would nudge one another and whisper whenever a coach would stop in front of Mr. Vaughan's to deposit a fashionable, properly veiled lady; and, sure enough, although this one was on foot and wore no veil, the wives exchanged nods and meaningful glances when they saw Marianna tread the shallow steps of Number 7 and ply the shiny brass knocker.

Mr. Vaughan was something of a personage in Cornhill. He was thin and quizzical; he dressed extremely nicely, sported a rather large boutonniere, and affected a walking stick and a powdered wig; he ate no meat and drank nothing stronger than iced water; and he proceeded according to the private motto: "Money is thicker than blood." When asked, from time to time, by the husbands of curious neighborhood housewives how things were going with him, he would invariably respond that he was doing "a little business here and there," or that he had "the usual balls in the air," or that he was tending "various irons in the fire." Mr. Vaughan, it was generally agreed, was a man who did what he could.

Mr. Vaughan was also a remarkably efficient businessman, for all of his affectations. He promptly greeted the young woman who was rapidly becoming one of his favorite clients. He immediately agreed to redirect Lady Westleigh's mail. He made note of her desire to purchase additional Consols. With an eye to diversifying her investments, he scanned the latest market quotations and offered South Sea Stock, Omnium, Navy, British North Borneo, English lottery tickets, and Exchequer Bills as promising possibilities. He accepted without demur her decision not to capitalize on the scandal about to rock Threadneedle Street. However, upon Marianna's departure not half an hour later, he could not resist saying, his fingertips pressed tightly together under his chin almost in an attitude of prayer, "You must sleep on it, my dear Lady Westleigh. India Bonds and Old Annuities! I can feel it in my bones!"

Marianna smiled in response and descended the freshly swept steps to the lane, Rachel in her shadow. Marianna's mind was clear now for the rest of the day, her heart light, with no burden heavier than the sunshine on her shoulders, no thought beyond the pleasant, sunny walk ahead of her. On a whim, she chose an alternate route back to Maddox House, one that would take her by Queen Anne Square and the outdoor merchants, the ones who sold doormats, brooms, lavender, spigots, combs, buckles, leghorns, holland socks, shoelaces, and matches; by Clare Market, where the shopkeepers still kept up the custom of having a 'prentice outside bawling an invitation of "Rally up, ladies! Rally up!"; and by the Turk in turban and red breeches who offered rhubarb and who, along with another Oriental known as the Moor, also sold kites.

To this end, then, Marianna descended Finch Lane in the opposite direction from whence she had come, turned the corner that would lead directly to Queen Anne Square, and had not walked more than half a block before her attention was idly caught by one of the innumerable little confrontations between coach and cart that seemed to occur at every other corner in the brawling streets of London. This time, Marianna saw that a carter carrying sand had

received the worst of an encounter with a plain black
chaise drawn by two horses.

The accident must have happened only the moment before, for the carter had apparently just begun to curse the
quantity of sand strewn across the cobbles and to gesticu-
late angrily at the broken axle of his cart, while the man
driving the chaise was just then descending from his high
perch. A small crowd was beginning to gather to enjoy the
entertainment.

Marianna glanced over the scene and was ready to walk
on when her attention was completely arrested. She
blinked once in disbelief, but neither her vision nor her
memory were faulty. The man who was driving the chaise
reminded Marianna strongly of the man she had seen two
months ago burying the box in the cemetery at Stanthorpe.
In the cheerful sunlight of this balmy April morning, the
man driving the chaise did not look as fearsome or as cadaverous as the one who had stood in the cold pall of a
February dawn with his black cloak whipping wildly about
him. Still, his overall severity, his height, his gaunt mien,
and the intensity that characterized his movements, even
the simple gesture of descending from the chaise, forcibly
brought to Marianna's mind the stark figure digging at the
hard, cold earth. She blinked again, but there could be no
doubt: the man standing not ten yards away was one and
the same as the man who had been in the cemetery.

She wanted a better look at his face but was surprised to
discover that by the time she had crossed the street, the
little incident was already being resolved. She saw the tall,
gaunt man shove a wad of bills into the carter's fist. As a
result of the quick exchange of money, the straggly group
of pedestrians was dispersing almost before they had really
gathered. It was a disappointment, really. These incidents
usually lasted much longer and at a higher volume, with
blame liberally distributed between the two opposing parties. The tall, gaunt man, it seemed, wanted no public display and no questions asked. The carter himself hardly

knew how to respond and, in his dumbfounded perplexity, had kept his hand held out. Before another moment had passed the gaunt man stuffed more notes into the carter's fist with the harsh, clipped pronouncement that that should cover it. Marianna caught the cadence of a foreign accent, but she had not heard enough to be able to identify it exactly. She guessed it to be French.

The next moment the man had climbed back up to his perch and had taken up the reins of his restive horses. They reared, snorting impatiently. He then cast a swift, disdainful glance over the few remaining onlookers, a silent command to disperse. Marianna felt an irrational stab in her breast at the wintry snap of his dark eyes as they fell momentarily on her and then passed on. She took an involuntary step backward at the force of his black, granite stare and felt a cold shadow pass over her heart.

She had never thought herself a coward, but then again, she had never before looked in the face of death. The spontaneous thought surprised her, that his was the face of death. He was not ugly, by any means. His gaunt face and features might have been handsome once, or fascinating at the very least, but something so hard and cold and naked and final, something so much like death, looked out from those eyes, that Marianna was quite sure she had never seen the like.

The glance lasted the veriest second, but the vivid memory of it accompanied Marianna home. She hastened back to Cavendish Square, oblivious of the noisy sounds and bright colors of street life. His dark, cold eyes hovered in her memory throughout most of the rest of the day. It was only while she was dressing for the theater later that afternoon that she decided, once and for all, to put him out of her mind. Here was an intriguing mystery, but one that did not concern her, or at least, one she could do nothing about. Had Lord Edward been alive, she would have discussed the cadaverous man with him at length. Had she enjoyed a different relationship with her husband, she would have been sure to tell him the unusual story.

Of her husband Marianna saw nothing in the hours before Everly's coach came to fetch her to the theater. Of Anthony Maddox's arrival in London, nothing was said as the carriage clipped over the cobbles. Her carriage companions were all very gay this evening, and the party included Susannah Marsh, looking lovely in daffodil and silver, Julia Thrale, a handsome widow, and Baron Childe, an amusing middle-aged exquisite. Presently they turned down Bow Street, which opened onto the square at the end of which stood Floral Hall and, next to it, under the harmoniously arched piazza, Covent Garden.

Marianna was naturally curious to witness firsthand the goings-on in and around the notorious Covent Garden Theater, since complaints had been lodged in the papers just that morning that the lobby of Covent Garden was mightily infested with gangs of pickpockets, pimps, and punks. Soon the party entered that dangerous, exciting, brightly lit lobby, and Everly pointed out to Marianna the door to the tavern where met "The Sublime Society of Beefsteaks," a coterie of the most jovial and witty individuals, who could demolish a steak and a bottle of port at one sitting and commit debaucheries all the night long, and among whose ranks was included the much celebrated thespian, John Kemble, who was playing the title role of Macbeth this evening.

Just before the beginning of the first act, the complete party, including the Hesters, had arrived and were comfortably ensconced in Everly's green box, which was well placed on stage with an excellent view of the actors and the rest of the theater. The ceiling of the large hall, which had been painted by Signor Amiconi, was lit by a thousand candles that clustered in the chandeliers hung with sparkling crystal prisms. Tiaras, necklaces, bracelets, and brooches winked in response, and the mellow light was thrown over all.

Below Everly's box was the pit, the chosen home of the critics. All the wits went to the pit; the macaronis went to the pit; the young bloods went to the pit and spent the greater part of their time ogling the ladies in the boxes. Between the acts the orange women with their baskets walked up and down in the pit, bawling and offering sweet China oranges, apples, and stout. At the first entr'acte, when the candles were relit (at a constant hazard of fire), Everly obligingly procured for the ladies a basket of the succulent oranges and produced, seemingly from nowhere, several bottles of champagne.

Toward the end of the second entr'acte, Eliza Parrish flitted over to their box. She was a talking flame, her hair dressed with crimson plumes, her cheeks rouged and patched, her dress a bonfire of satin. Wasn't Kemble the most marvelous performer alive, didn't Lady Morgana look dreadful, did one go after the farce to play picquet at Tom's or Will's? She chattered inconsequently as her dark, avid eyes roamed restlessly over the crowd below and then exclaimed, for all to hear, "Oh, look! There's Arianna Besant! Is Tony back in Town? Arianna must be in heaven!"

Then she gave a small start, artfully done, and covered her blaze-red mouth with a white-gloved hand, the perfect way to signal to everyone present that she had just said something she should not.

Without missing a beat, Susannah remarked, "You have your destinations confused, Eliza, for I had already noticed that the Besant is with Arthur Kingsley tonight. She is shockingly inconstant. She should take better care of her reputation."

Everly smoothly followed Susannah's lead. "You are entirely correct, Lady Marsh," he said lightly. "And if she is with Kingsley, it is quite a comedown for her. Why, he is not even half as amusing as her own husband is. And to flaunt him so publicly . . . ! But I daresay she is not acquainted with my theory, that not inconstancy but only a bad choice can blight a lady's reputation."

This observation was met with scandalized laughter, and so the barb of Eliza Parrish's comment was deflected in the ensuing volley of repartee surrounding the fine point of whether it was inconstancy or a bad choice that did the most damage to a lady's reputation.

Susannah engaged Marianna in trivial conversation, at the end of which Marianna thanked Susannah with her eyes. Susannah returned the acknowledgment with a tiny shake of her head, signifying that no thanks were necessary.

Not many minutes later, the candles were snuffed to begin the third act, and Marianna was understandably glad of the darkness. Her thoughts were quite chaotic, her one clear feeling being that of gratitude toward Susannah and Everly for having so deftly saved her face. She had willed herself not to react to Eliza's exclamation, nor to look in the direction that she had pointed, but even with Susannah and Everly's protection, Marianna had been stung by Eliza's careless words.

But was she jealous? In truth, she did not think so. Was she shocked? Hardly. Hers was a marriage of independence. Certainly her husband would amuse himself where he chose. So, why had she reacted so powerfully to the discovery of her husband's amours? Perhaps it was her very ignorance of them that affected her. Yes, perhaps it was her ignorance of his life before their marriage or, for that matter, since. She knew so little about the man, save what he had chosen to show her. It dawned on her now that her comfort in Society in the past weeks had been largely due to his absence from Town. With his return, everything had changed. The effect of his presence in her life was now incalculable. She had been caught off guard, and here was a lesson: the unpredictable was never comfortable.

Marianna had difficulty concentrating on the action going forward on the stage before her. Then, midway through the third act, on the dark stage eerily lit with flickering torches, Kemble's richly modulated Macbeth magnificently intoned to Banquo's ghost:

> Thou hast no speculation in those eyes
> Which thou dost glare with!

The words caught and echoed in Marianna's ears. Her mind fastened on one: *Spéculation.* "Intelligent scrutiny," Mr. Vaughan had written, "sight reinforced by mind, perception joined to conception." *Sleep on it, my dear Lady Westleigh. India Bonds and Old Annuities!* Speculation. The power to predict, the power to reap the reward. Speculation. Power. Reward. Arianna Besant. *Is Tony back in Town?* Arianna Besant. Anthony Maddox. *I do not intend to be an interfering husband.* Speculation. Speculation. Yes! *India Bonds and Old Annuities!*

Once having admitted to herself a sudden, passionate desire to make a killing on 'Change, Marianna hugely enjoyed the rest of the dark, despairing tragedy.

V

Maddox Cultivates His Wife's Acquaintance

Not many mornings later Marianna rose to read the delicious reports, "Twenty-Four Lame Ducks Waddling out of the Threadneedle Stock Exchange" in the wake of the scandal; then, hardly another week had passed before the startling news splashed in the papers that the prices of India Bonds and Old Annuities had rebounded vigorously. The swift reversal in their fortunes seemed miraculous to Marianna. According to the reports, it had something to do with the combined effects of government intervention, the reestablishment of national confidence, and an anonymous consortium of speculators halting the falling prices, but the result seemed far grander than the sum of its parts. It was, at first, bewildering. Then, the more she read, the more it began to make a peculiar kind of sense to her. She intuited (rather than fully understood) how Mr. Vaughan had guessed that the price per share of her stocks could reverse itself so dramatically and practically overnight; and the best part of it was that she had made a spectacular amount of money with very little effort. Speculation, she found, was an exhilarating pastime.

And it was not simply a case of beginner's luck. Her next few market purchases demonstrated a peculiar genius for what Mr. Vaughan called "intelligent scrutiny." Marianna laughed and said that he could call it whatever he pleased, but she knew it to be more a case of "feminine intuition." She now devoted some time every day to poring over the curling sheaves of the latest market quotations. These were printed daily in the back room of Jonathan's Coffee House in 'Change Alley, and Mr. Vaughan saw to it she received them every afternoon. And profit was heaped upon profit.

Nevertheless, for all of her "intelligent scrutiny," she did not guess that when she had made her most personally satisfactory financial gesture (what she privately called her "Declaration of Independence," after the Americans'), she had sown the seeds of her own undoing. The beginning of the end of her extraordinary career as a shadow investor on 'Change came one fine May morning, when the Maddox family financial manager requested an appointment with Lord Westleigh.

Mr. Charles Duguid was a very precise man, who arrived at Cavendish Square precisely at ten o'clock with the intention of alloting precisely one half hour to this morning meeting. Mr. Duguid was shown into the library.

Maddox, at his desk, nodded briefly at his entrance without looking up. He then scratched several more lines before sanding the page, shaking it out, and putting it in a thick dossier labeled *Chaumonot*. Only then did his brow clear. He rose to shake his visitor's hand, greeted Duguid conventionally, and gestured him into the chair facing the desk. Mr. Duguid perched himself on its edge and positioned his portfolio on his knees.

Settling himself back into his desk chair, Maddox looked almost as if he was going to enjoy this interview. "So, Duguid, what is it today?" he opened amicably. "Family finances?"

"Yes, in fact, yes, your lordship," Duguid answered.

"I am intrigued," his lordship continued with every evidence of good humor. "I thought we had pretty thoroughly gone over the budget in your offices only—when was it now?—last week or the week before."

"The week before, my lord."

"You see, then! When I got your note yesterday desiring this meeting, I could not help but wonder what matter could be so pressing."

"Yes, indeed, I quite understand how you might wonder!"

Maddox smiled. It was an attractive smile. He had a trick of lifting an eyebrow at the same time as the corner of his mouth. "It is, I believe, your very good understanding of my wishes concerning family finances that has brought you here today, no?"

"Exactly so, my lord!" was Duguid's response, and before he could come to the heart of the matter, Maddox surprised him by saying, "And if I do not mistake the matter, you have come to discuss Lady Westleigh's account."

Duguid had always admired his lordship's quick mind —and in such a very large man. One did not expect it. "Exactly so, my lord!" he said once again. "And now that you have mentioned it, let me say that—"

Maddox interrupted him with the flat demand, "How much?"

"How much, my lord?" Duguid repeated blankly.

"How much are we talking about? That is, in reference to her ladyship's account?" Maddox repeated, still with that affable note in his voice.

"I don't know precisely, my lord."

"Come, come!" Maddox encouraged genially, with a gleam in his eye. "Shall we say hundreds?"

"Hundreds, certainly hundreds, my lord, possibly thousands, but I don't—"

"Thousands?" Maddox echoed, the gleam having become a glint.

"Possibly. But you see, your lordship, I don't really

know the precise figure, for I do not have access to the complete account, and I was hoping that you would be able to—"

"You don't have access to the complete account . . .!" Maddox ejaculated, mobile brows shooting upward. "Good God! Could she have gone to Gin Lane already?"

To this extremely fastidious accountant, "Gin Lane" evoked the highly unsavory image of unswept alleyways, of back rooms and darkened windows, of ruined men and women, and illegal moneylenders. "G-gin L-lane?" Duguid stammered in horror. "What are you talking about, my lord?"

"The Twenty-per-Centers, of course, and I could not agree more with your shock and distaste." Then, seeing the bewildered look on Duguid's face, Maddox asked, "But what are *you* talking about?"

"Lady Westleigh's account, my lord!" Mr. Duguid replied, becoming more baffled with each passing second.

Maddox favored the hapless accountant with a lengthy stare. At last he said, "Well?"

Duguid was trying keep pace with his lordship's sudden change in humor. He proceeded to babble: "You desired me to keep you informed of any . . . ah, ah . . . irregularities in her ladyship's account, my lord, and it seemed that one had arisen, or at least I thought I had detected one a few days ago . . . hardly more than a few days ago! . . . and then I got to thinking about it, but I see now that I have made too much of nothing, and that your lordship has been laboring under a misapprehension with regard to her ladyship's expenditures, and no doubt you are already aware of them, and have made other arrangements, so that the mistake lies wholly with me!"

"I know nothing more now than I did when you came in!" Maddox's voice had completely lost its earlier pleasantness. "What is it with my wife's account?"

"Nothing, your lordship. Exactly nothing!"

"But a few moments ago, you were talking in terms of

hundreds and thousands of pounds," he rapped out. "Something about not having the precise figure, nor access to the complete account!"

"Well, as to that, your lordship, perhaps you have already contacted our offices about the bank draft, and I mislaid your message . . . ?" Duguid suggested, not unhopefully.

"A bank draft?" Maddox shot back.

"A draft from the bank, my lord!" Duguid explained.

"I'm warning you, Duguid!"

"A draft from the Bristol Bank, my lord!" Duguid rushed on, thoroughly discomposed, "For the precise figure—down to the penny!—of the amount that her ladyship has spent since she opened her account in March, so that her debits are at zero, not a single pound spent! That is what I meant when I said that the irregularity in the account was 'nothing': exactly nothing! Which struck me as very strange, of course, that she should have replaced the amount—*the exact amount*, mind you—of what she had spent in the first quarter even before the second quarter's transfer from your funds into hers. I can tell you that she was very far from having overdrawn. Her expenses to date had been modest . . . minimal, even! But that is not for me to say, of course. I would not presume . . . ! Yet, as you know, Duguid and Sons has built its reputation on serving the most distinguished families, and so we handle the accounts of some of the finest ladies in all England—of the first consequence, I can assure you!—and well, the fact of the matter is that very few of the ladies' accounts balance in a three-month period. I am sure you can well imagine what I mean! And so in comparison, all I can say is that Lady Westleigh's expenses have been very prudent and well within budget! That is why I was taken quite aback to receive that bank draft bringing her balance back to the very figure it was when you opened it for her, since it was not at all necessary. With a draft from the Bristol Bank, no less," he said, bethinking himself of the most egregious irregularity in the entire matter. "And in face of the fact that the Maddoxes were charter subscribers to the Bank of England nearly a century ago! And, well, as I've said, it seemed to me to be a trifle . . . ah . . . irregular!"

His lordship was attempting to master the details of this rather tangled, and very mysterious, recital of the irregularities in his wife's account. It was very murky indeed, but Maddox had regained a measure of control over his temper and was sitting back in his chair, his face closed, his eyes narrowed to slits of green light.

Duguid had cleared his throat and was plunging manfully on. "But, you know, it did occur to me that perhaps her ladyship's family . . . I believe I noted that her name is Lowth, is it not? Well, I do not presume an acquaintance with the Lowth family. They have not been clients of ours, or of any other management house that I know of! Nevertheless, I am sure that it is an excellent family, given the conditions of his lordship's will . . . Lord Edward's, that is! . . . and . . . well! Perhaps her ladyship's family is from Bristol? Although I do believe you told me once that she is from Stanthorpe, like your own family, but perhaps she has been left some kind of inheritance . . . ?"

Maddox smiled at this, not his pleasant, disarming smile, but a smile nevertheless, and Duguid heaved an inward sigh of relief. "Yes, perhaps you are right," his lordship replied after a moment. A faint note of humor had crept back into his voice. "An inheritance. Yes, in fact, I am sure that her ladyship mentioned it to me. But, you know, I have been rather preoccupied of late. I am aware now . . . yes, I am fully aware now that I have not given her a proper share of my attention. Call it an oversight!"

Duguid accepted these patent lies without a blink, but something in his lordship's voice prompted him to say, nervously, "But I have not meant to disturb you unnecessarily, or . . . or to have caused her ladyship any trouble, for I see now that I have come over a trifle!"

"No, indeed!" Maddox waved this away, affable once

again. "I am delighted that you have come, Charles! And I perfectly understand your concern over my wife's account and her ... ah ... apparent defection from the loyal services of Duguid and Son."

"No, no, *no*! Let me reassure you that I was not in the least concerned about *that*, your lordship!" Duguid replied, offended. "Where and with whom her ladyship chooses to bank is none of my concern! But the fact of the matter was this: I hated to see all that money sitting there idle, not being spent and doing nothing. It just didn't seem right! And so my intention this morning was to discuss with you the possibility of investing some of the balance of her ladyship's account. Investing on 'Change, that is! Now, it seems to me that some prudent investments might be the very thing for her ladyship, if she is not of a mind to spend her allowance. I ... I would have gone directly to her ... and not bothered you at all! ... except that when it comes to high finance, it has been my experience that ladies do not show the ... the ... precise understanding that we men do, and so my purpose this morning was to ask you if you thought I might arrange a meeting with her ladyship to explore the possibilities of investment opportunities. Very conservative ones, I assure you! Perhaps we might start with Government Bonds?"

Maddox applauded Duguid's suggestion, appended some observations that the Maddox family had all the more reason after today to count on the excellent services and foresight of Duguid and Sons, and finished his gentle remarks with the suggestion, "Let it ride! There's no hurry. I'll let you know when you should arrange to meet with her ladyship about investment opportunities. You know my policies! No Jamaican companies just now, or Yankee slavers." Then he asked to see the figures involved in his wife's account, the dates of the withdrawals and, in particular, the date on the draft from Bristol.

Duguid hesitated.

"Come now, Duguid!" Maddox cajoled. "You have

brought her file with you, have you not?" Maddox smiled effectively as he gestured to the bulging portfolio balanced on Duguid's knees.

Duguid cast a distracted glance at the lyre-shaped dial of the clock on the mantelshelf. He had not planned to spend this amount of time on what he was sure was to have been a routine errand. But almost from the start, this interview had not gone the way he had expected, and some indefinable instinct warned him that he had not done her ladyship a good turn by coming to his lordship. However, now that he had come, and now that his lordship had asked to review his wife's account (after he had so pointedly ignored it in their previous meeting!), Duguid did not very well see how he could refuse.

Thus it was that Charles Duguid ruined his entire day's schedule by spending the next half hour reviewing the debit and credit columns of what must have ranked as an exemplary account among the ladies of fashion. Not a penny overdrawn, not a penny out of place. Quite a credit to her character, Duguid would have thought, and what a relief and a delight it must be to her husband! Nevertheless, when Duguid took his leave from Cavendish Square, he could not quite shake the distinct, disquieting feeling that Lord Westleigh had been neither relieved nor delighted with Lady Westleigh's account; which thought led him to the uncomfortable conclusion that he might have done better by Lady Westleigh to let her entire allowance remain on their account books, unspent and accumulating a paltry bank-rate interest, for the rest of her natural life. "Let sleeping dogs lie" had been his father's motto, Duguid recalled, concerning that old scandal of Lord Harvey, the jeweler's bill, and la comtesse de Cambise. He wondered now whether his father's wisdom would have applied in this strange case as well.

It would have. After Duguid left, Maddox did not return to the file labeled *Chaumonot*, as he had intended. Instead, a storm on his brow, he prowled the library, stopping on occasion in front of one of the long, graceful windows to gaze unseeing over the burgeoning freshness of the May garden, and in the grip of an anger he had not felt since that dreadful day of the reading of his Uncle Edward's will three months ago.

This time, however, he was fired by an anger of a very different sort. If he had been in a mood for self-examination (which he was not), he might have realized the difference. Instead, he bent all his considerable mental energies on unraveling the more concrete financial puzzle at hand.

Maddox had been anticipating, with relish, a financial disaster in his wife's account; and for that contingency, he had been entirely prepared. He had known from the day he proposed marriage what he was going to do when Marianna Lowth overstepped her bounds. He had even given her the extra rope, metaphorically speaking, with which to hang herself; and he had been only too happy, upon receiving Duguid's note the day before, to think that her ruin had come so soon.

Maddox had been used to thinking of his wife—*his wife!*—in extremely unflattering terms that took no account of the patent facts that she was uncommonly pretty and possessed a lively mind and a lovely figure. Uncle Edward may have been played for a fool, but he, Maddox, would not so easily fall for a glorious head of curls, a pert tongue, and a few curves in the right places. That did not mean, of course, that he had not been willing to enjoy his marriage rights. He had, but he had not bargained for a wife he would actually have to woo! Dark, sultry women who had nothing to say for themselves were more in his style. His wife was clever, all right, but he had been confident that she would outsmart herself. He had determined that when she had overplayed her hand and overspent her funds, her game would be over, for good.

Now, however, he was baffled. If Marianna Lowth was not motivated by a desire to spend the Maddox money, as it seemed she was not, Maddox was forced to reconsider what her motives had been in befriending his uncle and in accepting his offer of marriage. He gave brief thought to why she had made such a point of returning her balance to zero. But this interesting consideration was quickly consumed in his blaze of anger. Having failed to control this woman in one way fired him with the desire to control her in all ways. For the first time in this marriage of independence, he knew just where he wanted his wife-in-name-only, and that was under his thumb.

He could contain himself no longer and hastily left the house to vent his anger in a round or two with a professional bruiser at Humphrey's Bear Garden Boxing Ring. The first order of business was to discover how she had come by such a large amount of money in the first place. The physical release helped him to regain his equanimity. With his connections, he hardly thought it would be difficult to discover the nature and sources of her financial dealings. He was confident to have the mystery of her bank account solved within the week.

When the week was over, and he was frustrated in his attempts to trace his wife's financial tracks, Maddox decided that a certain cultivation of her company would be necessary. This was easy enough. He began to circulate more widely in Society and, although piecing together her circle of friendships presented no challenge, it gave him a little clue into her finances. Instead, he learned what the rest of the world knew: his wife was warm, witty, and well liked.

He happened to cross paths with her on one occasion at an exclusive gathering at the home of the Italian ambassador and his wife. That evening, Lady Westleigh was to be found in company with Susannah Marsh, Peter Everly, and an assortment of other fashionables. When Maddox bowed and joined their group, they were deep into discussion of imminent war on the Continent and the inability of both the Austrian and Prussian generals to stabilize the situation in

France. To this Everly observed that war was far too serious a matter to be left to the military.

In the wake of the ensuing laughter, they hit upon the topic of laughter in general, and various witticisms were bandied about until one wag proposed: *"Rira bien qui rira le dernier!"*

"Diderot," murmured one voice, apparently fond of sources.

"Too, too banal!" another speaker complained.

"Surely we can do better than 'He who laughs last, laughs best,'" yet another agreed.

Marianna rose to the challenge. "She who laughs," she quipped, "lasts."

All very amusing, Maddox had thought at the time as he strolled over to discuss the latest from the Hanoverian court with his host, but he would eventually learn something about his wife's dealings that amused him not at all. He was to come by the information quite by chance, through an unexpected turning on the tortuous path in pursuit of Chaumonot, and this chance encounter would lead him directly to the doorstep of Number 7 Finch Lane, Cornhill.

In the meantime, however, Maddox's return to Society was generally noticed and remarked upon at every event he attended. He was alternately accused of having abandoned his friends without a word only to return to Town just as precipitously, looking fit as ever; or of having been a boorish slave to his work, whatever the devil it was that he occupied himself with anyway; or of finally realizing that he had heartlessly cast his very new wife adrift into Society (where she was doing very well without him, any number of people were happy to inform him). Peter Everly, for one, wanted to know whether Maddox had any intention of explaining the reasons behind this most mysterious marriage. Not that he would have to, of course; Lady Westleigh was a most charming woman. Still, when Maddox had left Town last February for Stanthorpe, Everly did not think marriage had been on his good friend's mind!

Marianna had also begun to notice her husband's presence in Society. She saw him, in passing, on occasion at Maddox House, but more frequently now he appeared at small, private gatherings, often enough that she had formed the most vexing habit of keeping half an eye out for a tall, broad-shouldered gentleman with a thick queue of unpowdered hair. Whenever she did meet him, she did not flatter herself that his presence had anything to do with her, for though he did not seem to avoid her, neither did he seem to seek her out. He would bow; she would curtsey; they would exchange the usual pleasantries. It was as if they were acquaintances—yet they were not. They were rather more like intimate strangers, as she had come to phrase it to herself, bound by the curious circumstance of sharing the same name and the same roof; and thus they were not, she was inclined to think, as totally independent one from the other as they had both thought they would be when they began their arrangement. She admitted to herself that he intrigued her, and she wondered what it would be like to get to know him better.

She was to have her chance at the large subscription ball known as the City Assembly. It was said that to become a member of the Assembly required as much interest as to become a member of Parliament, and seemed to rival the King's Birthnight Ball for exclusiveness. The City Assembly was held at the London Tavern, one of the finest rooms in all the city. The walls were light blue, ornamented with carvings and paintings, and the curtains and sofas were of blue silk with gold fringe; a large recess at the lower end of the room was entirely of looking glass. Magnificent lustres were spiked with wax candles, and the light they shed glanced on gentlemen in French satin coats with waistcoats of silver tissue, ruffles and frills of fine point lace, and swords at their sides, and on ladies in richly embroidered skirts ballooning over hoops and lace decolletages and feathered headdresses. Some of the elderly women were almost covered with diamonds. The room was so large that one hundred and twenty couples could dance in four sets, divided by ropes. The fiddlers, lodged on a balcony, scraped out minuets and country-dances.

This evening, once again, Marianna found herself in a small company organized by Peter Everly, and she was, at the moment, alone with him during a lull in the dancing. Maddox, elegant in his own particular way in a moss green coat trimmed with narrow gold lace, was strolling through the idle crowds. He came upon the couple as if by chance.

Marianna and Everly had just engaged in a light and amusing topic, but rather absorbing for all of that, when Maddox stepped up to them. They immediately broke off their discussion. Cordial greetings were exchanged all around. Maddox made reference to an encounter he had had with Everly the week before. Everly invited Maddox to join his party.

Maddox did not respond to the invitation, but looked about him, idly, and asked, "Oh, you have formed a party?"

"Why, yes, Lady Westleigh and I are in a party of eight this evening," Everly replied.

"And the other six are, I believe, invisible?" Maddox remarked.

Nothing in her husband's voice or demeanor suggested to Marianna that he was the least bit annoyed to find her alone with another man. The banter was meaningless, the words a pretense.

Everly kept it up. "Excellent chaperones, all of them, I assure you!"

"You need assure me of nothing, Everly," Maddox replied, indifferently. "I am only happy that Lady Westleigh" —he made a bow to Marianna—"should be so well entertained . . . and so regularly, it seems."

"Yes," Marianna said to this, "when I first met Mr. Everly—weeks ago it was already!—he was recommended to me as a friend of yours, my lord, and presented as London's most amusing gentleman! It has been my good fortune that he consistently lives up to his reputation! One is never bored in company with Mr. Everly!"

The musicians took up their instruments just then and announced the opening notes of a country-dance. Marianna felt the tiniest, most ridiculous twinge of disappointment that she had promised the next dance to Mr. Everly.

Everly bowed with a flourish and said, "My dance, I believe, Lady Westleigh."

"I think not, Everly," Maddox said bluntly and unexpectedly.

Indeed, Everly looked surprised. "But, Maddox! I am engaged to Lady Westleigh for the evening!"

Maddox did not, apparently, feel obligated to respond.

"But, Maddox," Everly said again, this time alluding slyly to the meaningful silence, "if you had wished to dance with your wife, you could have bought her a ticket and escorted her yourself. For these past three months and more, it seems that you have been chained to your offices and wedded to your work."

"I am not, as you see, at my offices now," Maddox said.

"And in fact, dear old boy," Everly continued, "I have never in all these years known you to frequent an assembly."

"I am not much of a dancer," Maddox admitted. "Yet, here I am at the City Assembly. With a modest desire to dance with my wife."

Everly eyed his rival with mock disapproval. He injected a note of light gallantry into the exchange. "Surely you do not mean to talk me out of my obligation—my very pleasant obligation—to her ladyship! She has promised me the dance. You know better than to break the Rules of Etiquette!"

"I know better than to bandy words with you, my dear Peter," Maddox replied gravely.

Everly sputtered with a laugh. "And I know better than to cross swords with you, I suppose? Very well, Tony! I bow, perhaps for the first time in my life, to the husband."

Everly spoke with all good humor, for he and Maddox
were, in truth, fast friends, but his imp of mischief
prompted him to say, "And what a perfect opportunity to
discuss the proposition that I had just put forward to Lady
Westleigh the moment you happened upon us!"

The music had begun. Maddox put his arm out to Marianna, and she laid her hand on it. Never, thought Marianna as her husband led her to the nearest set, could two
men have formed a stronger contrast: polished Peter
Everly, the very mirror of the elegancies, and Anthony
Maddox, brute masculinity come to life. Mr. Everly's
company was always light and undemanding; he was never
at a loss for words. In Maddox's presence, however, dis-
plays of verbal wizardry did not reign supreme, and Marianna was aware again of undercurrents churning just
below the surface of their seemingly polite relationship. As
they took their places, she was conscious of a change in
her heartbeat.

Marianna apparently had not been listening, for as they
took their places in the set, Maddox said, as if repeating
himself, "And the proposition?"

"The proposition?" she echoed, blankly.

"The one that you and Everly were discussing. Or was
that just another of his amusing remarks?"

Marianna gathered her wits. Her pretty blue eyes suddenly danced with merriment. "How perfect! So *that* is
what he meant! I hadn't thought of it!" she laughed. "You
see, Mr. Everly proposed that the country-dance was the
very emblem of marriage. I was disinclined to agree with
him until this very moment, but now I think he is perfectly
right!"

"Indeed?" Maddox replied, looking down at his wife
enigmatically.

It was a daring topic, but she was well practiced now at
this sort of thing, and the topic so perfectly suited the occasion that Marianna could not resist it. "Don't you see?"
she said, throwing out her first argument. "They both entail

contracts of fidelity and mutual agreeableness. Those are the duties of both dancing and marriage."

Maddox apparently did not find the topic objectionable, for he tossed back, "Explain yourself, my lady! The duties of the two do not strike me as similar."

"But yes! When one agrees to dance, or to marry, one enters into a contract that two people belong to each other, exclusively, till the moment of its dissolution. No outside party is allowed to interfere." She reflected on that point, the image of Arianna Besant rising up before her, and added, judiciously, "That is, in theory, at any rate."

"Ah! So much for the theoretical fidelity," he said. "But the mutual agreeableness?"

"It is the duty of the couple, be they dancing or married, to give each other no cause for wishing that he or she had bestowed themselves elsewhere," she pronounced with satisfaction.

"That is all very well, as far as it goes," he approved, "but it surely goes no further."

The figures of the country-dance kept them in close proximity. They met, they parted, but never farther than the space of an arm's length, making conversation as important a skill in the exercise as executing the steps.

"But consider this, then," she said. "In both, it is an engagement between man and woman, formed for the mutual advantage of each."

"Mutual advantage?" he pressed.

She preserved her even countenance. "It is not for me to say, of course, where those advantages are to be found. But, in general, I think you must agree that the two people come together for a purpose, be it for social pleasure or business."

"I will allow it," he conceded, excusing her from further explanation. "Any other similarities?"

She replied, on an inspired note, "In both, man has the advantage of choice, and woman only the power of refusal."

He conceded the point with a nod of his head. "Still, I think you omit a rather strong dissimilarity."

"Well," she said, "two people that marry must stay together. Two people that dance only stand opposite to each other for half an hour. Is that what you had in mind?"

"Not exactly," he replied. "Listening to you just now, it occurs to me that in dancing and in marriage the duties are exactly reversed."

"How so?"

"In dancing, the man need only be agreeable, as I have been doing thus far," he explained, "while the woman furnishes the support—here, the conversation!—as you have been doing."

"And in marriage . . . ?" she prompted, curious.

"It is the opposite. In marriage, the woman smiles, the man purveys. The woman is to make the home agreeable for the man, and the man is supposed to provide the support." He looked down at her. "Do you agree?"

"When you put it that way, I suppose I do agree. But certainly, all marriages—and I know many—do not conform to that pattern."

Maddox objected. "I know none which do not," he said. "Not even ours. You have undertaken the responsibilities of running my households, and I," he said, with an inscrutable look in his eye, "provide your support."

A tiny pulse leapt in Marianna's throat. Somewhere along the way, she sensed the topic had taken a serious turn. She dared to look up at him as their hands met for a figure. She felt his strength, and shied away from it. She said, with some deliberation, "I had not interpreted our marriage or seen our respective duties in quite that light."

"But you uphold your end of the contract by running my homes, making them agreeable to me."

"I am only too happy to do so! It is no trouble at all!"

"I am, naturally, glad to hear it, for I willingly provide your support." He added, still holding her eyes, "And, of course, there is a duty, exclusive to matrimony, that we have not yet spoken of."

She had been looking straight in his eyes. An unfair chemistry made her blush.

He continued. "A duty we discussed when you accepted my offer of marriage. I am to receive into my household a young ward, and I told you that it would be among your responsibilities to see to her tutelage and entertainment."

"I remember very well," she replied, as evenly as she was able, though she could not quite recover from the impression that he had exposed her in a most ungentlemanly fashion.

"Good. You should know that Miss Charlotte Armitage will be arriving soon," he replied. "I received a letter just this morning informing me that arrangements have been made for Miss Armitage to arrive at Maddox House on the morrow, before noon. Do you think that you can arrange to be at home to make her welcome? I should like us to lunch together tomorrow. Dine together, too, if possible."

Marianna replied she was sure that she could manage it. She then fell silent momentarily. She was wondering whether the imparting of this news had been the object of her husband's unaccustomed appearance at this Assembly and of his unprecedented action of asking her to dance.

After a very short space of silence, Maddox said, with a provocative glint lurking in his eyes, and a certain blunt charm he did not ordinarily exercise on her, "Since this is a dance, my lady, I expect you to purvey the conversation, while I am all complaisance!"

She imagined, for a split second, that he was flirting with her. She accepted the small challenge by regaling him for the rest of the dance with amusing accounts of her entertainment and diversions since coming to Town. He listened closely, asked a few leading questions, and did indeed hover, in his own unconventional fashion, on the edges of flirtation with his wife. However, he learned nothing more about her circle of acquaintance, or about her

possible financial associations, than he had known before
entering the room.

Soon the music stopped. Their contract of fidelity and
mutual agreeableness was at an end.

As he handed her back into Everly's care, she looked up
at him and said on an impulse, "You could have reminded
me of my matrimonial duty to Miss Armitage without the
dance, you know."

The light in the depths of his luminous eyes flickered
momentarily. "I could have! But then I never would have
heard your views on dancing and marriage." He smiled
down at her, his brow and the corner of his mouth lifting,
making his smile every bit as effective as she imagined it
might be. "You made some persuasive points, my lady,
but, you see, we disagree on the fundamentals. Perhaps we
shall have occasion to review them in the near future."

Marianna was left to make of that what she could.
Everly insisted that Maddox join their group. Maddox declined, pleading a standing late-night engagement. He
bowed then and left them.

VI

Lady Marsh Sees a Ghost

If Marianna was disappointed by Maddox's departure, she certainly did not show it. However, shortly thereafter, she noticed that the assembly had suddenly lost its appeal, and so she was glad when, not much later, Everly whisked the group off to another diversion.

Everly was at all times an amusing spirit, but he seemed, to Marianna, to be particularly so this evening.

For instance, as the group was milling outside the Assembly Rooms, separating into the various carriages which would convey them to their next destination, the Baron Childe demanded as he heaved himself into his coach, "Where are we for now?" Once inside, he flipped the catch on the side screen and pushed the glass pane out so that he could hang his head out and ask, "Do we go to Sheridan's or Carlisle's? Is it to be a drum or a rout?"

"We go to Sheridan's," Lady Hester called back, laughing. "But, dear me, is there a difference between a drum and a rout?"

Everly was at that moment handing Marianna into his well-sprung coach. He shook his finely rolled tye wig and exclaimed, shocked, "Lady Hester! I will not allow that you blur such an important distinction! Now, we might all agree," he improvised rapidly, "that a drum is not unaptly styled, from the noise and emptiness of the entertainment. But it should be distinguished from a drum-major, and then, perforce, from a rout, by the increasing degrees of multitude and uproar. Of no mean distinction, I hope you can see!"

This speech drew a laugh from Marianna, who looked down at him from the carriage step, her very pretty blue eyes twinkling with merriment. Everly smiled back, an oddly arrested expression on his thin, handsome face.

And, later, at Sheridan's, Everly declined the card playing, although Marianna knew that this pastime was the chief attraction for him at this sort of private party. Instead, he remained in the salon for talk, within the circle of which Marianna made a part. The absorbing subject of love was raised and ran a merry course from the delights of flings, fancies, and fickle loves to the very real peril of the fall, headlong and heedless, into love. All of this led to the topic of marriage, at which point Everly strongly protested.

"What, kind audience, may I ask, does our favored topic, love, have to do with marriage?" he demanded.

Eliza Parrish had joined the circle, and she rapped Everly's knuckles coquettishly with her fan. "Why, nothing at all, Everly! Whoever said it did?"

"No one, my dear," Everly replied. "And one does not demand much in the way of wit at Sheridan's, as we all know, but one must surely object to all gross lapses in logic! It was the transition from one topic to the next that drew my censure! I hold that our topic, love, has very little to do with that institution too often called 'the politeness of two indifferences.' Correct me if I am wrong!"

Many rose to his challenge. Everly was too severe, too cynical. Cudgels were taken up in defense of the institution of marriage (if only for the sake of discussion). Everly denied conjugal love. Where, then, were honor and fidelity and lifelong devotion? In short, where were all those emotions that were delicate, ingenuous, and tender? Accusations were launched that Everly himself could not know, never having been married and never having been in love.

"But I have been in love," Everly countered. "Many times!"

"Only with married ladies!" came the sly response.

He riposted deftly. "How else would I know so well the fireless hearth that is marriage? Indeed, you may well ask, where are all those delicate and tender emotions? I do not know! They are certainly not found in marriage. For it is a charming fairy tale of conjugal love you tell me, utterly charming but, nonetheless, a fairy tale!"

Susannah Marsh had also joined the group, in dazzling white with a daring decolletage. She had never looked more alluring, never more aloof. It had been whispered of late that the Duke of Kensington had almost made a conquest of her, but that she, unruffled goddess, had not quite permitted him to capture her, yet. Having caught the duke's interest had been considered something of a coup. Having caught his interest and dangled him along, still desirous, was nothing less than a tour de force.

"A fireless hearth—marriage?" she said. The catch in her voice was pronounced, but the ivory sculpture of her features betrayed nothing more than mild amusement. "You deny, then, the possibility of passion within the bonds of marriage? Something we might all agree comes close to a definition of true love?"

Everly laughed. "We have hopelessly confused the issue, I fear! I thought the topic was merely love, whimsical and insatiable! What you are talking about is a phenomenon rather like measles. Either you catch it young and are then immune; or, if you leave it to later, it can be fatal. Is that what we speak of? What you choose to call true love? Then, no, I have never been in love."

Marianna had been unusually quiet at Sheridan's. But this talk revived her, perhaps by its very contrast with the conversation she had had on a similar topic earlier in the evening.

"Fie on you, Mr. Everly!" she said, now joining the raillery. "You say at one moment that you have been in love many times and at the next that you have never been in love! Never mind our lapses in logic. You equivocate shamelessly! And I heartily wish that all the married ladies might learn of your views, so that they will no longer fall victim to your blandishments . . . or barring that, that you succumb to a severe case of the measles!"

"I would love catching a case from you, Lady Westleigh!" Everly replied immediately with a delightful twinkle in his eye.

Before Marianna had a chance to reply, the Viscount Stoke, who was hanging on Mrs. Parrish's arm, had chosen to enter the lists. "Why, if all married ladies henceforth refused Everly, that alone might improve the rate of success of conjugal fidelity—in London, at least!" The viscount was rather pleased with the witticism.

"But, no, you misunderstand me!" Everly said, holding a hand over his heart, as if to defend himself. "I am no philandering cad, seducing married women against their will! I cannot be held personally responsible for the marital infidelity running rampant in London! I feel a victim of your harsh criticism, and find my reputation in peril!"

"What, Everly, you call yourself now chaste?"

"No, merely fashionable," he replied easily. "Let me quote you the words of the immortal bard: 'As for love, I conceive it a mere empty bubble,/ And the fruits of success never worth half the trouble;/ Yet as Fashion decrees it, I bear the fatigue,/ That the world may suppose me "a man of intrigue." ' "

"The immortal bard?" Susannah questioned, laughing with the rest. "Yourself, in this case? Everly, where *do* you find your material?"

"I would tell you that I make it up, but then you would

just accuse me of puffing off my particularly fertile imagination!"

More in the same vein followed. Eliza was determined to show off the pretty diamond bangle she had won the night before playing at ombre and loo, and she had several amusing stories to tell of her amazing run of luck in cards during the past few weeks. Somehow, Marianna was restored to her usual spirits, although she had not quite admitted to herself that she had been out of spirits.

Then they were off again. The nucleus of Everly's constellation had attracted more stars, among them Susannah Marsh and Eliza Parrish. Others fell into the orbit. The suggestion—no one could have said whose—was made to attend the Pantheon ball, for more entertainment of a rather less genteel nature. The idea was instantly taken up.

The Pantheon ball was a masquerade. Dominos and masks were hired at the door and distributed to the ladies before they descended from the carriages. At the Pantheon could be found many a peer and gentleman of rank, but the balls were not recommended for the ladies of fashion. There one rubbed shoulders with the mixed company of the demimonde. It was a gay and gaudy throng made up of the entire gamut of city life, from tradesmen and journeymen looking for adventure, to those men living on the very margins of respectable society and below. The masked balls were frequented by lottery insurers and quack doctors, those men who had financial interest in the women from the commonest classes, the women who found coarse insults flattering and who took a certain cowed pleasure from short struggles in coaches. The Pantheon was the City Assembly stripped of its guineas and its decorum, but not its glitter and intrigue. It was a world of few restraints, where urgency reigned, allowing brutality and insolence as approved methods of courting. It was thus a world of great attraction to women of the highest rank, but only when they were sure to be shielded from its brutality and insolence by the proper escorts.

Everly's party, noisy and laughing, dominos cloaking their finery and masks in place, debarked from the carriages and plunged into the dimly lit, debased, frankly fascinating hall of the Pantheon. Everly's party had disbanded and recomposed: Everly had wanted to have Marianna to himself, but Eliza, in the mood for a mad flirtation, was demanding his undivided attention; the Hesters had formed a set with three other couples; several of the single gentlemen had known just what to do at the Pantheon and had no further use of Everly's party; while Susannah and Marianna had fallen in with each other and were reassured of their safety by the hovering, comfortable bulk of Baron Childe.

"Enjoying yourself?" Susannah asked lazily, looking about her.

"Immensely!" Marianna returned.

Susannah smiled and regarded her friend. "Why, I think you *are* enjoying yourself," she said.

"Of course I am," Marianna replied. Then, laughing unself-consciously, she asked, "Are you still trying to make me out to be a prim and countrified innocent to be shocked at the goings-on at the Pantheon ball?"

"No, you are no wide-eyed country rustic. I have remarked on that before," Susannah said. "And, remarkably, you do not look out of place here."

"I don't?" Marianna answered, rather pleased. "I suppose I have my father to thank for that! I have much more in common with the present company than you might think. You see, I spent a large part of my youth lounging in the coffeehouses in Milan—that is, if a girl of eight or nine or ten may be said to lounge! In any case, my father was something of a personage in those circles . . . and not the most elevated ones, although Italian society is so very different! In any case, I accompanied my father everywhere, petted and cosseted as *la ragazza inglese*—the little English girl—with the blond hair and the perfect Italian accent. My father taught me everything—except how to behave like a perfect lady. But perhaps I should not admit all of this!"

"Your candor is what one likes best about you," Susannah reassured. "Did you enjoy your upbringing?"

"If one can call it such!" Marianna laughed. "Of course, I enjoyed it. I loved it, in fact, just as I now love being in London. I had forgotten what it was like to be out and about, and I am thoroughly enjoying myself. Even more so now, I think, than I did as a girl. Society is far more entertaining as an adult!" She paused. "Or, should I say that Society is far more entertaining when one is a rich and respectable adult? And what a relief it is to be out of Stanthorpe! I feel so free!"

Susannah's finely arched brows rose a little above her mask. "Good heavens! I never thought about it. You went from the coffeehouses of Milan to a country village. Did you hate it? What did you do with yourself?"

"No, I didn't hate it." Marianna smiled. "Well, a little, at first! I spent an inordinate amount of time reading. But then, you see, I made a great friend in Lord Edward— Maddox's uncle—and that made my life tolerable. No, better than tolerable." Marianna bit her lip. "He died about three months ago."

"And you were very sad?"

"Yes, but you see, I was married almost immediately after his death, and so I have not been unhappy." Marianna smiled warmly. "Sometimes I think that Lord Edward would have wanted me to be married and well off! And then I can hear his voice, very clearly, accusing me of sentimental drivel!"

"So that is how you met Tony, then? Through his uncle?"

Marianna could have said yes, and left the conversation there, for Susannah never pried. However, the false face of the mask made personal conversations so much easier, and it came as a relief to talk.

"Not really, although, in a way, I suppose you could say

that I met Maddox as a result of my friendship with Lord
Edward," Marianna said.

Susannah's brows arched again. "Are you telling me
that your friend, Lord Edward, did not introduce the two of
you, throw you two together, and then pull you aside to
extol his nephew's virtues?"

"No, as a matter of fact, he never threw us together, and
he said very few things about Maddox that I can recall."

"Ah, so he took the other tack and promoted your many
virtues to Tony!"

Marianna had never considered that possibility. "No, I
do not think he did."

"My dear, you *did* spend too much time in the village, if
you think that!" Susannah teased.

"No, I honestly do not think Lord Edward would have
meddled in our lives like that."

"Perhaps not," Susannah said lightly. "After all, Lord
Edward would only have had to mention that you speak
perfect Italian for Maddox to recognize your political as a
political man's wife. Then, of course, one look at you
would have settled the issue for him!"

Strongly pulled by the trend in conversation, Marianna
would have liked to pursue it, but then her attention was
completely diverted. Into her line of vision came Arianna
Besant, with a tall gallant at her side. Marianna's heart
skipped a beat. There was no mistaking the Besant. She
had brazenly untied her mask and had let her scarlet domino fall open to reveal a dress that made all others modest
by comparison.

Marianna had been curious enough to want to glimpse
La Besant on a previous occasion. Tonight confirmed her
first impression. Arianna Besant was undeniably ravishing,
opulent even, with melting sloe eyes and luxurious black
hari against an expanse of white skin. A true vessel of
pleasure. It did not take much to imagine what Maddox
might see in the creature, for hers was an idolent beauty,

which would no doubt show to advantage on a couch, a languid Odalisque waiting be be adored and courted.

The Besant had raised her lips to her gallant, open and very red, a mute invitation for a kiss. The man bent his head and obliged her, thoroughly, passionately. The Besant quivered visibly in response.

Watching this seductive little scene, Marianna was suddenly conscious of her own innocence and inexperience, and of the stirrings of desire. A tiny doubt that she was as free as she had just claimed to be took root.

Aloud, Marianna said, "There she is," with no further explanation. She added, slowly, "But I don't think she is with Maddox."

Susannah's eyes followed Marianna's. Dispassionately regarding the couple locked in embrace, she agreed coolly, "No, it's not Maddox."

Marianna glanced at Susannah Marsh. She guessed that Susannah's approach to the gentle arts was very different from the Besant's. The Besant, all fire, would make herself frankly available to her man as a way of keeping his attention focused on her. Susannah, all ice, would keep him dangling with only a whisper of promised pleasure.

Even Marianna could not guess how Susannah had kept her duke on a string for such a long time, anticipating the end of desire only when she would become desperate, knowing that giving herself to him would be a blessed forgetfulness, a soft, warm drowning, but a giving that would nevertheless fall woefully short. She would never be able to give the whole of herself to any man, for any giving would not erase the haunting memories of Jean, the ghosts that followed her everywhere and gave her no rest, those memories of perfect passion and true devotion that would have to last Susannah a lifetime.

Of this, the world knew nothing.

Susannah said merely, "I do not know if it will matter to you, but Maddox has not singled her out publicly since your marriage."

To another person, Marianna would have laughed and waved away the remark with the airy "Of course it is of no consequence to me!" To Susannah, she said honestly, "I'm not sure it does matter, but I am glad to hear it. Thank you for telling me."

"Not at all," Susannah replied. "And from the looks of that little scene over there, I would imagine that he has broken with her entirely and that she has been driven to seek consolation elsewhere. Ah, well!" Then, regarding the Besant a moment longer, she commented, "All body but no heart."

"Do men care about a woman's heart?" Marianna asked.

Marianna could not read Susannah's face behind her mask as she replied, "Some do, perhaps, but then men are so unpredictable." There was an odd catch in her voice when she said, "Have a care with yours." Then Susannah half-uttered an exclamation, a gasp. She suddenly clutched Marianna's arm so tightly that Marianna was in pain.

"Lady Marsh! Susannah! What *is* it?"

Susannah was suddenly as white as the frock under her domino. She asked in an edged whisper, "Who ... who is that?"

"Where?" Marianna asked, startled.

"That tall man," Susannah said, "there."

Marianna looked where Susannah had pointed with such distress. Whoever it was, he was no longer there.

"He's gone!" Susannah breathed in suppressed agony.

Then, without another word, she left Marianna and the protection of Baron Childe to cross the room alone. She moved like a sleepwalker. She drifted across the dance floor, absently removing the roving hands of very drunk cavaliers from her person as if they were annoying flies, and disappeared behind an archway.

Just then, Eliza and Everly returned to her side, laughing, chatting, speaking of nothing. Everly drew Marianna off into the next dance with the mock serious pronouncement, "At last we are alone, my dear!"

Within the minute, Susannah came back to face Eliza and Baron Childe.

Eliza chirped, with a suggestion of malice, "And just where have you been, Susannah?"

Susannah had shaken herself free of whatever had gripped her. "Why, chasing a ghost, Eliza," she said, with a light laugh, tinged with an almost imperceptible trace of bitterness. "Only a ghost!"

Eliza cocked her head and thought herself very knowing. "I'll bet a handsome, well set up ghost."

Susannah's voice was composed and pleasant. "Betting will bring your ruin someday, Eliza," she predicted.

VII

Encounter at Jonathan's Coffee House

Just then, across town, Anthony Maddox was bending his head to enter the low portal of Jonathan's Coffee House in 'Change Alley. Inside, he found the usual arrangement: a front room with a low ceiling that had heavy beams running across it, and beyond there was most likely a warren of smaller rooms. Along the walls of the front room, which were wainscoted breast-high, men were drinking, talking, playing cards, smoking.

The host met Maddox at the door. He had never seen Maddox before, but it was his business to size up new clientele. He greeted Maddox cheerfully and ran down the bill of fare he was offering this night. Could he tempt the newcomer with some mutton pie? Maddox declined, but the ensuing exchange was sufficient to decide the host that, although the newcomer was not an easy man to place, he was neither a Mohawk nor a Bold Buck. No doubt the guinea slipped into his palm helped in the decision. Entry to the establishment was granted by a nod of the host's head.

Since the kind of talk Maddox wanted was not usually conducted in the front rooms, he penetrated the second room, where he found a staircase, shallow and broad and dark. He climbed it and made his way into the backmost of the upper rooms.

Several tables and chairs filled this room. In the center stood a crowd of men, mildly absorbed in the turn of the cards on the table. The stakes were low. The play at Jonathan's was not known to be deep. Several side conversations were in desultory progress. When Maddox approached the little knot at the table, room was made for him. He watched idly for a while, rapidly determined that not one face in the crowd looked a promising source of information on the activities of French revolutionaries, then took a place at one of the side tables. He always heeded Robert Armitage's wisdom: "Never drink less than a pint at the least promising tavern. Never drink more than a pint at the most promising."

A window was open. Noises drifted up from the street below, snatches of conversation of the passersby; the rumble of a cart, the click of carriage wheels; birds nesting down in leafy green trees swaying in warm May breezes; the sound of the watch prodding a drunk from the gutter, the drunkard's strident response; the sound of the watch telling a courtesan to move on or see herself in Bridewell, the courtesan's dulcet reply.

Inside, a tavern girl attended to Maddox. She was comely and buxom, and her virtue hung by a button. Maddox cast an appreciative glance over her charms, but his thoughts were elsewhere.

In the past several weeks, he had frequented an endless parade of London coffeehouses, clubs, inns and taverns, but with no luck. Still, he persisted, always hoping that the next tavern or the next coffeehouse would offer new leads into Chaumonot's activities in England. For Chaumonot's trail led surely to London, and Maddox could not rest until he had stopped the blackguard cold in his tracks. Maddox's progress was hindered by the fact that he did not know Chaumonot by sight. Robert Armitage had known Chaumonot well—too well. And now Robert Armitage was dead.

It took an ungodly amount of time, this frequenting of taverns: a whispered question here, the name *Chaumonot* dropped there; what rumors were circulating of the French revolutionaries come to London to plot? and what of the exiled French aristocrats who had begun to counterplot? Maddox had little taste for it. He operated best in the open halls of Parliament, not in the back rooms of taverns. Despite the fact that he fit in here remarkably well, he had neither his dead colleague's patience nor his uncanny methods of coaxing crucial facts out of unsuspecting informants.

Once again, he mentally cursed the loss of his longtime colleague and friend, Robert Armitage, the best and most seasoned agent in the Foreign Office. Once again, Maddox renewed his vow to avenge Armitage, who had been murdered in France last January. Of course, the Foreign Office had seen to it that English agents were spread all over the city, visiting the taverns and gaming hells night after night, searching for leads; and although Maddox would not normally have mixed in the affairs of the Foreign Office, he could hardly sit by, idle, after the man who had been his mentor had been ruthlessly killed. It was Armitage who had recognized Maddox's flair for finance and taken him out of the pool of Foreign Office aspirants in order to promote him in Parliament. It was Armitage who had taken the young lad of twenty with a lode of raw knowledge and forged him into a man with a steely grasp of politics. Now it was Maddox's turn to do something for Armitage. In fact, so deeply did Maddox feel the debt to Armitage that he had had to rein in his magnificent temper and accede to annoying stipulations in order to secure his inheritance of Maddox Hall in Stanthorpe. It would have been unthinkable to have let the property slip from his grasp, for it provided unparalleled access to the seafaring activities of the Frenchmen now swarming on English shores.

Hardly had the pint of foaming wet been placed before him than Maddox was approached by a very slim man of indeterminate age, dressed extremely nicely. No one could have called him a fop, but a more fastidious man in all of London would have been hard to find. He wore a wig, of course, and carried a hat and a stick. These hand-held accoutrements he laid across the table after begging purely perfunctory permission to be seated. This was followed by a gentle flow of words on the warmth of the lovely evening, on the coincidence of two men alone, on the friendliness of Jonathan's ambiance, all of which ended with the greeting, delivered in mellifluous tones, "Good eventide, kind sir."

Maddox returned the greeting, briefly.

"I do not believe we have had the honor of your company at Jonathan's before. It is a friendly coffeehouse. Indeed, I have just said so! And to what do we owe the pleasure?"

A man alone was not usually approached at the clubs. He either found a group and mingled in, or was left to himself. In a club where he was unknown, a man might, of course, be taken for a country flat by some operator running a rig, usually a shady one. This seemed to be one of those occasions. Maddox would tolerate the man, but only until he had drained his tankard.

Maddox gave the customary reply. "I've come for talk."

"Talk, sirrah? But why, then, come to Jonathan's?" the man asked. "It has no fame abroad for talk. You might try the Cocoa-Tree if it is talk you want!"

Maddox was being asked to account for himself. Although at no time did he want his identity to be known, it was still not his object to be taken for a country flat. "The Cocoa-Tree?" he said. "There the conversation turns chiefly on bribery, corruption, and mistakes in government." He shook his head. "Little interest there."

The fastidious man laughed gently. This was no pigeon for the plucking. He tried another tack. "Tedious topics, I agree! Well, then, you might prefer the sort of talk that centers on equipages, horse matches, and tupees, such as that at White's or St. James's," he suggested, naming the most exclusive of all the clubs.

"If I were a member," Maddox said.

"Which you are not?" It was a leading question.

Maddox merely smiled.

Decidedly, thought the fastidious man, this newcomer was a tough nut to crack. A challenge, in fact. Wearing his own hair like the commonest man in the street, and with the face and build of a prizefighter. Had the newcomer ever broken his nose? A difficult point to decide! But he sported a well-tailored coat and had a knowing look about him.

"For a man who has come to talk," the fastidious man tried again, "you do surprisingly little of it."

Again Maddox smiled and took a long sip of ale. "What talk do you have to offer me?"

The fastidious man was pleased. He came straight to the point. "Stocks and bonds and prices of pepper." He paused. "We like to think of Jonathan's as the stock market, as you must know."

Maddox was hardly surprised to discover that the man was a stock jobber. He shook his head dismissively. "Not for me, I'm afraid!"

The clever expression on the jobber's thin face sharpened. "Lost a bundle on 'Change already, have you?"

When Maddox did not immediately reply, the jobber drew his own conclusions. If the newcomer, wearing his own hair and a well-tailored coat, was a once-rich merchant down on his luck, the jobber might do well to hook him.

"You are wary, then," the jobber said. "I understand it. But, you have never invested with me. My investments are as safe—or as adventuresome—as you care to make them. I do not press! No, I never press!" The jobber's gentle voice lowered to a confidential whisper, but his eyes were bright and alight. "I think you should know that I have had quite a run of success lately." In truth, the jobber's success had been remarkable. It had, unfortunately, gone to his head. "I am sure that my rather phenomenal luck will continue for some little time to come," he said. "I can feel it in my bones!"

Maddox repeated that playing the market was not unlike casting dice at Hazard.

"You are a cautious man, I perceive!" the jobber said to this, searching for another angle. "A man who seeks an advantage, however small, where it may be found." He was warming to his topic. "Then, I am sure, you will appreciate the same quality in me. You see, for instance, I do not bank in London, where they charge positively usurious rates for every minor transaction—and I perform quite a lot of them." His thin lips curved up in a smile. "It is a measure of my success, you see. But, no, I bank outside of London, where a man gets more for his money. It is an advantage that not all my fellow stock jobbers have discovered."

Maddox had lost patience. "Again, no." Then, to end the discussion, he said, "At a guess, I would say you bank at Liverpool. Its banks are famous, along with their low rates, and the reason they can offer them is that every pound in them has been earned by the blood of a slave." Maddox regarded the jobber levelly. "It's the slave trade that makes Liverpool so prosperous these days, and I am not one to throw my money after that industry."

"So well informed! And a man of scruples!" the jobber exclaimed softly, with a hint of derision.

"No, foresight," Maddox replied. "As for scruples . . ." he merely shrugged. "I am not one to moralize. But the wind is blowing against the slave trade, and I don't want what little money I do have tied up in it."

"You refer, I suppose, to Prime Minister Pitt's bill before Parliament, kind sir?" the jobber said. "Yes. You see, I, too, am one to keep up with the times . . . and the laws! But the bill was defeated. Roundly defeated, if I remember correctly. And so you can see, sir, that I never participate in financial affairs that are against the law, and the slave trade is not illegal."

"It may soon be," Maddox said.

"Perhaps, but there is such a lot of money to be made in the meantime!"

For an answer, Maddox raised his tankard to finish it.

The jobber switched tactics. "But, as regards my banking practices, let me reassure you that we are of the same mind! I do not bank at Liverpool, where, as you so correctly point out, the present cash surplus may soon dry up. No, indeed, I bank only at Bristol."

Bristol! The name operated on Maddox with the effect of a magic word. He was glad just then to have been tossing off the last of his ale, for his face was hidden, and thus so was the look of sudden interest that must have crossed it. What Maddox lacked in the late Armitage's experience, he more than made up for in presence of mind. Bristol: could it be? For a man who had initially found nothing of interest in a pair of wide blue eyes and a mass of blond curls, Maddox found this bit very appetizing. Very appetizing! As tasty as a good lead to Chaumonot or a resounding victory on a tax bill. Better!

Maddox would have to be careful. Apparently, thus far he had done nothing to discourage the jobber. He put the empty tankard down on the table. He placed his hands in front of him on the tabletop and regarded them, as if considering an investment or two. In the soft candlelight, the table shone like a deep brown pool. In it was reflected the dull gleam of the pewter tankard and candlesticks, which seemed to float upon the surface.

Maddox looked up. "The bank rate at Bristol?" he asked.

The jobber told him.

"And your terms?"

Again, the jobber explained.

"So I do not need any of my own money, initially, to begin to invest?" Maddox asked with the proper display of thoughtful hesitation and speculative interest.

The jobber smiled. Finally the tables had turned, and it was the newcomer who was asking the questions. The jobber thought the large man a strange puzzle, wearing his own hair like the commonest merchant but with a well-tailored coat and a certain knowledge of financial affairs. Decidedly, thought the jobber, the newcomer might well qualify as an "irregular investor," the kind he so well liked.

The jobber came to a final decision, an impulsive one, perhaps, but his luck had been so very extraordinary lately. He could not lose!—he could feel it in his bones!

"I never discuss such matters here, as relaxed and pleasant as the atmosphere is," the jobber said. "I find it so much more . . . efficient to help my clients in my very own office, where all of my facts and figures are at my fingertips." He paused, for effect. "Should you like to make an appointment to visit my offices?"

Maddox agreed to that.

"My card," the jobber said, extracting one from his note case and, with a little flourish, flicking it over to Maddox.

Maddox looked down and read the delicate scroll: *Mr. Morgan Vaughan, Number 7 Finch Lane, Hosier, Hatter, and Stock Broker.*

"Shall we say tomorrow, late afternoon?" Mr. Vaughan suggested with a smile. "My place of business?"

Maddox agreed again and slipped the card into his inside pocket.

Mr. Vaughan was satisfied. He rose, picked up his cane and hat, and took a very correct leave of his newest, and most intriguing, client.

Maddox watched him go. Soon thereafter he also left the coffeehouse, with a surprising sense of satisfaction and anticipatory relish. He would go to the next tavern, and would continue on to the next after that, but if he turned up nothing at all on Chaumonot in the next few hours, he would still have had an excellent night of it.

VIII

Maddox Reveals His Character

The next day, before noon, Marianna went out to the imposing brick portico of Maddox House to greet the arrival of a hackney coach. Its passenger, a very young woman, bounced lightly down from the coach, and before Marianna had a chance to say anything, greetings were tripping off the traveler's lips.

"You must be Lady Westleigh," she said. Her smile was wide and dimpled in an open face ringed with chestnut curls under a jaunty little hat. "And I am Charlotte ... Charlotte Armitage! ... as I am sure you must have guessed, because Harry—Harriette Harriman, my former governess, but no doubt you know that, too!—wrote Lord Westleigh yesterday, (or was it the day before?) to tell you that I was coming. And, well, here I am! And I must say," she babbled on, gazing at the large edifice in front of her, "that I knew his lordship was very well to pass, but I would not have thought him so *very* rich. Nor had I dared hope," she continued, turning back to Marianna with a twinkle in her pansy-brown eyes, "that you, Lady Westleigh, would be so *ravishing*! And I know," she said frankly, "that Harry would say that I am rattling on to no purpose, but there it is! I always talk when I am happy, and I am *very* happy to be here!"

Marianna was not put off by these ingenuous disclosures, rather the opposite. She replied, with a warm smile of her own and a little hug of welcome, "And we are very happy to have you, too, Miss Armitage. But let us not stand in the street. I shall instruct the footman to carry your baggage into the house, so that we may go to your rooms and settle you in first thing!"

Miss Armitage thought that an excellent idea and made wide eyes when she saw the man standing behind Marianna begin to direct orders to the linkboys for the handling of the large array of bandboxes. She confided that Harry had told her how everything in London was very grand. "And now I see that 'everything' must include London footmen as well, for the one standing behind you looked so very grand that I thought at first he must be Lord Westleigh! But of course it is not he, for I remember him very well from the times that I met him—oh, last year and the year before—and he would be a very difficult man to forget!"

Marianna laughed at this tangle of ideas and replied that, of course, Lord Westleigh was memorable and that, yes, Maddox House was served by only the finest footmen. She explained that Lord Westleigh was not home at the moment, but that it had been decided only yesterday that he would be joining them for lunch in order to welcome Miss Armitage personally.

Miss Armitage thought that, too, was a grand idea. She was, apparently, of the type to say whatever popped into her head. Almost without pausing for breath, she made a dozen observations on the elegance of Cavendish Square, and when they turned toward the house, she hardly paused to observe before she exclaimed, "I've never seen so many windows in one house! Do you suppose that one person cleans them all?" Then she and Marianna were ushered past the low iron gate in the wake of the "very grand" footman, whose pace was eloquent of dignity and age, and through the arched doorway. She kept up a running stream of conversation as they made their way through the hallways, remarking on everything she saw, most of which was "grand," and reserved her highest praise for the staircase, which was "very, *very* grand!" After mounting the stairs, they turned down the private wing on the first floor and were led to the end, where they arrived at Charlotte's chambers. The footman rattled open the door to the suite and bowed the two ladies into the antechamber, where Charlotte was struck absolutely speechless at sight of the prettiest rooms she had ever seen.

She quickly recovered her tongue. "Are these really to be mine? I can't believe it!" she cried, and was about to launch into a dithyramb on the beauty of her rooms when she caught herself, and smiled, bringing her dimples into play. "No, I won't say another word! But I can assure you that I am *more* than happy! These rooms are the most beautiful, the most perfect, the *grandest* I have ever seen! I know very well that I am a prattlebox, for Harry has told me times out of mind! And she was not the only one, mind you! I remember that Father positively shuddered when I asked him to give me French lessons. He could speak it like a Frog, you know. But he just laughed and said that no one would ever get a moment's peace if I had *two* languages at my command!"

Marianna laughed at this enchanting child. "And so you never learned any French?"

"Not a word," Charlotte answered cheerfully. "Isn't that fortunate!"

"Very!" Marianna managed, choking a little. Mention of Charlotte's father reminded Marianna of the reason for Charlotte's presence. "But you must tell us if there is anything you need. This cannot be a happy time for you. I am sure that you must miss your father terribly."

Charlotte gave this a moment's consideration. "Well, of course, I am sorry that Father died and am not at all happy to have been left an orphan," she said. "He used to tell me not to worry . . . and always in such a serious way that it made me laugh! . . . and that if anything should ever happen to him, I would be taken care of by Lord Westleigh. Well . . . in the end, Father was right. Something *did* happen to him, and Lord Westleigh *is* going to take care of me! But as to missing him, I cannot say." A tiny frown puckered her brow. "You see, he spent most of his time abroad, away from me. In France, in fact. That is why he spoke such perfect French. I thought of him more as a favorite uncle, I suppose, than a father. I would have thought that the person I would miss the most was Harry but, you know, I don't think I will miss her very much now that I have seen *you*!" She paused and added, "And you needn't tell me not to tell her *that* next time I see her, for there are occasions when I know to be quiet!"

"I am sure there are, my dear!" Marianna managed to insert.

"But I am incurably honest," she continued, matching word to deed, "and say what I think, which is often taken for rudeness and tactlessness, although I do try to avoid either. Harry says in the village it is one thing to speak your mind, but quite another in London! Oh, no! She says that, if I am not careful, my tongue will put people off." Charlotte paused, and Marianna saw the slightly anxious question in the girl's eyes. "What do you think, Lady Westleigh? Do you think that you will be able to bear me?"

"I am sure we will deal famously, my dear," Marianna reassured her kindly. "I, too, am known for saying what is on my mind—I am called 'literal.' But it amounts to much the same thing in the end. So speak your mind, my dear! We can cultivate our honesty together."

Presently, after assuring Miss Armitage that she had time to change her traveling dress if she liked before descending for luncheon, Marianna left her young charge to talk the ear off of the newly engaged serving woman.

Marianna went first to the kitchens to review the menu. Then, on her way to the dining saloon to arrange the

flowers, she was handed a folded note from his lordship's
valet. She opened the paper and scanned the brief message
written in a bold fist. Owing to an important financial
meeting, she read, Maddox was excusing himself from the
luncheon. Beyond feeling a twinge of disappointment, she
gave Maddox's defection from the first meal with their new
guest no further thought, the only immediate consequence
of his absence being the rearrangements of the luncheon
seating.

Marianna was thoroughly delighted with Charlotte and,
if she had been apprehensive about being able to entertain
her young ward before they had met, she had no such fears
after an hour of Charlotte's acquaintance, at which point
they had already agreed to use first names. Charlotte, like
Marianna, wanted to see and do everything in London and
had the energy to accomplish it all. She scorned the idea
that she should take an afternoon rest after the midday meal
and enthusiastically seconded Marianna's suggestion that,
the day being so very fine, they visit a park. Unlike Marianna, however, Charlotte had not the least desire to visit
London on foot, so that when the coach was brought
around, the idea evolved that they need not visit anything
so tame as a mere park, but rather (having the coach at
their disposal) could go to a pleasure garden.

Marianna smiled and chose Marylebone, at a half an
hour's coach ride from Cavendish Square. Charlotte was
thrilled by the idea and thoroughly enchanted by the gardens, which were arranged around a circular basin of
water, with boxes around it in which the company took
refreshments. There were also bowling greens, Dutch-pin
grounds, and a cricket field upon which the Marylebone
Eleven had won many a silver cup. The Maddox footman
who shadowed their meanderings through the gardens lent
them countenance and consequence, and Charlotte was un-
flaggingly fascinated by the sights and the people and the
elaborate toilettes and the diversions. Marianna naturally
did not tell Charlotte that Marylebone was the least fash-

ionable of the gardens, having had its heyday in the Restoration, when all the world went mad after amusements.

They traveled back to Maddox House in the late afternoon not at all tired, and Charlotte insisted that she did not need to make an early night of it. Marianna had told Charlotte that she could attend the assembly this evening at the Great Concert Room in Soho, provided Maddox would allow his ward such license on her first evening in London.

Upon their return to Cavendish Square, Marianna learned nothing of Maddox's whereabouts. He had left no further message indicating whether he would be present or absent at dinner. Of course, Maddox was not in the habit of communicating with his wife as to his plans or engagements. It was only that since he had made such a special point of saying that they would all lunch and dine together the day of Miss Armitage's arrival, Marianna wondered where he was.

She was soon to guess, fairly accurately, where her husband had spent his day.

It was at the very beginning of the evening, the moment of the promise of twilight. Marianna was dressing for the assembly in Soho. She was seated at her dresser, wrapped in a wisp of lace fichu through which peeped the flattering lines of a snug, unboned corset of Jouy cambric. Her shoulders rose, sloping and very white, above the lace, which was caught at the shadow between her breasts with little gold ribbons tied down the bodice to the waist. There an underskirt was gathered and held together by a gold satin sash, from which the skirt fell in a swirl of silk about her pretty slippered feet. Her skin was fresh and very white, enhanced with a peach-and-pearl loveliness from her afternoon walk through the gardens, and charmingly exposed in her deshabille. Her curls, pale as candle shine, floated in a cloud about her shoulders and down her back.

Signor Luigi was in attendance. His mood was serious. Absorbed in the possibilities of this evening's creation, he had peeled off his coat to expose a white shirt of lawn with

cuffs of lace falling down to his knuckles. He was alternately posturing over Marianna's hair, pulling a golden
lock this way and that, and striking poses of deep thought.
Inspiration would soon visit him.

He had wrought significant changes in her ladyship's
dressing room. He was almost satisfied with them. He had
had two little bells installed on the closet, to provide a
lovely jingle-jangle at the dressing hour. He had demanded
that Lady Westleigh's bower be filled with a profusion of
freshly cut flowers. He insisted that she dress before total
darkness fell, when the half-light of the evening still gave a
glow through the long windows of her dressing room, facing north. He had seen to it that her dressing table was
surmounted by a large mirror. The table was smothered in
muslin, decked with lace, and littered with trinkets and
philtres, cosmetics and creams, perfumes and patches
(which her ladyship, for some obscure reason, refused to
wear), and hung with ribbons and tresses and plumes.

Signor Luigi had transformed the formerly utilitarian
little room into a charmed world of vanities, but grave de-
fects remained. He had not yet succeeded in convincing her
ladyship that she desperately needed a lapdog, yes, a little
lapdog to snuggle in her lap during the dressing hour. Nor
had he succeeded in persuading her that she should hold
court during this hour. Signor Luigi liked the flutter and
flattery of flunkies and lovers: a marquis here, a cock-robin
there. But no fawning attendants lounged in her ladyship's
dressing room, no scented love notes passed through her
ladyship's hands during the dressing hour. None of this for
her ladyship! Signor Luigi disapproved. The brilliance of
Signor Luigi's art alone could not release the beauty that
dwelt in her ladyship. The perfection of feminine beauty
was not a task for brushes and combs and pins and powder
and plumes alone. *Ma no!* Only love could bring the glow
from within to the light of day. Only love could unfurl the
petals of latent beauty that burgeoned inside, that begged to

open to expose their fragrance and fragile beauty to the sunshine. Only love!

But what did her ladyship concern herself with? Only long sheets of paper lined with columns of numbers! Bah! Instead of columns of numbers, she should be reading love notes! Verses to her dazzling health and to the full battery of her charms scribbled by ardent lovers. Verses to set her into the proper frame of mind for the night's entertainment. But not just verse! Boxes of sweetmeats, tender bouquets of Marseilles sprays, or violets. Signor Luigi was devoted to his mistress and the perfection of her beauty, but he could not do it alone! He disapproved of her unhealthy solitude!

Then, this evening, into this private, powdered world stepped Anthony Maddox. He entered the chamber, shoulders first, it seemed, and instantly filled it.

Upon sight of the large gentleman, Signor Luigi exclaimed with pleasure, "At last, my lady, you invite your cavaliers to wait upon you as you dress!" Then, noting that the gentleman was alone, he frowned to his mistress. "But only one, my lady? It is very bad form!"

"I am Lord Westleigh," Maddox informed the hairdresser with a brief bow.

Signor Luigi did not appear to think this any better form, for he looked pointedly at Maddox's hands, which were empty, bearing no trinket, no token, no note, no charm to tempt his mistress. "So!" he confined himself to saying. Then, recalling himself, he bowed with a flourish, straining the seams of his slim breeches. "*Su Eccellenza*, I am your 'umble servant, Signor Luigi."

"Yes, her ladyship's . . . er . . . *parruchiere*," Maddox replied.

Signor Luigi took a quick step back, his brush poised midair in a fencer's salute, with a fencer's *sa-sa*! on his lips. "*Parruchiere*?" he echoed, a flash of Mediterranean fire in his eyes, a throb of dark passion his voice. "*Parru-*

chiere? Non va! Signor Luigi is"—he struck an attitude—
"*uno scultore della testa!*"

"A sculptor of the head." Marianna translated on a point
of information and kept her smile inward when she commented, dryly, "You've been burned on that one before."

Maddox's "Quite" was equally dry. Then, after Marianna had soothed Signor Luigi's wounded dignity with a
few rapid phrases in his mother tongue, and encouraged
him to continue with his work, she turned back to her husband to find his eyes resting on her. Her pulses leapt that
he should find her in such an utterly charming state of
undress. She was very aware of the darker undercurrent, a
little threatening, a little thrilling, that had entered her gay,
gilded world.

"I trust I do not intrude," Maddox said without further
preliminaries. "We have several matters to discuss, and I
don't want them to wait."

"Yes, certainly, I understand," Marianna said. She assured him that he was most welcome to attend her in her
dressing room and invited him to be seated.

Maddox eyed with disfavor the dainty white-and-gilt
stool and declined the invitation. He took up a standing
position against one wall by the fireplace and propped an
arm on the mantelshelf.

Marianna turned back to her mirror. "But we missed
you at lunch today," she said, taking the initiative. "And I
am sure that you have come to discuss Miss Armitage."

"That, and other things. I was sorry to have missed
greeting Miss Armitage upon her arrival, as I had promised
to do last night. Pressing business kept me away from
home today."

Marianna glanced over quickly at her husband and wondered what it was in those simple statements that made her
heart beat suddenly more quickly, as if some hidden meaning lay behind them. She saw nothing in his expression,
which was bland, and he was inviting her, as a matter of
course, to tell him about his ward. "Since you will have the

lion's share of her care," he was saying, "I am interested to have your impressions."

Marianna replied with perfect honesty, "Charlotte is a charming girl! I am already so happy that she is come. She will be such a welcome companion for me! She is quite unspoiled and as eager as I am myself to explore the varied pleasures of London. I think she will prove a delightful addition to the household," she said. Then, with a twinkle in her wide blue eyes, she added, "That is, if either of us will be able to fit in enough of our own ideas to carry on a conversation with her. Charlotte, by her own admission— or at least that of her former governess—is a prattlebox. But a perfectly delightful one, as you shall discover for yourself when you get to know her better. Do you dine with us this evening?"

"No," he replied. "Again, I regret. My first meeting with Miss Armitage will have to wait until tomorrow. A series of unexpected appointments will keep me occupied far into the night."

Marianna wondered again what was in his voice, which was easy and melodious, that should cause her stomach to turn over. Certainly he had said nothing out of the ordinary!

"I shall breakfast with Miss Armitage tomorrow morning," he continued, "and with you, of course. You still hold to the hour of eight-thirty?"

Marianna affirmed this.

"Now you must tell me what you have done with Miss Armitage today," Maddox invited, "and what you have planned for her entertainment in the near future."

Marianna was happy to tell him about their excursion to Marylebone. She mentioned that she had withheld permission for Charlotte to accompany her in the party that had been arranged for the assembly at the Great Concert Room in Soho. "I told her she could go, my lord, if you would countenance this outing on her first night under your roof."

"Under yours, too, in fact. Do you go with Everly?" Maddox asked.

"Why, no, not tonight," she answered, and since Signor Luigi had just bent her head in the opposite direction from Maddox, she did not see the gleam in his eye. "I am going in a less dashing party, with Lord and Lady Bruton. Do you know. . .? Oh, of course, you do!"

Signor Luigi had let the tress fall, for he had not achieved the effect he was seeking. He stepped back from the dressing table to study the matter and began to pace back and forth, in a circuit of two steps either way.

"Lord Bruton is a member of White's," Maddox offered by way of explanation, "and yes, of course, I approve," he said. His voice struck an indefinable note. "Miss Armitage has my permission to attend the assembly with you."

Marianna was not pleased with his phrasing. Her husband's "permission" was, in her opinion, not necessary. That she had asked him at all was merely a courtesy. "Why, thank you!" she said with a touch of irony. "I am sure Charlotte will be thrilled to hear that you have given your permission." She slanted him a glance and asked, "Am I to understand that you would deny your permission, if I were going in Everly's company?"

"But his company is, by your own estimation, rather more dashing than Lord and Lady Bruton's."

"Indeed! But I shall certainly not leave her alone—or throw her to the wolves! I shall be with her every step of the way."

"You have implied that Miss Armitage is a handful, and the dangers are everywhere, my lady. Even for you."

Marianna laughed, prematurely. "Why is it that everyone tries to make me out to be a green girl from the countryside? I assure you I am not!"

His smile in response to this disarmed her. "Of course you are not, my lady," he replied. "Nevertheless, the dangers are everywhere. Especially for the most fashionable. Perhaps even for you."

"Dangers?" Marianna tossed it off. "For the most fashionable? What can you be thinking of?"

"Why, just this afternoon," Maddox said, leaning at his ease against the mantelshelf, "I heard rumors that women —titled and fashionable women—were investing on 'Change." His tone was offhand, his manner still agreeable. "I can hardly think of anything more dangerous than playing on 'Change. Since you move in those circles, you might be drawn into such foolhardiness."

Marianna had been taken completely unawares. She kept her expression immobile, but she paled a shade, the peach of her skin taking on an ivory cast. She struggled to grasp the implication of this disclosure. So! Here was the real object of this intimate, provocative little interview!

"'Change, my lord?" was all she could manage.

"The stock market," he replied. "Surely you have heard of it?"

She dared to glance at him. He held her eyes steady. She saw in their depths a disconcerting look she had seen there before. Marshaling her wits, she replied evenly, "You must suppose that I have."

"I suppose very little," he replied carelessly and quite pleasantly, but his voice had only a veneer of rough charm. Below the surface struck a faintly ominous note. This, too, she had heard before. "I wished only to warn you, to spare you trouble, if you . . . or Miss Armitage! . . . should take it into your heads to follow the feminine fashion of investing on 'Change."

Marianna could play this game, too. "I am at a loss, my lord. Even if I did take it into my head to invest, how should I go about doing so? It does not seem to me to be a particularly easy thing to do!"

Maddox moved away from the wall and came toward the dressing table. Marianna rose, to meet him on equal terms, putting Signor Luigi out of all countenance. She waved the little man away impatiently and put a hand out onto her table for support.

"There is a broker who lives in Saffron Hill . . . or is it Cornhill?" Maddox said. "My memory is not perfect! And this broker goes by the name of Martin . . . or is it Morton? . . . Vanbrugh, I believe . . ."

For all of these hesitations, Marianna would have just then bet her very conservative Four per Cents that her husband knew Morgan Vaughan's exact name and address.

"In any case," Maddox continued, "Mr. Vanbrugh has developed a business, a rather clever business, over the years but one which has suffered a reverse in the past several days. The result of a gross miscalculation on his part . . ."

Marianna schooled her features to polite interest.

". . . and I believe that Mr. Vanbrugh is, as of today, no longer in the business of investing on 'Change for ladies of fashion," Maddox finished.

The message was unmistakable. Marianna's knees shook slightly. It was on the tip of her tongue to exclaim, *And you told me that you did not mean to be an interfering husband!* Instead, she said, "Then this particular danger no longer exists. If this Mr. Vanbrugh is not now in business, then neither myself nor Charlotte can possibly take it into our heads to invest, no?" The words rolled off her tongue, and she was pardonably pleased.

"That is correct. I see that you have a ready understanding." Maddox bowed. "But, then, I have never doubted your intelligence. Yes, we agree, then, that there are many dangers in Town, and that this particular one no longer remains to draw the . . . unwary."

Marianna was not going to let this pass so easily. "Unwary?" she said, and then appeared to give this her consideration. "I would guess that the only unwary ones are the ones who lose money."

He looked down at her, his eyes slowly roaming over the masses of her unbound hair, resting on creamy white shoulders, then coming to rest on her face, a very pretty face, which was dignified and ever so provocatively defiant.

The look that flickered in the depths of his gray-green eyes made her catch her breath. It was as if he had just undressed her, ribbon by ribbon, folding back the lace at her corset and parting the silk of her underskirt.

"The market is," he said, "volatile, in the best of times. Prices fluctuate. And these times are damnably uncertain. Many trading practices are under review in Parliament. The stocks of some companies may plummet, in the near future, while others may rise. It is hard to predict." His gray-green eyes were suddenly no longer bright and appraising, but hard and inscrutable; and his voice held the muted ring of steel. "I have my own interests in these affairs, both political and economic, and as for interference —*especially from my wife*—I will tolerate none."

Abruptly he changed tone again, and said, as if it were a light afterthought, "This talk of finance reminds me that I am to convey to you the information that Mr. Duguid has requested a meeting with you. To go over your account, I believe. Some irregularity or another. I begged him not to bother me with it, and I was sure—as you have once again reassured me just now—that your understanding is sufficient to take care of the matter yourself."

Marianna said, as coolly as she was able, that she would certainly not trouble him to make her appointments but that she could perfectly well arrange her schedule for herself.

Maddox smiled again, charmingly. "I have already made the appointment for you. It shall be tomorrow morning. Mr. Duguid will await your convenience at ten o'clock."

She could hardly believe her ears. Was he to strip her of all her independence? She opened her mouth to speak, then folded her pretty lips firmly. She began again. "Thank you, my lord," she said. Her voice sounded too brittle, even to her own ears. "I certainly hope nothing is seriously wrong with my account. I have taken such pains to stay within budget, you see!"

Maddox had come a step closer, so close that she could practically feel his powerful length against her. Her stomach and knees began to dissolve, and she wondered whether he could hear the pounding of her heart.

"I believe you, my dear, and think you should be rewarded for your pains. So in case you have overdrawn," he dared to suggest, "I am prepared to cover you!"

Marianna, enraged, wanted to stamp her foot in vexation. Overdrawn? She knew he did not believe a word of it! She had a blistering retort on her tongue, but before she had a chance to utter it, he was to infuriate her still further with his next words.

"Where is your smile at my generosity, my lady?" he asked provocatively. "Or were you not persuaded by my arguments last night that, in marriage, the man provides—and I have been generous—while the woman smiles?"

Generous? Marianna could not find her tongue to speak, so her response to this piece of provocation was a blazing blue regard.

"Much better!" he approved, with a deep bow.

Then he was gone.

Marianna sank into the chair at her dressing table, consumed with anger. Signor Luigi began dancing about her hair, posing, posturing, and making a general nuisance of himself. Suddenly, Marianna could stand it no longer and pushed away from the table, causing Signor Luigi to squeak in surprise and dismay. He had just been on the verge of a creation!

She took several rapid turns around her little room, struggling with anger and frustration and a wild array of other unnamed emotions that she dared not examine. What had happened to their marriage of independence? She railed inwardly against the humiliating defeat she had just suffered at her husband's hands. She should have known better what to expect from marriage! Marriage to a man who could strip her of what little independence she had achieved for herself with a snap of his fingers! And it was of no consequence that the thrill of investing on 'Change had begun to pall on her and that she had contemplated stopping the practice of her own! *He* had no right to tell her what to do! No right whatsoever! *I do not mean to be an interfering husband*, he had said! That was a far cry from *the man provides and the woman smiles*! A very far cry indeed! She tossed the phrase around angrily in her mind. She would show him: she would smile if it killed her! Marriage, she sniffed scornfully. This was no marriage! And as for anger...! She was the only one with a right to be angry! The gall of the man, the unmitigated, interfering gall of the man to have shown her, if only momentarily, that he had been angry at *her*!

She stopped short. She stood in front of the fireplace, where her husband had been only moments before, and stared at the empty grate. Then, all at once, she remembered the strange scene of Maddox's proposal to her on that cold, dreary day in February. Something in his manner had puzzled her then and later that night when she had thought back on it. She recalled now that something in his manner was out of place, did not fit with the situation, something she had been unable to name. It was the tone in his voice, the look in his eye, but she had not known him very well then, and had not been able to identify it.

Then it came to her, the blinding, wholly unexpected— and still completely puzzling—realization about the state of Anthony Maddox's temper the day he had proposed to her: he had been angry. She could understand, perhaps, coldness as a mask to his grief at the recent death of his uncle, or even, perhaps, coldness at the prospect of marrying a woman he did not know for whatever ends he hoped to achieve. But anger...?

Marianna thrust both hands through her thick curls and flopped the blond mass on top of her head in a wild tangle. The muses came then and sat on Signor Luigi's shoulder. "*La corona d'amore*!" he cried, rapt in the happiness of the discovery, "ze Crown of Love! Yes, I shall execute *la corona d'amore*, ze curls piled high, entwined with flowers." He began plucking fresh flowers from their vases. "It is a difficult style, oh, yes! But I am equal to it. Nothing less than perfection will do! That is the style for you this evening, my lady! *Ah, si*! *Bella*! *Bellissima*!"

Marianna was not equally transported by Signor Luigi's raptures this evening. She sat back down with reluctance and took no interest whatsoever in the unfolding of his genius, in the creation of the Crown of Love. Bah! thought Signor Luigi. That is what comes from allowing a husband into a lady's chamber at the most important hour of the dressing!

IX

Of Money and Mistresses

Marianna soon realized that Charlotte's presence in Maddox House meant an end to peace, an end to quiet, and an end to the distant decorum established between husband and wife that had already begun to crumble as a result of the episode in her dressing room.

The very next morning, in fact, at the hour of eight o'clock, Charlotte tapped at the antechamber door to Marianna's suite and, without ceremony, bounced in, buoyant and ready for the diversions of the new day. Marianna was in her dressing room, being assisted by Rachel, and so Charlotte crossed the bedchamber, agog at every charming detail, and poked her head around the open door leading to the dressing chamber.

Her eyes popped. "Ooh!" she breathed in awe and reverence.

"Do you find it very grand, Charlotte?" Marianna asked, with a teasing smile. "Come in," she said. "Come in and meet my good friend Rachel!"

Marianna introduced the two young women. Rachel bobbed and flushed with pleasure, for she was a true slave to her ladyship. Charlotte gravitated like a magnet to the mysteries of the dressing table and proceeded to touch every object thereon, opening any number of vials and jars and bottles, sniffing and dabbing on an equal number of potions, all the while maintaining an unbroken stream of conversation.

Marianna invited Charlotte, belatedly, to help herself, at which point Charlotte dimpled charmingly and said, "Am I too terribly nosy? Do you mind company while you dress? If you do, just tell me, and I shall leave you!"

"Would that all visitors to my dressing room were so easily dispatched!" Marianna exclaimed, tartly. Since Charlotte was riveted by the fascinations of the dressing table, she did not wonder what Marianna could have meant.

While part of Marianna's attention was given to answering Charlotte's myriad idle questions, the other part was given to Rachel, who had penetrated into the depths of the closet and had returned with several frocks. Over the past months Marianna had grown into her role as Lady Westleigh. She had not initially liked the fuss, but now she allowed Rachel to replace her night rail with a rather pretty underdress over which was floated a white gown of worked cotton. Marianna shook out the lace at the cuff while Rachel arranged the ruffles of the chemisette inserted into the modestly cut neck. The tapes at the waist were drawn, and the cloth was brought into shape around Marianna's neat figure. The morning dress was finished off with a very pretty tiffany sash.

Marianna then sat down at her dressing table to have her hair dressed by Rachel's simple hand. Charlotte drew up the little stool and plopped comfortably upon it. Charlotte was speaking in dreamy terms of the assembly and asked Marianna if they could go to another just as wonderful as the one last night.

Marianna replied that they could go to one every night of the week, if they chose. "But, you know, Charlotte, I think that would become a little dreary after a while, and I

wonder whether we should not take it slowly in these early
days, so that the delights of London do not so quickly
fade!"

Charlotte did not think there was any danger of *that*,
and asked, her brown eyes bright, "And, so! What do we
do this morning?"

Marianna could not resist. "Well, I usually read in the
mornings," she replied.

Charlotte's face fell ludicrously. "Read?" she echoed,
much surprised. Then, thinking she had failed to grasp
Marianna's meaning, she added, "You mean, read books?"

"Books, yes," Marianna said, letting her head sway
with Rachel's brushstrokes. "Don't you read books, my
dear?"

"Of course I read *novels*," Charlotte replied, "but only
when there is nothing much more pressing to do!"

Two combs were withdrawn from their cases to catch
the curls away from Marianna's forehead. Marianna observed the effect and nodded approval. "I, too, read
novels, but I now also read journals, since I have become
especially interested in political events, and I make a particular point of reading the daily newspaper."

Charlotte was genuinely shocked. "The *newspaper*?"

"Is that so marvelous?" Marianna asked, quizzing Charlotte with her eyes.

"Well," Charlotte admitted, speaking her mind, "I never
thought anyone read the newspaper."

"Not anyone?" Marianna laughed. "Then why do you
suppose it is printed every day, if no one reads it?"

"Perhaps it's because," Charlotte said, brightening, "the
lists of the balls and assemblies are printed there, and so
one reads it to find out where one can go that night!"

"Actually," Marianna informed her, "it's quite the reverse. One reads it to find out what went on the night
before! Perhaps there is a report of the assembly we attended with the Brutons."

"With our names included?" Charlotte asked, suddenly

perceiving the interest of this otherwise incomprehensible pastime. "Well, that *would* be grand!"

"I shall make sure, then, you have a copy of the *Times* to read this morning at breakfast," Marianna said.

Charlotte's smile dawned, and a knowing look lit her eye. "I am not a complete simpleton—I see what it is. You want to make sure I do not talk my way through breakfast! My father always hated my early morning chatter. I promise you that I shall be as quiet as a mouse," she said, then amended, "that is, as quiet as I am able!"

Marianna had to be satisfied with that. Some ten minutes later, with her tresses pulled into a roll secured at the nape with a satin ribbon, she and Charlotte descended to the dining saloon. Charlotte was dying, as she put it, to see Lord Westleigh again. "Do you think that he will be at home this morning?"

"I believe so," Marianna replied, with a touch of frost in her voice. She was not at all looking forward to seeing her husband this morning. "He said that he would make a point of greeting you at breakfast."

"That is very grand then! Father used to speak of him as one of the finest fellows he ever met. Of course, I certainly do not think him the *finest* gentleman I ever met, although he certainly is rich—I can see that. But I suppose Father meant something about his character. As far as I am concerned, I met the finest gentleman last night, Marianna. And he was so handsome that I am quite sure I fell in love with him!"

"You did?" Marianna replied, startled. "What man?"

"Well, I think his name is Mr. Johnson," Charlotte offered.

"You *think* that the name of the man you fell in love with is Mr. Johnson?" Marianna asked, a little weakly.

"I am not very good at names," Charlotte explained. "But do you not remember him? He was introduced to us early on—that very handsome man who asked me to stand up with him for the gavotte. And it is a very fortunate thing that Harry insisted I learn some of the dance steps, for otherwise I should have embarrassed myself—and you!—but as it was, I could follow along pretty well, and when he wanted to ask me for a second dance, you refused!"

Marianna had a vague recollection of a downy youth, dressed in the height of fashion. Other than that, however, she did not have a precise memory of who Charlotte's Mr. Johnson might have been. In truth, the assembly had passed in something of a blur before Marianna's eyes, so absorbed was she with her own thoughts. However, with Charlotte now professing love for the first personable young man to come along, Marianna realized that she could not take lightly the guardianship of this charming, guileless, all too open hearted creature.

"Dear me!" Marianna said. "I am not exactly sure that I do remember him. But, as for your falling in love with him after just one dance . . . !"

"As he did with me!" Charlotte answered, dreamily.

"But, Charlotte, my dear. Love at first sight?" Marianna protested. "You cannot believe that nonsense!"

"But, of course, I do. So do you and Lord Westleigh," Charlotte said matter-of-factly.

"I am surprised to hear it!"

They had descended the stairs. Charlotte frowned a little and said, "Oh! But I had thought . . . that is . . . well! It's just that once, last year perhaps, when Father was home and was telling me so seriously about Lord Westleigh and that he would take care of me if anything should happen to Father while he was away, I asked him if there was a Mrs. Maddox. My father laughed and said that Anthony Maddox was a bachelor and likely to remain one! So you see—you are so very beautiful, and according to Harry, she said that Lord Westleigh had married you only recently, since coming into the title, and so why would he have proposed to you if he had not fallen in love with you at first sight?"

Of course, what Marianna wanted to know now was why he had proposed to her in anger. Since they were al-

most at the dining room, she patted Charlotte on the hand
and said, "I thank you for the compliment, and that's a
lovely story, Charlotte, but it's one, perhaps, that you
should keep to yourself—as your Harry would advise
you!"

Charlotte nodded and said cheerfully, "Oh, I know
that!"

The footman held the door to the dining saloon and the
two ladies were swept in. Marianna's eyes fell immediately
on Maddox, who had risen from his place and was already
crossing the room to greet them. He took his wife's hand
first and bowed over it.

Marianna felt a little dizzy at his touch and avoided
meeting his eye. She withdrew her hand, so that Maddox
could greet his ward. She was suddenly glad of Charlotte's
presence, for she, delightful child, was prattling on about
how wonderful it was to see his lordship again, how much
she loved the house, how exciting was London, how generous everyone was being to her, and about any other chance
thought that occurred to her fertile brain. Thus, she
smoothed over the awkwardness that otherwise would have
attended this next encounter between Maddox and Marianna.

After a minute or two of this, his lordship handed Charlotte over to a waiting footman who would seat her. Maddox then escorted his wife to her place, saying sotto voce,
"I had forgotten what a charming young lady is Miss Armitage. I am sure we shall have no trouble in marrying her
off . . . rather quickly! Strange that her father was such a
taciturn man."

Marianna looked up at him, her blue eyes twinkling.
She was quite sure she could hear the word *"prattlebox"*
hovering on the tip of his tongue. "Oh, yes, no trouble at
all, especially if you double her dowry. But, I find her such
a delightful companion that I would be very sorry if she
left the household anytime soon. Why, I find her presence
positively salutary!"

Maddox did not respond to this. Instead, he drew Marianna over to the table and seated her with great care. Accompanying this spuriously solicitous gesture, he said, in slightly mocking tones not lost on Marianna, "You see, my lady, I have respected the seating arrangement that you yourself established. You shall sit on my right, and Miss Armitage on my left. I thought that this morning we should begin to take our meals together on a regular basis, so that we may see more of one another."

Marianna was determined to smile. She smiled, sweetly. "Excellent idea," she said. "For Charlotte's benefit."

"Of course, for Miss Armitage's benefit," he agreed.

While they were being served and throughout the meal, talk ran easily. Maddox was obviously exerting himself, in his own particular way, to make Charlotte feel at home and comfortable. He directed most of his questions and comments to her; and when, on occasion, he addressed his wife, Marianna could feel that he was teasing her, testing her. Charlotte, glowing from the attention shown to her by his lordship, waxed expansive and did not lack for words.

Presently the mail was delivered, whereupon Charlotte gave a squeal of delight. "Is that the morning newspaper?"

Maddox leveled a curious glance at his wife but made no comment.

Marianna suppressed a smile and handed her copy of the paper over to Charlotte. "You must read it from cover to cover, my dear, and tell me if you find anything interesting."

Maddox raised his brows in acknowledgment of Marianna's little ploy, and it worked rather well for the next while. A cozy silence reigned in the room. Marianna, sorting through her mail, was aware of the charming picture of family comfort and harmony they must have made. She was also aware of the less than comfortable presence of her husband. Charlotte, she thought, made an excellent buffer.

"Not a word about the assembly!" Charlotte cried in disgust after several long minutes of quiet.

"Maybe next time," Marianna encouraged. "You cannot expect to find what you want the very first time you read it." Then, to change the subject, she glanced at Maddox and said, "We have received a flattering invitation from the Duchess of Marlborough to attend a country house party she is having. It is extended to the both of us," she said. "The Duchess—Gabrielle—has been very kind to me. I met her recently, at the Montenegros', in fact. At that party you attended as well a week or so ago. She told me, of course, how well she knows you."

"Yes," Maddox replied, "she and I have had a few dealings over the plight of the French refugees in this country. She is very devoted to aiding the cause of her former countrymen and women, and I have been in a position to help see some measures through."

When he elaborated no further, Marianna said, "Well! Now, she has invited the both of us to join her at Marlborough Park." She scanned the note that accompanied the invitation and said, "How lovely! Lord and Lady Hester are invited. Susannah, as well. Oh, and Eliza Parrish and Mr. Everly. It is sure to be amusing!" She gave Maddox the dates of the party, which was to be held several weeks hence. "Will you be free to go, my lord?"

Maddox had very specific plans for the month of June, and they did not include rusticating, however elegantly, in the country. He considered Marianna a brief moment. His eyes lingered. Then, slowly he said, "No, I am afraid that I must regret the invitation."

"Then, I shall accept for myself," Marianna replied immediately. "That is, if Charlotte may also come with me. I shall write the Duchess at once. We shall miss you!"

Marianna dispensed with the rest of the invitations easily enough. The hour advanced. When it was time to proceed with the business of the day, they all rose together. Charlotte, anxious to get on with the day's activities, ran on ahead.

"I am glad we shall be doing this regularly now," Maddox said, escorting Marianna to the hallway.

Marianna forced herself to agree to this pleasantry. "Indeed, very nice!"

"And I do not think, my lady, that you should shoulder the entire burden of Miss Armitage's entertainment," he began.

"Oh, it is no burden!" Marianna assured him. "I welcome the opportunity. It's one of my most pleasant matrimonial duties!"

"Neverthless," he continued, ignoring this allusion, "I should like to take you and Miss Armitage to Drury Lane this evening. I know how much you like the theater, and Sheridan's comedy is playing."

She arched a brow. "Do I take the invitation at face value, or should I wonder whether you mean to keep a closer eye on me, now that you have become aware of the many dangers that await unwary ladies of fashion?" she asked sweetly.

Maddox acknowledged the hit with a slight bow of the head. "I regret that you interpret my invitation in such a light."

She forced herself to smile. "Do you?" She was not used to thinking herself a contrary person, but no force on earth at that moment could have prevailed upon her just then to accept her husband's invitation. "You see, I have been engaged to go to Sadler's Wells this evening and thought to take Charlotte with me."

"Then you may change your plans."

"I would not like to be so rude!"

"I have found that most of one's engagements are only made to be broken," he observed.

"Well, in that case—" she began.

Maddox was as quick as his wife. "Social engagements, that is," he interrupted. "Now, business engagements are a different matter. I am quite adamant about keeping to one's business engagements. Which reminds me, of course," he said, with a glint in his bright eyes, "that you have a business engagement this morning. In a few minutes, in fact. I detain you. Until this evening, then, at dinner, before you embark for Sadler's Wells." He bowed slightly. "Give Duguid my regards."

Marianna swept down the hallway in some little temper. Her refusal to go to the theater with him had not got the better of him. She did not like the balance of forces in this so-called marriage of independence. She resolved to redress that balance, but had not the least idea how to accomplish that admirable goal.

She did not have time to give it much thought. The meeting with Mr. Duguid was upon her, and although its purpose infuriated her, she was to find that it would also enlighten her.

The preliminaries of her meeting with Duguid were taken up with formalities. There were the papers to sign to close her account in Bristol and the papers to sign to transfer those monies to her account in London. None to her surprise, she saw that these papers had been initiated and subscribed by her husband. She had not believed him for a minute when he had said he knew nothing about what Duguid wanted with her!

Mr. Duguid, faithful steward that he was, did not give any indication that all the paperwork represented anything out of the ordinary. He behaved as if this appointment had been arranged for the sole purpose of instructing her ladyship in the management of her account—not, Mr. Duguid stressed, that he had doubted her ladyship's ability to do so on her own, not for a minute!

Marianna lent him her polite attention throughout the rudiments of juggling the debit and credit columns, but when he began to instruct her on making modest investments on 'Change, her docile courtesy threatened to vanish. She firmly suspected her husband of a rather wicked sense of humor, and she had to suppress the desire to give Mr. Duguid a few good market tips of her own. However,

when Mr. Duguid explained that she was not to invest in
Royal African for the next year at least, nor in any company which traded in sugar or rum, she could not help but
object.

"No sugar or rum? But that applies to the stock of almost every merchant in London!" she pointed out.

"Yes, well, it is very complicated, but I do believe his
lordship objects to those companies whose *principal* goods
are sugar and rum."

Marianna did not hesitate to ask why this should be so.

Mr. Duguid did not think it seemly to discuss complicated world affairs with ladies. Still, he could not be rude.
He chose a middle ground. "That is because his lordship is
supporting a bill before Parliament now, one put forward
by Mr. Wilberforce, that will no doubt affect the price of
those commodities in the near future," he explained,
avoiding the central issue.

"His lordship thinks them bad investments, then?"

Mr. Duguid's smile was a little patronizing. "Let us just
say that his lordship believes that the economic system that
supports the cheap production of these commodities will
soon become illegal."

Marianna considered this. "But we are speaking specifically of Jamaican plantations, no? As far as I know, sugar
and rum are not produced illegally in Jamaica."

"No, not at all, my lady!"

"And Royal African? What is wrong with investments
in Royal African?" Marianna asked, thinking how well she
had done with that particular investment.

Mr. Duguid would not answer directly. "His lordship is
a very fine economist, as I suppose you must know, and is
supporting some remarkable measures to promote the
pound on the world market. Some very fine measures! And
he does not want them threatened. Now, I am not quite
sure I understand all of it myself, and perhaps there is a
moral issue at stake, but I do not think that morality is a
prime consideration of his lordship's! Not but that there

isn't a beneficial moral side effect, of course, if one chooses to look at it that way, but I am sure that anyone can see"—forgetting, in his passion for the subject, that he was in the presence of a mere woman—"just how important is the growth and the stability of the English pound, both here and abroad! Why, it is perhaps the most important way of keeping the French threat at bay! Our economy cannot be permitted to fall into the shambles that theirs has. Otherwise the Frenchies will export their chaos to us along with all their illegal brandy!"

Marianna grasped the essentials and was fascinated by this view of international politics and finance. She also saw that Mr. Duguid had said about all he was going to on the subject. She paused to add it all up. "Ah—so that was it!" But she could not decide whether it was the specific pattern of her investments that had occasioned her husband's interference, or simply the mere fact of them; and so, after another moment had passed, she added, thoughtfully, "Or was it?" Then, further reflection prompted her to exclaim, "Well, he certainly could have told me all of this himself, but I suppose that would have been according me too much respect!"

Mr. Duguid, listening to these ruminations, exclaimed, "But I never meant to cause you a moment's difficulty, your ladyship!"

"Difficulty, Mr. Duguid?"

Mr. Duguid's poise had been precarious from the start. This question put him into quite a fluster, and he tried, with woeful inadequacy, to explain quite how it was that this meeting between himself and her ladyship had come about, the most prominent theme being his evident mishandling of the draft from the Bristol Bank.

Further particulars did not interest Marianna. She had the gist. She had also taken pity on the poor man. "My dear Mr. Duguid, there is no difficulty whatsoever and no need to explain yourself," she said.

"But I had gathered," he said, making a clean breast of

it, "begging your ladyship's pardon, that something of a
... how shall I put it? ... storm had arisen between yourself and his lordship!"

"Then it is surely the most trivial of storms in the tiniest
teacup that anyone, even Gulliver," she replied, smiling
prettily, "has ever encountered."

Mr. Duguid was enslaved for life. He gathered together
his sheaves and thrust them into his briefcase, collected his
hat and walking stick, and left Maddox House with profound relief.

Marianna quickly put this meeting behind her. She went
about her life, which was a very fashionable and active
one. She took Charlotte everywhere with her and was
happy of her company, especially during mealtimes when
she now regularly saw her husband. These dinners were
generally agreeable occasions. Maddox did not make any
attempts to provoke Marianna unduly, but his mere presence struck her somehow as unspoken provocation. Often
she would find his eyes resting speculatively on her, and
she did her best not to let him get under her skin.

Then came that disastrous dinner when she took no
pleasure from Charlotte's company, when she thought that
Charlotte should have been strangled at birth, or at least
soundly beaten with a stick, when she felt all her husband's
lurking interest in her rise straight to the surface, when not
all her aplomb, finesse, or quick wit would save her.

It had begun so innocently. Charlotte had been singing
the praises of yet another young man. The handsome Mr.
Johnson of the city assembly was long forgotten in the
veritable parade of eligible bachelors whom she had met in
the past weeks.

"But my dear," Marianna said with a laugh, "it seems to
me that you fall in and out of love with amazing regularity.
This Mr. Edgecombe you speak of now must be, what, the
third or fourth young man who has taken your fancy in the
same amount of weeks!"

"A *fancy*!" Charlotte echoed, offended. "It is not a

fancy, Marianna! Oh, no, my feelings for Mr. Edgecombe
are deep and true! You see, Mr. Edgecombe is very different from all the rest! He is so very handsome, and says
such lovely things to me, and dances so elegantly!"

"I think you have said the very same thing about almost
every other young man you have met thus far," Marianna
observed. "So I do not know exactly how you can distinguish this attachment from any of the others."

"But Mr. Edgecombe has such a magnificent estate!"
Charlotte said, quite enraptured.

"Miss Armitage," Maddox said, amused, "remind me
when you receive your first offer to lecture you on the
subject of mercenary materialism."

"What's that?" Charlotte asked.

"Cupboard love," Marianna replied. "Now, don't you
think that you should try not to fall in love so very often?"

"But I can't help it!" Charlotte cried.

"Or at least try to limit yourself, my dear. Be more
circumspect! You will get a very bad reputation for flighti-
ness if you continue this way. Now, wasn't there that nice
young man—what was his name?—a Viscount...
Viscount..."

Charlotte searched her memory. "A Viscount? I don't
remember, exactly, but, then, I am so very bad at names!"

"I'm sure I'll remember it," Marianna said. "Ah, yes—I
have it! The Viscount Eldon. A charming young man, excellent address with a lovely estate, as well, and he seemed
to be quite taken with you."

Charlotte considered this. "The Viscount Eldon. Yes.
Well, perhaps he is a possibility after all. He was much
more in love with me, I think, than Mr. Edgecombe, and a
husband who is in love with his wife is infinitely preferable
to one who is not! Don't you think, Marianna?"

"Yes, of course, my dear," Marianna said, raising her
goblet.

A stray thought had popped into Charlotte's head. "Oh,

but that's not what you and your friends were saying the other day," she said.

Marianna stared at Charlotte over the rim of her glass. Before taking a sip, she asked, "What are you talking about, my dear?"

"Last week," she replied. "At the tea. Have you forgotten the conversation? Why, it was you and Mrs. Parrish—and I don't remember who else! perhaps Lady Marsh—and all of you were talking and laughing about your husbands and their *other interests*. And if you think that I don't know what it means, I do and—"

Marianna had choked on her wine. "*Charlotte!*" she gasped. "To talk like that at the table! My dear! It will not do!"

Maddox reproved calmly, "Lady Westleigh is right, my dear. Such talk at the table—or anywhere else—is most objectionable." The devil danced in his eyes. "But you were given such a poor example at the tea, when the ladies were apparently discussing very unsuitable things in front of you, that I understand why you would not think it unsuitable for the dinner table. In fact, I think it an excellent topic that will benefit from discussion."

Marianna shot her husband a withering look. "It is even more unsuitable now than then," she stated. Turning to Charlotte, she said calmly, "My dear, I really do not think this appropriate for the dinner table, and I will be most happy to—"

Maddox interrupted, smiling charmingly, maddeningly. "What is more suitable, my lady, than this family setting? Why, here you were, not a moment ago, instructing Charlotte in the proper conduct in Society. Something about advising her not to fall in and out of love so easily. Something about her being more circumspect, no?" Before Marianna had a chance to intervene, Maddox exhorted Miss Armitage, "Tell us what this is all about. Leave no detail out!"

Thus encouraged, Charlotte was happy to make a clean

breast of it. "Well, the ladies said that it was so much better
for their husbands to have *other interests* and to not . . . to
not bother them! I am not precisely sure what *that* means,
but I think it has something to do with the husband paying
court to another woman, telling her all manner of pretty
things and giving her gifts, and . . . well, I have to say that I
would not like my husband doing that for other women.
Not at all!"

"Yes, my dear, that is all very interesting," Marianna
said as if nothing out of the ordinary had been said. She
took up her fork, making every effort to eat normally. "So
let us get on with our dinner now that we have discussed it!
And the lesson to be learned here, of course, given your
views on the subject, is that you must find just the perfect
husband for you, one who will not pay court to another
woman. Now, about the Viscount Eldon—"

Marianna's heroic efforts to change the subject failed.
"But, Marianna," Charlotte interrupted, a little frown on
her pretty brow, "that was not at all what *you* were saying
last week."

"I?" Marianna questioned, a little weakly.

"Yes, you, my lady," Maddox repeated with great interest. He enjoyed seeing his wife lose her composure for
once, and wanted to see her squirm a little longer. "Surely
you must have aired your thoughts last week on the subject
of husbands and their . . . er . . . *other interests.*"

"I had no part in that particular discussion," Marianna
said with as much dignity as she could manage.

Charlotte wrinkled her brow. "That is true, you did
not," she said.

"Now you are showing the sense I know you have,
Charlotte," Marianna approved. However, if Marianna
thought she was going to be let off this very ticklish hook,
she was much mistaken.

Charlotte continued, "You did not say anything directly,
but it was Mrs. Parrish, I think, who turned to you and said

something about some woman. Now what was her name...?"

Marianna was afterward quite sure that some evil spirit must have come to jog Charlotte's memory in that split second, for the young scatterbrain was normally not able to retain a name she had not heard a dozen times or more.

"Oh, yes! The Besant," Charlotte said happily. "Yes, Besant! Well, anyway, you told Mrs. Parrish that you were not in the least concerned about her, and then you called her—the Besant, that is!—some name. I don't think it was a very nice name from the way Mrs. Parrish reacted, but I don't remember exactly what it was...."

Marianna's fork had clattered to her plate. When it appeared that Charlotte had indeed forgotten the extremely unflattering way she had referred to Arianna Besant, Marianna threw up her hands and breathed an exasperated, heartfelt, "Thank God for small mercies!"

Maddox had given himself over to his amusement and was laughing outright.

"But I have not said anything improper!" Charlotte cried out, at these unexpected reactions from her two guardians.

"You don't need to, my dear," Maddox replied. "I can imagine well enough!"

Sensing that Marianna was not quite pleased with her disclosures, Charlotte wrinkled her brow anxiously. "Should I not have said anything, Marianna? What do you think?"

The situation was so hopeless that Marianna did not even attempt to retrieve it. "I think, my dear Charlotte," she said with great deliberation, "that you should experience the great joy of the married state without delay. Preferably before the week is out."

"But no!" Maddox exclaimed, and wickedly quoted back Marianna's earlier words, laughter still shaking him. "I would be very sorry to see Miss Armitage leave the household anytime soon. Her presence is, as I think you once said, positively salutary!"

The nerve of the man! fumed Marianna. It was not enough that he had stripped her of her independent bank account! Oh, no! Now he was actually laughing at her over his mistress! Or rather his former mistress—not that the distinction mattered one little bit!

Charlotte was looking crushed by these comments from Marianna. "But you were the one who told me that my honesty was charming, Marianna! You were the one who told me to speak my mind!"

"I should have known it would be my fault!" Marianna exclaimed.

"And excellent advice it was, too, my lady," Maddox approved. He had an elbow on the table and was leaning across it, quite close to Marianna. "Yes, excellent advice. And I have some even better advice to give to you."

"I am sure I do not need it!" Marianna shot back, thoroughly embarrassed. She glanced up at him, briefly, through lowered lashes. Seeing the mirth lighting his gray-green eyes, she wondered how she had not always thought him devastatingly attractive.

"But you do, my dear. On the very topic of husbands and their mistresses. And I would be happy to give it to you now!"

Marianna struggled for poise. She schooled her features to composure but could not quite meet his eyes again. "I am sure that will not be necessary."

"Later, then. When we may be private. Unlike you, I believe some subjects unsuitable for the tender ears of unmarried maidens," he said, humor modulating the rich melodies of his voice.

"I can hardly believe it," she replied stiffly.

"No?" he laughed. "I will show you what I mean later, then. Yes, definitely later."

It was a promise.

X

Where Marianna Calls the Tune

It was, Marianna thought, as if the ice had broken. She was hard pressed to describe the exact nature of the change in her husband's attitude toward her, but she knew exactly when it had started, and that was the night of the disastrous dinner.

Maddox had said that Marianna should not have the entire responsibility of entertaining Miss Armitage; he was true to his word. He breakfasted with his wife and his ward regularly, dined with them when he could, and squired them to one or two select parties. He did not, for all of that, overexpose himself. He kept to his rigorous schedule of work. He spent long hours away from home, dined often with his cronies, and was usually and mysteriously gone from home on most nights. On those rare evenings he spent at home, he would more often than not closet himself in his library, poring over documents at his desk.

So, while Marianna was not inclined to think that her husband was actively pursuing her, he nevertheless showed signs of increasing interest. He toyed with her on occasion and teased her, as if drawing her into a flirtation with him. She noted that his eyes often came to rest on her when they

were together. She was stimulated by his watchfulness; she
was even roused to curiosity about what the speculative
gleam in his eye might prompt him to do. But, she was
determined not to fall for him. He was rapidly becoming
irresistible to her, but resist him she would. She would
hold him at arm's length as long as she could.

Maddox had been, all along, a very different sparring
partner from any other man she had ever met. Through
closer contact, she began to know him better. He was not
as light and witty as Peter Everly, nor was he as serious or
as scholarly as Lord Edward. He might have reminded her
of her father, with the scope of his interests and the range
of his knowledge, except for the fact that she could not
picture Maddox lounging in the coffeehouses of Milan with
quite the same grace and elegance as her father, frittering
his day away in discussion, dallying with the ladies. Nor
could she, for that matter, picture her father debating economic issues in the House of Lords with the brutality for
which, she had learned, her husband was famous.

It was the very subject of her father that Maddox unexpectedly introduced one very fine late May day. Maddox
had come home unexpectedly one afternoon, when the
spring was spreading its green glory over all, to find Marianna in one of the saloons peacefully writing letters with
Charlotte. He proposed to take the ladies on an outing of
their choosing. Charlotte promptly exclaimed that she
longed to visit the Bartholomew Fair. Maddox, in an indulgent mood, agreed. Marianna was mildly surprised, for
she thought the idleness of the adventure better suited to a
man of Peter Everly's tastes.

At the fair, the threesome strolled the gaudy stalls, past
the women frying sausages, past the exhibiting contortion-
ists and tightrope dancers, past the theater decked with
green and pink hangings and yellow columns striped with
red. While Charlotte's tongue was unnaturally stilled by
her absorption in the sights around her, Maddox turned to
Marianna to say, rather abruptly, "I read Dr. Lowth's gram-

matical essays in my earliest youth, and have forgotten everything in them, but I remember very well several of the essays he published on Italian politics ten years ago or more. What else did he write?"

Marianna was happy to oblige him. She filled in those details of her father's intellectual life that she thought might be of interest to him.

He listened agreeably, content to be beguiled by her voice. At the end of her reminiscences, he remarked, "Your father was a most unusual man. A free spirit in many respects, almost a rebel. Given that, it surprises me that this broad-minded gentleman should have sired a son who is content to be a village vicar."

Marianna laughed at that. "How angry Father was with Jonathan's defection into the ministry!" she said. "And that was the very word he used—defection—to the day of his death." She then recounted, with some amusement, her father's stories of how he had opposed Jonathan's ordination, how he had even written an angry letter from Italy to the principal of Jonathan's college, protesting his son's course of study. That incident, Marianna claimed, had brought an end to communication between her father and her brother.

"Your brother was never able to bring your father round to his way of thinking?" Maddox asked.

"No, I'm afraid not. But that is hardly a surprise. My father died without believing in anything, I'm afraid."

"An ironic twist for the father of a pious reverend," Maddox remarked.

"Oh, yes, it was quite devastating to Jonathan," Marianna admitted.

"You mean your brother was aware of your father's state of mind at the time of his death?" Maddox queried idly.

"More or less," Marianna replied. "You see, I was with my father in Italy, and when I returned to live with my brother, I fear that I told him more than he wanted to know about the last years of our father's life."

"How did your brother take it?"

"Not very well, I'm afraid, although I consoled him with the thought that old atheists seem less wicked and dangerous than young ones," she explained.

"And why is that?"

"Oh, I suppose because one feels that there is something of the ancient Greeks in them," she replied, offhandedly.

A smile of genuine amusement touched Maddox's eyes. "Sometimes I wonder how you survived in your brother's household," he remarked, after a moment.

"I was vastly irritating to Jonathan at times," she admitted with a chuckle. "How amusing it was, though, to see him bluster so hopelessly and confidently when he did not understand the least thing! I always knew that I had won an argument when he would recommend me: 'Mend your tongue, Marianna!' It was practically my only form of entertainment!" She flushed a little, for she had just drawn a rather unbecoming picture of herself. "But I hope that I was not reduced to finding my satisfaction in life from baiting my brother!"

"Reduced?"

"Well, as you can very well guess, Stanthorpe was not the most exciting village to spend my early adulthood. It lacked a certain sort of something after my childhood in Italy. And without your Uncle Edward I am sure my life there would have been nearly unbearable. He was my savior!"

"Savior? Was that not your brother's role?"

Marianna chuckled again. "Jonathan certainly thought so in all events! And he had every reason to despair, for I think he feared that he would never get me off his hands!" She was about to elaborate on that aspect of her relationship to her brother, but she remembered to whom she was talking, and abruptly changed the subject. "But, you see, although I lived in a community of good people, I think that my life without Lord Edward would have been . . . would have been . . ." She groped for words. "Well, as you can see, I truly hate to think what my life would have been like!"

"And why was that?" he asked.

"Because Lord Edward was such a very good friend," she answered. "Such a good and very dear friend that he made it all worthwhile!"

"Good friends, you and Uncle Edward?" he said, a faintly skeptical note discernible in his voice. Maddox was not burdened with the prejudice that a woman could have no qualities worthy of a man's friendship. He himself always appreciated a well-informed opinion, be it from a man or a woman. However, he had explored in depth only one form of communication with beautiful young women. "Do you mean that the two of you enjoyed a ready meeting of the minds and were in perfect harmony on all subjects?"

"Good heavens, not at all!" Marianna exclaimed. "We did not always agree with one another. In fact, we often violently disagreed—agreeing only to disagree!"

"On what issues, for instance?"

Marianna was in fine form this afternoon. She replied, with an attractive sparkle in her blue eyes that he had encountered before, "Oh, I remember one rather violent argument we had about the position you supported on raising taxes—two or three years ago, I think it was. Lord Edward thought your position was scandalous."

"And you?"

"I thought it reasonable, but badly argued, which was probably why the measures were so soundly defeated." She bestowed on him a gracious nod of concession. "But the entire blame cannot be laid at your door, for the coalition was a shaky one from the start!"

Maddox had to smile at that. "Kind of you, my lady!" he retorted, perceiving now some humor in one of the worst defeats of his political career. "And just how did you come to know so much about it?" Before she could reply, he said, with a flash of insight, "But I keep forgetting! You are an avid reader of the newspapers, and I recall as well that my Uncle Edward is to blame for having introduced you to the practice."

"That," she said, slanting him a rapier glance, "was exactly what Jonathan used to say. Shame on you!"

The look he returned was equally effective. "I begin to perceive just how irritating you were to your brother. My sympathies are firmly with him!"

Such personal conversations were, however, rare. For the most part, if she found herself in Maddox's company, it was at home, and Charlotte was the center of attention. Few were the occasions they were together in public, and then always as a threesome.

Then came the evening of the Montenegros' grand dinner. Maddox had informed Marianna that they were to attend this dinner together, and he said that Charlotte was to stay at home. It amounted to a command, but Marianna was not displeased, for it would be the very first time that she would appear in public alone with her husband.

That evening Marianna dressed without hesitation. She chose a gown of her favorite peach crepe, which she wore over a slip of cream satin. It flattered her figure in a modest sort of way, for it had snug sleeves that showed off her dimpled elbows, below which fell two deep tiers of cream lace, and a close-fitting bodice lavishly stitched with seeded pearls. Her hair was unruly this evening, and although Signor Luigi had difficulty subduing the more refractory curls, Marianna was not displeased with the final effect, which was tumbling and natural and would, in its way, complement Maddox's own uncluttered style.

When she descended the stairs at the appointed hour to meet her husband, she was confirmed in her impression that she had achieved satisfactory results.

Maddox cast a critical, appreciative eye over his wife's toilette, and said, "Pretty!" She had received compliments from Peter Everly as elaborate as Cleopatra's necklace, but Marianna found that Maddox's "Pretty!" pleased her beyond all others.

After exchanging a few pleasantries, Maddox excused

himself and came back moments later bearing a thin box, which he presented to her with a bow.

Marianna opened the box and stifled a gasp.

"The Maddox diamonds," he explained. Lifting the jewels from the velvet lining, he said, simply and with unaccustomed gallantry, "Allow me," and proceeded to clasp the heavy necklace around her throat. The effect of his touch, mingled with the feel of cold, fiery stones at her neck, caused a tingle down to her toes.

Maddox did not notice, for he was applying himself to inserting the diamond drops in her ears, which required him to touch her nape while wisps of her hair grazed his face, and he was lost, for a moment, in contemplation of the graceful curve of her neck and the allure of her scent.

The next moment he straightened and said, conversationally, that the carriage was waiting. He called for Lady Westleigh's cape and cast it lightly about her shoulders. It was only when he was handing her into the carriage that Marianna found her voice to thank him for the diamonds.

"The pleasure is mine," he replied. He then inquired into news of Miss Armitage's latest flirts and whether there were any serious contenders to Miss Armitage's hand. This neutral topic carried them comfortably through the streets of London. It was only when they were coming to a halt in front of the Italian ambassador's brilliantly lit villa that Marianna realized the gift of the diamonds to her this evening, flattering as it was, was perhaps more an indication of the importance of the evening to her husband than a signal honor he chose to confer on her.

Indeed, Marianna soon guessed from the composition of the guest roster just how important the occasion was. The guests—and there were over sixty of them—were of a quality unrivaled in all of London that night, including as they did, a dazzling mix of the most gay and glittering of the London fashionables, along with a great many members of the diplomatic set. Foreign dignitaries were everywhere. The babble of French and Italian drifted in and out of English conversations. Two cabinet ministers and their wives, as well as several of the old-guard political establishment, made up the backbone of the guest list. However, it was the younger men of vision—those new agitators of international finance and reform, a set of men best represented by Anthony Maddox—whose interests formed the hidden agenda of the evening's entertainment.

The Montenegros had not lost the touch of their Florentine heritage, but they had cleverly absorbed the best of English culture. Among the Italian masters that graced their saloons were interspersed the rival English masters: the street scenes of Hogarth, the portraits of Gainsborough, the landscapes by Wilson and Scott, and a wonderful collection of wickedly amusing caricatures by Gillray. The Montenegros had lured into their personal service as well the famous chef of the Anchor Tavern in the Strand, John Wollams, who was especially popular now with his nationalist approach to English food; and their guests ate off Wedgwood.

The moment Lord and Lady Westleigh left the receiving line and were announced, Marianna stepped into the large front salon, insensibly aware how right, how fitting, it felt for her to be present at such a gathering. She hardly questioned her place in it, nor ever thought she should be any place but here. She had never seemed more alive, never more wholly, excitingly alive. It was as if she had slumbered those eight years in Stanthorpe; but when she had been in Stanthorpe, her participation in such an evening would have seemed like a dream, not like the life she was born for. But it was no dream. It was a true awakening, as if she had been born again.

With her husband at her side, she fell into conversation with the first group they came upon. She aired her opinions with freedom. The Montenegros, admirers of Addison, used for the social tenor of their home his oft-quoted statement, "Women are more ardently political than men."

Marianna and Maddox were engaged, side by side, in separate conversations. Marianna advanced an idea and had it tossed back to her. She modified and returned. Maddox had overheard her last point, and disagreeing, turned to question her. She replied, with emphasis. He argued the point, but they came to no conclusion, and he turned back to his partner. For the rest of the evening they exchanged no further words.

Husband and wife were not, of course, seated together at dinner. Marianna was, however, at the same table as Maddox, one of two long tables seating more than thirty persons apiece. Relaxed, almost in a retiring mood, she confined her conversation at table, most correctly, to the gentlemen on either side of her.

Toward the end of the elaborate meal, there arose one of those moments when a social group spontaneously expands itself from small conversations of twos, threes, and fours to encompass fifteen or more. It might have begun when the prime minister's name entered the conversation. The host, Marcello Montenegro, presiding over one end of the table, explained that Pitt had gone north for the week; otherwise he would have been in attendance this evening.

Pitt's name was tossed about for a minute. Then was heard Maddox's reply to some comment or another. "But in the Age of Pitt," he said distinctly, "there is no sliding by on personal charm, good bloodlines, or a firm grasp of the obvious."

By now, side conversations around that end of the table were tapering off. The group was recomposing itself around the large discussion.

Several of the men laughed. "But it still takes a good deal of wit, Westleigh! Just as it did in the old days," one old-timer remarked jovially. "It still takes as much wit now to stay in power as it ever did!"

Peter Everly, on his toes, remarked that he had never considered a political career, for he abided by the motto, "The monuments of wit far outlast the monuments of power."

The comment drew laughter and the recommendation that his wit would stand him well in Parliament.

"Don't encourage him," Maddox commented genially. "Given Everly's political allegiance, we don't need men of wit in the opposition."

"Dear me! I fear that my firm grasp of the obvious," Everly returned with equal good humor, "would undercut my effective wit every time. But, good Whig that you are, Maddox, I suppose you cannot see that my allegiance to the Tory platform is prompted by the very obvious fact that my personal interests are so very much better served there."

Murmurs of an approving "Hear, hear!" ensued.

Encouraged, Everly continued. "As for my allegiance to the Tory cause, then call it my lamentable lack of imagination!"

"I will," Maddox returned.

"Don't debate the issues with him, Everly," Signor Montenegro warned. "He'll draw blood. Why, just last week, I heard reports of the meeting in the pit of the House of Lords. It was not a pretty one, and Maddox did not lose! And when there is a particularly brutal issue to debate, Maddox is sent to the House of Commons to fight it out!"

"Is that why you wear your own hair, Tony?" Everly queried. "So that you can impose on the commoners whatever scandalous bill you propose, while making them think all the while that you are one of them?"

"No," Maddox replied. "So that I can impose even more scandalous taxes on hair powder without taking a penny out of my pocket."

This comment drew laughter, in its turn, but one of the old guard was heard to grumble, "It's your demmed democratic philosophies, young man, that will bring our ruin! Together with the disuse of hair powder, we shall soon all be wearing pantaloons and trousers, cropped hair and shoestrings, without a buckle or a ruffle anywhere!"

"We won't be able to afford those buckles and ruffles, if

we continue on our present course," Maddox said calmly. "We're on the brink, you see."

He was accused of being a Jeremiah, a doomsayer. Marianna watched with interest her husband's methods. He was as talkative this evening as she had ever seen him, but still far from loquacious. Maddox let the topic be bandied about for a while, then chose his moment to punch in his points. And he had many to make: the inability to coordinate sound economic policies with Continental governments, irresponsible fiscal behavior in the wake of the American folly, the national debt. "For we cannot expect the South Sea Company to finance the deficit forever," he said. "Shall I mention the figure we're at now?"

"Don't spoil our appetites, man!" came the response. "Your stomach may be made of cast iron, but ours are far more delicate!"

Noises were made over the government's economic strategies, to which Maddox replied at once that the only active economic policy at the moment—if one could call it such—was the driving down of the value of the pound on international markets. Such a policy, Maddox argued, with no change in taxation, no action to reduce the debt, no coordinated trade policy with foreign governments, led him to believe that it was not a question of whether a crisis would occur, but only how soon.

Could one not put any hope in the upcoming international meeting in Brussels? Voices rose to denounce the blasted Dutch with their fat paunches and their trading practices.

"We would do well to follow their lead," Maddox remarked. "At least they trade with the Americans. What we do cannot be called trade. Ruining American industries by flooding their markets with our cheaper goods—government-subsidied!—is not sound trading policy! If we continue on that course we will, no doubt, soon be in another fruitless war with the Americans, which will only lead to more ruinous fiscal policies."

So, what was the solution?

Maddox wanted to see a restructured banking system.

A harsh exclamation came from a cabinet minister, followed by the bitter words, "The bankers are all robbers!"

"They're all Whigs," Maddox corrected. "You should be happy they are there looking out for your interests. We cannot have any more bad money circulating. The counterfeiters are the only ones these days doing good business. And who can blame them? It's bad enough that Spanish dollars flood our market. I, for one, am galled by the impudence that some of those dollars even have George's head stamped upon them!"

A nice touch, that, calculated to rouse nationalist sentiments, and Maddox said nothing more than was necessary to turn the conversation to the next order of business.

The dinner and the evening came to an end. Maddox was escorting Marianna across the foyer to the front door, when a sashed and medaled Prussian envoy came up to them and engaged him in discussion. Marianna moved away so that they could speak in private. The discussion looked serious, if the florid countenance of the Prussian were any indication. A few minutes later, Maddox looked over his shoulder at Marianna, paused a moment, then turned back to the envoy. He said that he would see his wife off and then would be happy to attend the meeting that the envoy was convoking in the Italian ambassador's library.

He crossed the foyer to Marianna and explained to her that she would have to return home without him. He smiled, very correctly, and bowed over her hand. It seemed to her that he released it with reluctance, but she hardly dared read anything into the gesture.

She did not see him again that night. When she arose the next morning, she was greeted with a brief note, written in his bold fist, that he had to leave Town for a day or two. He would see her upon his return and sent her his most respectful wishes.

"Far more flattering to inspire desire than respect!"

Everly had once said, and Marianna was a little disgusted with herself for wishing that Maddox had shown her less respect and a good deal more desire.

The next two days dragged, unaccountably. Happily, she had had an invitation to Ranelagh and had that outing to anticipate. It was to be a gay party, and a very large one, for every one of her very dear friends was to attend. Charlotte was in a fever of excitement. Marianna could not rouse herself to the same state, but she was nevertheless pleased that the weather, which had turned hot and heavy, was going to hold for the evening, and that the party would not be spoiled by rain.

Ranelagh's principal attraction was the "Rotundo." It was a fine circular hall around which the company promenaded. Seats were ranged against the walls. Mirrors were hung up everywhere. There was a profusion of lights. The crowded company was well dressed and well behaved, and with the good orchestra, everyone agreed that the scene was pleasant and bright.

Indeed, it was a very pleasant and bright party that Marianna arrived with at Ranelagh, almost too bright, one might have said of Eliza Parrish, whose luck at gaming had been decidedly out of late. She lamented loudly that she was losing her jewels and her debts were mounting. She laughed it all off with a metallic titter. She hoped her luck would soon change, for she had just discovered a marvelous new gaming hell in Cheapside and wished everyone to visit it without delay. So many Frenchmen frequented it! Her luck would surely change there! Or perhaps it was only the horrible weather, hot and heavy. It ruined her concentration! And it made her so tired!

Hearing this, Susannah Marsh chuckled. Eliza turned on her. "What, Susannah, are you never tired?" she asked, with a nasty undertone.

"I am never tired," Susannah replied with equanimity.

It was true. Susannah Marsh was never tired. She was known for her even temperament and her tireless energy. A

long time ago, years before, she had been tired for weeks
and months on end, so tired that she had wanted to die. But
she had not died. She came to England instead and discovered in herself a tremendous reserve for the diversions of
Society. She was a model of the perfect lady of fashion.
She was always present at whatever entertainment was offered and was always beautifully turned out. She never
complained of headaches or ailments or querulous hair-
dressers or frocks that had been cut wrong by a stupid
dressmaker or unpaid bills or lack of funds. She never said
an unkind or unweighed word. She had never been known
to insult anyone. She had never been seen to yawn or to
show any other sign of ennui. She was a charming companion, for anyone, for everyone, at all times. The endless
round of parties did not affect her behavior. She appeared
always relaxed and refreshed, as if just rising from a rest.

Eliza Parrish knew nothing of Susannah's history, and
Susannah's perfect equanimity was only one of the things
Eliza hated about her. Eliza turned away, huffily, to engage
Marianna in conversation.

The dancing began. Marianna danced. The dancing
stopped. Marianna left with the others to stroll in the fresh
air of the parapet. One group decided to meander down one
of the four orderly walkways, paved in mosaic and fes-
tooned with lanterns, leading away from the Rotundo. The
pathways were defined by high clipped hedges. Formally
bedded gardens laid out in circles, crescents, and squares
intersected the paths in geometric precision.

By some miracle, Marianna suddenly found herself strolling down one of the paths alone with Anthony Maddox.

It took her an instant to realize it. "You!" she exclaimed,
wholly off guard. Then she stammered, "M-my lord!"

"My lady," he replied.

She said the first thing that came to mind. "How did you
get here?"

"Through the entry," he informed her. "Admission is
half a crown."

"I know that!" she said impatiently. "What I mean is, what are you doing here?"

"My dear, I believe you have been taking your duty as chaperone to Miss Armitage too seriously. You are beginning to sound like her!"

Marianna was instantly sobered. She said, in perfect command of herself, "I suppose you found out where we were by asking at Maddox House."

"A simple expedient. Is this my greeting?" he inquired.

She eyed him, warily. "Yes. Did you return today?"

"This evening."

A small space of silence intervened. "I wonder where the others have gotten to!" she said brightly.

"I have no idea," Maddox replied, as if the matter did not concern him in the least which, of course, it did not.

They found themselves strolling down a side path. The bright lights from the Rotundo cast a glow over the entire gardens, but it was a faint one, and the moon was hidden away behind a thick bank of clouds. The sounds of the orchestra drifted over them. A concert of voices rose from the terrace.

They walked a few steps together in silence in the direction of the canal and the bridge, beyond which was the Chinese building.

"But I do wonder where they have gotten to," she tried again.

"I don't," he replied.

She looked up at him but could not read his face. "I suppose you know your way," she said.

"Tolerably well," he replied.

She took a deep breath. "Well!" she remarked, trying to keep her voice light. "How very lovely this evening is!"

He did not immediately reply. "Such a perfect time for me to give you that advice."

"Advice?" she echoed, and before she knew it they had arrived at an unlit alcove fashioned from an arch of a wooden trellis with vines and ivy rambling over it. It was a leafy, sweet-smelling arbor, and in its center was a carved stone bench.

"Shall we?" he suggested. The shadowy gesture he made indicated that she should be seated.

"Oh, no," she said quickly, her heart beating a little faster. "I prefer to continue on our walk."

"Very well," he replied.

However, as his eyes rested on her in the darkness, her feet refused to obey her, and she was not able to leave the little alcove. She simply stood before him, submitting to his lazy scrutiny.

He came closer by a few steps, moving without apparent purpose, but Marianna felt the strong surge of his intention, and so took a step backward.

"And that advice?" she began, groping for words, catching at the first wisp of an idea to occur to her.

"Ah, yes, the advice," he said, as if he had forgotten that he had mentioned it. "Long overdue, and not unrelated to the whole of our marriage."

"Our marriage?"

"It might be wise to review some of the terms first, and then I'll give you my advice," he said.

"I thought we had settled the terms on the day you offered for me," she said, a little breathlessly. "I thought we had a marriage of independence."

"You will also recall, I think," he said, "that on our wedding night we had a difference of interpretation of the bounds of that independence."

"I do," she said, retreating but determined not to be completely overpowered by his presence.

"And has your interpretation of those bounds changed in the past few weeks?" he asked. "Do you still think we have a marriage of complete independence?"

"No, in fact not," she conceded. She still had a score to settle with him, a rather important score. "At least, not since you interfered in my finances," she said, daring to mention the topic that they had never addressed directly. "Why did you do it?"

She felt, rather than saw, the gleam in his eye, and heard him chuckle softly. "Why did *you* do it?" he countered.

The backs of her knees were against the stone bench now. She shifted quickly to the side but did not free herself. She backed into the trellised wall of the alcove, so that the small of her back was flattened against it. He put his hand up against the wall and leaned slightly into it. He was so close to her that the lapel of his coat brushed the lace at her breasts.

"I was minding my own business," she said at last.

"So was I."

"No, that was my affair. Not yours! So, once again: why did you interfere?"

"You can't guess?" he replied. When she did not answer, he chided gently, "Once again, you do not play your part. You should be smiling and thanking me for the intervention. Surely you have seen the latest market figures. By my calculations, at your former rate of investment, you would have been crippled by now. Royal African, for one, has suffered resounding losses. I saved you from total ruin."

She had indeed noticed the bad market and had thought herself well out of it. However, this explanation was utterly beside the point. Perverse woman that she was, now that she had his desire, she wanted his respect. "You could have told me all of this, you know."

He did not take his eyes off her. "You didn't ask."

They had reached an impasse. "I am to smile and you are to provide," she recited.

"Such is my definition of marriage."

"But we do not have a real marriage!" she pointed out.

"That may be repaired," he said, "immediately."

He was so close to her that she was conscious of every movement he made, of every breath he drew. She seemed to be separately conscious of every bone in his body, and of the muscles rippling over them, and of his skin, his scent, his eyes upon her. When his hand lifted to touch her, to light a fire at the pulse in her throat and to trail the flames over her shoulder and down to her breast, she was quite sure that she could easily be lost in his strength, in the passion she knew dwelt within him, which was focused wholly on her.

No, she would not give in so easily. She feared the strength that lay behind his calm. She feared the masterfulness of his hot but hidden nature. She would not surrender to such a man, for in the crucible of his love, her own nature would be dissolved, transmuted, and rendered part of his. She would not abandon her personal territory for his pleasure. She would not give up that last province of her independence over which she had control.

"When we agreed to this marriage, you told me that you would make no unreasonable demands on me," she reminded him.

"Unreasonable," he repeated huskily, on the shadow of a laugh. "No unreasonable demands." His lips were very close to the tiny crease in her neck that had begun to fascinate him in the past several weeks. He pressed his lips to that enchanting crease. "I also recall saying," he murmured, "that at issue was the interpretation of 'unreasonable,' that it was a question of what you desired from the marriage."

There was no denying that she desired him at just that moment.

"And I also recall," he continued, thinking to clinch his arguments, "that you tossed the ball back to me and asked me whether I intended a marriage of convenience with regard to the physical demands of the relationship."

"To which you replied 'marriage of independence,'" she replied swiftly.

"And on that point we had a difference of interpretation about those physical demands, as you have already pointed out," she continued. "But as for my desire, I happen to recall that your original offer did not include such persuasive methods."

He trailed kisses down her neck to her breast. "No, but of course I did not know you then." His lips came back to her ear. "Do you refuse me?"

Marianna held an iron grip on her resolve, which was rapidly dissolving. "I refuse to smile for you," she said. Her voice was hardly above a whisper. "You had the power of choice. You gave me the power of refusal."

"So. The difference of interpretation continues," he remarked into her neck. Then he straightened slightly, but he did not remove his hands from her breast. Her heart beat against it thunderously. "But you consented to marry me. You did not refuse me."

"Upon conditions."

His eyes narrowed. She was so close that she could see the tiny flames of passion that flickered in their depths. "Still we dance, then?" he said. "You are to provide, and I am to smile?" He did not smile at that. "We cannot dance forever. Ice water does not run in my veins." He drew away from her. "And now for my advice: do not provoke what you do not want. You have been very provocative of late."

She could not, in all honesty, contradict him.

"You cannot refuse me indefinitely," he repeated. "A woman cannot refuse her husband forever. A man grows weary of dancing, and a husband will claim his rights."

"Do you mean, force me?" She regarded him speculatively. "I wonder if you would."

"And I wonder whether you really think I would not," he said.

XI

Lady Marsh Meets Her Ghost

L ady Susannah Marsh was escorted by the Duke of Kensington, a handsome widower with six estates and three grown children, from the seats inside the Rotundo to one of the arched doorways that led to the terrace. Susannah accepted his solicitous gesture graciously, and they crossed the dance floor together.

The fiddlers who scraped in the ballroom were temporarily silent. The pavilion was emptying of its revelers. Some had chosen to take a turn in the various corners of the gardens, and some preferred to partake of the light supper laid at the interval.

The duke and Lady Marsh made an exceptionally handsome couple. The duke was aware of it, but one would have said from Susannah's demeanor that she did not give it the least thought. As they left the Rotundo, she did not gaze once at their splendid reflection in the mirrors that covered the brightly lit walls.

Outside, the sky was darkening and covered with clouds bellying with rain. The trees had their summer burdens. Old oaks fluttered their new leaves in the warm, sticky breezes. Mingling with the soft sounds of spring could be

heard the murmur of disembodied voices rising from
hedged walkways and the gentle lapping of water against
the gondolas drifting along the artificial waterway circling
the pavilion.

They walked toward the low parapet that ran along the
edge of the terrace. Susannah turned and leaned against it.
She gazed back serenely upon the pleasant, bright orb of
the pavilion set against the night sky. Ranelagh was
crowded this evening, and the company, as always, was
decorous to the point of being sedate.

The duke had seen Susannah earlier in the evening. He
had left his own party and singled her out, speaking to her
at length. He had taken her hand at several moments. At
times she had let her slim, white hand rest in his, at others
she had withdrawn it. He made specific plans with her for
the next evening. She accepted. The duke felt himself fortunate. He did not understand this beautiful goddess, this
gorgeous queen. He knew only that he wanted her to be
his, that if he could possess her, he was sure he could make
her love him.

A clock tower chimed the hour. The evening had advanced and the velvet curtain of night had crossed the sky.

Susannah had not come to Ranelagh in the duke's company. She turned to him and said, with her lovely smile,
"I'd better find my party now, Your Grace."

"Gervase," the duke corrected, a little ruefully. He
sensed the dismissal. He was still the humble suitor. "You
do me an honor by accepting my invitation for tomorrow.
Have I bored you this evening with my stories, my lady
. . . Susannah? I thought for a moment that . . ."

"No," Susannah denied, "you haven't bored me." She
gave him her hand again and smiled. "Tomorrow night will
be amusing."

The duke was sure that he had bored her, this slow-spo-
ken woman with the unexpected sense of humor and the
perfect equanimity. This lovely woman, whom neither jeal-

ousies, nor gossip, nor scandal had the power to affect. So cool, so remote, she seemed a law unto herself.

The duke offered to escort his goddess to her party. Susannah shook her head and said that she knew where they were. He bowed deeply and left her on the terrace.

Alone, Susannah did not seek her party. Instead, she turned and placed her hands on the parapet. She stood leaning against it and looking idly down at the lily pond a few feet below. Little colored lights ringed it round, and clusters of artificial flowers, designed to hold tiny lamps, floated on the still water. These had provoked a great deal of laughter and admiration earlier in the evening.

Susannah saw a great many things reflected in the depths of the lily pond. She saw a nineteen-year-old girl, hurrying deep into her mother's garden in France. A young girl, looking over her shoulder, afraid of being seen, dressed as a simple country maid in a sheer chemise with a brief corset laced over a heart so demanding, so avid that the woman who remembered wondered it had not burst the flimsy trappings. She saw a tall, thin man, painfully thin but with muscles like whipcord, waiting in the shadowy recesses of the cedar grove. A man with a stark, melancholy face, a stern face even—ugly, some would have said, but hauntingly ugly, passionately ugly. As the man pressed the girl to him, she felt his lips against her throat and she heard him speak to her, in French, "You came to meet me, then, *ma chère*. You do not deny yourself. You have shown courage. You have done well."

Then he bent his head and his lips met hers, and although she had intended no more than a brief salute, she was startled to find herself clinging to him, bound by invisible cords as her lips parted beneath his. An eon of time floated past, and, as if under the influence of a potent wine, her senses were submerged in a surge tide of emotion. She wanted him. The touch of his hands on her body sent every nerve singing, demanding more, giving more. She unlaced her bodice and hitched her skirts for the man who, so the world had told her, was not fit to tread the same ground she walked on, not worthy to stand even in her shadow. This rough upstart from the village whom she had known from her earliest childhood, this tall, thin, ugly steel whip of a man, with blazing black eyes that devoured her so thoroughly. This man with the peasant speech, but no plain peasant brain. The man with the fiery ideas, like his eyes. With the fiery words that bore into her mind, her heart, her stomach so that she would do anything for him.

Deep, dark forests, without the moon, beds of cool moss by night. Sun-scorched fields; hay, dry and brittle or damp and fragrant. Heat of summer and trees brown under the brazen sky. Light, dark, day, night, morning, afternoon, and always Jean. Tall, thin, gaunt Jean, a man fifteen years her senior, who demanded and demanded, taking more and more, and always she was willing to give; a man whose passionate melancholy could alter to a terrifying temper if she displeased or reminded him, inadvertently, of her high birth, his low birth. "Get back to the manor, bitch. I can do better with the village slut."

Then weeping. A promise to do better. Tears pleading, words pleading, hands pleading. She would not displease him. It had been a mistake. She would try again. She would do better. She would please him, if he could tell her how.

He told her. And he showed her. And he pleased her, as well. Repeatedly. He saw her beauty but was not overwhelmed by it. He was not circumspect. He dispensed with wooing. He put an end to all pretense of respect or honor. He was a bold lover with bold talents. He reached her heart without appealing to it; he subdued her without so much as mentioning sentiment. Sometimes he was gentle with her, and patient. Other times, he was not. Then he was hot and triumphant and indecent. She had loved him as a little puppy loves its master, hopelessly, humbly, a special worship, quivering at his casual touch, slinking, cringing from an angry word, a hand lashing out to strike her.

He did not strike her often. Only when he had been drinking, only when he had been with that group of men who had the new ideas, the angry ideas, the *revolutionary* ideas. The men who thirsted for blood. But he did not share her with these men. For that she was grateful. She was not to blame for the state of poverty, the peasants in rags, the populace gone hungry. She was not at fault for that, with her privileges of birth, her beauty, her title, her estate, her clothes, her health, her body. Her beautiful body. That was his. He would take and take again. She was happy she could please him better than the village sluts.

"But why *can't* we be married, Jean?"

"*Dieu*, do I have to tell you again? You can't marry me, *ma chère*. I don't have a right. Not with the laws the way they are. But things will change. You will see. Then we can be married."

She did not think that Jean cared to marry her. The words he gave her were just so many excuses, and things did not change quickly enough for Susanne. She would fly in the face of her mother. She would fly in the face of convention. They would live on the *dépendance* of her mother's estate. He would continue to work in the village and meet with that group of men that met every month. But now there were more and more groups of men. Growing, restless groups with ideas. Those groups had begun to travel the country. Inciting. That was the word whispered by the old blood.

Again: "Sure, I want to marry you. Why wouldn't I? You doubt me? Let me show you. There. Let me show you. Now."

Eventually, her mother had discovered the liaison. Or rather the extent of the liaison, for she had suspected all along that her daughter was involved. But once Susanne had ruined herself, her mother pushed for the marriage, forced it, for she was still in a position to force it. So Susanne and Jean were married. Quietly. Jean and the girl she had been.

Less than a year it had lasted. Less than a year, then he was gone. Without a word. Without a trace. In the weeks and months of their marriage, she had been deliriously happy. There was nothing elegant about the man. Nothing sensitive. Only dark and mysterious and passionate and insatiable.

"Don't you love me, Jean?" she had asked.

"Leave me alone, bitch," he had snarled. But then, having said it, he would turn to her and please her very well.

She would ask again. "Don't you love me, Jean?" And the more she had asked over the course of the months of their marriage, the more he withdrew, the more he spent time away from her and the *dépendance*, the more time he spent in the village, or traveling with the dangerous bands of men with angry words on their lips and hatred in their hearts and blood on their hands. Blood. They had a thirst for blood. Blue blood. Well-born blood. The blood of her friends and acquaintances and family. The blood of her mother. Her own blood.

Then one day he had left the *dépendance* where they lived and never came back. Was never heard from again. Presumed dead. Killed perhaps. The body was never found. Less than one year of marriage. Four years after that first, angry, hungry night deep in the dark woods of her mother's estate.

She had been taken back in by her mother's family. Disgraced beyond words, of course. Thoroughly ruined. Susanne de Crécy, exquisite daughter of a distinguished French family and the late English Lord Marsh. Married to a common, semiliterate tradesman, himself son of a miller. Susanne Desmoulins. Left. Or widowed. And so tired. Spent. Exhausted. Empty of passion and hope and life and breath. So empty that she had wanted to die. So depleted that she had almost died. But no. It was not so easy. She would live. She suffered from too much youth, too much vitality, too much health.

Instead, it was her mother who had died. The passing of

another year had brought the death of La Baronne de Crécy. With her died also Susanne's French identity. Her mother dead, Susanne, at the age of twenty-five, gained legal control of her father's estate in England. She chose then to assume the other half of her heritage to which her birth gave her right.

Less than another year had passed before all of England had seen the star of Lady Susannah Marsh blaze across the firmament of London fashionables and permanently stud the sky with her beauty.

Susannah stared into the pond. Who would believe such a tale? But she had never told the story, had never tested anyone's credulity.

She thought, How would her life with Jean have been different, had he lived? She had never quite doubted that her mother had had him killed. Her mother. Her very own, beautiful, cold-blooded, icy shrew of a mother. Her mother, who had lived for years apart from her husband, had not shed a tear when news of her husband's death had reached Anjou, had almost forgotten to inform Susannah of her own father's death. It had slipped her mother's mind.

Susannah would never marry again. Wouldn't marry if the man had the face and fortune of the Duke of Kensington, the wit and charm of Peter Everly, or even the brains and brawn of . . . of Anthony Maddox, if he were available, which he was not. And, she thought, leaning against the parapet, what had she done that she had been cursed with the ability to love once . . . and no more . . . to love a man tall and gaunt, with a face like a broken cliff side, all jagged and granite, a face that could be ruthlessly passionate and passionately cold. A man who . . .

She would not pursue this tonight. She had been too much haunted of late, by these thoughts that she had thought so many, many times before. This night, last week, last year. Nothing served to obliterate them. She had had other men, not many of them, and discreetly. She had known many, many more who were attracted to her. But

she could not love them. She could fall deliriously in love
for a little while, she could give her lips and her hands and
her beautiful body. She could give, perhaps, a little of her
heart. But that was not the surrendering love the nineteen-
year-old Susanne had known for Jean.

She could not keep the duke waiting much longer. It
would not be entirely satisfactory, for mere physical rela-
tionships seldom were, but at least she could hope that she
might drown herself in it—if only for a little while. She
might feel her pulses pound hotly behind her eyes, but she
could not forget entirely. And she knew that it was her
deliberate reserve, the part of her kept hidden away, which
was the part that men most longed to possess, which drove
them mad for her and kept them panting for more.

The irony was almost amusing.

The irony was that she would have been happier had she
been born a peasant.

A shadow moved among the hedges close to the pavilion. Susannah caught the movement of the long, shadowy
form out of the corner of her eye. Her heart skipped a beat.
She shook her head. Her mind was playing tricks on her.
She had been too nervous since that night at the Pantheon
Ball. She had grown fanciful. No, worse. She had grown
maudlin.

"There you are, Susannah!" a voice shrieked. It was
Eliza Parrish. "We've been looking all over for you!" She
came tripping up, several gallants in tow. "But alone?" she
said. Susannah heard the implied malice. "Where is the
duke?"

"I don't know," Susannah replied. She smiled serenely.

Eliza plainly hated the woman before her. She hated her
beauty, her social success, her stunning conquests, her serenity. "Still not tired?"

"Not at all," Susannah replied.

"Then why not come cast dice with us?" Eliza invited.

"To the gaming hell you mentioned before, Eliza?"

Susannah asked. "Where did you say it was? St. James's Square?"

Eliza bared little white teeth. "Hardly there, Susannah! It's much more amusing! In Cheapside. And such a varied clientele," she said. "So many Frenchmen. Fleeing their country, it seems, and from all walks of life. I've been there once. Stoke took me. And everyone is mad to go there tonight. Do you join us?"

A poisonous woman, Susannah reflected, not for the first time. "I think not," she answered.

"Not even to be among your countrymen?" Eliza queried. "Why, you're fond of the French, are you not? That's what you've always said!"

A poisonous woman who carried a knife. Susannah had never said anything of the sort. But Eliza did not have the power to affect her. Susannah shook her head, her serene smile unchanged. She shifted her glance back to the gardens. "Not tonight, Eliza. I'm sorry to say that even the attractions of gaming and Frenchmen do not have the power to draw me. Everly will take me home."

Susannah's voice had trailed off, a little, at the end. Her attention had been caught again by that furtive shadow in the hedges. The tall, gaunt form had been joined by others. It was no lover's tryst. Susannah could see that it was a group of men.

Eliza, noting the direction of Susannah's gaze, and always greedy and hungry for gossip and scandal, thought, What is happening with Susannah? But then Susannah turned back to Eliza, and nothing in her face betrayed the least reason for curiosity. Eliza gave it up. "Suit yourself, then," she said and added, waspishly, "As long as you're not tired." Motioning to the court of drones she kept buzzing around her, she made a few parting remarks, and they proceeded to leave the terrace.

Susannah peered into the dark shadows of the garden stretching out and away from her. Suddenly the impulse was stronger than herself. She headed straight for the shallow stone steps that led to the path in front of her. She did not look around her and, thus, she did not notice that Eliza had cast a backward glance at her over her shoulder. The look of menace and malice never far from the back of Eliza Parrish's eyes would have stopped Susannah dead in her tracks.

But Susannah did not think of Eliza again. She hurried —as much as Lady Marsh could ever be said to hurry— down the steps, onto the path, and into the shadows. Chasing ghosts again, she thought. Would she never learn?

Would she never forget?

Cautiously she approached the pathways where she had seen the shadows disappear. She passed a strolling couple. They acknowledged her presence with the slightest of nods, but were far more absorbed in each other. So much the better. A woman alone, a slightly distracted woman alone in the gardens had raised no eyebrows.

Then, voices. Low voices, faint voices, whispering. Perhaps four or five men. Susannah knew the gardens well enough to judge which side path to take, which alcove would serve her best for listening. The thought came, Had she gone mad? Then, a decision. If the alcove were occupied, she would abandon this chase. A stroke of luck—or was it? The alcove was empty. She sat down, the voices directly at her back, her own person hidden by a screen of high hedges.

So intent was she on listening to the voices, straining to hear familiar cadences, familiar inflections, that it took a moment or two to realize they were speaking in French. Rapid French, a mix of Parisian and provincial, and not from the highest orders of society. A French she knew well enough. Too well, her mother had complained.

She did not care about the content of their conversation. She was listening for a particular voice, but she could not at first distinguish any one voice from the whispered jumble. Finally, her ear was able to discriminate the separate

parts, and she identified the voice of the man she thought
might be the leader of the group.

"We're all here now," he said, low.

Several affirmations.

"That is good. Now let me tell you why we have come."

"But why here?" a voice interrupted.

"Our contact insisted," came the reply. "This place.
Only."

With contempt: "A pleasure garden for aristocratic
dogs. May they roast in hell."

Murmurs of agreement.

The leader cut this off with a quick, hissed curse.
"Fools! We've more important business for now!"

"All right, then. Tell us, Chaumonot, have you met the
contact man?"

Chaumonot, the apparent leader, replied, "Once."

"And the money?"

"We shall see. It is promising."

"The contact man knows what to do?"

"Yes." This from Chaumonot again, with emphasis.

"But if he fails us?"

A low, bone-chilling chuckle from Chaumonot. "Then
we know what to do. With him. Or anyone else who gets
in our way."

"We've done it before," was the gist of several replies.
Notes of satisfied relish.

More in the same vein. Expressions of hatred and violence and blood lust. Slogans: Death to the aristocrats; long
live Mirabeau, Robespierre, Marat. Ideas for bringing the
Revolution to England. This very night. Beginning in this
very garden. Death to the aristocratic English dogs. Free
England of tyranny.

"Shut up!" Chaumonot's whisper.

Two or three voices rose to accuse him of cowardice,
lack of commitment to the Revolution.

Chaumonot stopped such talk with another of his horrifying cackles. "You babble like fools. You are impatient. We accomplish nothing with impatience."

Susannah strained her ears harder. Uncertainties remained. Still, she had heard enough now for her heart to have flipped over.

"Why wait?"

Chaumonot answered. He asserted his authority with a stinging note of contempt in his hard voice. "Think! Think, you fools! Marat does not need stupid men! He does not want stupid men! Listen. We have much to do first. This is not France. Here a man dies, and there is an investigation. It ruins everything for us. Police come. They ask questions—Who killed this man? Why? We jeopardize our plans. We need English money much more than we need English blood."

Susannah's own blood ran hot. It ran cold. The uncertainties were gone. She sat, rooted to the bench, herself a stone statue.

Discussion followed. She was not listening. She had been stunned. When she heard the group make plans to leave, it took a herculean effort to shake herself free of her immobility. Two or three of the men left. Two remained to speak.

Susannah stood up on her side of the hedge and held her breath.

"We'll meet in an hour," said Chaumonot.

"At the same place?"

"The same place," Chaumonot confirmed: "*L'Abeille*."

"The winnings are good."

Chaumonot laughed. "The winnings are decent. Gambling is one thing. *L'Abeille* draws the rich—and when they leave our tables they are less rich. But," he continued, "we need more money. Thousands of pounds. Perhaps millions of pounds. And I have a plan to get it."

"Et alors?"

The relish could be heard in Chaumonot's voice. "We

buy our way into the English stock market—and then sell off our bonds from the Banque Royale."

A pause. Then, an admiring "Very good!"

"And that, Mersenne," Chaumonot replied with finality, "is why Marat chose me to lead this mission to England."

"So," replied Mersenne. "Tell me about the contact man. Is he going to buy us into the market?"

"Yes. I see him in a few minutes. At the first canal." Chaumonot paused to reflect on the man he was about to meet. "A pretentious dog. With aspirations. We can use him to our ends. I have reason to think that he is, at present, hungry for money himself—and hungry for revenge. Yes, such a man we can surely use to our ends." Chaumonot laughed again. "He has recently lost a considerable amount of money, and if I have my information correct, the loss was caused by an aristocratic dog, but I have not found out yet which one. I am not sure that it matters to us, in any case. We can still use the hungry man as we wish. It is well."

The two men were on the point of departure. An afterthought: "Ah, Mersenne. I'll be needing you to travel in the next few weeks. First to the coast and the harbor to lead the next group ashore. We'll have to see, after that, for you are the only one among us who can speak English intelligibly." Chaumonot paused. "We all have our uses."

Then, brief valedictions. The crunch of gravel underfoot. Chaumonot and Mersenne departing in different directions.

Susannah was caught and had to chose which way to turn. Her peace of mind depended on it. Her life.

She paralleled one set of footsteps to the end of the hedgerow, where the two paths merged. She would have nothing to lose if she had chosen the wrong man to follow. She would have everything to lose if she had chosen the right man.

She turned the corner.

The moon darted from behind a cloud. The light fell on

the man's face. It was gaunt, deeply lined, as if carved from granite. It was without expression, the dark eyes cold as ashes in a winter's fireplace.

"*Jean*," she breathed.

The man looked at her, curiously, contemptuously. He nodded, bowed briefly, and made as if to go around her. "*Madame*," he said distantly.

Susannah clutched his arm. "*Jean, nom de dieu!*"

His face did not change. He looked down at her. The moment stretched endlessly. Then, he removed her cramped hand from his arm. "So," he said at last, recognizing her with his eyes, but he would not acknowledge her with words. He had nothing more to say. No words of explanation.

Susannah's heart writhed. Her voice betrayed all her anguish. "I thought you were dead. All these years, I thought you were dead."

The man nodded grimly. "That man is dead."

"Jean Desmoulins," she said on a sob, "stands before me."

"Jean Desmoulins is dead."

She shook her head, a little wildly. "Who are you?"

"You don't want to know me."

"But I do know you," she said pitifully. "You are Jean. And I am Susanne." She added in a rush, "Susanne Desmoulins. I must see you again."

"Susanne Desmoulins?" he echoed, the scorn in his voice like a whip. "She, too, is dead and gone."

He stood looking down at her. He had always been aroused by her beauty. He had always been aroused by her fear of him. Brutal and ugly he had been to her then, years ago. Experience had made him far more brutal and ugly now. It was tempting. He had tasted that particular lust many times since the day he had left her. It had not been quite as hot, not quite as salty, not quite as bloody. He had had other satisfactions. And he had other plans awaiting

him now. The same decision he came to all those years
ago, he made again. Easily. He wanted to be rid of her.

When he did not answer, Susannah asked, "Who is
Chaumonot?"

He grasped her arms then, so strongly that it caused her
head to snap back. He held her wrist in such a wrenching
grip that the pain shot up her arm. She loved it. She hated
that she loved it.

The violent movement of his arm had caused a button
on his shirt to come undone, exposing a part of his chest.
Susannah glimpsed a part of a medallion he wore around
his neck on a thin chain. Without seeing the whole, she
knew that the silver disk bore the imprint of a small gristmill perched over a running stream.

So. He still wore it. A fresh tide of memories washed
over her. She nodded at the medallion. "Jean Desmoulins
is not dead," she said.

He quickly released her arms and rebuttoned his shirt.
"A reminder," he said. "One, only." He placed his hands
on her shoulders. "And I have a reminder for you," he
hissed. "You have never heard the names *Desmoulins* or
Chaumonot." It was a threat. "You have never heard the
names. You have never seen me. You will never see me
again. Understood?"

Susannah nodded dumbly.

He smiled down at her, a shadow of the smile she had
formerly found so compelling. It was a thoroughly cruel
smile now. "Can I trust you to stay out of my way?" he
asked, pulling her toward him in a vicious grip.

Susannah could not speak. All the questions stuck in her
throat. Why are you here? Why did you leave me? Who
are you now?

"Stay out of my way," he said roughly into her ear. He
had bent low over her. His hands were lightly clasping her
throat, resting heavily against her collarbone. "Stay out of
my way, Susanne Desmoulins."

Susannah looked up at him, her eyes wild, his broad

hands resting heavily on her throat and shoulders. She could not think of what he was saying to her. She did not care. Only one question formed itself in her mind.

"Why did you leave me?" she asked, pitifully, plaintively.

For an answer, he cast her bodily aside. She stumbled slightly, almost fell.

"Out of my way," he snarled.

"*Jean, non!* Wait! Come back!" she called. But he had disappeared into the shadows.

Susannah found her way to the nearest bench, trembling as if weakened by extreme illness or lack of food, and sank onto it. She felt a hundred years old. She pressed her hands to her maltreated wrists and throat. She passed a dizzying second trying to steady herself, wondering how she would get out of the gardens and back to her house without being seen. She had come in a large party. They had seen her earlier with the duke. With luck, they would not be looking for her or curious about her prolonged absence. With luck, they might think the duke had escorted her home.

No such luck. She had been seen. One person was mightily curious about her activities.

Eliza Parrish, her nasty little black dog of envy nipping at her heels, had eluded her gallants minutes before in order to follow Susannah into the gardens. She found her, the moment Susannah had sunk to the bench. Eliza caught the veriest glimpse of a man's face and the view of a retreating form, dark and tall and distinctively thin. A face she might have seen before. A figure that was unforgettable.

One she had seen recently.

One that had caught her eye.

One she had seen in not the most elegant of surroundings.

But where? Eliza had been many inelegant places in the past several weeks. Where had she seen him?

Then it came to her. Well, well! Her first thought: *What*

does Susannah Marsh have to do with him? Her second thought: *Whatever it is, my luck has turned!*

Eliza was not stupid. Experienced card player that she was, she was not about to tip her hand to Susannah's viewing. Still, Eliza wanted some immediate satisfaction. She slipped behind the bushes and made her way back to the terrace of the Rotundo to wait.

Eliza's reward came several minutes later. Susannah Marsh made her way out of the gardens, looking very changed from the woman who had entered them. Eliza was awaiting her at the head of the stairs.

Gazing down at the beautiful, blond goddess as she slowly mounted the steps, Eliza asked, "Not tired yet, Susannah?"

XII

Country Pleasures

After Ranelagh, Marianna did not see Maddox again until one evening, a good week or more later, just as she was leaving for the theater.

Charlotte had already gone out the front door, when Maddox emerged from his library and, upon seeing his wife, crossed the foyer to where an attending footman was helping her with her shawl and her gloves.

"I'm off to Stanthorpe in the morning, my dear," Maddox said, striding toward her and taking the light shawl from the footman's hands, as if he were in the habit of doing so.

"Stanthorpe! Why, I haven't thought about Stanthorpe in months!" she exclaimed spontaneously. She turned around to look at him and wished she did not feel her pulses quicken at sight of him. "How long shall you be there?"

"The week, at least," he replied, neatly disposing the shawl across his wife's elbows. "Maybe more. I cannot now predict."

"What takes you there, my lord? Business?" she asked, making an attempt at a normal conversation.

He hesitated, slightly. "Yes, business. The usual."

"Still, it is rather nice for you to be going to Stanthorpe," she repeated.

She was about to pull on one of her gloves. He took it from her unresisting hand and performed the office for her. "But not nearly so amusing as in Town," he remarked.

"I'm not so sure!" she answered lightly, permitting him the liberty with her hand. "This next week will be rather slow, I think—although it will come as a welcome change for me, I can assure you! I don't doubt, however, that Charlotte will complain miserably of boredom! In all events, she and I will be leaving in less than a week for the country."

"The country?"

"Yes, Marlborough Park. The duchess's country party. The one you regretted. Had you forgotten?"

Having neatly fit the kid glove over her fingers, Maddox replied, "In fact, I had forgotten it," and then applied himself to the task of closing the long line of tiny seed pearl buttons on the inside of her arm, from wrist to elbow. "Do you think the duchess's party shall be amusing?"

"Oh, I don't suppose it will be dull," she replied. "But I do know something of the variety of country diversions, and I am sure that they cannot be so very different, save for the elegance, at Marlborough Park from at Stanthorpe."

"Then, you might just as well be going to Stanthorpe," he said.

Marianna looked up at him quickly. Gray-green eyes met blue, blandly. She was not quite sure of him, and chose caution. "Is that an invitation?"

He was securing the last button. "Were you fishing for one?"

She flushed and protested baldly, "No!"

"Then, you put me in an awkward situation," he said gravely, but she heard the teasing note in his voice. "For now that you have inferred an invitation from my comments, I am hardly in a position to gainsay you. Let us say, then, that it stands. The other glove, please?"

"What about Charlotte?" she asked quickly, handing him the object in question.

He renewed his efforts with the glove, saying, "The second is always the trick." Fixing his eyes on the task of smoothing the soft kid over her softer skin, he replied that Charlotte could come or stay as she pleased, and anticipated a possible objection by mentioning that Browne could easily find a chaperone for her, if she chose to stay in Town.

"But the Duchess's country party . . . ?"

"You've just told me that the diversions there will be no different from those in Stanthorpe," he replied, "and I've heard the guest list. It's a rather long one, and Marlborough House will be filled. I doubt very much that anyone will miss you."

"You are not very flattering!" she said.

He said, at his most formal, "Indeed, I had hoped to be very flattering!"

Marianna bit back a smile. He was teasing her. She was mightily tempted to accompany him to the country. "By inviting me to Stanthorpe?"

"It might be amusing to go back to our beginnings." He deftly fastened the buttons on the second glove.

"Start over, you mean?"

His eyes twinkled devilishly. "Start over? Perhaps I mean to start in the first place." He was still holding her wrist in a light clasp. "Are you cold, my dear?" he asked. "You shiver. Perhaps you need something more than your light wrap this evening."

She knew full well that he did not think her frisson was due to an evening chill. She would not let him bait her so easily. "A heavier wrap? Well, I don't know! But, then, I am an indecisive person, which makes me think that I cannot be sure after all," she said, "that the country attractions

at Stanthorpe are really equivalent to those at Marlborough
Park!"

He let go of her hand. "No? Well, you shall have to suit
yourself." He was not going to beg. He said, with a bow
that held the suggestion of mockery, "We are agreed that I
am not much of a dancer." With that, he handed her back
into the care of the footman and sent her off with a highly
unsatisfactory, "Enjoy the country pleasures at Marlborough Park, my lady!"

That was the last she saw of him that week, for the next
morning, by the time she had descended for breakfast, he
was gone.

Summer had come. June, not more than a week old, had
heralded its arrival with lashings of warm rain, washing the
world clean. The rains came and went, bringing in their
wake delicious, summer-scented breezes wafting into the
city. The kind of breezes that Marianna remembered from
summers in Stanthorpe. The kind of breezes that had accompanied her over fields and fells during her long walks
alone. The kind of breezes that had swirled about her and
Lord Edward as they used to sit on the terrace of Maddox
House, drinking tea and laughing and arguing.

She firmly suppressed these memories and all her second thoughts about having refused Anthony Maddox's invitation to Stanthorpe. She set her sights instead on the
forthcoming journey to Marlborough Park.

Nothing could have been more pleasant. The burden-
some chores of packing for herself and for Charlotte were
placed entirely on other shoulders, while she savored only
the anticipation of departure and reveled in a flurry of last-
minute, seemingly necessary, but entirely frivolous purchases.

The journey itself was a joy. Marianna was happy to be
leaving Town and in such style. As easily as she had grown
into her role as Lady Westleigh, she would still never quite
forget what it was to be a penniless young woman, traveling from Italy to England with little but her dignity. It was

certainly much more agreeable travel than any she had previously experienced to be bowling through the green English countryside in a fashionable, well-sprung chaise-and-four, the postilions handsomely liveried, rising so regularly in their stirrups, and the numerous outriders properly mounted.

Whereas her previous traveling experiences had been, for the most part, exercises in tedium, she found that this one passed extraordinarily quickly. During the long hours, she hugged to herself all her private thoughts on the past few months as she gazed out across the countryside, her eyes embracing the sweep of the placid fields rolling away, merging with the line of woods rambling over undulating hills off into the distance. They passed through benevolent green hills cradling ancient villages slumbering in an air of changelessness. They passed snug little farms nestled everywhere, whose lichened stone fences were brownish-gray and creeper-covered. They passed myriad threads of streams stitching together a rolling countryside flocked with ripening orchards.

The exceeding pleasantness of the journey was only slightly marred by Charlotte. Now, Charlotte had fallen in love again. This time, yes, this time, she was sure that she had found True Love. It came in the form of a handsome —and indigent—French nobleman who had, after many harrowing adventures, sought refuge on English shores. So while Marianna was inclined to enjoy the passing scenery and spin her own thoughts, Charlotte had a tendency to pout and to sigh.

"You are whining again, my dear," Marianna said as they stopped on the second day at a charming inn for luncheon. "The whole of the world is spread out at your feet, and you choose to close your eyes and to whine! I would certainly hate to think of your spending the next fortnight in such a humor. Why, what could be more exciting than being a part of a most fashionable and select country party given by the Duchess of Marlborough?"

"Staying in London," Charlotte replied immediately.

"But there is nothing doing in Town right now, as you know, and so I do not think that we would have so very many opportunities for gadding about—"

"Gadding about, Marianna? Gadding about? Is that what you call it?" Charlotte demanded hotly.

"You are always taking me up on what I say, Charlotte! That is exactly what I call it! What name do you put to it?"

"Love!" Charlotte wailed.

"My dear, we have had this conversation! How many times have you been in love already? Four, by my count. Possibly five. You must forgive me if I have lost track. So, if you are now going to tell me that there is a new one that I don't yet know about, I feel that it is my duty, as your—"

"You know very well who I am talking about, Marianna! And this is serious! You met him for the first time at the assembly last week."

"The assembly? Then, *you* met him there for the first time, as well. I hardly think one week's time is sufficient to be extolling a new love!"

"That is how much you know!"

"Whatever happened to that nice young man, the Viscount Eldon? The one with the magnificent estate?"

Charlotte turned accusing eyes on Marianna. "You were the one who told me not to fall in love with money—you did! You called it cupboard love. And now I have met *him*, and I don't care a pin that he is poor!"

It was Marianna's turn to sigh. "My dear, how poor is he?"

"Very!" Charlotte breathed rapturously. "He's lost everything. Everything! And he behaves so nobly about it, that I can tell you I have never been so impressed with his suffering in the face of adversity."

"Lost everything?" Marianna queried. "Do not . . . I beg of you, Charlotte . . . do not tell me that he is a gambler!"

"No, he's French!" Charlotte replied angrily. "He's been dispossessed!"

"Oh, yes, well, then, that would account for it," Marianna said, with an amazing lack of feeling for the poor, dispossessed nobleman.

"You met Gaston, Marianna! Last week. At the assembly!"

"Ah! So you managed to remember his name after only one meeting," Marianna commented. "Perhaps this *is* serious!"

The import of this remark was not completely lost on Charlotte. "Are you still angry at me?" she asked, suddenly contrite. "About the dinner table conversation?"

"You must know that I wasn't happy about it! But we've been over this ground, too! Several times already, and I think you must know how very . . . how very inappropriate it was to speak of *other interests* at the table in front of Lord Westleigh. I am afraid that it gave him a very odd opinion of you!"

"I don't think he cared at all that I said it and, anyway, he provoked me into telling him about it!"

Marianna had to agree. "He is a provoking man, I'll grant you that! But you started it all by letting your tongue run away with you!"

"Did I cause you trouble with Lord Westleigh, Marianna? I did not mean to!"

Marianna found the question impossible to answer.

"Forgiven and forgotten?" Charlotte ventured, her dimples peeping.

"I will forgive you everything, my dear, if you drop this subject! And all talk of Gaston for a while! Be a brave girl, do. I would so much like to enjoy the passing scenery. And who knows? You cannot now say what new love you will find among the guests at Marlborough Park. Perhaps an equally indigent Frenchman!"

Marianna was to prove an unexpected prophet.

They arrived midday, on the third day of travel, at the entrance of Marlborough Park drive. The heavy wrought-iron gates had been thrown open, and before them was spread the magnificent emerald carpet of lawn sloping gently up to the crest of a slight hill atop which stood, proud and aloof, the nobly proportioned Marlborough House. Its sublime facade was decorated with massive fluted columns and pilasters rising the whole height of the building to support a scrolling frieze. Giant keystones thrust up from the windows, the two central ones of which were framed by voluptuous garlands, and a tall figure of Athena on the pediment of the entrance projection emphasized the ascending character of the design.

The duchess herself was greeting her guests, who were arriving throughout the day. She met all thirty or more with hugs and chaste kisses and the news that she had invited the most amusing company of French men and women—with such tragic stories, all of them!—who would be coming the next week. And would it not be great fun to put them on the cricket field and see what they could make out of bats, balls, wickets, and all?

Marianna nodded significantly to Charlotte, who received this news with a sniff of affected indifference.

The duchess, upon hugging Marianna, informed her that her dear friend Lady Marsh would be arriving later. "Such a curious note I received from Susannah," the duchess said in her charming French accent, "who regrets her absence and says that she will try to attend, but cannot promise anything! You know, I simply cannot imagine that she is indisposed, but what else could it be?"

Eliza Parrish, overhearing this, smiled like the cat with the cream.

The rest of the day was marked by an endless flurry of arrivals. Since most of Marianna's dearest friends and most cherished acquaintances were coming, she predicted to Charlotte that the duchess's country party would prove a lovely fortnight.

So it was. The first week proceeded at a leisurely pace. Al fresco luncheons were counterpointed by exquisitely formal dinners of five courses and three removes. There were ridings and outings, mild flirtations, passionate seductions, walks and talks, and a seemingly never-ending variety of things to do, all unfolding at a refined pace.

In the opening days, a topic of conversation was established. It was to carry the conversationalists among the guests throughout the first week at least. Marianna became aware of the topic on the second day, and noted thereafter that it was either the source from which all discussions departed, or the point at which they all eventually arrived. The topic, which was inaugurated by Lady Louisa Hester, was the Rights of Woman.

A group was taking a tour through the rose garden when the conversation turned to women and their accomplishments.

Lady Hester's judgment was severe. "Oh, in an unguarded moment, I suppose, we women have tossed off a Queen Elizabeth or a Joan of Arc, but for the most part we have preserved a glorious mediocrity that allows men to believe themselves dominant in administration, art, science, war, and finance."

Everly had stopped to bend a particularly lovely rose to his nose. "Oh, but my dear Lady Hester, I cannot agree!" Everly replied, straightening quickly, ready to take up this most delightful topic.

"But, Everly, I hardly make a controversial statement by saying that women stand out in history only rarely!"

"It was not the first part of your statement that I objected to," Everly explained. "No, rather, it was the second part: your assertion that man believes himself to be superior to woman. I wish merely to note that not all men believe themselves to be superior to women—no matter what the man's accomplishments."

Lady Hester refined her point. "In fact, I said that women *allow* men to believe in their superiority. But let us not quibble! Let us speak instead of your beliefs, Everly! I take it that you do not think poorly of woman's intellect?"

Everly bowed. "Once again, Lady Hester, I wish to turn

your statement around. I think very highly of the understanding of all the women in the world. Especially of
those, whoever they may be, with whom I happen to be in
company."

"I should have expected no better from you, Peter
Everly!" Lady Hester said repressively, but she had a sense
of humor for all of that and had to bite her quivering lip.
"But this is not a laughing matter, my good man! Do be
more serious!"

Everly tried again. "Lady Hester," he said, "no one can
think more highly of the understanding of women than I
do. In my opinion, nature has given them so much that
they never find it necessary to use more than half."

"I will agree with you, Everly, that the average woman
makes a very creditable concealment of intellect," Lady
Hester said, looking him straight in the eyes, "as do some
men that I know!"

Everly was about to retort to that, but Marianna intervened. "We shall get nothing more serious from him now,
Lady Hester," she said. "He is not in a sober mood, and if
you wish to wait until one comes upon him, I fear that you
shall wait forever!"

A few more inconsequent remarks were made in response, and the discussion ended soon thereafter when
Everly invited Marianna to stroll with him down a side
path in the rose garden, on the pretext that there was an
extraordinarily beautiful bloom he wished to point out to
her.

"So it is a sober mood from me you want, my dear?"
Everly asked smoothly, leading her along. "If it is, I am
happy to oblige you. Behold me in a sober mood!" So
saying, he picked up the hand that Marianna had lightly
laid on his arm and intertwined his fingers in hers. The
intimacy of the gesture took Marianna, at first, aback.

"But you need not conform your moods to my wishes,
Everly," she replied lightly, allowing her fingers to rest
passively in his.

"Oh, but I do!" His tone, this time, was indeed remarkably sober.

"Good heavens, sir!" she bantered, slanting him a glance. "This does not sound like you at all! Have you had a touch of the sun? Or are you ill, perhaps?"

"A case of the measles," he replied, serious still.

"My goodness!" she exclaimed, looking at him a little alarmed. Then, although he returned her regard seriously, steadily, and even warmly, she narrowed her eyes and said suspiciously, "I knew it couldn't be true! You are joking me again, are you not? But I am afraid I do not understand the joke."

"It's no joke," he said, his handsome eyes and lips unsmiling.

"But the measles . . . ?"

"A disease not unlike true love, did we not once agree?" he said. "It seems I have succumbed . . . at last," he said. The pressure of his fingers increased on hers. They had stopped walking, and he had drawn her slightly closer. "And I am hoping for a cure."

"C-cure?" Marianna took a step back and disengaged her fingers from his. She had not expected this from him, and yet she could not quite say that she was entirely surprised.

Everly did not attempt to retrieve her hand. He immediately perceived that he had been too precipitate. He bowed. "Yes, a cure, and I was hoping for your help in, ah, securing the lady's affections," he said easily.

"How can I help?" she asked.

"I thought that you, as a married woman, would be the perfect confidante, for there is a lady here at the party who attracts me greatly . . ."

"And who is also married, like myself?"

"Precisely," Everly replied. "And she, as I say, attracts me as no other woman has before."

"Oho! Do you expect anyone to believe *that*?"

"It is quite true! I have never felt this way about a

woman before," he said, "and I have never told another soul that I have such a feeling."

"Not even during a . . . let us say . . . most auspicious moment?" Marianna suggested. "An auspicious moment when you were pursuing a married woman? For you are, after all, infamous for your pursuit of married women."

"Slander! I cry slander on my reputation," he lamented, mock-tragically. "This time, I feel very different, I can assure you," he said, surprisingly earnest. "And I wish for you to believe me."

"And what of the lady's husband?"

"Absent," Everly answered.

"How convenient!" Marianna said.

"Yes, isn't it?" he replied, laying her hand again on his arm and proceeding to meander down the path. "I am a practical man, as well as an amorous one, and so noting the husband's absence on the first evening, I asked myself if this were not the perfect occasion to declare myself. Well, I hardly need tell you that my better self rose to the occasion and delivered a rather stern warning to my baser self on the improprieties of making love to a married woman!"

"And . . . ?" Marianna prompted.

"And my baser self won!" Everly replied, quite cheerfully.

"So easily?" she asked. "Do you not feel any . . . scruples about the husband? That is, what if you were a friend of the husband's? Or do you only establish liaisons with married ladies with whose husbands you have but scant acquaintance?"

"You see, my dear," Everly said, serious once again, "it is not only that the husband is absent from this particular party. It seems that he does not pay his wife—his very charming and beautiful wife—the attention she deserves. It seems a shameful waste, but there it is! I can only think the husband somewhat of a dolt for neglecting her so!"

Marianna bit her lip. "And how am I to help you secure the lady's affections?" she asked cautiously.

"It is simply this," he said. "It is important for me to know whether the lady wishes to bask in the golden glow of my attention . . . or not. I shall be happy to shower it on her, and make of this country party a true idyll, if she so desires it. But I need to know whether you—as a married woman—would yourself appreciate such attentions."

Marianna could think of absolutely no response.

"Ah, here is the bloom I so wanted you to see!" Everly said just then, to bridge over the highly charged moment. He cradled in his palm a rose he had chosen at random. "The color! The fragrance! Is it not exquisite?"

Marianna obligingly bent over the rose. "Lovely," she agreed, hardly noting, in her momentary confusion, either the color or the fragrance of the rose in question.

"So like the lady whose regard I seek."

Marianna gathered her wits. She stood back up and regarded Everly openly. "I cannot speak for the lady in question, of course, but, as you say, my being married myself gives me some insight. On the other hand, I am perhaps not yet dashing enough to think of receiving the attentions of a man who is not my husband, so I am not sure that I can give you the advice you need . . . or want."

"Ah, well! Yes, I see how it is must be." Everly sighed, as if over a trifle. He paused, as if conjuring an exceedingly pleasant vision. "But the opportunity of these next few days and weeks is so enticing as to be irresistible! Just the thought of it makes me think that I have truly fallen in love!" Then he sighed again and said, "Perhaps I must be a little more patient. Or perhaps I shall abandon the notion entirely."

This he said in an offhand way, so as to relieve any embarrassment she might have felt at what could have become, with a little encouragement from her, a declaration.

They had begun to walk again. Marianna had always liked Peter Everly and had never taken his occasional amorous bantering seriously before. She was still not quite sure how to take it now.

They emerged just then on the other end of the path, not far from a group of people already waving to them, beckoning them to join.

Wishing to keep their friendship intact, she said, "But abandoning the notion so easily does not argue much for your having truly fallen in love, does it now?" She scoffed gently. "You, Everly? Fallen in love?"

"Anything is possible," he said lightly. And since he, too, did not want to jeopardize their friendship (or, perforce, create any awkwardness between them that might spoil future opportunities to secure her affection and regard), he added with his charming, careless smile, "Already fallen? Perhaps not, after all. But most certainly teetering on the precarious precipice."

XIII

Lady Hester on Women

Marianna did not see Everly again until dinner the next evening, at which time he made her an elegant leg and drew a smile from her with several light comments. Marianna was pleased to think that their relationship was to continue on its established terms of easy friendship.

Dinner that evening was an altogether entertaining interlude. Lady Hester had only just begun to warm to her topic of the Rights of Woman and had formulated some fascinating views on the story of the Garden of Eden that she was determined to share with her audience.

With a little encouragement, Lady Hester gave out her opinion. "The romance of Adam and Eve was written by so subtle a hand that I feel sure the novelist must have been a woman. Her timeless allegory of Eden contains the whole situation of the sexes: it shows the superiority of woman, while seeming, for his own good, to show the superiority of man. As it must have required a woman to write the parable, so perhaps it requires a woman to expound it."

All other conversations around the long dinner table virtually stopped. There were chuckles of derision and snorts

of disapproval from the men, and murmurs of encouragement from the women, with one unabashed feminine voice
rising to a "Bravo, Louisa!"

One of the bolder men demanded that Lady Hester explain herself. Was not Eve the temptress, causing man's
fall? Was she not the one easily seduced by the snake,
which any reasonable man knew to be the embodiment of
evil?

"Well, now!" she replied. "It is a question of interpretation, is it not? I read in the story that Eve was more capable
of initiative, the bolder to act, as well as the braver to
accept the consequences of action, while Adam, I observe,
was unconscionably lazy and mopish!"

"*Mopish*?"

"Yes, mopish!" she replied without hesitation. "What a
dolt he was! What a lump! For no one knows how long,
Adam had been bumping into that tree without once seeing
it for what it was. Now, Eve plainly saw that it was, first of
all, good for food, and second of all, pleasant to look
upon. Man did not notice its beauty until woman told him
so. Now, thirdly, and of course here is the key, Eve saw
that the tree was to be desired to make one wise. We all
know how Eve's motives have been impugned, for when a
man is ready to die for knowledge, he is called scientific,
but when a woman is ready to die for knowledge, she is
called inquisitive!"

Peter Everly, who seemed to have recovered from his
rebuff in the gardens the day before (if rebuff it had been),
spoke up. "You know, I have noticed something similar,"
he said gamely. "It is customary to say that when a man
speaks, he is having a serious discussion," he added auda-
ciously, "but when a woman speaks, she gossips."

It was safe to say that after these broad openings, food
for conversation did not lack. Arguments for and against
woman's superiority continued far into the night. Everyone, down to the very last guest, advanced an opinion on
this, the most universally appealing of subjects. Even Eliza

Parrish had her say, and some highly original and entertaining opinions were proposed by those who were not otherwise drawn to the rarefied circles of good talk. The
duchess remarked happily that Louisa was singlehandedly
turning her "modest little party" into an *event*.

Nor did it stop with the dinner.

One early evening a day or two later, at the blue hour,
the company had assembled in the magnificent receiving
saloon that ran almost the length of the back of Marlborough House and gave onto the terraced garden, facing
west. The afternoon had been a golden one, with guests
variously occupied. Charlotte had agreeably passed the
hours fishing with several personable young men and
women, while Marianna had played croquet. Now the
company had changed into evening toilette in anticipation
of an informal dinner, buffet style. They were disposed in
small groups, relaxing over sherrys and clarets, occupied
with cards or dice or embroidery or knotting fringes, as
befitted their temperaments and their sexes. A perfectly
magical sunset was gathering on the vast horizon of the
park, promising an equally magical night ahead.

Of all people, it was Lord Hester who provoked the
evening's discussion. He, not so innocently, accused his
wife of a lack of logic and reason in her assertion that
women writers were uniformly superior to men writers.

"A lack of logic and reason!" she exclaimed, in a voice
that drew the attention of those within earshot. "My dear
man, listen what I have to say about *that*!"

Lady Hester had a good deal to say about that. "As to
woman's mental mechanism"—she plunged in—"it is so
much finer than man's that, out of pure pity for his clog-
ging equipment, we let him think logic and reason better
means of traveling from premise to conclusion than the airy
flights we encourage him to scorn as woman's intuition.
Nothing is more painful to a woman than an argument with
a man! He journeys from given fact to deduced truth by
pack mule, and she by air balloon. When he finds her at

the destination, he is so irritated by the swiftness of her passage that he accuses her of not having followed the right direction, and demands as proof that she describe the weeds by the roadside, which he has amply studied. He calls this study his reasoning process." Lady Hester paused for effect. "Of course, no woman stops to botanize when the object is to get there!"

"Ah, Louisa!" the duchess exclaimed, once more delighted with the entertaining turn in conversation. "I am so endlessly fascinated by your thoughts that I wonder why you don't write all of this down!"

"That," Lady Hester acknowledged, "is a great problem. I am currently working on *A Treatise on the Natural Gifts of Woman*, but I have discovered that a woman must have her house in order first, to be able to write."

The Fifth Earl of Choate, a longtime friend of the Hesters, was unwise enough to protest. "But, Louisa! You have an army of servants to do that for you!"

Lady Hester treated this remark with the disgust it deserved. "Just like a man! I was speaking metaphorically!"

"You should have known better—really, Vernon!" Lord Hester reproved from his corner.

"But Vernon's chuckleheaded remark only serves my point," Lady Hester continued. "Vernon cannot know the least thing about it, poor man that he is! Let me explain: it needs the whole woman, acting harmoniously, to write. A man can retire to his brain and make a book, and often a fairly good one, leaving all the rest of his personality in confusion. But a woman must put her whole house in order before she can go off upstairs into her intellect to write. Man is put together in pieces: body, mind, soul. But a woman does not move in pieces like a man or . . . or an earthworm—"

"You never disappoint, Louisa!" Lord Hester interpolated on a grin.

"—but functions as a whole human being and, therefore, amounts to most intellectually when she amounts to still more personally. I have found that my literary productiveness is far more precariously dependent upon my peace of mind than is a man's, so that my writing goes very much more slowly. In woman, body and brain and soul are inseparable. I must keep all three parts in harmony in order to write! No easy task, I assure you!"

Everly, who seemed to be considering these points, then mused aloud, "If, as you state, Lady Hester, the soul and brain of a woman are inseparable from her body, then I wonder, why is it that women continually complain that they want to be loved for themselves alone and *not* for their bodies?"

Since this remark was plainly unanswerable, it was fortunate that Lady Hester was spared the necessity of replying. Her comments had struck deep chords in the feminine half of her audience, at least. Charlotte, who was still trying to make amends to Marianna for having spoken so thoughtlessly on husbands and their other interests, had been making efforts this week past to improve the tenor of her conversation. She said, immediately on the heels of Everly's remark and quite spontaneously, "Perhaps that is why, Lady Hester, I so much prefer reading women writers! That is, when I do get around to reading. For I have always thought that the novels that women write are . . . are like visiting someone's home. And I think it is the women who make the home, isn't it? A home that people like to visit, where everything is in order, as you say, and . . . and so welcoming!" She glanced anxiously at Marianna for endorsement of these remarks and received an approving nod in return. Then, to Lady Hester, "Do you see what I mean?"

"Perfectly!" Lady Hester answered.

Marianna, who was sitting rather near the door to the main hallway but with her back to it, had been listening, rather bemused, to this conversation. She heard, far off behind her, the sounds of arrivals at the main door. A little bell was sounded in the saloon, and the duchess excused herself in order to greet her newest guests. Marianna was hoping that it might be Susannah Marsh. She did not have a moment to consider it, however, for her attention was drawn back to the conversation at hand.

"Does any of this make sense to you, Lady Westleigh, as a writer?" Lady Hester was saying. "As I have told you, I used to read your articles in the *Anglican Mirror*. But you wrote those, of course, before you were married, and I have seen nothing that you have written since, which is too bad, for your articles were very amusing, my dear!"

Marianna thanked Lady Hester kindly but declined being referred to as a writer. "I am not sure that my little scribblings count! But, as I was listening to you, I was weighing your comments against my own experience. However, I think that my writing was more a means of escape from the very real 'chaos below' created by my nephews, than of commitment to the craft! When I was living with my brother and his family, I could retire to my brain, as you say, and spin out my stories. Since coming to London, I will admit that I simply haven't had a desire to write—or a reason, really! I have things on my mind now other than writing—"

"Of course you do," Lady Hester replied. "And no doubt you will have more when your children come."

Marianna could not adequately respond to that, but she continued, "All of which makes me think that I did not have the soul of a writer to begin with, only an amusing point of view!"

Lady Hester was, paradoxically, pleased by that admission, for she said that Lady Westleigh's remarks only proved yet another of her points: the life of a woman writer is a desperate compromise between writing and living. "And Lady Westleigh has chosen to live her art!"

Marianna laughed at that and said that she felt a heavy burden now to make of her life a work of art. "But, in any case, I agree with your observation, Charlotte," she said, encouraging her ward's participation in the conversation,

"that there is something special about the novels women
write. Like you, I often find them so vastly more welcoming than those written by men!"

It was at this moment that the duchess returned to the
saloon, but since Marianna was facing the terrace doors,
she could not see who was with her. The duchess was
speaking to her newly arrived guest, saying something to
the effect that his arrival was unexpected and, what with all
the French guests about to descend on Marlborough Park,
there were no extra chambers immediately available, unless he should desire her to open up a suite in the north
wing? The duchess mentioned that, of course, his wife's
suite was most charming, and quite large.

A richly textured masculine voice dismissed any notion
that the duchess should trouble to open up another wing for
only one person and said, with utmost cordiality, that it
was certainly no hardship to be chambered with his wife.

Marianna's heart leapt to her throat, and she quickly
turned around to confirm with her eyes what her ears had
heard. She felt a flush creep up her face.

It was indeed Anthony Maddox. He bowed, greeted
those closest to him by name, and entered the saloon. Marianna was struck, once again, by the figure he cut: it was
one of rough presence and, to her eyes now, of undeniable
masculine beauty.

He crossed first to Charlotte, then to her side and bowed
over her hand. She met his eyes, fleetingly, and read in
their luminous gray-green depths the message: *We'll now
proceed on my terms!* She murmured a polite greeting, and
he took up a standing position behind her chair.

Marianna suddenly realized what had been missing from
these discussions during the past week: Maddox's opinion.

After this little interruption, the conversation took up
precisely where it had left off. "Now, I could not agree
with you more, Lady Westleigh," Lady Hester was saying,
"that the novels written by women are more entertaining
than those written by men."

Lord Hester, who had a way with his wife, mentioned that they had not been speaking specifically of novels when the discussion began, but only of men writers and women writers.

"Well, I daresay gentlemen never read novels written by women," Charlotte offered brightly.

"Why is that, my dear?" This from Peter Everly.

Charlotte was surprised by the question. "I don't know! I've never thought about it, and I suppose I could tell you all the reasons why I've never thought about it, but Marianna has asked me to limit myself to just a sentence or two when speaking... to begin with, at any rate! And so it seems to me that gentlemen don't read women's books because... because they aren't clever enough. Gentlemen read better books."

"I wouldn't say that," Everly replied.

"Well, have *you* read any novels by women, Mr. Everly?" Charlotte asked, innocently wandering into fascinating territory.

"What a charming young lady you are, Miss Armitage!" Everly remarked. In fact, it happened, he said, that none had ever crossed his hands. "But I don't have any prejudice against them! It is a question of chance that I have simply never taken one up." Everly was happy to toss the slippery topic away. "What about you, Maddox?" he asked, a little slyly.

"I have read all of Mrs. Radcliffe's books," Maddox replied matter-of-factly, "and most of them with great pleasure."

Marianna turned her head around to regard her husband in some astonishment. He was smiling down at her in a way that made her pulses leap.

"Why, Maddox, you unman me!" was Everly's comment.

"You, Tony?" Lady Hester was also surprised into saying. "The only serious man among us? And a political economist, no less!"

"Why is that so extraordinary?" Maddox replied. *"The Romance of the Forest* was most entertaining! I must have read it . . . what, several months ago already . . . and I could not lay it down once I had begun it. I remember finishing it in two days, my hair standing on end the whole time!"

"But a novel written by a woman?" Lady Hester pursued.

"I am not sure that I was aware when reading it," he said, "that it was written either by a woman or a man. I do not recall thinking once about the author's sex, only the story."

"So you are not against the rights of woman, then?" Lady Hester asked.

"I cannot answer that," Maddox said, "unless you define for me what a man who is against the rights of woman might believe."

"That would be a man who considers himself superior to women," Lady Hester informed him. "That is, a man who does not believe woman is his equal."

"Actually, a man who does not recognize woman's inherent superiority, according to your arguments earlier this week, my lady!" Everly interjected.

"That, ultimately," Lady Hester acknowledged. "But we cannot expect too much at once! Well, Maddox?"

Maddox was too experienced a politician to fall into the trap. "I have an abiding suspicion that I will answer 'No, I am not against the rights of woman' only for you to point out the next instant how wrong I am!"

"An equivocation!" Lady Hester frowned.

"Perhaps I can help," Marianna said, looking up at him. Her blue eyes were sparkling irresistibly. "A man who is against the rights of woman, one might say, is a man who does not allow a woman to make her own decisions. For instance, a husband who does not allow his wife to spend —or invest—her own money as she pleases. What is your position on that?"

Maddox looked down at her. "But now we have two

issues at hand. The first is how man in general treats woman in general. The second—the one you bring up, my dear—is, I believe, how a husband treats his wife. I firmly distinguish between the two."

Needless to say, this position sat well with the husbands present.

Not so for Marianna. "Here, then, is the crux of the matter!" she said. "And I think it would benefit a thorough examination!"

"Readily!" he said, without hesitation, and coming round to stand in front of her, he took her hands and raised her from her chair. "Let us examine it at once!"

"But, here," Marianna said, protesting weakly, "in a public forum."

"However, we have hit on a private issue, no?" Maddox countered.

Everly had a puckish comment on his lips, but thought the better of uttering it. It was just as well, for the dinner gong reverberated, and the duchess invited her guests to serve themselves in the dining saloon and then to find themselves a comfortable spot to eat. Everly rose from his chair and requested of Charlotte, with the deepest of bows, that she might bestow on him the pleasure of escorting her to dinner.

As the company in general were rising and forming small groups to proceed into the dining saloon, Marianna made some halfhearted comments about joining the other diners, but Maddox merely shook his head and regarded her with an inquiring lift to his brow.

XIV

Garden Enchantment

"Where to?" Maddox said.

Marianna was on her feet. "I don't know! What are the choices?" she asked.

"You're leaving it up to me?" he inquired, and Marianna realized her mistake in having so thoughtlessly given away the initiative. "Well, then," he said, as if considering the matter, "may I suggest the gardens?"

"Oh, yes, the gardens!" Marianna approved quickly. She thought them a safe enough place. In her inexperience, she wanted to defer the inevitable. She wanted to be very sure of herself at that moment when he would demand, as he surely would, that the dance end and the marriage begin. She thought the gardens a welcome middle ground between the dance floor and the bedchamber.

"The gardens, then," Maddox repeated. He thought the gardens a delightful spot to exact his wife's complete and utter submission. He tucked her hand into his elbow, and they left the saloon through the open French doors.

An enchanting half-light lingered abroad when they strolled across the terrace, which was wreathed in pink and purple bougainvillea and flanked by stone urns cascading

flowers. They stepped onto the sloping velvet lawns leading to secret, meandering paths.

The gardens drowsed, and in the hush the cicadas
pulsed. The shadows of the tall trees stretched across the
lawn, and full-blown roses pouted on their stems, scenting
the warm evening air. From their rooftops the doves cooed
and murmured and indulged in sudden bursts of flight,
their wings spread white. The sun had slipped below the
horizon, and a full moon, amber-gold, was rising against a
sky of indigo, soon to be mazed with stars. The summer
night was upon them, full and flush.

They did not speak at first. They were both content to
wander to the first path that presented itself. They were
immediately surrounded by a wild tangle of vines and untrimmed bushes and low, leafy trees. It was an untended
undergrowth, which stood in sharp contrast to the mani-
cured lawn, a thicket where brambles and wildflowers and
self-sown saplings rioted as they pleased. The air was
fresher here and cooler, and as expectant as the darkness
that surrounded them.

"And now for the distinction you make between women
and wives?" she said.

"An irrelevant one at the moment," he answered.

"Which was my point to begin with," she returned.

Suddenly, he stopped. "Do you know that I have never
fully kissed you?"

It was a breathtaking change in subject. "Yes," she said,
stepping away from him. "I know."

He caught her, bent his head, and kissed her.

Marianna had been standing in the midst of an untamed
garden, but suddenly everything became filtered, through
Maddox. He stood between the world and her senses, re-
fining the particles of the moonlight, the hum of the cicadas, the scent of the leaves and the earth underfoot, so
that her breath and her blood beat in rhythm with their
surroundings through him.

He kissed her two times. The first kiss lingered briefly.

His lips were warm and slightly parted, touching hers with a feeling of misplaced nostalgia, as if he and she had been lovers in a similar garden long ago and their passion was long past, a frenzy remembered rather than anticipated, and this first kiss merely the remnant, a little dangerous, a little teasing. And so sweet.

The second kiss was more insistent and promised what was to come. It was a rapid beating of the blood, a mixing of the currents that ran between them: his fiery nature, her calm one. But she was not calm now and met his kiss with a rising passion of her own. From the first time she had recognized the light of interest in his eyes, she had feared her loss of independence. Kissing and clinging to him now, she suddenly discovered something quite unexpected. A new, unknown spirit sang and danced in her blood, a spirit imprisoned and longing for release. The longer she kissed him, the stronger became the need for its release, and she was testing out, through lips and hands, the dazzling theory that giving herself to him might not be a submission, but rather a very different and very most exciting form of independence.

He was aware of her response. He moved his lips away, with regret. His goal was the pond, grassy and private. He wondered if they would make it. A third kiss might keep them in this very spot for the rest of the night.

When he broke off the kiss, she said, in a shaky attempt at humor, "You argue unfairly." She tried to move away.

He did not release her. She was pressed to his length, and he thought that this was where she belonged. "Not at all," he said.

"We were speaking of the difference between women and wives," she reminded him.

Since he had no doubts about the outcome of this encounter, he would not force the pace; and he had learned enough of his wife in recent weeks to know that wooing her first with words would make the end so much sweeter. "Were we?" he replied. "But before I address the question,

I would like to ask two myself." When she nodded mutely, he said, "The first is, Wife, how you managed to do so well with your investments."

"It is something to hear you admit it!" she said, on a low laugh. "I thought that I was supposed to be an idiot only able to be protected from disaster by my husband!"

"You are an idiot, for having refused me for so long," he said. "But your investments were, for the most part, solid. How did you do it?"

"Air balloon," she replied.

"My dear?"

She laughed. "Nothing! I was intrigued by some of the names of different stocks. It was guesswork, you might call it. Or intuition."

"You gambled thousands of pounds on intuition?" he asked, in accents of amazed admiration.

"Well, no, actually, I used the skills I learned as a child in Italy playing a game—a café game, really, played with cups and pebbles. The idea is to move as many pebbles from one cup to the next in as few moves as possible, and the entire exercise struck me very much like buying and selling on 'Change. I can't explain it exactly, but I can tell you that I was extraordinarily good at the game!"

"Were you?"

"Well, yes, you see, I had so much practice. I practically grew up in the cafés."

Then, with an idle interest, for he was happy, in his turn, to be seduced by the sound of her voice, at least, until they arrived at the pond, he invited, "Tell me about Italy." They moved on. He wanted to reach the pond without delay.

She drew a deep breath and followed his lead down the overgrown path. "Oh, it's a remarkable country, with eccentric plumbing and plaintive music and a language that owes as much to hands as to tongues. A land of fountains and cypress trees . . . How prodigal Italy is with her fountains and cypress trees! And there are dark-eyed children with shy smiles—"

"Children?" he interrupted, with interest.

She cocked her head as she looked up at him. "But is this not all beside the point?"

"It seems, to me, rather to the point." He stopped again, unable to resist another kiss.

This time she drew away first. "But you tell me nothing of yourself. Somehow I have the feeling that you know Italy well enough."

"Well enough," he agreed.

"The Grand Tour?" she asked.

"No, a great friend of mine, my superior at the Foreign Office, took me by the hand and showed me the way of foreign governments."

"You men are so lucky with your fathers and mentors. While I," she said, "did not even benefit from a mother!"

"Poor Marianna," he remarked, without sympathy. "But we were speaking, originally, of your investments, and you would have me believe that you made your gains solely through your skill at an Italian café game?"

She admitted reluctantly, "Of course, there was also Mr. Vaughan . . . who, no doubt, bears you a certain grudge—"

"No doubt!"

"—and he helped me a little at the beginning and then some later."

"It does not seem that he was going to help save you from ruination in Royal African," he remarked. She tried to push away from him, but she was no match for his strength.

"I have no idea whether I would have sold before disaster struck," she said, still resisting his embrace, for she was not yet willing to give up the unequal struggle. "And neither do you!"

"But since I happen to know that Vaughan took a beating on it himself, I have reason to think he would not have bailed you out. I can give you the exact figure of his losses, in case you are interested."

"I am not! I will not smile for you, and I will not thank you!"

Maddox merely laughed.

They had reached the end of the path. They had to bend their heads at times, so thick was the summer growth over the exit. Then before them lay an idyllic little clearing.

"Where are we going?" she asked.

"To the pond over there. You see?"

"And, then . . . ?"

He smiled and led her on. "My second question."

"Which brings us to the real question of the evening?" she pressed.

"From my point of view, in all events," he replied.

They approached the willow-draped pond. The moon made a silver ladder across the water, which was strewn with lilies, and its hem gently lapped the thick blades of grass that had ventured to its edge where they met leggy reeds and rushes.

"I wonder," he said, drawing her arms up around his neck and running his hands down her back to her waist, to the curve of her hips, where they rested, "why it was that you made such a point of returning your bank balance to zero?"

She smiled at that. "You were so angry," she mused.

"So were you," he said, touching his lips to her neck, her cheek, her ear, "but I am not angry now. And reconciliation is so sweet. Why?"

Just before his lips came to brush hers, she said, with ardor, "No, I won't tell you the reason, for that would be pandering shamelessly to your vanity."

He considered her response and then said, on a low laugh, "Uncle Edward had his moments."

Marianna did not think that she had heard aright, but she was untroubled by the comment. Forgotten was the unresolved conflict between husband and wife. Now was the time for untying the more basic knot that lay between a man and a woman. So when he kissed her, she responded with every part of her being. Then, he drew her over to the shelter of an old willow and quickly eased off his jacket, letting it fall to the ground. When he put her hands to the buttons of his shirt and began to unlace the bodice of her gown, she fully realized what he intended. Her heart began to beat so hard that she had difficulty breathing.

She leaned into the trunk of the tree for support, the small of her back pressed against the bark. She said, dazed, "But, Maddox, do you mean to continue this? Here?"

"I do," he said, trailing kisses down her throat to the swell of her breasts, blazing a fiery path. "You agreed to the gardens."

"I didn't think . . . ! I mean . . . now?"

Her bodice now open, he brushed his lips against the rosy tip of her breast, causing a shudder down to her toes. "Now."

Marianna argued no further. Everyone was at dinner. No one was concerned with their whereabouts. No one would heed her cry of protest, certainly not Maddox and, in all honesty, she had none to make. Her defenses were down, it was true, and while his hands bruised her shoulders and his lips drew the breath from hers, she could not have chosen, if offered the chance, to have put him off any longer. His wide shoulders had shut out the rest of the world, and with her bared breasts pressed against his chest, she had forgotten the world beyond that which was held in his rough, ungentle hands as they explored her skin.

Then his lips came again to hers. His kisses were slow and savory, and although he was a man who had waited far longer than he thought necessary, he was in no mood, this evening, to rush.

A thought occurred to him. He broke off. He took her face in his hands and looked down at her. She opened her eyes and saw first, beyond his shoulder, the sequined sky,

and then, back to his eyes, the desire in them, staining the
gray-green depths black.

"The terms of our marriage," he said, "were that I
would make no demands on you, unless you desired me."

She smiled her response and began to draw his head to
hers.

"No," he said. "Pander to my vanity. Say it."

This time, she obeyed. "I desire you."

He nodded with satisfaction and kissed her again,
deeply, passionately, savoring the smell of her, the taste of
her. She responded, the flat of her stomach against his
loins, aware of his arousal, afraid of him, aroused in her
turn by him, knowing that he desired her, and that no feeling had ever been this powerful. She felt an answering
desire for him, and she let it have its way with her. Delight
and desire foamed through her suddenly heated veins,
seeking an exit, but she had no experience with the flood-
tide of passion, nor its release.

His strong hands roamed over her, down her neck to the
creamy swell of her breasts, to her waist and down her
thighs over the silk of her heavy skirts, then back up to her
face. She sighed and trembled both at once, hardly knowing whether to fear or urge on what was to come. He
plunged his hands into her hair, sending a shower of pins
down to the ground and her hair tumbling across her white
shoulders, and murmured something indistinguishable into
her ear to the effect that her hair intoxicated him.

"Hm?" This from Marianna.

"And to think I was never partial to blondes," he said.

Marianna staged a feeble protest.

One strong hand kept her pinned against the tree, while
his other hand caught up her skirts and petticoats. "Which
makes me wonder..." he said, leaving the sentence delicately unfinished as his hand slid over her bare thighs toward the center of earthly pleasure.

She was surprised by the boldness of the exploration
and was suddenly, unexpectedly, taut with longing.

His fingers having gained their end, he smiled slowly and looked down at his wife, whose desire was as evident as his own. Marianna's curls fell forward over one shoulder in a golden cataract that flowed almost to her waist. The oval of her face, the slenderness of her bare forearms and her well-rounded breasts glowed palely in the moonlight. Her white field was his for the taking. His. By rights. He had not thought beyond his desire of taking her, making her his, forcing her to his will. Until that moment, he had not thought of her as his wife, inviolate and inexperienced. Until then, he could have imagined a leisurely, perhaps even provocatively half-dressed passage at arms, amusing, satisfactory, effective. The woman had defied him. She had provoked him, and now he had her just where he wanted her.

Or almost. He found that his own moment had come far sooner than he had anticipated, that his desire fanned far more urgently than he had previously experienced. Her skirts were decidedly in his way. Nothing less than a thorough seduction of white skin and bare flesh would do, and he was determined to have no wisp of clothing shielding her from him.

"It occurs to me, belatedly . . . ," he began.

She murmured something, too intoxicated with his prolonged touch to speak.

"It's your skirts," he breathed in her ear. "I want them off."

He withdrew his hand from her skirts and directed her hands to the buttons of his breeches before he reached for the ribbons at the back of her petticoats. Their lips were hot, their tongues were wild, their bodies searing, still pressed together throughout the gestures of undressing, swept away with a passion that had taken them both by surprise. He was drawing her down to the ground. The full satisfaction of desire was soon to be.

It was not to be.

Crashing through the underbrush at that moment was

one of Maddox's newest pages. Jeremy Wilton had been honored to be selected from a vast pool of government office aspirants, to accompany his lordship and his lordship's secretary to Marlborough Park. It had been impressed upon him that the assignment was an important one, and his fellow juniors, from whom he had been chosen, had clapped him on the back and congratulated him on his good fortune. He was anxious not to misstep in any way or to fail in the execution of his duty.

It was a part of his duty to inform his lordship of the movements of the Frenchmen they had been following from Stanthorpe. In fact, relaying this information comprised the whole of his present errand. Lord Westleigh had had reason to think that the Frenchmen were headed toward Marlborough Park. Thus, Jeremy Wilton, after consulting with his lordship's secretary, dutifully set out to find his lordship to tell him the news that he had been right. Jeremy discovered, rather easily, that he was last seen heading out to the gardens.

Jeremy had a very good idea what a man might be doing in the gardens, especially a man of his lordship's reputation. "Work hard, play hard" summed up his lordship. But to a young man of Jeremy's idealistic trend of mind, a walk in the gardens under a starry sky called forth visions of coy glances, a shy handclasp, a tender kiss or perhaps, just perhaps, if a man was lucky, a further liberty. So while Jeremy did not necessarily think that profuse thanks would be proffered by his lordship upon receiving the important news that the Frenchmen had arrived, neither did he entirely expect to be consigned in no uncertain terms to the deepest pit in the inferno. For this was indeed the gist of Maddox's remark when Jeremy happened onto the clearing by the pond and, upon seeing some shadowy figures under the willow tree, called out, "Oh, I say, Lord Westleigh! I have some news!"

It took a few moments longer to sort out the confusion in Jeremy's, and indeed, everyone's, mind. As Jeremy started forward to approach the willow tree, Maddox's next, biting words made him retreat quickly to the far side of the clearing.

"Oh, no," Marianna moaned when Maddox turned back to her. He was not done fondling her. He slid his hand down her back to press her hips to his. She quivered in response. A few layers of fabric was all that was keeping them apart.

"He shall be horsewhipped," he replied roughly into her ear.

"But who is it?" she whispered back.

"It is Jeremy Wilton, my lord!" came the voice from across the clearing, inadvertently answering Marianna's question. "And it's urgent!"

"Good God! *Urgent*?" Maddox called back, the rich melodies of his voice striking harsh notes.

Jeremy was beginning to realize, hazily, that he had interrupted something rather more involved than the exchange of a few chaste kisses and a caress or two. He cogitated rapidly and came up with the answer that he had, indeed, done his duty by seeking Lord Westleigh out.

Jeremy spoke loudly across the expanse of the clearing. "Yes, you see, my lord, it's the men you think are involved with—"

"I know who you mean!" Maddox shot back angrily. "You need not bruit the names about, especially if the men are on the premises!"

Maddox bowed his head into Marianna's hair. He ran a finger down her breast. She shook her head as if to say "no more," but her hands were shaking when she began to gather together her bodice and to lace it. With her head, she gestured to his shirt.

"What should I do, my lord?" Jeremy called out.

Maddox began to fasten his buttons. He had a few choice suggestions, which he did not utter. "I'll be with you in a moment, lad." It was not a pleasant response, for Maddox was in truly bad case. Marianna reached up to

smooth his hair into some orderly disorder. She did not
think that she could so easily put herself to rights.

"Well, you know," Jeremy continued, feeling awkward
(as well he should), and in his confusion, babbling a little
as if to explain himself, "I really do think it's the men who
are involved with *L'Abey*...*La abi*... well, *The Bee*, at
any rate and—"

Maddox had bent in a fluid movement to retrieve his
coat from the ground and had flung it across his shoulder.
"Don't make matters any worse, Wilton!" he said with fire
as he swiftly crossed the clearing. "I've told you not to
bandy those names about. I'm going to have a hard enough
time getting close to any one of the newcomers. They are,
no doubt, wary enough of me as it is!"

"But, I th-thought, my lord," Jeremy stammered, looking up at Maddox, whose bright eyes were blazing in the
moonlight, "that you said you wanted to be apprised of
every detail of their movements, that it was our most important mission here to—"

"It is not necessary for you to repeat to me my own
instructions!" Maddox flashed back.

Jeremy was truly quaking in his boots now. "But I con-
sulted with Harris and he and I decided, well...we
decided...that is, I thought," he said in a rush, "that
Chaumonot was a prime consideration for you!"

"And is Chaumonot here?" Maddox asked.

"Oh, not him, but his henchmen!" Wilton explained
nervously.

Marianna had put herself together enough to cross the
clearing. She was curious to hear what the conversation
was about. "Who?" she asked, catching the name as one
she had never heard before. She slipped her arm through
Maddox's elbow.

Maddox was still struggling to master his temper and
had no desire to engage in this discussion, or any discussion.

"And shall you introduce me to this charming young

man?" she inquired of her husband, when he did not respond.

"Lady Westleigh, this is Jeremy Wilton," Maddox informed her.

"*Lady Westleigh?*" Jeremy exclaimed involuntarily, entirely shocked, somehow never guessing that his lordship would be in the gardens, in an amorous passage, with his very own wife. Then, recalling himself, he sketched a deep bow.

This was too much for Marianna, who began to laugh helplessly.

"And this, my dear," said Maddox, completing the introduction, "is Jeremy Wilton. My former page."

XV

Of Birds and Bees

By the time Maddox had left her side and was crossing the clearing with Jeremy Wilton, Marianna had cooled to a simmer. She was momentarily warmed by the glance of desire and promise Maddox relayed to her over his shoulder just before he plunged into the underbrush of the path leading back to the house.

Once he had been swallowed by the grove, however, Marianna experienced waves of doubt. As she went back to the willow tree to attempt to find her hairpins, her face flamed with her thoughts. She had—vain woman!—thought her husband had followed her to Marlborough Park with the sole intention of seducing her. She had been, evidently, willing to fall in with his wishes. More than willing! She had been eager, aching, desirous, hungry for his touch, inflamed by it, heated by a passion she had not known could exist. And he had known it, too—to his equally evident satisfaction.

Her thoughts moved sluggishly. Now it seemed that he had not come to Marlborough Park for her. He had come for—who was it—Chaumonot? Who had something to do

with what must be a code name: *the bee*? It meant nothing
to her, and she could not guess at its significance.

Neither did she care. She was bent on quelling the sensations that welled up from her stomach to her breast and
that threatened to overcome her. It had been quite a shock,
this meeting of hands and lips and bodies in the gardens.
Yes, hands, she thought, not without a blush. She wondered if she would ever be able to look on his strong hands
again without feeling the stirrings of desire. And not just
any hands. The hands of her husband. A strong quiver
passed over her.

She found what she could of her hairpins and flopped her
hair into a wild coiffure. She managed, somehow, to pull her
dress into some order, but she was still shaking with unquenched desire which, in Maddox's absence, translated into
a ravenous appetite for food. However, she could hardly
present herself in the dining saloon in her present state, and
so she determined, as she made her way back across the
clearing and back through the enchanted grove of kisses and
caresses, to repair herself in her chambers, which she would
attempt to reach by means of a back staircase.

She judged accurately enough which outside door to
enter in order to reach the wing that housed her chambers,
and she was running through her mind how she would arrange her hair if Rachel did not happen to be immediately
available when, by chance, in the alcove of the stairwell,
she met Susannah Marsh.

Susannah had been looking down the hall, away from
Marianna, as if she had been following the form of a retreating figure who had just disappeared from sight.

Marianna exclaimed her surprise and pleasure to see her
friend, at last, at Marlborough Park.

Susannah turned toward Marianna, her beautiful face
perfectly composed, and they embraced warmly. When
they had finished, Susannah looked her charmingly disheveled friend up and down and said, her voice full of humorous suggestiveness, "Well, well, my dear!"

Marianna laughed and blushed and said that it was not what Susannah thought.

"It is exactly what I think! I know the signs when a woman has been thoroughly and most expertly kissed!" Susannah contradicted amicably. "Let me say that I am happy for you! Besides which, I am also very discreet!"

"But Maddox is here."

"Then I shall be doubly discreet!"

"No, Susannah! I was just with Maddox!"

Susannah smiled. "Ah! In the gardens with Anthony Maddox. Almost I envy you." Before Marianna had a chance to reply to that, Susannah remarked, conversationally, "But I did not think that Maddox had accepted the duchess's invitation. In fact, I am quite sure that you said he had declined. No?"

Marianna answered that he had declined weeks ago. She said she had thought he had gone to Stanthorpe, but that this evening, quite unexpectedly, he had turned up.

"To see you, one might suppose?" Susannah said.

"Heavens, Susannah—I don't know!" she said. "I . . . it . . . but I'm not sure!" Susannah did not press, and Marianna continued, a thought occurring to her, "But, Susannah, you might know! Does the name *The Bee* mean anything to you?"

Susannah laughed at her friend. "You are moonstruck, my dear. Let me be the first to tell you that you are speaking nonsense!" Then, she paused, as a shadow crossed her face. "The Bee?" she repeated slowly. Then, firmly, "I know nothing about it! Why do you want to know?"

"No reason," Marianna said, and shook her head clear of its longings and unfulfilled desires. "I must be moonstruck. Forgive me. Tell me instead: have you just arrived? The duchess said that she received a curious note from you explaining your delay. We were wondering if it were truly possible that you were ill?"

"Not at all," Susannah said pleasantly. "I had several

things to do in Town before I came. Nothing important, but they could not be put off!"

"Well?" Marianna said, expecting more. "Did you accomplish them?"

"In fact, no," Susannah said, without further elaboration, the catch in her voice attractive and mysterious.

"And you don't mean to tell me!" Marianna said, putting her arm affectionately around Susannah's waist. "Well, I can be as discreet as you, and I won't even hazard a guess as to your activities. And since the duke is here, anxiously awaiting your arrival, I gather that you weren't with him."

"No, I wasn't," Susannah said, as if she had entirely forgotten his existence. She added quickly, "I look forward to seeing him."

"Yes, I imagine that he is at supper now, and that is where I am headed myself, after I repin my hair. Have you greeted the duchess? No, not yet? That's odd! Well, I am sure she shall be delighted to see you, now that so many French guests have arrived and will be needing your entertainment."

"Why, yes," Susannah said, her voice polished and neutral. "How lovely! I look forward to meeting them."

Nothing more on the topic was said. Marianna reiterated her need to go to her chambers to make herself presentable. Susannah said that she intended to find the duchess without delay in order to discover where she was to be lodged. Marianna hugged her in parting and lifted her heavy skirts to trip lightly up the stairs, without once wondering why Susannah should have been in that alcove if she had not yet greeted her hostess and did not know where her rooms were to be.

Within a short space of time, Marianna had put herself back to order and restyled her hair by herself, since Rachel had been given her *congé* for the evening and was not spending the time in her mistress's chambers. Marianna rejoined the company, ate heartily, bantered with Everly, whose wit this evening was honed to a sword's point, met some of the French guests, and kept an ear out for the name *Chaumonot*. She did not hear it, nor did she see anything of her husband for the rest of the evening.

It had been a long day of physical exertions. Many of the guests began to retire in the earlier hours. Another group of the guests, Eliza Parrish among them, had found a second wind and wished to lavish their energies on cards. That prospect did not capture Marianna's imagination, and so it was with a feeling of profound regret, bordering on a panicking despair at not having seen Maddox again that evening, that she excused herself for the night and sought her chambers.

Rachel, trusty servant, was this time at her post, ready to attend to her mistress's wishes. She helped her ladyship out of the full skirts that had been so bothersome earlier in the evening, wrapped her in a negligee of peach lace, and loosely bound her luxurious hair in one thick braid before pulling aside the coverlet and handing her mistress into the cool, empty bed.

Pleasantly exhausted, Marianna let her long-lashed lids flutter shut, and immediately to her mind's eye sprang the image of Maddox pressed against her, kissing, searching, demanding, giving. She sighed deeply and remembered the snatch of conversation she thought she had overheard as Maddox had entered the receiving saloon earlier in the evening. He had said that the duchess should not open a wing for him, that he would be chambered with his wife.

The question remained: did he mean to come to bed?

Before wandering in the gardens, Marianna had wanted to put him off, just a little bit longer. But no more. On the fine-edged sword of unfulfilled desire Marianna drifted into the margins of a land of warm lips and ungentle hands and rough skin and fine muscles.

Hours later, nestled in satin and swansdown, she was vaguely roused from her suspended state of languorous semislumber by a shifting weight on the bed. The next moment her mouth was covered by a strong hand to prevent a startled scream, and her eyes flew open.

It was Anthony Maddox, bending over her, replacing the hand covering her mouth with his lips. He kissed her, not as he had in the gardens, with provocation and promise, but with full possession. The kiss lasted and lingered, a forceful statement of his claim as her lord and master. She belonged to him; her body existed for him, to do with as he pleased. And what he pleased, this night, was mutual delight.

Marianna had raised herself onto her elbows to more fully savor his kiss. After a long moment, he eased away from it. He smiled down at her, desire on his lips and in his eyes, and ran his hand down the white column of her throat. He had shed his jacket and boots, but he still wore his shirt, which was open and stuffed loosely into his breeches.

With one hand, he placed hers against his chest; with the other he trailed his fingers down to the curve of lace covering her breasts and caressed them before continuing his journey downward across the slightly rounded plain of her stomach to her thighs and down her ankles, before traveling upward again. His eyes never left hers as he slid his fingers up under the negligee and over her bare thighs to the place where he had so importunately left off in the gardens. She trembled as he touched the very seat of Venus, stroking and caressing, so that she was instantly on fire. She caught his face between her hands and pulled him to her.

"Much, *much* better without the skirts," he breathed into her ear, and with a fluid movement he removed the weightless nightdress of lace and ribbons.

A movement of his head indicated that she was to help him off with his clothes. The shirt was easily cast off to expose the broad expanse of his chest, while the breeches were caught, momentarily, on the most natural of impediments, provoking a deep chuckle from Maddox and a gasp of astonishment and trepidation from Marianna.

"It can't be true!" she exclaimed low, shifting instinctively away from him, but not succeeding in getting far.

"It is very true," he replied, gathering her into his arms, pressed for the first time against the whole of her unde-

fended loveliness. Awash with desire, he buried his face in
the crook of her neck and shoulder, breathing in the intoxi-
cating scent of her skin and hair.

She tugged at the ribbon holding the thick poll of his hair
in place and pulled it away from his neck. The dark masses
were released across his shoulders and fell to tickle her
cheek. When she brushed the lock away, he grasped her hand
in his and pulled it above her head, so that she was fully
stretched out beneath him. He ran his hand, once more, down
her length to her breasts, proud-nippled, across her belly,
which quivered deliciously, to her thigh, where his hand
pressed between her legs, spread them to find the tenderest of
treasures in its silken nest. And when he touched the pearl of
bliss itself, hot fires of desire shot through her. Marianna
shifted now, waiting and ready to receive what she had
previously thought of as her conquest, but she was now sure
that this sweet moment of surrender would come as a surprising, even gratifying form of liberation.

Their moans mingled in the meeting of their lips, and
his throbbing weapon was thrust, at first searing and painful, deeply into her sugared pleasure-trove. They drew together, crushed to one another, moving to a rhythm that
would bring them rapidly to the precipice, and then over its
edge into the infinite moment. But he was not satisfied
with the usual coup de grace. He wanted complete mastery,
and so grasped her buttocks at that moment and pressed her
white limbs fiercely around his. She responded, transported beyond all expectations by the thrill of his gesture.

Moments later they shuddered together, as if releasing a
flock of doves.

They dozed, arms and legs entwined, for long hours as
the dawn crept over the horizon, Maddox's powerful body
heavy in repose against hers, a strong arm flung across her,
his slumbering head against her breast. One of her hands
held his hip in an unconscious caress, and the other, fingers
spread, crossed his nape, keeping the heavy fall of hair
away from his neck. They were breathing deeply, both

drugged from the intensity of their lovemaking, reluctant to awaken from the depths of sensual satisfaction into which they had so willingly plunged.

Upon retiring those few hours before, he had not pulled the bed curtains. Soon the pink flush of the very early summer morning came to lie golden across their happiness. A large assembly of birds had gathered on the eaves and ledges of the upper storeys of the west wing, and were engaged in strident discussion. The cacophony penetrated the bedchamber.

Still submerged and replete, Marianna stirred slightly. At length the ceaseless chatter caused her eyes to flutter open, and she became fully aware of the weight against her. A swirl of pleasure coursed through her, and she drank in the feel of his flesh and bones molded against her curves and contours, breathing him in through every pore.

She lazily surveyed the scene spread around her: the gathered silk canopy drawn to a tight center and knotted with tassels, the bed curtains sashed to a liquid billowing, the tumble of dark hair against her fair skin, powerful shoulders defined by corded muscles, a broad back that tapered down to hips that disappeared into the satin drape, the lazy, silken waves of hectic sheets and bed covers that did not cover.

It was a lovely vista, marred only by the horrible noise. Marianna tossed her head back and forth on the pillow, trying to find a comfortable arrangement for her ears. She let her lids close over her eyes and snuggled into Maddox, hardly able to get close enough to him.

Maddox surfaced, slowly. He became aware first of a delightful embrace, and when he opened his eyes, in full possession of his senses, his return to animation instantly communicated itself to Marianna who, in turn, opened her eyes to meet his. The sun had not yet risen. The shadows still crouched in the room, blurring objects, but there was no mistaking what lurked in the depths of his frank, gray-green eyes. She blushed but could not look away.

"Marianna." He pronounced her name slowly. "But no longer Lowth." He ran his hand over wide expanses of her skin. It came to rest between her legs. "You awoke for more?"

She stirred under his touch. "No," she laughed low, "it was the birds. The noise is perfectly awful."

He became aware of it. "Have you grown so used to Town in so short a time? Surely this is no worse than the commotion on Cavendish Square."

"Much worse," she answered, "and it cannot be but four or five in the morning. The birds are a nuisance."

"This, from a country girl?" he remarked.

"I may have spent all those years in Stanthorpe, but I'm not a country girl," she answered.

"No?" he contradicted, boldly punctuating his statement with pressure from his long fingers. They prodded a moan from her, another stirring, another shift in position of legs and thighs.

"No," she protested. "You can't mean it."

"I do."

"It's too much."

He ceased his fondling and placed his hands on her shoulders, turning her toward him. It was quite a light touch, but an intention was there. "Do you mean to resist me?" he asked.

"To a certain extent," she replied.

He shifted and had suddenly lifted himself up on straightened arms, which he planted on either side of her so that she was pinned directly beneath him. He was then in position to achieve what he wanted with a minimum of further effort. "But not," he said, showing her exactly what he meant, "to this extent."

She shook her head, unable to speak, which was just as well, since he had taken her lips with his.

XVI

Unanswered Questions

*S*usannah was seated on the broad, bricked terrace in the late morning sunshine. The lush grass rolled away in front of her. The imposing pile of stones guarded her back, a stalwart presence, a monument to all that was enduring and respectable in the world. At several stations along the terrace, handsome bewigged footmen stood erect in their buckled shoes, ready to perform small acts of service. Her duke was seated with her on a scrolling wrought-iron seat, holding one of her hands in both of his.

Here should have been a moment of gilt-edged peace and serenity. Here should have been a rapt moment of perfection, when one rested replete, secure with the knowledge that all past desires had been satisfied and that all future desires would be met amply.

Susannah felt no such fullness or comfort or balance. For her, this charming tableau was merely useful. It was the sign to all her world that she had come to Marlborough Park to cement her relationship with the duke. Just by sitting there with him, hands and fingers entwined, she was announcing that she had withstood his epic siege, beautifully, but that she was now giving in, gracefully. She would give herself to him completely, this evening if not before, and no one would know that her present passion for the handsome English nobleman was fired by private purpose.

The duke was toying with each of her slim, white fingers in turn. She allowed this affectionate display. She encouraged it, even, communicating to him through her fingertips that his waiting was over, that she was his.

"I can hardly explain it myself, Gervase," she was saying to him, her husky voice intimate and attractively sincere. "I have hardly been ill a day in my life, but to have been so . . . gripped in the days following that perfectly lovely evening at Ranelagh . . . ! I was surprised, to say the least . . . and disappointed."

"It was food poisoning, my dear Susannah," the duke replied seriously, permitting this endearment, exulting in it. "From the description of your physical state that your abigail gave to me, I vow that it was food poisoning! A slice of bad ham, no doubt. And you must know that I went straight to the authorities at Ranelagh and told them what I thought about their kitchens!"

"You were very kind," she said, returning what had become a rather fevered handclasp. "And so was the note you sent me. Why, I was almost going to regret Gabrielle's party altogether, were it not for the lovely, thoughtful note you sent urging me to come."

"Imploring, more like," the duke answered, a little rueful still, "and I had almost given up hope of seeing you here when you declined my offer of sending you a Kensington carriage to bring you from Town to the Park."

Susannah did not say that it was her intense curiosity at his mention, in that same note, of the many amusing French guests who were coming that had persuaded her in the end. Instead, she arched her brows, and her laugh was low and alluring and full of promise. "Gervase," she said with a smile he had waited months to see, "you should know by now that I cannot give up all my autonomy at the drop of a hat. I would not have you think me so easily persuaded."

"Easily persuaded . . .!" He echoed her and then, checking himself effortfully from gathering her in his arms and crushing her in an embrace in full view of the company on the terrace, he said, "But it is my heartfelt desire that you give up at least some of your autonomy."

Her response to this was a smile full of passion. Just then, Everly strolled over to them and perched himself elegantly on the low wall surrounding the terrace.

Everly's opening words suggested that he had intercepted that smoldering regard and made the correct interpretation. He glanced around and about him, looking over the edge of the terrace, and remarked, "Somehow, in this perfect setting, I am reminded of the Spanish proverb: 'If your wife tells you to throw yourself from a balcony, pray God it's a low one.'"

"Oh, are you contemplating marriage?" Susannah answered him.

"Not at all! Rather, I had another couple in mind for that charming institution! And, while we are on the subject, I must say," he said, his tone as dry as fine champagne, "how disappointing you two have proved!"

"My dear Peter," Susannah said, without batting an eye, "you are impertinent."

"I trade on my impertinence," he said, and then, from his half-seated position, he bowed from the waist at his longtime acquaintance, the duke. "Ah, Gervase, and here I was thinking until a moment ago that you two were the last amusing people at this party."

The duke took this remark in the spirit of good-natured congratulations which, in effect, it was, and so merely laughed. Susannah ran her eye over Everly's lounging posture and remarked, "What, Everly, are you bored?"

"No, my dear! How could you think so?"

"No reason." Susannah's gaze became a little more penetrating. "Are you a little irritable, perhaps?"

"Does it show?" Everly asked smoothly.

"Well, the spate of acerbic comments you made last

evening was not exactly in your style, was it? You were
undoubtedly at your most amusing—but, dear Peter, so
many sharp points!"

Everly smiled down at her. "Do you notice so much, Lady
Marsh? I, myself, would say that you were not present long
enough last evening to have determined my mood."

Susannah had been present long enough to have ascer-
tained that Jean did not number among the French guests. It
had been a wild improbability that he would attend such an
affair. She shrugged, and looked up at Everly. "Perhaps I am
able to determine your moods since you and I are two of a
kind, dear Peter," she said, a little more seriously than she
had intended, and then, as if to cover up, she cast a dazzling
smile over the duke and squeezed his hand. "But if I did not
remain with the rest of you the evening long, it was because
Gervase had gone off—alone, so he says—into the village
for the night . . . and I became bored without his company!"

The duke's reply was prompt. "That was only because I
did not know you were arriving, my dear!"

Everly watched this byplay with a slightly skeptical lift to
one thin brow. He pushed himself off the low ledge, caressed
Susannah's shoulder casually in what was a friendly, reassur-
ing gesture, and departed on the flippant words, "I must seek
out Eliza Parrish at once! Her astringent company is, I fear,
the only one that will suit my mood today. Besides which, I
think she is thick as thieves with that new group of Frenchmen, and surely they should be able to provide me with some
suitably unhealthy diversions!"

Susannah followed Everly's movement across the terrace, long enough for her to spot where the tightest knot of
Frenchmen might be. She turned back to the duke to continue their flirtation, but her mind went with Everly. Even
though Jean was not among them, she had the visceral
intuition that one or another of the guests would provide
her with clues to his whereabouts in London. Perhaps even
one or two of them might have been with Jean that night in
the gardens of Ranelagh. She hoped to draw each of them

into conversation with her, in French. Perhaps she would be able to place a voice.

After her disastrous encounter with Jean, she had spent the next few days in her bed, curtains drawn, curled in a wounded ball, hardly able to eat. But then, recovering from the initial shock that he was still alive, she pulled herself together with great effort of will and spent the next week trying to track him down in London. She had come up empty-handed. She had never made it a point to frequent the parts of Town or the society where Jean Desmoulins would most likely be found, and so her random forays through the seamier sections of the city brought her no closer to her love.

She had not, for all of that, lost her head. She made some rather good guesses why he might be in this country, and she did not suppose that his activities here were in England's best interest. She had grown to love her adopted country, but her first, girlhood love was more powerful. She would do what lay within her power to protect Jean. As long as he lived and breathed she had hope, she had a reason for living.

Strengthened by her purpose, Susannah had successfully outfaced Eliza Parrish upon her arrival at the Park the evening before. Susannah derived immense satisfaction from the fact that Eliza had been unable to put her out of countenance. Admittedly Eliza had had the advantage over her at Ranelagh, but now at Marlborough Park, her wits intact, her nerves cool, she successfully parried all of Eliza's malicious little questions about her health, her delay in attending the party, her desire to associate with the French, her relationship with the duke.

Susannah had never liked Eliza, it was true, but she had never bothered to articulate to herself the reason. Over the next few days, however, as Eliza made her well-placed, public gestures of friendship, Susannah's dislike of Mrs. Parrish crystallized into the particular formulation that *Eliza runs with the hare but hunts with the hounds!* Susan-

nah was resolved that she would not be an easy hare for
Eliza to catch.

In the meantime, Marianna had been in serious danger
of finding herself wholly and madly in love with Maddox.
However, she was checked from the fatal fall by Charlotte,
who quite inadvertently gave Marianna several pieces to
the larger puzzle of why Maddox should have chosen to
come to Marlborough Park at just this time.

The very afternoon following Maddox's arrival at the
Park, Marianna and Charlotte were strolling to the river
where Charlotte had spent many agreeable hours fishing
with her young friends. It was entirely amazing to Marianna that Charlotte had not fallen in love with anyone in
the week past. Amazing but welcome, and so for once,
they could discuss other matters. During the walk, they
met other strollers. When they happened to pass Eliza Parrish with two French gallants at her elbows, Charlotte
pressed Marianna's hand and hardly waited until they were
out of earshot before she whispered,

"*That man*, Marianna! The funny, thin one with the
mustache and little beard! I was first introduced to him
yesterday evening as we were all going in to dinner. He
had just come in that group of new guests, you know. He
was introduced to me as a count, but you know, I don't
think I have ever seen anyone less *countly*! The Count of
Mersenne, I think, is his name! Anyway, when my name
was given he said, 'Ah! the demoiselle Armitage. I knew
your father!' Well, I was never so surprised! So I asked
him how he knew my father, because of course, I told him
right away that my father had spent so much time in
France! Then he became quite agitated, as if he had just
remembered something, and disavowed all previous acquaintance with my father! He said that he must have been
confused, for he had met so many Armitages since being in
England and that the name had seemed familiar but that he
had obviously misplaced it! Well, you know, Marianna,
there are not so very many Armitages in England—or at

least many he would run across in just the last few weeks of being here. It was very queer!"

"The one called Mersenne knew your father?" Marianna asked, glancing discreetly over her shoulder at the man's back. "You told me once that your father spent a lot of time in France, but I never understood why. What was he doing there?"

"Well, that is what Mersenne asked!" Charlotte answered. "I told him I didn't know but that he should ask Lord Westleigh, for I was sure that Lord Westleigh knew, because he and my father were close friends and because he is my guardian now that my father is dead!"

"Really? And what was the count's response, I wonder?"

"Then he became *very* queer and started talking a lot of nonsense. The one moment, he said that it would be impossible to ask his lordship since his lordship was not planning to come to Marlborough Park—as if he knew perfectly well where Lord Westleigh was planning to be! I pointed out that Lord Westleigh had arrived only minutes before he had. You know, it was true—Lord Westleigh came right before dinner, you remember? And so, then, Mersenne seemed very surprised and looked around and asked me to indicate his lordship among the crowd of diners. Well, I did look around but I didn't see him. By the way, I didn't see you, either. Did you have dinner with him last night?"

"No, my dear," Marianna choked out. "But do go on with your story."

"Well, it seemed to me that as he was asking me to identify Lord Westleigh, I gathered that Mersenne did *not* know him!" Charlotte concluded, performing a feat of logic. "So, naturally, I asked him whether he did or did not know my guardian, and he assured me that he did not but that he was looking forward to meeting him, for he had not known that he was so closely connected to Armitage!" Charlotte paused, looking disgusted. "Now, I ask you! *How* could he have known that my father and Lord Westleigh were friends when

he did not know either of them in the first place! That's a very
queer man—and no count, if *I* am any judge of the matter!
What do you think, Marianna?"

"Why, Charlotte, I think I will take your advice and ask
his lordship about what your father did in France," Marianna replied.

Marianna chose her moment, and it was very much later
that night. She was discovering, to her delight, that her
husband was an ardent lover, and he enjoyed her as well as
her enjoyment of him. He began that night gentle and undemanding, making her pleasure as sweet as the stroking of a
kitten's silky head or the deep intake of the fragrance of a
rose. Then pleasure changed to need, a need suddenly demanding and urgent and savage, and she came alive in his
arms, drowning in power and the feel of the hardness of
muscled shoulders, the ripple of skin across his shoulder
blades, the feel of a massive chest and the pressure of powerful thighs. When he abandoned gentleness for mastery, titil-
lation for possession, she found herself completely in his
thrall.

When she surfaced from this exceedingly pleasant
drowning, she forced herself to remember that he had not
come to Marlborough Park primarily to claim her. A flattering, seductive idea, that, but she was just as happy to
have kept her eyes wide open. Her clear-sightedness armed
her with a daring she would not otherwise have had.

He lay drowsing with his head against her breast. She
was running several fingers up and down his arm, which
lay across her stomach and thigh. While he languished so
happily in her arms, she remembered her conversation with
Charlotte.

"I'm wondering, Maddox," she said dreamily into the
velvet night air, "why it was that you chose to come to
Marlborough Park."

He murmured thickly, "You can't guess?"

"I know what you would like me to think," she replied
humorously, for she had found that nothing advanced their

intimacy so much as teasing. "But I don't think that's the reason."

A moment passed before he turned to nuzzle her neck, and when he spoke his voice held the same bantering thread as hers. "Don't you, my dear?"

"Oh, don't get me wrong! I am most impressed!" she tossed back lightly.

He rolled away from her slightly and propped his head on his fist. "Impressed?" he inquired. She felt the effect of the lazy scrutiny from his gray-green eyes and was glad of the darkness that defended her from its full force. "With what? With whom?"

"Why, with you! For having been so . . . so passionate in the execution of your . . . your matrimonial duty, I think we are calling it, as if you had not come here for some other purpose."

"Here's a new twist!" he commented. "Passion in the service of some other purpose." He paused. "I have never thought it could be anything but an end in itself."

Marianna persisted. "I have reason to think that you came here and made a union of this marriage as a pretense for . . ."

Maddox's indulgent chuckle cut her off. "I'm further ahead of you than I thought. Don't you know that a man can rarely make a pretense, as you say, of making passionate love to a woman? He either can or can't. It's as simple as that."

"But he can make love without loving," Marianna argued, diverted by this new trend.

"True," he answered. "But loving? I do not recall that loving and being loved was a condition of the marriage."

Marianna glanced up at him quickly from under her lashes but could see nothing of his expression. "Of course not!" she rallied lightly. "Only desire, I think you said. But we digress, and I would like to know why you have come."

When Maddox did not immediately answer, Marianna pressed, "It has something to do with the French who have just come, does it not? And a man named Mersenne and his relationship to Charlotte's father?"

The moment invited confidences, but Maddox was not a man who confided easily. It was early for Maddox with his wife, and he was not yet ready to open his thoughts to her. The bed was enough for now.

"Can you really wonder, after these past several days, why it is I have come?" he asked, with a discernible smile in his voice.

Since it was clear to Marianna that he was not going to answer her original question, she would try to win some wooing words from him. "Are you telling me, then," she asked slyly, "that you are not as indifferent to me as you once were?"

He was enjoying the teasing game as much as she. "I'm telling you that my arrival at the Park was a natural male response to your increased availability."

"*Availability?*" she echoed, piqued, then flipped back the covers and made to leave the bed.

He caught her easily with one strong arm around her waist. "Oh, no! We're behind the time on this marriage and need to catch up!"

"I begin by asking you why you are here just now, and you respond by flaunting my availability!"

"If you don't like the answers, you should not ask the questions," he remarked, and bent over to kiss her.

"No wonder I do not like your responses," she said, with what little breath was left to her. "They are not quite on the subject, I would say!" She attempted unsuccessfully to slip out of his grip.

"This, wife, *is* the subject," he said.

She could not have said, when he told her with his lips and hands and body exactly what he meant, that she was truly dissatisfied with his views on the subject.

XVII

The Noble Game of Cricket

O ver the next few days, Marianna did not again approach the question about the possible *other* reasons Maddox had come to Marlborough Park; nor did she particularly care to think about them. The following days spent in Maddox's arms were an idyll. Intrusions from the outside world were unwelcome. However, the question of her husband's involvement in the outside world was to intrude upon her once again, this time as she stood on the cricket field on the last day of the highly successful country party at Marlborough Park.

As the duchess had announced early on, the fitting climax to her party was to be a cricket match. Her object was to introduce her French guests to the English passion for sport and sportsmanship. The idea was enthusiastically received.

Now, Lady Hester, who liked nothing in the world so much as a rousing cricket match (and was a rather good cricketer herself, sport being very much on her program for the improvement of women), had agreed to take the organization of it into her capable hands. She would not have the match degraded into an affair of bettings, and hedgings and cheatings, like boxing or horse racing. Nor did she envision a pretty fête in a gentleman's park, where one club of cricketers encountered another such club, and where they showed off in graceful costume to a gay marquee of admiring belles, who condescended so to purchase admiration, and while away a long summer day in partaking cold collations, conversing occasionally, and seeming to understand the game—the whole being conducted according to ballroom etiquette, so as to be exceedingly elegant and exceedingly dull. No, there were too many expert cricketers among the duchess's party and, no doubt, in the village, Lady Hester argued, and thus she pressed for a real, solid match, where each team attacked the other for honor and a supper and half-a-crown a man.

She was to have her way. A scouting troup was expedited to the village to discover among the locals the most promising talent. Now, it was well known that the country lads, those accustomed to the flail or the hammer and who knew how to move their shoulders and had the free use of their arms, grew into outstanding cricketers. A dozen or so men from the village were easily enjoined to take part in the match, which was to be held, as tradition demanded, on the village green. The chief prize from the roundup was, of course, young Jake Smytt, the blacksmith, who had a reputation miles around as a capital hitter.

On the eve of the big match at the park, the Englishmen undertook explaining the broad outlines, the strategies, and the subtleties of the game to the French guests, who managed to look polite throughout and, evidently, understood not a word. Four of the Frenchmen agreed to participate.

The morning dawned unfavorably. The sky promised a series of showers and kept its word, as English skies are wont to do on such occasions, but then cleared to become bright and warm. The wickets could be pitched, along with a couple of marquees for the rest and refreshment of the contending parties, along with benches and tables spread with hogsheads and rounds of beef, and parasols for the

spectators from the Park. The whole of the village partici-
pated and offered, as their part, many kegs of beer and a
truly remarkable array of pastries. The men from the village went down in a body before breakfast for a plunge in
the cold bath in the corner of the close; and by ten o'clock,
although the game had not yet commenced, two or three of
the duchess's guests, along with a handful of the village
men, were amusing themselves with a majestic air by
throwing the ball carelessly from hand to hand. Several
other gentlemen had shed their confining overcoats to play
in their vests and shirtsleeves but were, as a rule, more
finely dressed than their village counterparts and were most
generally distinguishable by the fact that they kept their
wigs and hats.

Only one among the duchess's guests caused a moment
of confusion in the villagers' minds. Jake Smytt, seeing
Maddox take the field, thought at first that he might be the
new blacksmith from a neighboring parrish. Jake made a
rather bawdy comment to his fellow villagers about his
rival and was going to cross the field to engage in some
verbal sparring when one of his friends caught him by the
arm and hastily informed him that the man he wanted to
provoke was none other than Lord Westleigh. Jake ran a
practiced eye over the muscles in his lordship's arms and
shoulders and thought it just as well when, minutes later,
they were chosen for the same team.

It was to be a contest of Gentlemen versus Players,
which designations in no wise indicated the lineage of the
eleven members who composed them. For instance, Maddox and Everly found themselves together on the Players
team, a fact which Everly did not hesitate to comment
about as he flexed his muscles by swinging his bat several
times over his head as a warmup. He was in a perfectly
sporting mood today, and gave it as his opinion that the
Players would carry the day.

They tossed for innings. Gentlemen won the toss and
had first innings. When the first two players walked, bats

in hand, to their respective wickets, scattered applause and
taunts came from the spectators, depending, quite arbitrar-
ily, on which side any one of them had chosen to back for
the day.

Lord Hester was the bowler for Players. He had grown
quite stout of late. As he took the field, his body and legs
looked like a gigantic roll of knit worsted elevated on a
couple of inflated pillowcases. But he still had what it took
to be a fast bowler who opened with the wind, and he was
encouraged in that strategy by some rather full-lunged cries
from Lady Hester on the sidelines.

"Play!" Lord Hester cried suddenly.

"The play's the thing!" Everly quipped from his position
in the outfield.

The ball flew from Lord Hester's hand straight and swift
toward the center stump of the wicket. The batter was not
on the alert and was bowled out without a stroke. The next
Gentleman batter snicked one, making the Players appeal
noisily and en masse (at least the English-born players).

At the fatal snick, with the ensuing strident, razzing
yells of "Howzat!" erupting in the outfield, Everly attempted to explain these calls to one of the French fellow
outfielders, who managed to look only slightly befuddled
at the evolution of the play. Everly gave it up and took
another tack. During the next lull, he attempted to explain
to the young Frenchman the proper position for "looking
out," in different parts of the field.

"You must see, my dear Jean-Phillipe," he said, "that
even if you do not understand a moment of the game, you
may as well look the part!" Everly then fixed himself into
the proper attitude by placing one hand on each knee, and
stooping very much as if he were "making a back" for
some beginner at leapfrog. "All the regular players do this
sort of thing," he explained sagaciously to the Frenchman,
"and, indeed, it's generally supposed that it is quite impossible to look out properly in any other position."

The Frenchman essayed the position. Everly pointed

over to the vigorous young Jake Smytt playing long-stop off to his right as having assumed the position perfectly. The Frenchman, eyeing the blacksmith and imitating the position reasonably well, looked back to Everly with a hopeful "*Et, alors?*"

"Not bad!" Everly encouraged, then commented with a dazzling insight, "But you know, it occurs to me that if your *noblesse* had been capable of playing cricket with your peasants, your chateaux would never have been burnt!"

The spectators, meanwhile, had been eating, drinking, and talking without stop. At every good stroke they expressed satisfaction and approval of the player, while at every bad attempt at a catch and every failure to stop the ball, they launched into denunciations: "Ah! Ah!" "Stupid!" "Now, butterfingers!" "Muff!" "Humbug!" and so forth.

Marianna, quite like her French counterparts, hovered most of the day in a state of bewildered incomprehension of the action—or lack of it—going forward on the field. She laughed at all of Lady Hester's attempts to explain to her exactly what was going on. She was entirely convinced that one had to grow up in England to begin to understand this game, and said that even having spent eight years in a household with two growing young boys had provided her with little enlightenment. The noble game of cricket, she feared, was forever to remain for her an enigma.

Marianna was not, for all of that, completely ignorant. Now, when Players were at bat, the opening batsmen being of course Anthony Maddox and Peter Everly, she did not need to be told that Maddox's off-hitting was powerful, nor did she need it explained to her why he was never in his ground, except when his wicket was down. Beyond that, however, she could not keep up with the runs on the field, which began to be posted from the moment the first ball went swiftly to the center stump of the wicket, fell on the tip of Maddox's bat, and bounded far away over the heads of the scouts, who had just stooped low enough to let it fly over them. It was apparent from the beginning that Maddox was going to have a good day of it.

Everly, for his part, played with an intensity no one had ever seen from him before. Now, Everly had the reputation of being a good bat, not a great one, but this day he earned laurels. He almost matched Maddox for strength and endurance. In fact, one might have said that his true opponent was Maddox himself, and not the Gentlemen. Everly blocked the doubtful balls, missed the bad ones, took the good ones, and sent them flying to all parts of the field. The scouts were hot and tired; the bowlers were changed and bowled till their arms ached; but Everly and Maddox remained unconquered. If a Gentleman essayed to stop the progress of the ball, it rolled between his legs or slipped between his fingers. If a Gentleman tried to catch it, it struck him on the nose, and bounded off while the Gentleman's eye filled with water, and his form writhed with anguish. If it was thrown straight up to the wicket, Everly had reached it before the ball. In short, when Everly was caught out, and Maddox stumped out, Players had notched some fifty-four while the score of the Gentlemen was half that. The advantage posted by Players was to prove too great to be recovered by dusk.

After his innings, Everly admittedly retained little of his customary elegance, while Maddox was, in truth, none the worse for wear. The two convened afterward in the brief intermission, off on the sidelines. Maddox had planted his bat squarely between his legs, while Everly was holding his to one side and leaning against it as if he were idling, despite his slight dishevelment, cane in hand at some fashionable lounge.

"Well played, Peter," Maddox said. "Admirable strokes."

Everly thanked his good friend kindly and said that he had always prided himself rather on his ability as wicket keeper, but that today, at bat, he had been inspired.

"Very inspired," Maddox agreed. "I've never seen you place a pull shot to the square-leg boundary before."

"Yes," Everly preened, "that was an exceptionally well-placed shot, wasn't it?"

"Or stolen so many byes," Maddox continued, regarding his friend closely. "You ran like a flash."

"Yes, indeed. Like a flash."

"Inspired, as you say, no doubt, by the spectators," Maddox suggested.

"No doubt!" Everly replied. "A rousing crowd today! And I thoroughly enjoyed our French friends' bewilderment in the outfield. Having two Frenchmen per team naturally made us both fall short of the ideal eleven, and perhaps it was that disadvantage that gave me the impetus to play . . . why, almost as well as you."

Maddox did not respond directly to Everly's last comment. Instead, he said, "But was it only the French who inspired you?"

"Why, I don't know! What do you mean?"

"I was thinking, rather, that perhaps you were displaying your manly abilities for the benefit of some particular damsel," Maddox suggested, "or even some matron among the spectators."

"Dear me, Maddox! You are so brutally direct! But, no, I am bound to disappoint you. I am pursuing no amorous adventure this fortnight."

Maddox let this pass. He paused. Then, "I hear you spent a deal of time with my wife before my arrival."

"Charming woman!" Everly replied promptly. "I have told you so already! Yes, I do enjoy her company on occasion, but I confess that I have been rather drawn to the French guests—especially since your arrival."

"And speaking of the French, have you found out anything about them for me?"

"Yes! Well! After our little chat that first night of your arrival . . . some time well after dinner, I believe it was, do you recall? . . . you did indeed persuade me to do a little

investigating. You were quite right that there must be more
to some of our guests than meets the eye! I think the fellow
that might interest you most is the one called Mersenne."
Everly coughed deprecatingly into his fist. "A count, so he
would have us think, although I am sure that not even a
child would fall for his pose. The solving of why he should
want to pass himself off as a French count—beyond the
momentary thrill of bamboozling us!—I will leave to your
capable brain, Tony! I, for one, am convinced that he is a
fraud. Or, rather, that he is, at least, not a French count.
Have you met him?"

Maddox replied that he had not yet had a chance to meet
all the French guests.

"You have been busy." Everly's tone was equivocal. He
made neither a statement nor a question.

Maddox did not respond to this but said instead, "He is
one of the ones who have been so cleverly avoiding me and
my secretary and my page. But I had anticipated that,
which was why I asked you, dear Peter, to find out what
you could about them. Mersenne, you say? Point him out
to me!"

Everly scanned the crowd of spectators a moment and
nodded infinitesimally with his head. "He's with the Parrish at the moment, and they," he said with an interesting
edge in his voice, "are standing now with her ladyship.
Lady Westleigh, that is."

Maddox's gaze crossed the field and registered the man
on Eliza Parrish's arm, talking with his wife. "I'll see what
I can find out about him upon my return to Town."

There was time for no more. Play had been called
again, and the two men made off to take their positions.
Before parting, Maddox said to his friend's back, "Peter."

Everly looked back around. "Tony." This time his tone
was vaguely challenging.

Whatever had been on Maddox's mind to say, he
changed it. "Thank you for your help," he said pleasantly.
"I'm glad that you and I are on the same team."

Everly laughed then, charmingly, the trace of the rough edge completely smoothed over. "So am I, my dear Tony!"

Marianna, who had caught a glimpse of this exchange from her end of the field, saw nothing more than two friends exchanging congratulations after an extraordinarily successful innings. She did not have long to consider how the feelings ran between her husband and Peter Everly, for her attention was being claimed, rather stridently, by Eliza Parrish, with one of the French guests.

Marianna had noticed that Eliza Parrish had been roaming the crowds for most the day. Her clear high voice could be heard almost everywhere. She whispered conspicuously to different groups, made great plays with her fan, and then laughed immoderately. When she spoke, aloud, for all to hear, her comments were in the general vein of *Isn't it delicious?*, or *And at her age!*, or *He'll lose interest in her now!* and again, *Was it my fault that I happened to see her lure him into her bedchamber a few nights ago?* The general trend was painfully obvious.

Marianna had noticed that something cold and malicious had come into Eliza's sparkling dark face in the past few days; and with Eliza's wickedness today, Marianna had had more than enough of her by the time she and her gallant had drifted over to where Marianna was standing with Lady Hester.

"Marianna! Lady Westleigh!" she shrieked. "Here's someone who has been dying to meet you all week!"

Marianna wanted to get rid of the woman as quickly as possible. "Eliza," she said, distractedly polite, almost absent, keeping her eyes on the progress of the play, as if she were riveted by it. "Oh, yes, do present him to me."

Eliza sketched an introduction between her and the Count of Mersenne, at whom Marianna merely glanced. "Oh, I'm sure you'll have a lot in common with him, Marianna," Eliza said, slyly, "for he has told me that he shares the same interest you do: gambling!"

Marianna looked at Eliza, sharply, then at the man. His

was a thin face, one she had never seen before. "What do you mean?" she asked Eliza quietly, hoping that Lady Hester had not heard this odd comment.

Lady Hester had not. She hushed them all and said, very firmly, that there were those present who wanted to watch the game and not have their ears addled by pittle-pattle! "So do go away, I beg you, if you want to talk!"

Marianna took the opportunity. Eliza declined to join them, saying loudly that she was sure they would have a lot to say to one another. Eliza flitted off, and Marianna and Mersenne stepped away from the knot of spectators who were engrossed in the play and shouting taunts and encouragements.

"What do you mean?" Marianna repeated. "I have never gambled."

"Perhaps not at a gaming table, but then, there are many forms of gambling in this England, no?" Mersenne replied.

"Just what do you imply, sir?" she asked.

"Perhaps we have a mutual friend, madame," he replied.

"Who is . . . ?"

Mersenne shook his head. "You must guess that for yourself!"

These insinuations made Marianna distinctly uneasy—just as she knew they were supposed to do. The man was a toad, and it needed only a minute in his company for Marianna to agree with Charlotte—and everyone else—that here was no count. Marianna would suffer this man's presence no longer. She lifted her skirts to make her way across the lawn back to Lady Hester, saying over her shoulder, "I am no more fond of guessing games than I am of gambling!"

"Oh, but if you had a reason to be—shall we say—angry with your husband?" he suggested to her back.

"Which I do not," she stated firmly over her shoulder.

"Or liked quick money?" he continued, while she was still not more than two feet away. "Then you might want to invest in some French bonds. I predict that they will do well in the coming weeks on the stock market."

"French bonds?" she queried.

"From the *Banque Royale*," he affirmed. "Or, perhaps you might be interested in buying *les caisses d'escompte*?"

Marianna looked back at him, more disturbed than ever, trying to understand the puzzle of what he was saying.

"My French is not good enough to keep up with you," she replied with finality.

Mersenne merely smiled. "You can buy them at an advantage now—for a large reward later."

Marianna would not give the man another moment of her time or her thoughts. She took a further step away from him, shaking her head free of his insinuations. He could certainly not mean what she had inferred from his comments! No, she was determined to let nothing spoil her deep pleasure in this country party.

"Go to our mutual friend," Mersenne said, before she was out of earshot. "I think you know who I am talking about. You will be pleased with the return on your investment."

Marianna did not dignify that comment with a reply. She reached Lady Hester's side, whereupon she was informed, in detail, of all the latest action on the cricket field.

XVIII

Where Marianna Learns One Truth...

The journey back to Cavendish Square from Marlborough Park was of a far different tenor from the one in the opposite direction. Maddox had sent Charlotte off ahead, chaperoned by Marianna's Rachel, while he and Marianna made the trip back together. They lingered at roadside inns, not particularly caring about the quality or elegance of the establishment. They gloried in a love that was strong and rapturous and passionate, with a potential that would only grow. They shut out the world. They reveled in those few days, making them a tumultuous secret, to be hidden and treasured, not even to be spoken of. Maddox needed no words. He communicated with his hands and his lips and his body, wholly and with abandon, encouraging, persuading Marianna to join in his abandon. She did; and she was struck anew, every time, by the utterly impossible combination of excitement and security she experienced in his arms. She had no desire to hurry their return to Town; yet she looked forward to it. How lovely it would be to open, once and for all, the communicating door between their bedchambers on Cavendish Square, which had remained closed all these months!

When, at last, the coach came to a heaving halt in front of Maddox House rather early one morning (they had spent one last night not many miles outside of London; they had been unwilling, or unable, to wait until Cavendish Square before retiring), Maddox kissed and caressed his wife indecently and at length, and in full view of the goggling eyes of the footman waiting to hand her ladyship down. Marianna would not have believed, at just that moment, that the communicating door between their two bedchambers would not be opened this night, nor that the memory of this last, loving embrace in the coach would have to satisfy her need for his touch for some days to come.

"I won't descend here," he said. "I'm off to my offices." Another kiss. "Days overdue."

"Only two," she corrected. "No one could have expected you before yesterday. It took Charlotte and me two and a half days to get to the Park and only three and a half in return."

"Far, far too short," he said. "Were we in a hurry?"

"Once, at least!" she said, provocatively. "At the pond. Do you remember the pond? The one that was behind the charming little inn . . . but what was it called, now, that little inn?" She laughed at her inability to conjure a simple name, and attempted, without success, to wriggle out of his hold. "You know, I have completely forgotten its name."

"I forget as well, but the pond . . . ," he said, restraining her easily and kissing her again with full-blooded passion. "Yes, I remember the pond." He looked down at her when a thought struck him. "The pond was, after all, my original choice at the Park for the place to consummate this marriage." Then, caressing her, "A place you did not think quite as enticing as I did at first, if I recall correctly."

"Only until you showed me what you had in mind," she replied, returning his kiss.

"Pandering to my vanity?" he suggested.

"Not a chance!" she said, tartly. "Considering how stingy you are with your compliments, I am not about to reassure you of how quickly you convinced me of the excellence of your idea!"

"The excellence of my idea," he murmured against her lips. "And what a disaster!"

She laughed at the memory. "Poor Mr. Wilton," she lamented. "Did you indeed dismiss him?"

"What a woman you are for changing the subject," he said, kissing her.

"Well, did you?" she demanded. It was a simple question, and she wanted an answer.

"No, I did not," he said, with a kind of reluctance. "I took pity on him."

"That must have been a first, from what I hear," Marianna commented.

"You are a bad influence," he explained, "and seem to have nothing on your mind other than my business."

"While you," she returned, "seem to have nothing on your mind but . . . this!"

For an answer, he made as if to take her right there in the backseat of the traveling chaise as it stood, stationary, in front of their house. Marianna protested in earnest. "Good God, Maddox!" she breathed into his ear. "This time you truly cannot mean it! Besides," she said, determinedly shifting into an upright position against the leather squabs, "if we continue like this, you shall tire of me before the week is over."

He relinquished his hold on her. "Ah, and what a delightful time I should have doing it," he replied, sitting up as well.

It was a straight shot off a solid bat. Marianna fielded it easily enough. "But how sorry you should be the week after!" she tossed back.

He laughed at that.

She adjusted her clothing, and continued, businesslike,

"Now, what are your plans for the rest of the day and evening, if I may ask?"

"I shall have to see once I'm at my offices," he said, raking his hair with his hands and finding that he had to retie the ribbon holding his thick hair. Marianna performed this lover's office for him. "I'll let you know," he said. "I can send a runner over with a message sometime during the day. One of my pages—" he began, and Marianna laughed. "Or perhaps *not* a page, on second thought! Anyone available can carry the message to you. I need only to know if you have any plans for the day?"

Marianna shook her head. "None whatsoever."

"Then I'll have the message sent here. You'll be hearing from me. Most likely later this afternoon. I expect I'll be rather taken up today, but I'll try to disengage myself before the evening is too far advanced."

Marianna nodded. He pushed the door to the coach open then, handed Marianna down the steps to the footman, alit for one last, brief salute on her lips, and then hopped back in and directed the coachman to Westminster.

Marianna entered Maddox House as if for the first time. Here, suddenly, was her home. She was no longer merely a tolerated visitor. She was its mistress, unquestioned and cherished.

Browne gave her the news of Charlotte, who had not yet risen. Browne had seen to it that Charlotte had spent the evening before in very respectable company and that she had made plans for an equally respectable outing that day. Marianna nodded, patted Browne fondly on the shoulder, and then ascended to her chambers enveloped in delicious thoughts of spending her day in luxurious idleness. She would read, she would nap, she would have Rachel prepare her a long bath; and then after a pleasantly drowsy afternoon, she would begin to prepare herself for whatever lay ahead for the evening. She was whole and happy and radiant, and most unwisely in love.

Marianna's plans for a leisurely, voluptuous day did not materialize. A seemingly innocuous series of visitors to Cavendish Square not only altered the shape of her day but also radically revised the events in her life.

Early that afternoon and very much to Marianna's surprise Browne took it upon herself to announce to her that Lady Susannah Marsh was belowstairs and awaiting her ladyship's pleasure in the green saloon. Marianna had been reposing, with the most sensational book of the year lying unread in her lap, staring dreamily out the window. At the announcement of this visitor, she happily cast the book aside, rose from her chaise longue, and stretched languorously. She said, with a smile that took any sting out of her words, that she hoped Browne knew that Lady Marsh should not have remained in the green saloon but should have been shown upstairs immediately.

"And so I told her, your ladyship," Browne replied solemnly, "but she showed no inclination to come up."

Marianna was only mildly surprised by this and so tripped, quite unconcernedly, down the stairs to an elegantly appointed, formal room, one she would not normally have used to receive her dear friend. Marianna swiftly crossed the threshold, words of apology on her lips, but they died just as quickly.

"Susannah! What is wrong?" she asked with real concern, crossing to Susannah's side.

Susannah rose from the silk and gilt settee and accepted Marianna's outstretched hand. "Nothing visible, I had hoped," she replied, with that deep, attractive catch in her voice. She smiled then, her unconsciously lovely smile that had thoroughly captivated the duke, and said, "Is it so obvious?"

Marianna looked at her friend and shook her head. "No," she said. "It was just that the moment I came into the room, you looked so . . . cold, as if you had taken ill, and I was only worried that you weren't well." Marianna regarded Susannah closely. "But if you had hoped that nothing wrong showed, I am led to believe that something *is* wrong. Can you tell me about it?"

Susannah sank back down to the settee. "That is why I am come," she said, perfectly composed. "I had been awaiting your return, you see, and did not have the courtesy to send you a note first announcing my visit. And that is because . . . because . . ." Her composure had slipped away, and she did not finish the sentence.

Marianna sat down next to her and took one of Susannah's hands in her own. She was a little alarmed at how quickly Susannah's beautifully smooth face had crumpled into lines of pain. "Susannah, my dear," she said gravely, "is anything wrong with the duke?"

This brought a shadow of Susannah's lovely smile back to her face. She even laughed, a little. "No, nothing is wrong with the duke," she said, with light irony, misinterpreting, a little willfully, what Marianna meant. "He is a thoroughly charming man! And so thoughtful! Such a catch, from everyone's point of view! And so taken with me! It's quite beside the point that his devotion is absolutely *stifling* . . ." She stopped short and changed her tone. "Do I sound horrid? Do you hate me?"

"Good heavens, no!" Marianna replied quickly, pressing Susannah's hands reassuringly before letting them go. "I certainly don't hate you, but I don't think I quite understand you! I was under the impression . . . that is, I thought that you and the duke . . . well! I had thought that Marlborough Park was a sort of turning point for the two of you, was it not? Or, at least, so it seemed to me!"

"To you and to everyone else," Susannah interpolated, herself again, for the moment.

"And I could have slapped Eliza Parrish's face for it, too!" Marianna said with unaccustomed violence.

"Yes, how satisfying," Susannah agreed placidly. "But she cannot be held entirely at fault for having spread the news of my *affaire*. It was announcement enough that I went there at all and spent time with Gervase so publicly."

"Nevertheless, the woman is a menace!" Marianna declared. "How *can* she be like that?"

"I heard that her husband lost both his fortune and hers years ago and that she has been forever trying to recapture it." Susannah shook her head. "But none of this is to the point!" She looked down at the hands in her lap. Then, simply, "I need your help."

"Whatever you need, Susannah," Marianna said. "I can see that something is troubling you. Perhaps it has been for some time now?"

Susannah nodded, still contemplating her hands.

"Whatever do you need, Susannah?" Marianna repeated.

Susannah drew a deep breath. "I need to get in touch with someone. It is vital to me to get in touch with that person, to contact him." She glanced up, quickly. "Oh, yes, it is a 'he,'" she said, with a wry twist to her mouth, then she looked back down at her ringless fingers. "I have been looking for him ever since I knew that he was in London, but have had no luck. At Marlborough Park, I chanced to discover a possible address where he might be contacted. But it's only a possibility, and I cannot be sure . . . !" Susannah looked up to gauge the effect that this story was having on her listener. Seeing only concerned interest on Marianna's face, Susannah was encouraged to continue. "And don't ask me what Marlborough Park has to do with any of this, for a good part of this, I am sure, would be better for you not to know!"

"I need only know what you choose to tell me, Susannah," Marianna reassured.

"Well, as to that, I had not planned on telling you—or anyone else—any of it! But, you see, after I tracked down the address, I naturally went straight there, and then I found, to my horror . . ."

She broke off, unable to continue. Marianna waited patiently, expectantly, while Susannah struggled for composure.

It was a struggle she had been losing over the past days, had all but lost. Jean had made it plain to her that night at Ranelagh that he wanted nothing to do with her. Why, then, had she tormented herself with trying to find him, with chasing to Ranelagh in the hopes of any little clue, with deceiving Gervase, who certainly deserved a better woman than she, or at least one who was heart-whole?

Jean had robbed her, she thought bitterly, of her heart, her youth, her self-esteem. When he left her all those years ago, when he left her either at her mother's bribing—for her mother had certainly been capable of such an action— or of his own accord, he had taken everything. Or almost everything. His reappearance in London had taken the last little bit of what she had, that shred of the ability to escape, even briefly, into a little world of love that was not loving. And now that was gone, too. She could not continue with Gervase.

She was bound to the man she had married, something dark and compelling drew her to him, without illusion, without real desire. She had woven many a fantasy in the long, sleepless hours of the past days and nights. She would find him, persuade him from the course of disaster he was surely steering in England. They would go abroad, live quietly. Italy, perhaps. America.

It was of no use.

It was worth a final try.

"To your horror...?" Marianna prodded gently.

Susannah's beautiful eyes were full of unshed tears. "I discovered this morning, to my horror, that my resolve had deserted me," she said, with devastating simplicity. She drew a thick envelope out of her reticule. "I have written a letter. Everything is clearly spelled out. Where he can find me and under what name." She attempted a smile. It went awry. "Oh, Marsh *is* my real name! But I am not sure that he knows it. In any case," she went on in a rush, "I went to the address this morning, had my coachman drive by, and found that I could not descend, could not descend to ...

deliver . . . a . . . simple . . . letter." She looked down with an almost Oriental curiosity at the letter now trembling violently in her hand. "I could not deliver it! It was incredible. It seemed the end for me!" She looked up at Marianna. "Then I thought of you, and you seemed to me to be my last hope."

"Would you like for me to deliver the letter for you?" Marianna asked, knowing of no other way to ease Susannah's evident pain.

"Even simpler than that, I think!" Susannah said. "Somehow I would not like you to do the errand for me! But, contradictory creature that I am, I would ask you to accompany me in the carriage. Hold my hand! Give me moral support!" She paused, shocked at herself. "I feel a fool!"

Marianna took Susannah's hands again. She was grieved over her friend's grief. She understood little of what lay behind Susannah's most extraordinary story but did not think her complete understanding of the circumstances was what Susannah wanted. "Of course, I will come with you. I wish I could do more!"

Susannah shook her head, mute, as if to say there was nothing more Marianna could do.

"Shall we go now?" Marianna asked.

Again, Susannah could only nod mutely.

"I can be ready on the instant," said Marianna. She rose from the settee and gently raised Susannah by her elbow. "Is your coach waiting outside? Good. Then we need not wait for the Westleigh carriage to be brought around. Perhaps you will give me the address, and I will direct your coachman?"

Susannah fished in her reticule for another paper. She handed it over to Marianna.

Marianna gasped and stiffened in surprise and dismay. "Oh, no!"

Susannah stammered, "N-no?"

"But, Susannah! Mr. Morgan Vaughan, Number 7 Finch

Lane, Cornhill?" Marianna asked, doubts and half-formed fears crowding in on her. "I'm not sure that I can!"

Susannah had paled considerably. "You can't come with me?" Her voice sounded pitiful, even to herself.

"My dear, I want to! That is, I would! I mean ..."

"Marianna," Susannah said. "If I tell you something, will you promise never to betray me to another soul?"

"*Betray* you! Of course not!" Marianna replied immediately.

"Do you promise me?"

"Susannah, you need not ask! I promise you without hesitation!"

Susannah composed herself for one last admission. "Perhaps I am asking a lot of you, Marianna. Perhaps it is too much to expect! But the letter I want you to help me deliver," she said, "is intended for my husband."

Marianna made no further protest. All hesitations were swept aside. Not much later they were rattling down the cobbles of quiet Cornhill and pulling up in front of the charming bow window of Number 7 Finch Lane. Susannah nearly lost her resolve again, but Marianna pushed her gently out of the coach and encouraged her by gestures to deliver the letter. Susannah pulled a veil over her face, trod the steps, and paused a moment before the door, as if in fervent prayer. Then she let her fate slip from her hand, down the brass mail chute in the door, quickly turned on her heels and hurried back to the carriage.

Marianna had emerged from the carriage and stepped onto the fender bar of the carriage to await Susannah's return. When Susannah was coming back down the steps, Marianna nodded her approval and folded Susannah into her arms as she drew her shaken friend back into the carriage. A moment later the carriage moved forward.

From across the street, Anthony Maddox was standing, witnessing this affecting little scene, in the company of the Secretary of the Foreign Office and the Secretary of the Treasury.

Now, Maddox's personal involvement in pursuing Chaumonot had waned significantly during his days at Marlborough Park. Upon his return to his offices that morning, he suddenly found reason to renew his participation in the case. He had been involved from the beginning with those men whose principal task was to trace the activities of French revolutionaries in England. He had secured Maddox Hall in Stanthorpe for the very purpose of turning it over to the Foreign Office, which considered the Hall to be invaluably located for the surveillance of the hidden harbors and ports on the coast. Beyond this and his own searches through the inns and taverns of London, Maddox knew that his effectiveness was limited, and that the case of Chaumonot was being ably handled by other officers.

Thus, he would not normally have made the journey from Westminster to Cornhill this morning, except for the fact that he happened to learn that Chaumonot's trail led to the doorstep of one Mr. Morgan Vaughan. This little bit of news had whetted, once again, his appetite for the case.

It was, however, with a rather acrid taste in his mouth that he saw emerge from a carriage standing in front of that unassuming house in Finch Lane the lovely figure of a woman who bore a striking resemblance to his wife.

XIX

...*And Suspects Another*

Marianna helped Susannah into Marsh House near Pall Mall and saw to it that she received proper care from her staff. A thousand unasked questions accompanied Marianna back to Maddox House.

Although deeply disturbed by her friend's apparent and unexplained agony, Marianna had not lost her glow or her anticipation for the delight in the evening ahead. Not much later, when Signor Luigi arrived for his late afternoon work, he did not fail to notice the subtle flowering of his mistress. Marianna sat down at her dressing table and instructed her darling *parruchiere* to fix her hair in an uncomplicated way that would be easy for her to unpin.

The slim Italian easily grasped her meaning. "Ah, Signora!" he exclaimed with pleasure. "For this I was born! Yes, I will create for you the perfect style for the occasion —although I need hardly improve on your beauty. I shall merely enhance it! Yes! This is how I saw it from the very beginning. Call me a prophet! Call me an artist! Call me a genius! I shall achieve for you this evening the style simple, yet elegant and—shall we say?—easily handled!"

Marianna laughed her response, and it did not take

much for Signor Luigi's skilled comb to coax her luxurious curls into a charming arrangement. He coaxed as well Marianna's heart—her true Italian heart—to sing. Mistress and hairdresser chirped away in *la bella lengua*, which the mistress spoke so beautifully and which, in Signor Luigi's considered opinion, was the only language capable of fully expressing the heart.

Through the vigorous brushing, and the placing of a few ingeniously placed combs, Marianna had slowly regained the sweet anticipation that Susannah's visit had dispelled. She thought ahead to her clothes, atwitter with indecision, since she had not yet heard from Maddox, and changed her mind and her dress no less than four times. Charlotte bounced in midway through this elaborate process and augmented Marianna's euphoria by recounting her various activities that day, which Marianna, from her serene Olympian heights, smiled down upon as being so gay and charmingly youthful.

But for the evening ahead? Charlotte wanted to know, with an expectant look on her pretty, innocent face. Marianna had no plans. Charlotte was free to do what she liked.

"May I go out with Everly, then?" Charlotte asked. "He sent a note around to me earlier in the day. Actually, it was addressed to the both of us, and since you were out just then, I opened it, but, of course, I have not yet responded, since I did not have your permission, and then I went out in a party, which was a little dull, I'll admit . . . and well, now I have just gotten back, and it is getting so very late, and I really would like an amusing evening! And if you don't want to go," she added a little defiantly, "that is no reason why I should sit around here with you doing nothing! You've said yourself that Everly is the perfect escort!"

Marianna clapped her hands to her ears. "My dear! I've understood less than half of what you've said. Do what you like. Go with Everly, and with my blessing."

Charlotte vanished on a little skip. Time passed. It was

nearing seven o'clock. A rosy gold was spreading over
Cavendish Square. Finally came word that a visitor was
awaiting her in the library. She descended the stairs, happy
to receive the envoy who was sure to have come from
Maddox.

He had. But it was not a mere envoy, it was Charles
Duguid.

Marianna crossed to him and held out her hand with a
smile that held no hint that her previous meeting with him
had signaled a complete defeat for her. She greeted him
with the cordial words, "Why, Mr. Duguid, what a pleasant
surprise!"

He bowed low over her hand and said that this was
already the second time today he had come and had the
honor of bearing a message from his lordship, who was,
when he saw him much earlier in the day, knee-deep in
papers.

"My husband told me that he would get in touch with
me through a page, but I had not expected to see you in the
guise of an errand boy!"

Her warm smile caused Mr. Duguid to melt. He had to
clear his throat twice before he replied, in his rather tangled way, "Well, your ladyship! I am sure that his lordship
did not intend it either! You see, I spoke with him . . . oh,
hours ago it was already! . . . and he was occupied with
some details and so did not really have a chance to look
over the second-quarter statements that I had brought over
to him, and well"—he said, clearing his throat again—
"when he mentioned to his secretary that he must get in
touch with your ladyship before too much longer, I volunteered to relay to you personally any message that he might
have to give you, since Cavendish Square is only a little bit
out of my way! His lordship wouldn't hear of putting me to
such trouble! I insisted (feeling as I do that . . . that . . .
amends are still to be made to you for the trouble I caused
you on your account! which I was very sorry for after-
wards, I can assure you!) and so here I am!"

Marianna waved this away. She hardly cared about that anymore. It seemed so long ago, and so irrelevant now! "You were only doing your job, Mr. Duguid," she soothed, "and in all events, you make too much of it to give it a moment's thought more!"

Rather more at his ease, perhaps, than he should have been, and enchanted by her ladyship's smile, Mr. Duguid unwisely pursued the topic. "Well! It caused me some bad nights, I can tell you, your ladyship. And in light of the terms of his lordship's will and all ... I guess you can imagine ... ! But, there it is! Your husband never likes to have his hand forced, as I'm sure you must know, and I can hardly tell you what a heartfelt relief it is for me ... seeing you now ... to know that all's well that ends well!"

An odd weight fell from Marianna's heart to her stomach. She did not pause to ponder what Mr. Duguid had just said, but the smile on her face had become a little fixed when she asked, "And the message from my husband, Mr. Duguid?"

"Oh, yes, the message!" Mr. Duguid recalled the purpose of his errand. "His lordship told me to tell you that he would be arriving home by eight o'clock at the latest and that he would be bringing with him some dinner guests. He was sure that you had met them already and so did not charge me with their names, but he said that if dinner were prepared for no more than ten people, it would be most adequate."

"Ten here for dinner?" she repeated, distracted, but not by the thought of entertaining ten people on less than an hour's notice.

"He expressed complete confidence (and a very flattering confidence it was, to my mind, at any rate!) that you would be able to rise to the occasion," Mr. Duguid explained. "His lordship said the guests would not expect anything but the most informal of meals, and that he was only charging you with this burden because entertaining at Maddox House would be a welcome change for him from dining at one of his clubs! And, of course, the only reason why he gave me the message at all was because the very moment that I was speaking with him, a page from the Secretary of the Treasury came into the room with a rather urgent message for him—or so it seemed!—and his lordship was perfectly delighted by the news in the message (whatever it was) and dropped everything he was doing!"

When Marianna did not immediately reply to these disclosures, Duguid continued chattily, "And so he sent me to Maddox House at once with the message, and that is all he said! So you see, I came here hours ago, but you were not at home, and it simply did not occur to me to relay the message to the head footman or your housekeeper, since I was wanting to relay it to you *personally* . . . as I've said, I think some kind of amends are in order! . . . and so I returned to Westminster to inform his lordship that you were not at home and to discover whether he wanted to change the plans for any reason, and then it chanced that *he* had gone out, in a hurry, so I was told, and so I had to assume that the plans stood the way he had conveyed them earlier this afternoon. In short, my lady," he said, "if you are receiving the message only now, it is entirely my fault, and I hope I have not caused you undue trouble by the short notice!"

Marianna had composed herself with an effort. "No trouble at all!" she said, a little colorlessly. She cast back to Mr. Duguid's previous statement, as casually as possible. "But I really can't imagine, you know, why you should think that amends are in order, or should have worried about the . . . the . . . irregularity in my bank account, or what that has to do with the terms of his lordship's will."

"Oh, your ladyship, not the *present* lordship's will!" Mr. Duguid said, much shocked. "To think that I could cause you a moment's confusion over *that*! I fear I did not make myself at all clear! My goodness, you must know how your husband's will was settled on the day of your marriage! Oh, no, no, my dearest lady! I meant, of course, the *late* lordship's will, as I am sure you remember!"

"Yes, of course," she said, with a calm she did not feel. Strange, but she had not, for some reason, misunderstood Mr. Duguid's first mention of the will. She had known that he had meant Lord Edward's, but she could not have said why. A startlingly clear picture flashed into her mind. No, it had not flashed. Rather, a pattern that had been lying there all along had suddenly taken clear shape, like the child's game of finding the beast in the jungle or the figure in the carpet. Suddenly, all the unpredictability that she thought had ruled her life, all the purpose and mystery and passion that she had been swept up in of late, had not been the results of unpredictable factors at all, but were parts of a higher predictability, a more complex pattern discernible to her only after the essential fact had fallen into place. All the things said—and left unsaid—between her and her husband now had clear outlines that she should have seen from the moment he proposed marriage to her, but which, in her ignorance, in her foolishness, she had not even had the wit to suspect.

Still, she did not have all the facts just yet and would not be able to rest until she did.

Marianna saw Mr. Duguid off with a lovely smile that hid the sickening thud of her heart in her breast. She absently wiped her damp palms against her skirts, then wrung her hands, once. After taking a determinedly deep breath, she searched out Browne to begin the hurried preparations for the dinner. The menu was decided, the dining room prepared, a tentative seating arrangement devised. Simple tasks, all of them, easily executed. Marianna went about them in a way that should have steadied her, but the awful, nauseating weight in her stomach left her uncentered, unbalanced, and she found it difficult to concentrate on them.

Charlotte skipped down the stairs and airily informed Marianna that Mr. Everly's carriage had just pulled up at the portico. Now, Charlotte said that she knew perfectly well that it was just not the *thing* to be looking down into the street, anxiously, waiting for a man, but that is just what she *had* been doing, so there was hardly any reason to disguise the fact or to make Everly think that she did not have the least idea that he had arrived and to keep him waiting another half an hour or more.

Everly walked through the door a moment later to see the two ladies standing in the foyer. He greeted them conventionally, gracefully accepted Marianna's regret, and flattered Charlotte outrageously. Everly had made no further overtures to Marianna, since Maddox's arrival at Marlborough Park, but upon leaving, he took Marianna's hand and looked deep into her eyes.

A sickening thought came to her. Did Everly, too, know of the terms of Maddox's uncle's will?

"Everly," Marianna said, accepting his hand gratefully, returning the light pressure, clinging to it, momentarily, as if to a lifeline. "Enjoy yourselves this evening. I shall try to join you another time."

"At your service," Everly said, seriously, with a bow over her hand. Was she dreaming, or did his tone indeed suggest that he understood her pain?

Maddox strode into his house a second later, in time to see this touching little exchange of hands and regards that passed between Everly and his wife. Maddox saw Everly make a light, witty remark upon releasing Marianna's hand, which drew a laugh from her.

Never having experienced jealousy before, Maddox did not recognize the surge of the unnamed emotion he felt stir in his breast against his old friend, Peter Everly. He hardly paused to examine the feeling. Several long strides took him across the hallway. He inquired into Everly's evening plans for Miss Armitage and escorted the two to the door. Then he returned to Marianna's side and kissed her fully, the way he communicated with her best. She responded, savoring the bittersweet taste of his embrace. He broke off the kiss and looked down at her, his eyes touching her lips, her eyes, her hair.

"Did you countenance this outing?" he asked, with a gesture of his head toward the front door, and without quite releasing her.

"Yes, I saw no harm in it," Marianna replied, lingering in his arms, then stepping away from him. She had not been prepared for the feel and taste of him and had to steady herself with one hand on the ormolu side table. "You see, Everly sent a note here earlier this afternoon, requesting the company of Charlotte and myself at some event or another, which I somehow never received," she said, entirely distracted. "And so I told Charlotte, when she asked me about it, that she could certainly go without me." Marianna paused and pressed her temples. "Was that before or after I received your message about the dinner? I don't know! But, in any case, I encouraged Charlotte to take my place."

"I see," Maddox said. His head was turned from her when he asked, in distinctly bland accents for one with such a melodious voice, "And are you disappointed not to go with him this evening?"

"Oh, no!" Marianna assured her husband, a little shakily, finding it difficult to breathe properly and thinking how pleasant and undemanding would be Everly's company at just this moment. "I hardly paid attention to the invitation when I received it! This afternoon I was hovering in a dream world, I fear, and had my mind on . . . but then I was interrupted by. . . ." She did not wish to finish this thought aloud. She gathered her forces and said with determined brightness, "But enough of that! I would far rather have you tell me about the guests we shall be receiving this evening."

"No, don't demur!" Maddox said. "I'd be delighted to hear what you did to amuse yourself today. Do you mean to tell me?"

"Oh, my goodness, nothing!" she said, unconvincingly,

but she was not thinking of her encounter with Susannah, and even if she had she would not have betrayed her dear friend's most intimate secret. "I read a book," she offered next, and because she could not have given the title of it if he had asked her just then, she continued, "But about our guests? I shall need to know whom you have invited. And what a . . . what an excellent idea," she said, finding her way through the sentence, although it cost her a certain heartache, "to entertain at home. It shall be our first occasion! Shall we review the particulars in the dining room?"

Maddox had a sudden, visceral intuition that Peter Everly could have teased out the information how Marianna had spent her day with an amusing remark and a light caress. Maddox said, merely, "Yes, I had thought earlier today that the timing of the occasion was rather good." He followed her lead into the room that was quietly animated by whispering retainers and the muted ring of crystal glasses being set and silverware being laid. "I did not think you would mind receiving some of my colleagues or spending the evening in what must seem a rather dull fashion, talking finance and politics!"

"Dull, no!" she replied, turning around to meet his gray-green eyes. She thought she saw in their depths a rather searching look, but she doubted her perception. She quickly looked away. Her heart recoiled now that she had the key to what he must feel every time he looked at her. It caused her to say, with a lack of conviction that gave her words an unintended and faint note of irony, "You must know that I live for these occasions!"

"If I had only known earlier. . . !" he replied, but the words did not come out as lightly as he might have intended.

She turned, and said to him directly, "You must have known the general trend of my taste from Lord Edward."

He said, with a slight bow, "I am afraid that I knew very little of you from Uncle Edward."

Their eyes held a moment longer. Marianna's gaze faltered first. The conversation had entered dangerous territory, one that could not be explored at the moment. There was still a long evening ahead, and so she suggested that they discuss the seating arrangement. "Now, who did you say was coming?"

Maddox told her. She knew most of them from the general run of Society, and the others she had met, once, at the Montenegros' dinner. Maddox also indicated where everyone should sit and briefly outlined to her what he would like to see accomplished this evening in the way of policy statements.

Marianna nodded, a little dully, to the predinner briefing which, under other circumstances, would have been for her a great delight. She was very drawn to her husband just then, hearing him speak to her, however impersonally, about what lay at the heart of his actions and his goals; and when he asked her if she understood, she replied that she grasped perfectly what he was about and he could count on her to support him. Then, with what amounted to very bad grace on her part, she excused herself on the pretext of needing to repair a nonexistent rent in the flounce of her gown. Maddox bowed her out of the room with only a brief look in her direction, his face closed and unreadable.

Marianna's earlier euphoria had vanished like dew in the sun. She sought her chambers to calm herself by bathing her wrists and temples in cool water. When she descended minutes later to the sounds of the first guests arriving, she was steadier and knew from the first curtsy that she dropped, as she stood at Maddox's side, that she was going to prevail. The strange new knowledge she held about Lord Edward's will seemed to have sharpened her vision. When she sat down at the head of the table, hostess to a select group of her husband's choosing, she was aware that the lights were brighter, the room more alive with personalities, the table full, and her husband never more attractive than in his element.

She found a precarious center, deep within herself, and

held on to it, fragilely, during the meal. She was thankful, at least, to have the length of the dining table and ten guests between her husband and herself. She did not feel quite herself. She imagined that she was a cat whose fur had been rubbed the wrong way. She imagined that she was a bird whose feathers had been ruffled. This mild form of alienation did not seem to hinder her; rather it seemed to help her through the evening. Her tongue seemed to have a life of its own. She was a wit. It was a freak of temper. It usually took her much longer to warm up to people she did not know very well.

It was a gay, convivial party. The prime minister's latest attempt to reintroduce the excise bill was an inevitable topic of discussion. Marianna's interpretation of the events surrounding Pitt's efforts were considered to be original; they were even applauded, figuratively speaking. The identity of the mysterious columnist Gentleman X, who had all of London talking and guessing, was tossed about, at length; and while all feared that this columnist's trenchant wit might turn on any one of them, everyone agreed that it was even worse to be ignored by him. Once again, Marianna made some interesting guesses as to the columnist's possible identity, one of which, in fact, was correct.

The covers were removed, the ladies withdrew to a drawing room, and the gentlemen took their port at the table, but they did not linger. For the most part, the significant business had been concluded during the dinner, and the informal evening drew to its conclusion. Marianna and Maddox, standing together while seeing their guests off, were assured of the success of their evening by such parting remarks as, "Your measures have my support, Westleigh!"

To which Marianna replied, in a wifely spirit, that her husband advanced only the most reasonable of measures.

Another guest chimed in to say, "Charming wife you have, Maddox! You should certainly have her assert your

positions more often! Your measures—as reasonable as
they are—would go over far better from her!"

To which Maddox replied, gallantly, that his wife's as-
sertions were her own. He could only be flattered, said he,
when his modest opinions happened to coincide with her
intelligent ones.

"Oh, and Tony," yet another guest said, "let's plan on a
week at my shooting box in Leicester! We'll surely be quit
of these dreary politics by September! You'd like that, too,
wouldn't you, Lady Westleigh?"

To which they both replied that the idea was an excellent one.

When the last of the guests had left, a queer little silence
fell in the foyer. Marianna could stand it no longer. She
looked up Maddox and said in a rush that she desired him
to follow her into his library. Maddox acquiesced with a
brief nod. When they had entered the room, she leaned
back on the door, which closed with the weight of her
body.

"I think it time to discuss Lord Edward's will," she said.

XX

Hard Words

Maddox stopped in the middle of the room. He had not expected this. Nor did he want it. But when he turned to face her, he was ready.

"Uncle Edward's will?" he queried. "What is there to discuss?"

His tone, which was far from amiable, might have warned her off her present course, but the matter was too important for her to be diverted.

"It seems there were terms attached to the will," she said.

"And so?" he said, shrugging his broad shoulders. "I thought we had resolved the terms to our mutual satisfaction."

Marianna was genuinely surprised. "How could we have, when we have never discussed them?"

"My God, not in so many words!" Maddox shot back. "But what is it you want from me?"

She could hardly turn back now. "To know the terms," she said.

"You want me to spell them out for you?" Maddox said, rather surprised himself now.

She nodded and swallowed hard. "Yes."

"But surely you know them already!"

"Not . . . not all of them," she said. Throughout the dinner, she had been hoping against hope that she had misinterpreted Mr. Duguid, but the present trend of conversation confirmed her impression that there had, indeed, been terms to the will, and unpleasant ones at that.

"Really?" he said, with some irony. "You want . . . you *need* for some reason for me to tell you all of them? Let's start with the easy part. What do you know about them?"

"I know, for instance, that Lord Edward put some condition on your inheritance, tying Maddox Hall to me," she said, a little miserably.

It was out. She had spoken her fear. In some perverse way, the words seemed to hang there. Although they had been uttered, they did not vanish. They echoed from every corner of the room.

"Yes, he did," he said.

She had never seen so harsh an expression in his eyes. She had not expected him to deny it. She might have hoped for some help from him in discussing it, but he was, apparently, not inclined to give it.

She had to have it in words. "You had to marry me in order to inherit?" she said.

"Have it your own way," Maddox said, cryptically. "No, in fact, not," he corrected. "I was only constrained to offer for you. Your acceptance—or refusal—was irrelevant."

His statement hung there stark as a winter's branch.

She repeated, very slowly, "So you had only to offer for me?"

"Yes."

The matter he told her was too great to be swallowed at a mouthful. "But I did not have to accept your offer in order for you to inherit?"

Maddox did not think it necessary to respond to that. His silence confirmed that the terms were far worse than she had feared, or could even have imagined. The humiliation was great, but rising to her aid came an anger she did not yet understand.

"And how was anyone to know whether you had offered for me?" she asked, with a calm she did not feel.

"The lawyer was to check with you at the end of the week after the reading of the will."

"But you could have foregone the inheritance," she argued, trying to find her way out of this nightmare. "You did not need the land or the estate! Lord Edward once told me as much. You did not need to comply with the condition!"

"To have foregone the inheritance," he said brutally, "would have been unthinkable."

"You had your reasons, I suppose!"

"I had my reasons," he affirmed.

"Which you do not choose to share with me?"

"Not at present," he said. "Not now. They do not concern you."

She clenched her fists as if her temper were a solid thing held in her hands, raised her chin proudly, and said, "You might as well say that it is none of my business! In fact, nothing you have ever done has been, in your opinion, any of my business! So much about our marriage from the start has now become clear to me! But I digress!" She attempted to compose herself. "Simply allow me to point out that when you chose to comply with the conditions of the will and made your offer, you were not . . . you did not make yourself disagreeable."

"Neither was I particularly solicitous, if I remember correctly."

"Goodness knows, I realize now full well that you did not want to marry me! You could have been far *less* solicitous than you were—and without much effort!"

"I am not, perhaps, as polished as others that you may know," he said in a style he had always used to excellent effect in the debating pit in the House of Lords, "but I do not think myself a complete boor."

"Oh, no! In fact, you have a surfeit of social graces," she retorted bitterly, for she was hurt and humiliated.

"Enough not to have wanted this particular discussion, at least!" He struck back without a moment's hesitation. He, in his turn, was determined to win this one. "Enough to think that I am owed an explanation of why it is that *you* wanted it! Or why you chose this most curious moment to force the issue!"

"Good God! It's not obvious?" she cried. "To put a little honesty into this marriage!"

"Honesty?" he mimicked, with heavy irony. "You want honesty, do you?"

"Call it a product of my charming candor," she retorted flippantly.

"To borrow a turn of phrase from Peter Everly, am I to suppose?" he said. Before she had the chance to register the hot and ringing note of jealousy in his voice, he was continuing. "If you had wanted honesty in our marriage you might have told me—*honestly and hours ago*—where you spent the afternoon."

"Here, at home!" she said. Then, she suddenly remembered that she had told Maddox this morning that she was not going out. However, she had not been at home when Mr. Duguid had called the first time. Perhaps Duguid had relayed some message about her initial absence to Maddox?

In any case, her face had betrayed her. A flame spurted out of her rock of anger. "Are you accusing me of an assignation?" she fired back.

"No," he said baldly.

"Oh, are you paying me the tremendous compliment of assuming that no one else would want me?" she goaded him.

"No, I would rather pay you the compliment of assuming that you know the difference between flirtation and fidelity," he said in a tone that was far more threatening than it was complimentary. "But as it happens," he said, clinching his position in a way that his colleagues in Parliament would have recognized instantly, "I know exactly where you went this afternoon."

A terrible silence installed itself between them.

"You do?" Marianna said at last, choking over the simple words.

"I do. And I also expect to be told what you were doing there."

Marianna had no intention of betraying Susannah. Even if she had not been entrusted with Susannah's complete confidence, Marianna still would not have offered her errand for Susannah as her shield. There was something rather different at stake here than the question of Susannah's private life.

"I have no reason to tell you what I was doing there," she said. "No more reason than you to tell me why you should have chosen to comply with the conditions of Lord Edward's will. It does not concern you."

"Or you might have said that it is none of my business," he quoted back, matching her deliberate calm. The next moment the guard on his temper was dropped. "But as for it being none of my business—!" This, with real heat. "It is my business! It is *exactly* my business! My business and none other! I told you weeks ago that *your* business with Vaughan was over! Not another rendezvous at Finch Lane!"

"A rendezvous," she said coldly, "is an arranged meeting."

"And I believed your understanding of this matter to be entirely sufficient!" he continued, ignoring her comment. "A matter which, by the way, is far graver than you perhaps imagine! And to think that you could jeopardize months of careful planning!" He broke off, attempting to master his anger. He failed. "And I did not then, nor do I now, intend to be made a fool of by my wife. *By my wife!*"

Marianna was far from cowed by this display. "And I do not intend to be reduced to a chattel, begging for every penny from my husband when I am perfectly capable of making some of my own! My own! I can respect your economic policies! I can even understand them! Why this display of surprise? Did you not know that I have no difficulty grasping subtle financial issues? That is, I can grasp them only when and if my intelligence is respected enough that I am *informed* of them! I am not a moron! I've never heard one word from you about your policies or ideas! Good God, you said not ten minutes ago that my ideas were my own and that you would be flattered if yours coincided with mine! That's a laugh!" The laugh that punctuated her statement did not ring true. "And we have never, in this so-called marriage of independence, resolved the particular issue of money. A crucial one, do you not agree? We seem to get diverted every time. Or at least you do! That is, at Marlborough Park when we were going to the pond . . . and then, later, you had different ideas on what the subject of discussion should be . . . that is . . . that is to say that we never discussed . . ."

She could not complete the thought. She did not need to. Maddox knew well enough what now diverted his attention every time he was with his wife.

He was smiling. It was not his charming smile, which often transformed his unhandsome set of features into a face Marianna could not resist. It was rather a cruel smile —of satisfaction, or of derision, Marianna could not have said.

"Which brings me precisely back to my original point," he said, with a twist to his mouth, "that I thought we had resolved the distasteful terms of Uncle Edward's will to our mutual satisfaction. But perhaps I erred in thinking so! And so I wonder now, after all of this, what you had hoped to gain from forcing the issue at this late date."

"This late date?" she echoed, involuntarily. She struggled to remember that what was painfully fresh news to her was months-old news to him.

"Yes, this very late date," he repeated with a savage finality. "If you think that dragging all of this out into the open now will serve you in some way, you are sadly mistaken—"

"Serve me?" This, weakly.

"—for I have no intention now, or ever, of allowing you to invest on 'Change!" he finished, as if she had not spoken.

"Good heavens! The one has nothing to do with the other!" she said.

"You bring it up at this very late date," he continued, ignoring her again when she spoke, "when I am sure that we both agree the marriage—whatever its dishonest beginnings, as you have said—has gone too far to admit of undoing. As little as I wanted to marry you in the beginning, I will not, I repeat, I will *not* release you from it now!"

Marianna caught in her breath sharply. "But that is not at all what I meant!"

"No? Then, why, wife, do you bring up the conditions of Uncle Edward's will now? Tonight?"

"Because I just learned of them!" she cried.

"Come!" he blazed. "You can do better than that! You were aware of the conditions the day I offered for you at your brother's home. You say that you are not a moron. Well, I am no simpleton! You were my uncle's friend and confidant. You must have been aware of how he provided for you in his will! My God, you *were* aware of it. You said so yourself!"

"I did?" she answered, mystified. She was now having to assimilate the further shock that not only were thoroughly distasteful circumstances attached to her marriage, her husband had believed her complicitous in having seen them established.

He sketched an angry gesture. "You said that you were

aware of the reason for my call that day. You displayed no surprise when I made my offer." He paused. "And *you accepted it!*"

"I didn't know about the conditions then!"

"And you learned of them only today?" he demanded, derisively. "How could you possibly have learned of them today?"

"From Mr. Duguid! This afternoon!" she said. Her chin came up. "When I returned from Finch Lane," she added, defiantly. "Mr. Duguid was rambling on about, oh, I don't remember what! Perhaps the dinner guests we were to have, or my bank account, and he alluded to the conditions on Lord Edward's will. I'm not sure anymore what he said, or even how I knew what he was talking about. But somehow I just knew! And you have confirmed what I suspected. Far beyond what I had suspected, I will admit!"

He had placed his fists on his hips and planted his legs beneath him. "Could you possibly be suggesting that if you had known the conditions on Uncle Edward's will that day, you would have refused my offer?"

His voice flicked her like a whip. She felt tears spring to her eyes. She attempted to wink them away but failed pathetically. Before she totally humiliated herself in front of him, she had to leave. She turned to go.

"You choose not to answer my question?" he said angrily. The flames of love and fury made the same fire in Maddox. It was fury just then which was uppermost. "Or can't you answer it?"

She looked back over her shoulder. She looked very beautiful and dignified in her helplessness, and she was all that was dear to him.

"I don't honestly know," she said.

He had won, beaten her on all points.

"But if I had known that day what I know now," she said, moving toward the door, "I certainly would have refused you."

The moment she left the room, his victory rang hollow.

"No, come back! I didn't mean it, Marianna! *I didn't mean it!*" However, the words were never uttered. Instead, he swore violently and expostulated aloud, "My God! Words! Curst words!"

He took a quick stride toward the door, only to be brought up short by the entrance of his butler.

"I beg your lordship's pardon!" Steward said apologetically, for he had just seen her ladyship run blindly up the stairs.

"What is it?" Maddox snapped in his temper.

"It's Lord Carleton, my lord!" Steward explained quickly. "I thought you would want to know that he has returned to retrieve Lady Carleton's reticule and decided to use the opportunity to speak with you. I think he mentioned something about a tax bill that you were supporting. He is waiting in the saloon."

Maddox looked down the hallway and up the empty staircase. "Very well!" he bit out.

Marianna had found her chambers, shut all her doors, and flung herself across her bed, to weep in anger and frustration and humiliation. Her world was toppling about her ears. She sought an anchor, any familiar and comfortable point of reference, to ease the lurching, pitching, queasy nausea of her misery. She cast back to her family, all her dear friends, all her readings. She thought of Susannah and suddenly was sorry for all women who put their love in a man's careless keeping.

Nothing served. No agreeable thoughts, not even selfpity could settle her or soothe the searing ache of the sure knowledge that her marriage was a shambles, a travesty, and had been so from the beginning. Her marriage of independence.

Independence?

No. She could not hide from it. She knew strongly, starkly, distastefully but inescapably that something had started within her that would have been better not to have begun. It was true. She was already far more dependent on her husband than she could have imagined possible only a few short months ago. And for much more than his money.

But how? When? He was not even her type! Had the choice been hers to make freely, she would never have chosen him! She had always imagined . . . but what had been her girlish ideal? She could hardly remember! A man to talk and laugh with. A man to enter into all her thoughts and tastes and wishes and desires. A man who could make her laugh. A Peter Everly.

A man to dance attendance on her, she thought, bitterly, and Maddox did not dance.

"A masculine version of yourself," Lord Edward had said. Her dear friend, Lord Edward, who knew her so well! Who had entered into all her thoughts and tastes and wishes and desires. But they had not agreed on everything!

Her eyes widened, suddenly smoldering at the thought. Lord Edward. *Her friend?* Never! Her traitor, more like! Here was the true object of her anger, not Maddox! He was as much a victim as she! How could Lord Edward have served them such a turn? How could he have put her in this impossible, embarrassing, humiliating situation? How could he have forced it on his nephew? What on earth had he been thinking to have machinated this wild scheme? She simply could not understand it. She never would have entered into his scheme for putting such a condition on his will. She never would have agreed to allow him to use her so! Never!

But Lord Edward had done so. And Maddox had complied, and she had accepted.

Should she have been able to guess on that day the reason why Maddox had offered for her? Had Lord Edward not given her clues? Was not the end predictable from the beginning?

Predictable—there was a word! The pattern in the carpet. The beast in the jungle. A condition on a will. Two people thrown together. A terrible mistake. An ending as inevitable as tomorrow's sunset. But who would have predicted that she would fall hopelessly, madly, in love with a man who did not make her laugh, but who did make her live?

Her life was an open book. Could she rewrite it?

What if . . . ! she thought. What if she had known of the terms of Lord Edward's will on the day Maddox had offered for her? Maddox had asked the same of her just now, for his parting, insulting remark. She had said that she did not know, but she recoiled from the answer that came to her now; and when, treadmill-wise, she came back to that same answer again and again, she finally lifted herself up and out of the heap she had made of herself on the bed.

"I still might have said yes," she breathed aloud.

It was not a flattering conclusion.

Rachel came in to attend to her mistress. If Rachel noticed anything amiss in her ladyship's face or demeanor, she did not show it. She drew her ladyship into her dressing room.

Marianna sat down at the charming little table surmounted by the mirror, thinking, Why did I force the issue? What did I think to gain by it?

"*Brutta figura,*" Marianna said, quite spontaneously, to her reflection.

"My lady?"

"Ugly face," Marianna translated automatically, then explained to an uncomprehending Rachel. "The ill-mannered, the thing 'not done,' which all Italians abhor. Good heavens! I should have known better! What did I expect? Why, I am as bad as Charlotte. Ho! I flatter myself—I am a good deal worse!"

Rachel said nothing. Minutes later, Marianna was clad in her night rail, her hair properly braided, and in bed. The communicating door between her bedchamber and Maddox's was not opened this night, a night that, for Marianna, dragged interminably out into a very long and sleepless one.

XXI

Lovers Apart

Several mornings later, Maddox was in his offices at Westminster. He was handing a sheaf of documents over to Jeremy Wilton for delivery to Exchequer, clear on the other side of the sprawling government building, when Peter Everly arrived at the open door.

Wilton had been recounting indignantly to Maddox that the last time he had delivered important documents to Exchequer, he had been addressed as "Jerry" by the very haughty secretary there. "Just as if I were a . . . a schoolboy, your lordship," Wilton complained, "handing a letter of introduction over to a headmaster! And not as if I were your page delivering a vitally important bill!" He sniffed with indignation. "He called me Jerry! *Jerry!*"

Strolling into the large, mahogany-lined office, Everly remarked to this that bad manners always made him sick. "But is it any worse, dear boy, than referring to the present King of France by his Christian name, untitled, simply because he has lost most of his power?"

"Peter," Maddox said briefly, by way of greeting.

"But perhaps the French king will regain some of his power, after all. What do you think, Tony?" Everly asked pleasantly, placing his hat upon Maddox's heavily littered desk and standing his cane against it.

The two men shook hands.

"I doubt it," Maddox said. "After Louis's failed attempt to flee and his arrest at Varennes a few weeks ago, I would say that he is in very bad case." Maddox frowned in thought. "We'll see what developments July will bring."

"According to the rumors that were flying around Marlborough Park last week," Everly continued, "Louis will be restored to full power before the month is out."

"And rumors are also rife in Town this week that French bonds are a good buy on the Market," Maddox replied trenchantly. "Imagine what the bonds will be worth if Louis loses all his power and the Banque Royale is no longer functioning!" Maddox shook his head. "Louis can't last much longer. But what the outcome will be if he is dethroned is anyone's guess!"

In the next breath, Maddox dispatched Wilton on his errand, and Everly recommended the young man to keep his chin up and smile charmingly to the Secretary of Exchequer. Jeremy bowed himself out of the room and closed the door behind him.

"Well, Peter?" Maddox said, directly. "Have you taken the unprecedented step of coming to my offices to discuss international politics?"

"Dear me, no!" Everly replied. "Acquit me of any serious motives! Although I am sure, if we were to pursue our conversation, that you could edify me wonderfully well on the present state of international finance and politics. But I'd really rather not hear, don't you know, of the impending disaster that awaits this weary world!" Everly regarded his well-manicured fingernails. "No, rather it happens that I came to do some shopping."

Westminster, with its law courts and government offices, was also known for its stalls set down the sides of the Hall, at which could be bought books and barristers' wigs, and sergeants' coifs and women's clothing and household goods.

"Yes, you see, I am looking for a particular edition of Pope that I was sure I could find at one of my favorite booksellers below. But, alas!" Everly held up his empty hands. "No such luck! And so, I thought, since I was in the neighborhood, that I would come and visit you at your offices. To ask your advice."

"A first. On both counts," Maddox remarked.

"Indeed." Never having visited Maddox before, Everly walked around the office a moment. A nod of his head here and there and an admiring murmur or two indicated that he was impressed with the magnificence of Maddox's office and position. Everly paused at the large window, overlooking the Thames, and followed for a second the progress of a stately barge along the water.

"Sit down!" Maddox invited, watching his friend closely. "Now about the advice that you seek?"

"Yes, you are a busy man, so I will not detain you!" Everly said, taking the chair Maddox indicated, and disposing himself elegantly in it. "You see, I am in love."

Maddox's brows rose.

"I see that I surprise you by coming too rapidly to the point. That is also a first for me. So many of them today! No, indeed, I am not known for saying precisely what is on my mind—the way you are, Tony!"

Maddox had had ample time to regret how frankly he had spoken his mind to Marianna. She had threatened him in a way he had never been before. Their emotions had run too high that night; their intimacy had been too fragile to have withstood the punishing words he had poured out. Punishing words. Punishing for the threat to himself he perceived in her raising the issue of the conditions of the will. So many words to say to her now. So many to unsay! And he had not been able to see her again since that night.

Maddox's brows lowered, ominously. "For this you come to me?" he asked heavily, harshly. Everly's admission acted powerfully upon him. He felt, once again, that ill-defined threat. "To tell me you are in love?"

"Why, yes!" Everly replied lightly. "I have lost my heart, and I am sure you did not know I had even possessed one!" he said. "'Charm without heart,' I think you once said of me. But now, I have found it, only to lose it! And what is worse: I have lost it to a married woman."

"And so?" Maddox growled. "When has that ever stopped you?"

"Oh, but the case is very much different this time!"

"Do you seek my advice, then—or my blessing?" Maddox demanded savagely.

Everly held Maddox's angry gray-green eyes without flinching. "Surely not your blessing, dear boy!" Everly replied carelessly. "You see, she is the wife of a very dear friend of mine, and so I would think my attempting to win the affections of this particular lady would rather violate a basic code that orders the Society in which we live! I value my friendship with her husband very highly, you see." Everly paused. "However, that is rather a moot point, in this case, for it happens that the lady does not return my regard. I do believe her affections have already been rather thoroughly engaged. Now, whether she has given them to her husband or not, is not known to me! I am rather persuaded that he does not treat her as well as he should, and I have reason to think that they may be estranged one from the other at the moment—which would be a wonderful time for me to step in with the shoulder and the handkerchief, so to speak. But, as I have said, I shall not attempt it. Forgive me, I ramble! So, in fact, the precise matter of your advice, or blessing, with regard to my heart does not arise. I needed rather to unburden myself first."

"Get to the point, Everly," Maddox said, his brow lightening slightly.

"Ah, yes, the advice I seek," Everly replied, as if he had quite forgotten. "I am wondering what you would say if I were to pay my addresses to your ward, Miss Charlotte Armitage."

This surprised a crack of laughter from Maddox. "I won't be a party to murder, Peter!"

"Murder, dear boy?"

"Good God! Everly! You would strangle her within the fortnight!"

"Do you indeed think so?" Everly seemed to consider this aspect. "Well, she does talk quite a bit. Rather more, even, than I do, but I have been thinking this past day or two . . . especially since last night . . . when I happened to go out again with Miss Armitage and with your very charming wife, that perhaps I could fashion Miss Armitage into something rather more sophisticated and interesting . . . something more along the lines of Lady Westleigh, to take a chance example. She's a taking little thing!"

"Lady Westleigh?" Maddox shot back.

"No, rather, I was thinking of Miss Armitage, dear old boy," Everly replied without heat. "Now, don't, I beg of you, poker up on me. If you don't like the idea of me seeing more of Miss Armitage, just tell me and I will retreat!"

Maddox regarded Everly levelly for another moment or two. Then he sat back heavily in his chair, and said, "I would not like to think of my ward being courted on the heels of a disappointment on your part. It might not augur well for your role as her husband—that is, if you were to marry Miss Armitage."

"But there are so many ways to begin a marriage," Everly retorted to this.

Maddox merely grunted. "Tell me about your relationship with the woman you love," he invited.

"Perhaps I do owe you a brief description of the woman who has caught my heart, after all," Everly said. "So that you may judge for yourself if I have any hope of being the kind of husband you envisage for Miss Armitage." Everly paused and gazed in abstraction at the ceiling. "I should like to think that we are friends," he began. "Friendship is, after all, the finest balm for the pangs of disappointed love. I am, I hope you know, capable of friendship. With both men and women." His eyes shifted from the ceiling to Maddox. "But, yes, the lady in question. Let me see. No one knows better, perhaps, than I how impossible it is to keep the grand promises made by the exciting beginnings of a relationship! Or how inevitably the magic of these breathless openings yields to the plodding dullness of a development! You cannot imagine how quickly, in the past, I have tired of a woman! I never dreamt that a woman would come along who would sustain my interest over a period of time, who would still keep me waiting for developments, for things to come."

Everly paused to formulate further. "The woman who has captured my heart is, let us say, a woman of exciting beginnings. Like a very good book! And when I found myself reading her in earnest . . . well, that was when I decided that I should put her down, before coming to the end. She is a book that I love, but one whose conclusion can never be the one I desire." Everly smiled, satisfied with this description. "Yes, I think that is a fair enough assessment."

Maddox did not reply immediately to this. "And you think Miss Armitage could live up to such a woman?"

"She might well grow into it," Everly said. "With a little help from me, perhaps. As a boy I always loved the story of Pygmalion!"

"It might be that, sometime in the future, you would find another woman such as the one you have just described to me," Maddox suggested. "What then for Miss Armitage?"

"That might well happen, Tony. One can never predict such things!" Everly said. "But I have put off falling in love for this long, and I am inclined to think that such a woman does not come along twice. No." He shook his head. "And, in any case, I am a changed man. Some will say that this is the best thing that ever happened to me. Good God—how depressing! In any case, the frivolous, the entertaining is not enough for me anymore!" Everly regarded his nails again with absorption. "I would almost envy you your... work, Tony, if envy were not such a fatiguing emotion. But, work? What is it? I have always thought myself so well cast as a character in a light opera. In a former century I would surely have been a court jester. You see, I have come to think that we live in a world where there is no script and no director—or, at least, one without nearly the sense of humor I had once thought! And I even dare think that we live in a world where there rules no king. Not that George ever really counted—a fact that has been painfully obvious for years. Or the poor blighter Louis, needless to say. But I think you see what I mean."

Everly looked up. Maddox was regarding him meditatively and nodded for him to continue.

"Lately," Everly went on, "I have had a recurrent dream. A most disturbing one where I stand at a gate. As if I am some sort of a sentry. But who comes to the gate to ask passage? Why, it is I! Myself! None other! But I haven't been given the necessary password. And so I shoot myself."

Everly broke off. "Ah, but you see the depths to which love has made me sink! I am no longer amusing!"

Maddox considered this at length. "You're bending, but you won't break," he said, simply. Another small silence. "Do you think Miss Armitage is the one to help you back into shape?"

Everly rose from his chair. "I don't know, dear boy," he said, picking up his hat and cane and tucking them, as was his fashion, under his arm. "I thought merely to discuss it with you. To let you know where things stood with Miss Armitage. To unburden my heavy heart, so to speak. I feel ever so much better!"

"I am glad."

"So am I. I did not want you to receive the wrong impression," Everly said, "about my intentions toward Miss Armitage."

"I understand," Maddox replied, rising as well. "You have my permission to pay your addresses to my ward, if that is what you want from me. Perhaps I will have better advice to give you concerning a more serious match when I have seen the two of you together more."

"Quite! Yes, indeed." Everly moved toward the door.

"And, Peter," Maddox said, crossing to Everly's side and holding out his hand, "I thank you for seeking my advice."

Everly took the hand and shook it with a smile strongly reminiscent of his former, careless self. "It is I who thank you!" he said with punctilious courtesy. "You see, I remembered what you told me the other day about our being on the same team."

The two men stood, hand in hand, a moment longer, a study in contrasts: Maddox the rough-hewn oak, Everly the handsome, willowy reed.

For a response, Maddox nodded, once, decisively.

"Oh, and, Peter," Maddox said. "If ever you find yourself in a similar situation and need—"

Everly cut him off. "I never repeat myself," he said lightly, but with finality.

Then he was gone.

It was all Maddox could do to keep his mind on his work until he returned home that evening. He made it an hour earlier than was his custom, but he was not soon enough. When he arrived at Cavendish Square, he was informed that her ladyship had gone out with Lady Marsh only minutes before. No, it was not known what their destination was and no, the outside footmen had not noticed in which direction the carriage had left the Square.

Marianna had looked forward to spending the evening with her friend, Susannah, the one woman for whom she now felt a strong kinship. Marianna, still very bruised from her last conversation with Maddox, had agreed, in an act of defiance, to go gambling with Susannah at the hell in Cheapside that was all the rage.

Marianna had not seen Maddox again after their last conversation. She had known that he left the house very early the next morning and had returned very late. She assumed that he was avoiding her, and she had every desire to avoid him. She wanted no part of a man who made her so miserable. She was not going to allow him to have such a strong hold over her heart.

That next morning after their heated words, she had sat down at her writing table and dashed off, in one sitting, a very amusing story that she entitled "Footnote from Town." It was her intention to write Maddox out of her life. Never mind the fact that her vision had been at times as fuzzy as the blotting paper at her escritoire. She was certainly not crying over him!

The morning after that, when she arose and reread what she had written the day before, she was surprised to find that it really was one of her most amusing stories. She had it sent off that afternoon, after a few minor corrections, to the *Anglican Mirror*. That evening she went to some dull party or another. She met and laughed with Peter Everly, who she found was not his lighthearted self, but as he had made no further overtures to her since that walk in the garden at Marlborough Park, she had no reason to attribute his humor to his blighted love for her. Instead, she mused that the disease of seriousness must be going around Town, and that she and Everly had caught fatal cases of it.

Everly, it seemed, had been aware of it, too.

"Don't look so sad, my dear! There's magic in love and smiles," Everly said to her at one point.

"Do you read me so well?" she asked, amazed, for she had made every effort not to wear her heart on her sleeve.

He chucked her playfully under the chin. "Magic and smiles, my dear! Use them every day and see what wonderful things happen!"

Marianna laughed, bitterly, at that. "It seems to me,"

she retorted, "that 'brass cleaner' can be substituted for 'love' in that little maxim without at all violating its meaning! Love is merely a tool. Smiles are another. They are both just tools for accomplishing certain ends. There is no magic in love, merely chemicals."

"Am I speaking with Lady Westleigh?" Everly said, with exaggerated surprise, groping instinctively for his lorgnette to better survey her. "I do not think I recognize this woman!"

"No?" she said. The depths of her blue eyes drew him irresistibly. "We apply love, like brass cleaner, to the object of our affections. We polish and polish and expect that object to shine brightly enough to return our own reflection, enhanced and sparkling." She was thinking specifically of her love and friendship for Lord Edward. She laughed and stated, on a challenge, "A brass cleaner! That is what love is!"

"I am sure that I do not agree with you, your ladyship," he replied, infinitely sad and incapable of an appropriate retort. At the beginning of flirtation, Everly had always been able to strike all the right notes. All these years, he had kept himself immaculate of feelings. Just now, sophistication, lightness, and gallantry would not carry him through anything so dire as the passion he felt for Marianna Westleigh.

"Love is the pursuit of shadows," she continued. "And over the last few days, it has seemed impossible to me that anyone could ever really love anyone else, or if they could, that anything lasting or fine would come of it!"

Everly's propriety took instant alarm. He bowed with the formality of the previous century. "I am sorry that you think so, Lady Westleigh," he intoned, and resolved, at that moment, to seek Maddox out at the first opportunity.

Marianna immediately let the topic drop.

But that was last night, and this night Charlotte had gone off with Everly for the evening, and Marianna had unwisely chosen to attend yet another tedious party whose

utter boredom was alleviated only by the presence of Susannah Marsh, who was in the company of the harmless
and therefore popular cicerone, the Baron Childe. It so
happened that the very uncountly Count de Mersenne
chanced to show his face at the party midway through the
evening, but he did not approach Marianna.

At sight of him, Marianna's wits, which had been hopelessly addled since the moment Maddox had kissed her in
the gardens at Marlborough Park, suddenly came back to
order. She added up the column of clues in her head, but
she still could not make them total. She knew enough to
know that she needed more information. She turned to Susannah and asked how to say "bee" in French.

Susannah's lovely brows arched in question. "*Abeille,*
of course," she said, in her deliberate manner. "Why do
you ask?"

"It's that man Mersenne, over there..." Marianna
began, and had to elaborate no further.

"I think you must be referring to the gambling hell in
Cheapside, no? The one run by those Frenchmen. The one
that Eliza is always raving on about," Susannah said, with
a little smirk. "Eliza's been having a lot of luck there,
lately. Winning fistfuls, so she's said. I went there myself,"
she admitted. "Looking," she added, "but there was nothing doing."

Susannah explained no further. Marianna understood.
Susannah had been looking for her husband but apparently
had not found him there. Susannah had said no more about
her husband since the day before yesterday, when they had
made their fateful little visit to Morgan Vaughan's establishment and Marianna had not asked. When Marianna first
saw Susannah this evening, she had asked Susannah with
her eyes if Susannah had received any word. Susannah had
given a tiny shake to her head and formed a brief "No"
with her pretty mouth, and had then explained in an offhand manner why it was that she was not being escorted,

this evening, by the duke. Marianna had allowed the change of subject.

"Well, it was at the duchess's party last week," Marianna said, to pick up the earlier topic, "that Mersenne said such a very odd thing to me. About gambling and French bonds. It did not make great sense to me then, and it still does not now, but I am curious to look in at 'The Bee.' Are you interested?"

Susannah was interested. The Baron Childe was pressed into further service.

In the Baron's coach, they crossed the late-night streets of London and passed into that part of the City (it was often said) which, if buried "full fathom five" in the ground, would never be missed by the other. That was not entirely true, for although it was the case that the wealthy and titled great did not live there, they did come there for certain of their less healthy diversions and entertainments.

In this part of the City stretched scores of streets, which at night were utterly dark. It was a morass of misery, a vast space of low, damp land intersected by some noisome ditches and festering patches of garden ground broadening over a common, and hemmed in on the one hand by the long line of Walworth Road beyond the turnpike, and on the other, deep and far across, the Old Kent Road.

In the windows of almost every other inhabited house one saw bills announcing "Unfurnished Apartments to Let"; in almost every street numbers of houses were shut up, and padlocks hung on the doors, which told the tale that the late wretched inhabitants had been rendered still more wretched, their few goods sold and themselves either driven to the parish, or, with their beds of straw, housed in some new and equally wretched habitation. Houses there were which had not had a coat of paint on them for years, and many of these once must have been respectable-looking places. Here the broken windows were repaired with paper or filthy garments; there with the summer they had been removed. Lamps burned dismally.

They passed a police station, formed near the center of this swampy sector of the City, and then they turned a corner and found a bright-lit establishment, and above the door a fresh-painted shingle proclaiming *L'Abeille* emblazoned with a bee, whose shape and form struck Marianna as oddly familiar but could not quite place.

They entered and were given masks at the door. They tied the strings and, masks in place, approached one of the largest of the gaming-rooms by the first open door they came to. It was an apartment entirely given over to deep basset. About a dozen persons were seated round a table, all of them masked, and most of them so intent upon the cards that the entrance of the three newcomers passed unnoticed. A deathly hush brooded over the room, indicating that the stakes ran deep, and its silence contrasted markedly with the cheerful hubbub in the adjoining saloon, where the threesome next ventured.

In this saloon, branches of tallow candles, not wax, lit the tables and the walls. The people in this second room watched, drank, yawned, quarreled, were amorous or sleepy. There were random games of hazard, pharaoh, ombre, loo, quadrille, pope joan, bassett, passage, commerce, costly colors, Queen nazareau, post and pair; sometimes two or three different games were being played at one table. In this room, a man looked at the gamesters through a wicket. This man, who was little and was cursed with the face of a benevolent rat, exchanged the punters' rouleaus for money. In an establishment as successful as *L'Abeille*, it was usually the house that received the counters.

They passed on into another room. A faro bank was in full swing, as well as an E.O. table, which was being set in motion by a rather pretty young woman who, when observed at close hand, bore the signs of having been around the world more than once.

Marianna and Susannah and the baron chose to remain in this room. The ladies took a table, while the baron went to purchase some chips from the little rat in the adjoining room. When Susannah and Marianna took their seats, they could not have been aware, of course, that a slat of wood in the wall had slid back to reveal a disembodied eye, surveying all newcomers through a peephole. Even if they had been looking at that tiny corner of the wall (which they were not), the eye would have been difficult to discern. The eye, however, had no difficulty perceiving them.

After the baron had returned to the table, Eliza Parrish drifted into the room, glanced over at her dear friends, but did not immediately greet them. She was voluble this evening, more than ever. She had been drinking. Too much, perhaps. And talking too much. Laughing immoderately. After a time, she sidled up to the table where Susannah and Marianna were seated, wearing a sly face resembling the cat with the cream; and she walked as if she owned the place.

Eliza greeted each of the three of them in turn.

"Still winning, Eliza?" Susannah asked, glancing up from the glass whose fragile stem she had been twirling idly between her fingers.

"Now that you've walked in, Susannah," Eliza said. Her pretty dark eyes were bright, too bright, alight with too much alcohol and an unquenchable fever for gambling that made the blood roil in her veins, "I think my winnings will be very good tonight."

"Yes, I'd heard the news that Lady Luck has been sitting on your shoulder recently," Susannah responded.

"Oh, it's not a lady who has been sitting on my shoulder all these past days," Eliza said, her voice cloyingly sweet and with a double entendre even the least subtle spirit could seize.

"No?" Marianna said, entering the conversation. She glanced around the room. "Is it very wise of you to tout your winnings in a place like this so carelessly, Eliza? Should you not have a care with what you say?" Marianna meant this as a friendly warning.

Eliza's response was arch and dismissive. "It's what I *haven't* been saying recently that has brought me all my good luck here," she said over her shoulder, in a voice imbued with deep meaning, as she flitted off.

Marianna saw Eliza cross the room and disappear behind an unmarked door at the other end, at which she knocked, once, before opening, as if she were accustomed to going in. Marianna did not see Eliza come out again, but then Marianna had given Eliza no further thought beyond saying, "Eliza's drunk too much. She'll regret it tomorrow."

To which Susannah said, "She has gambling fever and will never sleep it off."

"She talks too much, if you ask me," the baron grumbled. "And what on earth did she mean about her good luck coming from what she doesn't say? I've never known her to be quiet about anything before!"

The question was purely rhetorical, and went unanswered. They played E.O. Marianna lost a little, Susannah won a little, the Baron broke even. Later, when the pleasure (what little there had been) of the hell had worn off, the baron graciously offered to escort the ladies home.

Once outside, Marianna was suddenly grateful for the fresh air. The hell had been a disappointment, she could not have said why. She had expected something to happen there, but it had not, and her head had begun to ache abominably. She asked that they walk to the corner and back before mounting into the coach, which the baron had already had called around.

The three set off down the uneven flags of the sidewalk. At the corner, Marianna looked down a deserted alleyway to her right. A shaft of moonlight dimly lit a heap in a far corner. She cried suddenly, "What's that . . . over there?"

Susannah and the baron looked. A strange lump filled a corner, near some overfull rubbish bins. The lump lay on the ground, whatever it was, sprawling, like an empty sack.

"Old clothes," Susannah said.

"A drunk, mayhap," the baron offered. "Not for us, I'm afraid," he said confidently. "That's the job for the constable and his watch."

"Yes, it does look like a person," Marianna said. "But not a drunk sleeping it off." She walked across the street and down the alleyway, heedless of the baron's calls to return. Susannah followed, and in her wake the baron continued calling after them, blustering that wandering down alleyways "just wasn't done in this part of Town."

Marianna had almost reached the dark blotch on the cobbled passageway. It was neither a sack of old clothes nor a drunk. It was a woman. That much Marianna could discern even without the benefit of light. It was a well-dressed woman. Young and with dark hair.

By the time Marianna had come up on the inert form and stood directly over it, she had covered her mouth, stifling a cry. Right behind her came Susannah and the baron, and as they came up and saw who it was neither of them could utter a sound.

They saw Eliza Parrish lying there, and Eliza Parrish was dead.

XXII

Stanthorpe Revisited

After a moment of utter, incredulous horror, Marianna spoke. "You see—that brick?" She gestured to the brick that was just visible through the tangle of Eliza's disheveled hair. "She fell against this brick and hit her head. She had been drinking . . . had too much to drink. You know, we all remarked on it! Perhaps she had even more to drink after she came to our table." Marianna licked her lips in agitation. "You see, then? It was a freak accident."

Marianna knelt down beside the crumpled body, heedless of the fact that her silk skirts were sweeping the filth. She put her hand at the back of Eliza's head, testing her theory, and felt the wound at the base of the skull. "It's possible that she fell," Marianna said, looking up at Susannah.

The Baron Childe, shaking his head, was muttering to himself, "Not my kind of party. No. Not at all my kind of party. Better get away. Notify the constable. His job."

"Oh, my God, Marianna," Susannah said, the horror still washing over her. "Are you *sure*?"

Marianna felt for a pulse. There was none. She put her

ear to Eliza's quiet heart and then sat back on her heels, her
hands on her knees.

"I'm sure," Marianna replied dully. "Or perhaps some
thief came and tried to take her purse . . . ?" she offered, as
a possible alternative. She played the scene out aloud.
"The thief approached Eliza, demanded her money. She
ran a little, darted down this alley, but caught her skirts up
in her heels or stumbled over a cobble. She was cornered.
The thief, who was also probably very drunk, picked up
the nearest brick. That brick and . . . Eliza fell."

Susannah knelt down then, too, and withdrew the brick
from behind Eliza's head, her fingers shrinking from contact with the flesh. She rose, slowly, turning the brick
around in her hands. It was old and jagged, not large, but
large enough to deal out death. However, something in
Susannah resisted that pat explanation. Her mind was a
blur of thoughts and images all rushing together. There was
Eliza Parrish, weeks ago, mourning over her losses at the
gaming tables; Eliza Parrish, more recently, gloating over
her winnings at the gaming tables. Several memories of
Ranelagh Gardens rose up to clash inside her head. Jean.
Eliza Parrish, again. Then, a stray image of the roulette
wheel spinning on its uncaring axis in a hot, greedy little
room not many yards from where they were standing. A
roulette wheel. Lady Luck. Fortuna.

Eliza's had just run out.

None of these images fell into place; one did not fit well
enough with the next to form a meaningful picture in Susannah's mind. Then a small glitter in Eliza's hand caught
Susannah's eye. She bent down again to peer at the glitter.
She pried open Eliza's clutched fingers, gingerly. Her eyes
widened. She touched a silver medallion that bore the imprint of a small gristmill perched over a running stream.
Carefully, she slipped the silver disk into her palm.

Still kneeling next to the dead woman's form and not
noticing Susannah's gesture, Marianna felt sick. She had
disliked Eliza from the beginning. Lately she had even

begun to feel that Eliza was a little inhuman. But now she
was dead. Marianna felt nothing but pity, and somber
thoughts of the brevity of life, of the things that could
happen, of the consequences of bad choices and bad luck
consumed her.

Susannah, standing next to Marianna, had never liked
Eliza Parrish either, and in the wake of recent developments had felt that the world would be better off without
her. Now the world was without her, and Susannah felt the
pity that Marianna felt. However, through Susannah's pity
surged a fear, and that fear—which was not for herself—
caused her to put some of the pieces of this nasty puzzle
together.

Marianna rose, also working through the implications of
Eliza's death, juggling bits and pieces of that same puzzle,
but for her the pattern was still scrambled and unidentifi-
able.

The Baron Childe performed no such mental gyrations.
He wanted to quit the alley as soon as possible. "Call the
constable," he repeated, still shaking his head. "His work."

Marianna held to her theory of the drunken thief. "This
looks to be very recent," she continued, ignoring the
baron. "Eliza must have been chased only minutes ago.
Or," she said, forcing herself to survey the figure awkwardly sprawled across the cobbles, "at least within the last
half hour. Perhaps the thief is still in the neighborhood and
can be caught."

This observation operated powerfully on the Baron
Childe, who at no time enjoyed courting danger or flirting
with death. He made more ineffectual noises about leaving
this godforsaken alleyway before the same—or another!—
drunken cutpurse came upon them. He attempted to draw
the two ladies away from the unsightly, unthinkable scene.
He tried more forceful tactics as his agitation grew. He
announced his intention of leaving the alleyway, immediately, with or without the ladies, as much as committing

such a gross discourtesy would go against his grain. Once again, he was ignored.

"But why Eliza?" Marianna asked, curious, almost detached. "Was it for her money? Could a human life be worth so little?"

Susannah replied, distractedly, "I don't know. It does not look good."

The baron had had more than he could stand. Words had achieved no success. He took bodily hold of Susannah, who was standing next to him, causing her to drop the brick at Eliza's feet, and began to pull Susannah out of the alley. Never much of a talker, he had been reduced to mumbling, a steady stream of mumbling, a nervous, shaken, incoherent mumbling.

Marianna raised her skirts and followed, protesting and gesturing. "But just *leave*? Leave her here?" Tears were starting to spill, unchecked, from Marianna's eyes. "Like a bag of forgotten clothing?"

"We'll go straight to the constable, and let him handle it!" the baron recommended, rather forcefully, his strength returning now that they were putting distance between themselves and the body that had once housed the spirit of Eliza Parrish.

"No, wait! We'll put her in your coach, Martin," Marianna said, a little desperately. "Take her to the parish. Find the constable. We can't leave her here!"

Susannah came to the baron's aid. She said harshly, "I couldn't. I couldn't be in the carriage with her. I'm sorry to be such a coward, Marianna, but it's . . . I . . ."

Without another word, Marianna left the place with her companions. She drew her brows together. That wasn't like Susannah to display her nerves. Even when Susannah had told Marianna of the husband she believed to be in London, she had been remarkably composed. But not now.

The three very sober companions made their way around the next corner, where the baron's coach had been called to await them. They fell in unison upon the unpaid constable of the parish, who was an able-bodied man and happened, this night, to be perambulating the streets in company with that posse of paid officials known as the watch, lanterns and staffs in hand.

The rather onerous and unpleasant matter of the female body in the alleyway was taken care of neatly, surgically.

The death of Eliza Parrish was immediately ruled an accident, of course. The constable had seen it dozens of times. The word *cutpurse* was uttered. The constable dismissed it with an airy wave of his hand. His gesture swept the burly men of the watch. Hadn't had a robbery in Cheapside the whole summer long! No! It was drunken women—gamblers all of them! Better off dead!—were always falling and hitting their heads. It was the shoes they wore! There would be paperwork. The grim business of the letter to the next of kin, the undertaker and death certificate, the notice to the *Times*. The constable would attend to all of that. The accident had occurred in his parish, after all. The Baron Childe, who had miraculously emerged as the spokesman for his party, congratulated the constable at some length on his efficiency. The constable was sure to receive a goodly sum of money in the morning mail.

The baron escorted Susannah and Marianna to his coach, and the three quit, at last, the terrible neighborhood of Cheapside, which each privately decided he or she would never visit again.

"Don't cry, my dear," the baron said to Marianna, now in full control of himself and the situation.

"I can't help it," Marianna replied, sniffing, the tears flowing again. "It's so terrible. There were times when I wished that her mouth would close, never to open again. And now it has! To see her ... in the street like that. She looked so young, so defeated, so quiet. Eliza Parrish quiet! It's not natural!" A sound, halfway between a sob and a laugh, caught in her throat.

"It was an accident," the baron reminded her with a friendly pat on her hand. "Happens all the time."

Susannah sat strangely quiet.

Nothing more was said in the somber coach as it bowled through the deserted streets in the dead of night.

When the coach pulled up at Cavendish Square, Susannah clutched Marianna's hand. Susannah's mouth was dry, her face burned as if with fever, and she shook her head as though to clear her vision. "I'm coming in with you, Marianna," she said.

Marianna nodded. The baron seemed to think this an excellent idea. It was his opinion that Susannah was suffering from the aftershock of the incident. The two ladies could comfort each other. He, for his part, intended to seek his consolation elsewhere, and without delay.

Once inside the foyer, Susannah spoke suddenly in an uncharacteristically flat voice. "If your theory of the drunken thief is true, then there should have been blood on the brick." She stared at her hand, as if she still held the brick. "A drop at least."

"What?"

"You felt the wound. Had it bled?" Susannah asked.

Marianna considered this. "Yes."

"But it did not bleed on the brick. There was no blood on that brick. I didn't realize it at the time. But in the coach, coming here, I began to understand."

Marianna came to the same horrible conclusion that Susannah had come to earlier. Eliza had not fallen and died as the result of a freak accident. Neither had she been set upon by a drunken thief who wanted her purse. She had been murdered. And for a reason.

"I think I know who killed her," Susannah said quietly. "And I myself might have provided the motive."

Marianna looked quickly down the darkened foyer. A sleepy footman drowsed in a chair. Marianna motioned Susannah wordlessly into the library. She plucked a burning candle from the candelabrum on the side table. They soundlessly entered the library, and Marianna closed the door behind her, giving only the slightest thought to the last, disastrous meeting she had had in this room with Maddox.

"Who?" Marianna asked, breathless.

Susannah shook her head. "No. It's just a guess. It can't be."

"Who? Susannah! Any guess is better than none!" Marianna cried.

When Susannah spoke, she was cool and composed. "My husband."

"But, no . . . ! You can't mean it!" Marianna replied, as a matter of course, but one look at Susannah's pale face in the candlelight confirmed to Marianna that Susannah did, in fact, mean it. The questions tumbled out all at once. "But who is he? Why should he kill her? Did he contact you, then, as you had hoped? Was he even there tonight? Did you see him?"

"No, I didn't see him. That was the curious thing. Although . . ." Susannah shook her head again. "I am imagining things!"

"Tell me, Susannah! Don't stop now!" Marianna entreated her. "You *do* know something, but don't wish to tell me!"

"It's not that I *wish* to keep something from you," Susannah replied, beginning to pace the room. "It's just that I cannot put it all together. It does not add up! I *am* sure, though, that Eliza must have guessed that he was connected to me. I doubt she knew that he was my husband. He still is . . ."

Marianna empathized with the pain she heard in Susannah's voice and said nothing. She would not prompt Susannah to say more than she could.

"I think . . . I think she must have seen me with him," Susannah continued, after a moment, "when I discovered him at Ranelagh. He is certainly distinctive enough to remember, even in the moonlight, and I know that he has a connection to *L'Abeille*. That much I overheard in the gardens." She laughed a little. "With that phony count, Mersenne."

"Mersenne?" Marianna echoed, surprised.

"What of it?" Susannah shrugged, uninterested in Mersenne's role in the intrigue. "But I think Eliza must have guessed enough of my relationship to him to have been blackmailing him. For that is where she had been getting her money recently. I am sure of it! Her luck hadn't changed at the tables! She punted just as badly this evening as she ever had done! And she seemed to enjoy a rather peculiar status at the hell. Did you notice it? I could not quite put my finger on it at the time. But she must have gotten too greedy, or perhaps, when we came in this evening, she had become too careless with her knowledge of what I might have been to him. Or, perhaps, she quite simply got in his way."

Susannah stopped pacing. She remembered, with a shiver, Jean's warning to her to stay out of his way. She could not accept this thoroughly cold-blooded image of Jean. She could not accept that he could hate better than he loved. To protect her own feelings, she devised, at random, an alternative explanation for why he would murder Eliza Parrish. "Perhaps he was losing money and could no longer pay Eliza off?"

"On the contrary, the gaming hell looked very successful," Marianna noted.

"Perhaps, then, he was losing money in investments. You remember that address we went to. Vaughan? That is what he does, Mr. Vaughan, does he not? Invest?"

"Yes," Marianna replied to this, a little dryly. "He specializes in the unusual investor, if I am not mistaken! But why should your husband invest?" Marianna asked, several new ideas exciting her tired brain to sudden life. "Why should he wish to hide, or deny, his relationship to you, enough to want to pay Eliza off—or to kill her—to keep her quiet?"

"I do not wish to know the answers to those questions," Susannah said, with a tragic little smile.

Marianna understood, after a fashion, but she did very much want to know those answers. Up until this moment, she had exercised scrupulous discretion with Susannah on the subject of her husband, but now was not the time for either scruples or discretion. "But who is he, Susannah? Can you, at least, tell me his name?"

Susannah laughed without humor. "I can tell you his name," she said. "It is Jean Desmoulins. But I do not suppose that means a thing to you."

"Not a thing," Marianna agreed, and tried another tack. "But, you say he is distinctive?" she said, and her heart had already begun to beat a little queerly, anticipating the description. "Could you describe him? It is possible that I have seen him here or there."

"Jean," Susannah said, and repeated, reflectively, "Jean. How to describe him? Tall, thin, ugly might serve as a description! But he defies description. He is like no one else I have ever seen!" She wiped something from her eye. It glistened suspiciously like a tear.

"Dark and gaunt?" Marianna prompted.

Susannah nodded.

"Tense?" Marianna continued. "No, more than tense. *In*tense, rather!"

"Yes," Susannah answered, hesitantly, cautiously.

"Snapping black eyes, and so cold! So very cold!"

"That is Jean," Susannah said, "But have you seen him? Do you indeed know him? I would find that quite hard to credit!"

"I saw a man of this description in the neighborhood of Mr. Vaughan...oh, weeks ago it was, already! And, of course, now you know that he has a connection to Mr. Vaughan...But, good heavens, what on earth is he doing here?" Marianna demanded. "In England, I mean." She glanced over at Susannah. Her eyes were still bright, but her tears were under control. Marianna did not think it would be too much to probe, a little. "Do I gather that he is French? When I first heard you speak of him, it did not occur to me that he would be anything other than English ... of course, I did know that you grew up in France, but, you know, somehow..." Marianna trailed off. Her thoughts were casting wildly about in her brain, all stray bits of information she had learned over the past months coming together "... but somehow, I never added it all up. Do I suppose correctly that he is French?"

"He's French. Salt of the earth. Peasant French," Susannah admitted. She marveled that she could make the admission so easily. Her husband—a peasant. She marveled as well that Marianna seemed to have accepted it so easily.

Marianna did accept it, and now it was her turn to pace. She did not care about the birth or background of Susannah's husband, or the reasons why Susannah had married him. Or even why she apparently still loved the man. "The gambling was a blind," Marianna said, her mind completely absorbed by the puzzle at hand. "A blind for something else ... something else ... Mersenne, a phony French count. Desmoulins, a French peasant." She was suddenly very agitated. "And with a connection to 'Change? Good heavens! But are you *sure* he killed Eliza?"

The reference to the dead woman drew their eyes together in wordless camaraderie, in sadness, in fear at where the tangled threads of this puzzle would lead them.

Susannah remembered the silver medallion she held in her hand. She opened her palm and held it out for Marianna's inspection. "I found this in Eliza's hand. It belonged to Jean. I remember it well. They must have struggled, Jean and Eliza. He grabbed her. She grabbed him and caught the chain. It was a thin chain, easily broken." Susannah's voice faltered. "It's the image of a mill. Jean Desmoulins. The Miller. And I am Susanne Desmoulins, the miller's wife." She laughed a little, then, in self-deprecatory irony. "Oh, but he does not call himself that anymore. No. Desmoulins is gone. It's Chaumonot now." She gestured with the medallion in her palm. "But is this not evidence enough that the killer was Jean Desmoulins, who must have been at *L'Abeille* this very evening?"

Marianna glanced at it, frowned, then looked up at Susannah. "Chaumonot, you say?" Then, "Stanthorpe!" she cried. She was suddenly all movement, all decision, all action. "My God! Chaumonot! The bee! The box! Stanthorpe! The graveyard!" she exclaimed. "Come! We've wasted far too much time here. We have to go to Stanthorpe! Without delay!" She hurried to the door and cast a glance over her shoulder. "Are you coming?"

"But I don't understand," Susannah said, bewildered.

"I'll explain on the way. There's no time now!" Marianna answered. "*Are you coming?*"

The answer came in a heartbeat. "Yes."

By the time the word had left Susannah's mouth, Marianna was already rousing the household to carry out wild preparations for a sudden, desperately urgent flight from Town. She had shaken the sleeping footman to life with the order to have the Maddox traveling chaise brought round immediately, then flew up the stairs with Susannah in her wake, roused Rachel, who was slumbering in the chair in her antechamber, waiting to do her bidding. Rachel cracked an eye and was startled full awake by an unusually peremptory request from her ladyship to pack her bandboxes and to be quick about it.

Marianna had no patience at the moment for her customary gentleness. She harried Rachel to hurry, put her own two hands to work, hastily grabbed a comb and brush off her dressing table, withdrew a supply of whiteclothes from one of her neatly arranged drawers, and several scarves as well, for which she anticipated no use, but which simply happened to be in the drawer next to the whiteclothes. She stuffed the lot into the largest of her tapestry traveling bags that was at hand, carelessly dashed the ends of the dresses that Rachel had been meticulously folding into several portmanteaux, clamped them shut, and carried them herself to the hallways, while an alert footman had already gone to fetch one of the Maddox traveling coaches.

They stopped momentarily at Marsh House and performed the same hasty preparations for departure in under a quarter of an hour. Soon they were rumbling over the London Bridge to Downe and then into Kent. The ride would seem to Marianna interminable, her anxiety only increasing when, after an hour on the road in the deepest dead of night, Susannah began to talk, sporadically and haltingly at first, then more fluently, about her relationship with Jean. The more Marianna heard, the more she was sure that she was on the right path, and the greater was her panic at what might be in the box in the cemetery and at what might be Maddox's stake in the whole affair. Still, Marianna did not want to expose Maddox's interested to Susannah, and it cost Marianna something to hold her tongue. She reasoned that her desire to protect Maddox would be as strong as Susannah's desire to protect Jean.

After four or more hours, the sun peeked over the horizon. Soon thereafter the familiar, rocky Kentish terrain came into view, and instead of comforting Marianna, as it should have done, the sight only increased her anxiety. They were coming ever closer to the mysterious box and the revelation of its contents, but the coach just did not seem to be going fast enough.

Another hour passed before Stanthorpe village proper appeared on the horizon. The old Norman church, where her brother presided, stood at the northern end of the road, like a benevolent godfather, with the vicarage behind it. From the church the houses ran down either side, half-timbered cottages, many of them with overhanging upper stories, and thatched with heather or with straw that had been golden when new, then had turned slowly to a rich brown, and now was emerald green with moss and lichen and shining, jewel-like in the brilliance of an early July dawn. Tiny dormer windows looked out, wreathed with honeysuckle and ivy. Thick untrimmed hedges fenced the houses off from the road, and there were small wooden gates, some of them spanned by arches of climbing roses. Above the hedges could be seen the confusion of blooming flowers, delphinium mostly, purple and pink and white, hollyhocks that reached almost to the eaves, an apple or plum or cherry tree, ripening regally in the full of summer.

It was Stanthorpe, a village Marianna knew well, but so very different from when she had seen it last in February; yet she hardly noticed the beauty of the village in summer, and did not give a thought to this, her first homecoming. All her thoughts were transported over the knoll just beyond the green at the far end of the road, where lay the cemetery.

Before they reached the end of the road and the knoll, the carriage turned off the main road, and soon they were jolting over the rutted drive to Maddox Hall. They passed the meadows, which were thick with clover and campion. They crossed the creek on the sturdy old bridge and passed the large kitchen gardens, where the cabbages and other vegetables grew, and then, at last, they came to an extremely uncomfortable halt in front of the stone-terraced entrance to the old Hall.

Marianna realized that she had never come to the Hall any way other than on foot. She had also not entered it since her marriage. She stepped out of the carriage, beckoning for Susannah to follow, looked down at her crumpled finery, which had suffered greatly in the past six hours, then cast her eye over the Hall: there was the old stone frontage over which ivy vines rambled helter-skelter, the roof a jumble of chimneys, each also muffled in ivy, the roof steep and of slate, the old-fashioned windows and the eaves at improbable angles, the brick-paved courtyard, the whole suggesting a house full of character and an active, useful life during many generations.

She trod the stately, crumbling stone steps and was met by Lord Edward's senescent butler, Reynauld, who stood at the front door, awaiting her, as if he had known all along she was to arrive at just that very moment.

The days and weeks and months rolled back for Marianna, and she could almost imagine that she was an unmarried young woman, come to call on Lord Edward, with not a crack in her heart.

Reynauld's opening remarks were to dispel that happy illusion instantly.

"Reynauld!" she said, gladly.

"Miss Marianna," he replied, equally glad, then recalled himself. "That is, *your ladyship* now, Miss Marianna! Why, and here you arrive on the very heels of the agents! We've a full house now. And pleased I am! But here I am forgetting myself, and not greeting you proper as befits your first visit to your new home, but you'll forgive me if I don't think of it as your new home, for ever since I've known you, all these many years, I've thought of you as a part of Maddox Hall!"

Marianna uttered but one word in response to these remarks. "Agents?"

"Yes, miss! That is, your ladyship, miss! Government agents. Come within the week of your marriage, don't you know, so that they could be here to do his lordship's work. The new lordship, that is! And what a fine man he is, too, and I should be congratulating you on your marriage! Which I did, I am sure, on the day of your nuptials. A wise man, his lordship. The new one! To have chosen you! I'm sure his lordship—the late one!—Lord Edward, my master, would have been happy to see it."

Marianna smiled a little sadly at that.

"But, in any case," Reynauld continued his narrative, "the agents have been here on and off since, oh, February or thereabouts, seeing as how Maddox Hall provides such a perfect spot for our government to keep on track of the activities on the coast. Clandestine activities, as I am sure I do not need to tell you! Oh, yes, Maddox Hall is excellently located for that! They nabbed, er, apprehended a Frenchie or two in the past months, but still don't have the big one, so I've been told. Oh, wonderful times we have been having! His lordship—the new one!—coming down here from time to time! I know for a fact that he's been mortal pleased with its strategic position and so he said, not more than a week or two ago when he was down here last!"

So now Marianna knew, at last, why Maddox had refused to forgo his inheritance, why he had obeyed Lord Edward's condition on the will, so that he would not lose Maddox Hall. She was not going to dwell on her own pain, but wished instead to make haste to the graveyard; and she wanted no help from the agents that Maddox had planted there.

Marianna presented Lady Marsh to Reynauld, briefly directed the placement of the little baggage that accompanied them, and then excused herself and Susannah rather abruptly from Reynauld's kindly, but garrulous, presence, and without yet stopping to change their fine feathers, Marianna showed Susannah the way behind the house that led to the path toward the cemetery.

Just before they began to make their way down the bramble-tangled path that Marianna knew so well, she remembered to go back for a shovel. She quickly ran across the back lawn to the garden shed, built of soft red brick and showing the aged silvery-gray oaken timbers of its frame, and hauled open the door on creaky hinges. She emerged a moment later with two shovels in hand and handed one to Susannah.

Marianna and Susannah plunged down the path, Marianna wishing to uncover the box to aid Maddox's cause, Susannah wishing to protect Jean from doing his worst.

XXIII

Chaumonot

Several hours after Marianna had flown London, Maddox strode into his house on Cavendish Square, tired and irritated. He had spent his evening and most of the night in a futile search for his wife, visiting an endless and very boring round of parties, only one of which she had actually attended, and had left, early on. He had learned that she had left the party in company with Lady Marsh and the Baron Childe, but it was not known where the threesome had gone.

Nor had Maddox learned their final destination. Periodic returns to his home had yielded the information that, wherever else she might have been in London that evening, she was not at Cavendish Square.

This time his return was different. Before he had even crossed the tiled foyer halfway, his butler greeted him with the alarming news that her ladyship had returned to the house only to have left again, having ordered the traveling chaise brought round.

Maddox's first thought was: *I'm too late! She's left me!* He snapped, "When was that?"

"An hour or more ago, my lord," Steward replied.

"And then she went out again, after ordering the traveling chaise?"

"So it was, my lord."

"And did you tell her that I had been scouring all of London looking for her?" Maddox demanded.

"Well, as to that, my lord, I did not quite have the opportunity."

"No, and why not? Just where did her ladyship go?"

"I don't know, my lord," came the nervous reply.

"*You don't know?*" Maddox expostulated. "Where were you, man, when your ladyship returned and ordered the chaise?"

Steward coughed delicately into his fist. "I was in the nether regions, my lord, playing cards and bending the elbow with Kennelly . . . as is my custom in the evenings when your lordship is out very late! As it was, I knew that you had been coming in and out the night long, to see if her ladyship had returned. And it was apparently just after your *last* return that her ladyship came home . . . you could not have missed by more than a quarter of an hour! . . . but she came in and out so fast that I had no time to learn that she had even come home, much less left again, if it had not been that Jem—the stablehand, who often sits in with us for a round or two, himself, on occasion—had come in a little later with the strange account of her ladyship asking for the traveling chaise in the middle of the night! Well, I can tell you that I was never so surprised! So, I did my duty and went to find her ladyship's Rachel immediately . . . as I am sure you would have wanted me to do . . . and she told a wild tale, as well, about cramming bandboxes with dresses and such like! Not to mention traveling off in all her silks and ribbons, and seemingly in the company of Lady Marsh, who (so I am told) was seen climbing into the chaise."

"Lady Marsh?" Maddox repeated, frowning, many more questions forming on his lips; but since it was obvious that he would get nothing more out of Steward and since, at no time was Maddox ever a man to waste words, he did not bother with asking the obvious questions. Instead, he delivered himself of a rather pungent critique of Steward's ability to execute his duties this evening (which invective had only a momentary satisfying effect). Then, after desiring Steward to have his horse brought around immediately—that is (with heavy irony) *if* Steward felt he were equal to carrying out this simple command!—Maddox strode swiftly the rest of the way down the hall. He entered his library and began, absently, to go through the various sheaves of paper littering his desk, as if they might in some obscure way reveal to him Marianna's destination.

The possibility that she had gone to Stanthorpe and the vicarage and her family loomed large. He would have taken off immediately for the coast, except for the fact that Lady Marsh's presence in his wife's flight did not, somehow, point to the idea that she was desirous of returning to her brother's fold.

Hardly had he riffled through one stack of papers when the front doorbell sounded, announcing yet another late-night visitor to Maddox House. Cavendish Square had never before seen such activity at this extraordinary hour of the night, and this latest arrival was coming with still more alarming news.

Maddox dropped his useless task. Hoping to find either his wife returned or someone who had news of her, he exited, full tilt, from his library and practically ran the new arrival down. It took Maddox a moment, in the dimly lit foyer, to recognize the face of the hapless Jeremy Wilton, and he would have dismissed the lad out of hand as an unnecessary annoyance at the moment, if it had not been that, in the next moment, Maddox perceived the extreme anxiety on young Jeremey's face.

Maddox felt a stab of cold fear pierce his breast, expecting now the worst of bad news.

Jeremy had indeed come with bad news, but it had nothing to do (so anyone in his right mind would have known) with Lady Westleigh. Wilton babbled out a story about the gambling hells in London, the French, the—

"Are you telling me anything I don't know?" Maddox interrupted peremptorily.

The irony was lost on Jeremy, and the fierceness of Maddox's tone caused him to jump back involuntarily. "You already know about what happened tonight, then?"

Maddox grabbed the poor boy's lapels and raised him an inch off the ground. "My God, what incompetence I have had to live with this night! If it does not end soon, I'll be ripe for murder! Where *is* she?"

Understandably shaken, Jeremy was rattled from his already precarious composure. "Sh-she, my lord? Sh-she? I-I don't know!" he stammered. But then he mastered his tongue enough to pour out the story that he had been sent to deliver. The essence of it was that the government man trailing Chaumonot had suddenly lost the Frenchman's scent.

Curiously (to Jeremy's mind) this very bad news had a calming effect on Maddox.

Maddox released Jeremy's coat, and commented, rather dispassionately, "And after all the trouble we had tracking him down in the first place? After all the work we did at Marlborough Park? Do you mean to tell me that Mersenne has slipped his jail cell as well?"

"Oh, no," Jeremy was happy to report. "He's locked up tight as a trivet but won't talk. Hasn't yet, at any rate! Not that he won't—eventually! Now, Vaughan hasn't been taken into custody, as you know, since we have nothing definite to charge him with, but"—he broke off hastily, seeing the fierce glower on his master's face—"you'll already be knowing all about that! And if I am talking too much, it is only because I am nervous! No, it's only Chaumonot that's slipped the trail. He was last seen this evening at *L'Abe* . . . *L'Abaya* . . . dash it! at 'The Bee'!—just where we all expected him to be, 'The Bee' being his favorite haunt of the past weeks . . . and although the agent who was

assigned to him had thought that when Chaumonot slipped
out the back door at one point, late on in the evening, he
would return . . . well! Chaumonot never came back! Reports were made to our office not an hour ago of a horseman riding furiously across Blackfriars Bridge—going
south, of course!—and paying no toll. Whether it was
Chaumonot or not is anybody's guess, since he had no
apparent reason for leaving 'The Bee' like that! They were
having one of their most successful evenings to date! Well
attended, many of the best names . . . oh, yes, that reminds
me, I think that I was told that Lady Westleigh was there
tonight, too! And she was with a woman named Marsh, I
think it was, who was also at Marlborough Park (but I
didn't meet her), and they were escorted by—"

Maddox did not remain to hear the rest of the sentence.
Nor did he thank Wilton for the valuable information. Not
many minutes later, a broad-shouldered horseman was
thundering across Blackfriars Bridge, also heading south,
straight for Stanthorpe, and also paying no toll.

Maddox rode the night through, changing horses only
once, ever gaining on the first rider who crossed Blackfriars Bridge, who was, in his turn (had he but known it)
following the Maddox coach, which had left London before either rider. Hours later, and stained with travel dust
and dirt, Maddox entered the village of Stanthorpe. He
stampeded down the carriage path to the vicarage, hoping
against hope that she had sought refuge there, never thinking that she would go to the Hall, and unable to determine
what, if anything, Susannah Marsh could possibly have to
do with his wife's flight.

Unaware of the riders on their way to Stanthorpe, Marianna and Susannah were, in fact, just then wending their
way down the path that led from the back of Maddox Hall
to the cemetery at the edge of the village. Shovels in hand,
they spoke little, bending often under the snarl of branches
that grasped and tore what little elegance was left to their

evening finery and disheveled further their once-elegant coiffures.

Marianna was understandably tired after having lost a night's sleep, but the fresh and familiar tang of the sea air revived her, as did the undeniable curiosity and excitement and presentiment of danger she felt ever more strongly the closer she came to Lord Edward's grave. At last, they emerged onto the placid clearing that was the cemetery. The gentle mounds and gravestones seemed to swim indistinctly in the morning ether. It was too early for the sun to have poured out its gold to part the Channel mists and to send them back to sea, and so wispy white tatters, the ghosts of the night, still trailed aimlessly among the headstones and swirled around their ankles and up around their skirts.

"Over there," Marianna said to Susannah, nodding toward the far side of the cemetery. Her throat was dry, her voice hardly above a whisper. "Your husband buried the box right at the foot of Lord Edward's grave, as I've said. It's over there, just before the row of thornbushes that marks the village limits. See there? And behind the bushes is a path that branches off one way to the sea and the other to my brother's vicarage. After we've dug up the box, we'll take it to his house and decide what to do with it, once we know what it contains. We can't risk the government agents breathing down our necks if we return to Maddox Hall. And I have no intention," she said, looking about over her shoulders at the eerie setting, "of examining the box here. In any case, I believe it is padlocked, but I do know where my brother keeps his saw. Follow me."

Since they had agreed on their course of action hours ago, Susannah merely nodded mutely to these remarks. She was satisfied that Marianna would not expose Jean unless it was unavoidable.

They lifted their skirts and hurried to Lord Edward's grave. Marianna paused a moment to look for signs of digging but saw only seamless grass over unbroken ground.

She doubted her memory for the space of a heartbeat, then shook her head clear of its sluggishness.

"We're in luck!" she breathed. "There's not a blade of grass out of place. It means that no one has been back since the winter to dig up the box. The crazy thought hit me, just now, that perhaps I had imagined the whole!" Then she began, without further discussion, to dig.

Susannah pitched her shovel into the summer earth as well, and began to turn the previously unturned ground. They exchanged no conversation. Marianna was desperately hoping to uncover the box before the day advanced any further. She knew that soon the Stanthorpe folk would be up and about, using all the pathways in and around the village, and that the only protection she and Susannah had against the eyes of any chance passerby was the thickly foliated but rather low row of thornbushes.

After she had spent a good twenty minutes or more of digging, Marianna's spirits began to flag. Apparently the box had been buried deeper than she had realized. Or perhaps it was no longer there. She paused to uncramp the muscles in her back and arms and shook her head in an unconscious gesture of lost hope. "And to think that we have to put back all of this heavy dirt, even if we don't find anything!" she said, wearily.

For a response, Susannah's shovel struck the ground with a decisive *chink*, the sound of metal hitting metal.

Marianna and Susannah regarded one another with widened eyes, faces lit with discovery. Marianna's shovel eagerly joined once again with Susannah's in pitching the damp, loamy earth away, to expose to view ever more of the tarnished gleam of the top of the buried strongbox.

Then Marianna knelt down, in her excitement, to scrape the dirt away with her hands, and the next thing she heard were the deathly cold words, "That will be enough."

Then she perceived, all at once, that Susannah had ceased digging and stood, frozen, beside her and that the unearthly voice belonged to a tall, gaunt, stark, forbidding

form that had materialized from behind a nearby grave-
stone.

As Marianna rose, slowly, to her feet, the tall, gaunt
man came forward, and by the time Marianna was fully
upright she had come face to face with the barrel end of a
very long pistol. It was held by a man known by the British
Foreign Office as the most dangerous and ruthless of the
French revolutionaries, but she hardly needed to be told
that for her to understand that her life was in grave danger.

Marianna's heart was in her throat. She forced herself to
look her fate straight in the eye. The depth of the cold she
read there made her life flash before her. *Her life was an
open book. The end was predictable from the beginning. A
pattern in the carpet. A box buried in the earth. To think
that her last exchange with Maddox could have led her,
indirectly, to this. Worse! To think that she and Maddox
might have to part, forever, on such awful terms. Should
she have guessed—could she have guessed—that she
would now have to trade the knowledge of the contents of
the box for her life?* For she was determined, at least, to
win that knowledge before her life was over.

The next moment, Chaumonot had done surveying the
two women in their ragged finery. He did nothing more to
register his wife's presence than to flick Susannah with his
eyes. He gestured at Marianna with the pistol.

"And you," he said. "Who are you?"

Marianna felt suffocated. She fought for breath. "Marianna," she choked. "Lowth."

Chaumonot did not seem satisfied with her response. He
tried out, awkwardly, spitting with distaste, the foreign
name on his tongue. He shook his head. "I don't think that
is your name."

"Marianna Lowth," she repeated, "from Stanthorpe."
She waved her hand in the direction of the thornbushes.
"I'm the vicar's sister, the Reverend Jonathan Lowth's sis-
ter."

Chaumonot's black eyes narrowed. He recognized her

now. She had been wearing a mask the night before at *L'Abeille* when he had spied her, through the peephole in the wall, in company with his wife and another man. "A country vicar's sister at a London gambling hell?"

Marianna saw no use to deny it. She glanced at Susannah, whose beautiful face was rigid with pain. "I was there, and my name is Lowth," Marianna insisted. She held to a faint hope that she and Susannah would leave the cemetery alive, but in order to do so, she knew she had to hide her married name. To have the name Westleigh uttered could prove fatal.

"And here?" he demanded. "What are you doing here?" With the menacing pistol, he indicated their shovels and the deep hole next to Lord Edward's grave. The top of the box was just discernible, keeping alive Marianna's curiosity and her will to live.

"You can see what we are doing," Marianna said boldly. "We're digging up the box you buried in February." She paused to lick dry lips. "My name is Lowth and I'm from Stanthorpe, as I've said. I saw you bury it all those months ago."

"I don't believe you," he stated flatly.

"How else could I have known it was here?"

Marianna could see that Chaumonot was calculating the response to her question. He would not dispose of her, or Susannah, until he had the answers he sought. She had told him only the truth, and yet it seemed that the truth had bought her some time to think, to act.

It had given Susannah time, as well. She emerged from her speechless immobility, a dead woman come back, momentarily, to life. "You killed Eliza Parrish, didn't you?" she asked, her voice low and husky.

Chaumonot transferred his wintry gaze to his wife, who flinched at what she saw. He was not desirable; but it was not remembered nor renewed desire that had held her prisoner to her memories these past few weeks, alone behind curtained windows, sometimes sobbing and sometimes

stretched out immobile for hours on end with dry eyes, and
sometimes cursing him in the peasant French she thought
she had forgotten. It was not a reawakened limitless love
that had brought her to the cemetery. It was nothing good
and hopeful that fueled her wish to protect Jean from himself. Her girlish passion for life and love and Jean was
over. The feelings of Susannah the woman went deeper
than desire. She felt fury and fear and anger and humiliation and blind commitment. She was bound by a naked
attachment to the man standing before her, a love stripped
of the trappings, a tie as naked and ugly as her husband's
face.

"I killed her," Chaumonot admitted with a chilling pleasure. "Stupid woman." His lips twisted into an inhuman
smile. "Does it matter?"

But why—for God's sake—*why?*" Susannah did not
ask that question. In any case, it had nothing to do with
Eliza. The real questions were, rather: *Why did you leave
me? Why was my love not enough for you? Why am I
bound to you?*

"No," Susannah said slowly. "It does not matter." Then,
quickly, "Do you need money? Jean, I have money. More
money than we'll ever need for the two of us." She
begged, pitifully. "Quit what you are doing. Come away
with me. We can go abroad. Live quietly. Away from all
this."

"You don't see, do you?" Chaumonot replied to these
pleas. They were speaking French now.

"I've always loved you, Jean."

"Still?"

"I haven't stopped." Susannah raised her hand toward
him in an unconscious, imploring gesture. "It isn't love as
I used to understand it, or as you might understand it now.
There is still something for us in this world."

Chaumonot shook his head. "That was over years ago,
ma chère. Over and done with. The day I left you. Before."

The words took a moment to sink in. "Did my mother pay you off?" she asked.

"Handsomely."

"She died a year later."

"May she roast in hell," Chaumonot answered.

"I have more money," she offered, again.

"I know just how much you have. It is not enough."

"It is enough. I know it is!"

"Not for the Cause."

"For us, then! For us! *I love you!*"

She thought she saw, with a little wild hope, one brief second of hesitation on his part. His next words indicated how profoundly she was mistaken.

"I made my decision years ago. We're through. You do not understand. You are a stupid woman, too," he remarked brutally.

Susannah dropped her hand. "To be dealt the same fate as Eliza Parrish?" she asked, hollowly. She was crying now, but it was not out of fear. He had been capable of murdering Eliza. She knew now he was capable of murdering her and Marianna as well, to achieve whatever ends he thought necessary. She took a step toward him. She had one weapon left. She would use it, flaunt it. "Not with a gun, Jean," she said, through her tears, taking another step toward him. He was ugly, and he drew her. She was beautiful. Even in her torn dress and hair, her beauty could still rouse him, bring the taste of blood to his lips.

"You did not use a gun on Eliza," Susannah continued, still moving toward him. She stopped only when the metal barrel of the pistol was against her heart. She looked into the cold abyss of her husband's eyes. Her voice was low and suggestive. "You did not shoot Eliza. You put your hands around her neck and you choked her. I saw the bruises. They were faint. Too faint for your strength. So, perhaps she struggled and got away from you, momentarily. You came after her. You lunged at her. You fell against her. And she fell against a hard object. The blow killed

her." Susannah shook her head. "Not a gun. Don't kill me
with a gun, Jean. Should you not sting me like a bee? The
bee that is your trademark?"

Watching this extraordinary scene, Marianna did not
fully understand the words they were saying, but she intuited the depth of Susannah's passion for the man who
held her life in his inhuman hands. Then, out of the corner
of her eye, Marianna saw a figure move. She dared not
look in that direction, fearing even the slightest movement
on her part might draw Chaumonot's attention, which was
focused now on Susannah. She held her breath, hoping that
Chaumonot had not also perceived the figure.

He had not. "I was wrong," he said with a cold appreciation of her tactics. "You are not as stupid as the little
Parrish."

"But you wish to kill me, do you not?" Susannah
goaded. "Kill me, if you will, Jean, but leave Marianna
out. She has nothing to do with this."

"I spare no one," was his answer.

Susannah would taunt him. "You can have only one of
us. Take me, Jean. Spare Marianna. You are a bee, Jean,
are you not? Will you not sting me?"

Susannah was pushing him to his limit. She was hoping,
if Jean chose to pull the trigger and she should die, that at
least Marianna would have a chance. Marianna could use
the shovel as her weapon against Jean and, possibly, save
herself.

Marianna had indeed thought of the shovel at hand, but
she thought of it more as a way of saving Susannah. Still,
Marianna hesitated to use it now, for with the pistol pressed
at Susannah's heart, Marianna did not wish to provoke
Chaumonot into firing. Out of the periphery of her vision,
Marianna saw that figure move again. This time, it came
closer.

"Well, Jean?" Susannah challenged coolly through her
tears.

The split-second moment of truth had come. Chaumonot moved his thumb, fractionally, to the trigger. Then, the name *Chaumonot!* rang out from across the cemetery at the instant a shot was delivered from the same direction. Chaumonot was distracted momentarily and a lightning-swift, dead-accurate bullet hit his pistol at the moment of his release. Chaumonot's pistol spun out of his hand, and its bullet went awry, missing Susannah, to find a different victim.

XXIV

The Box Unlatched

"*O*h, God, no!*" Susannah cried out as she bent down to gather into her arms Marianna's crumpled form.

Not fifty feet away now, and running forward, Maddox fired again. Chaumonot, on the run now himself in the opposite direction, did not falter in his steps. Before Maddox's third shot had been delivered, Chaumonot had ducked behind the thornbushes and quickly disappeared down a path that would lead him, most probably, to a private harbor, and then out across the Channel, beyond the arm of the English law.

Maddox did not pursue the man; and if Maddox's usual cool aim had been off, it was because his heart, just then, was very much ruling his head. He had thrust aside all thoughts of avenging the death of Robert Armitage, of stopping the blackguard Chaumonot dead in his tracks. Maddox had ceased to care about Chaumonot. As he swiftly crossed the cemetery to where Marianna lay, so still it seemed, in Susannah's arms, he did not even reason (as he would have done in less emotional circumstances) that his personal pursuit of Chaumonot was most probably superfluous. So many English agents were dotting the fields and fells of the coastline, on the alert to stop any man who answered to Chaumonot's physical description, that they would do a better job catching the man than Maddox.

A moment later, Maddox was at his wife's side and had knelt down and scooped her into his arms. His initial heart-stopping fear was quickly allayed when Marianna turned limpid blue eyes to his ashen face and said, in a perfectly normal voice, "It's a flesh scrape only, and it's already beginning to clot."

Maddox had no words to respond adequately to that. He simply proceeded to take out his handkerchief and began to examine Marianna's wound.

Marianna struggled into a seated position, with Susannah and Maddox kneeling on either side of her. She surveyed her shoulder, which Chaumonot's bullet had merely grazed. Her already ravaged evening gown was now further tattered by the bullet and spattered with flecks of blood and a ring of black powder, since Chaumonot's pistol had gone off at such close range.

"I look far worse than I feel," she said, with a touch of fugitive humor, "and I'm in no danger. You need not stay with me," she reassured her husband. Then, with conviction, "Go, do what you have to do."

As if in answer to this, a volley of pistol shots rang out from the distant thicket of trees and resounded for a long moment. This eruption was followed by an echoing, sickening silence.

"The agents," Maddox commented briefly. "It is good." With grim satisfaction, he dabbed and pressed at Marianna's shoulder.

Susannah stood up then, slowly, her face drained of color. The savage pistol reports could mean only one thing. "No," she breathed. "It can't be. *Non! C'est Jean!*" Then she began to run, lifting her grass- and dirt-stained skirts high over her ankles, tripping over little clumps of earth that nipped and tore at the heels of her dainty evening shoes, but never falling, running straight into the woods, not bothering to find a path, running blindly through brambles and vines and low branches, arriving, as if by instinct, at the very spot she was praying not to discover.

Government agents had been swarming the woods. At the sound of the volley, they, too, had begun to converge on the spot. Susannah stumbled into the little knot of men that circled a long, extremely thin body sprawled across the earthen floor.

"It's Chaumonot," one man was explaining to another, who had just joined the group before Susannah. "He's the one that the Foreign Office has been wanting for months. Westleigh alerted them to him. Of course, it was only since last night that the case broke wide open. You see—" he broke off. "My lady!" he said, aghast.

Susannah had crossed to the side of the dead man and had knelt down into the soft, early morning earth to take his head in her hands. She explained, looking up, fastening her eyes on the man who seemed to be in authority, "His name was not Chaumonot." Her eyes were very large and dazed. She was shaking her head. "Chaumonot, I do not know who that is. This man, here, he was Jean Desmoulins. A miller from Anjou. He was my husband."

No one spoke.

After a moment the man in authority began gently, "My lady—"

"Susannah Marsh," she interrupted. "I am Susannah Marsh, or Desmoulins, if you prefer. I have come to Stanthorpe with Lady Westleigh. You will know where to find me. I simply want . . . that is, when . . . when your arrangements have been completed . . . I wish to claim the . . . I am the one who should make the . . . that is, I wish to bury . . . the . . . the. . . ."

She dropped her head into her hands, then flung her arms across the body. The word *Jean!* was ripped from her. It was a painful, pitiful sound. The man in authority bent over her bowed figure and coaxed gently, "My lady, my dearest Lady Marsh, please come away."

It was an ugly, despairing scene, beheld by the circle of men, a scene wherein a human spirit had snapped and broken, a scene that should have had no witnesses.

The man in authority understood this. He raised the weeping woman bodily and then, half lifting her into his arms, supporting her, he said to the staring men, "Let's get her out of here." He nodded down at the slack body on the ground. "Him, too."

The men obeyed. Susannah was taken back, on foot, as much as she was able to walk, to Maddox Hall. She had stopped crying. She was cold and still, a woman who had died, but who would, shortly, return to painful life.

Every now and then she spoke her thoughts at random. "I always loved him," she said to the man. "I tried to make him take me back. He would not have me." And, after a while, "He did not want me. My mother paid him off." Later, "I knew what he was capable of. I must have guessed what he intended. He killed Eliza. He could have killed Marianna. I could forgive him Eliza. I could never have forgiven him for Marianna." She laughed a ghostly laugh. "Is that not terrible of me, to pass such a judgment? But he didn't kill Marianna. He was capable of it, of course. He was even capable of killing me." She paused and laughed again. This time it was a particularly chilling sound. "He did kill me. I could have stopped him. I could have informed the authorities weeks ago."

The kind, concerned voice of the man holding her arm penetrated these musings. "Please, my lady, say no more. We will not hold you responsible for Chau—your husband's activities. But please, say no more."

Susannah said no more. She had begun to cry again.

On the other side of the woods, in the far corner of the cemetery in the shadow of Lord Edward's headstone, Maddox finished ministering to his wife's wound. Marianna insisted on standing up. She had overestimated her strength, however, and so wobbled slightly before sinking into Maddox's arms. The curtain of tension that had fallen between them at their last meeting had understandably vanished in the anxiety of the last minutes.

Maddox cherished the woman in his arms, but instead of kissing her, he opened his mouth to voice strong protest and even stronger relief, which he intended to take the form of a severe scolding and a hot demand for an explanation of the circumstances that had brought her to the Stanthorpe cemetery at this hour, to look down the barrel of Chaumonot's gun.

Before he had a chance to launch this invective, Marianna shook her head vigorously and pushed away from him. "I'll explain everything later," she said, finding her balance on her own two feet. "For now, it's the box. We must find out what is in that box."

A man of action, Maddox wasted no further words. He had indeed noticed the hole that had been dug next to his uncle's grave, and the two of them set about the task of unearthing the box, whose top was just barely visible.

The next moment he was transported back into anger. "You've just been shot! Put that shovel down, Marianna!" he commanded hotly.

"I am perfectly all right, Maddox, as you yourself know," Marianna retorted. "And if I sit idly by at this moment, my health will be far worse off than it is now, for I shall suffer a stroke from frustration!"

Maddox desisted. Not a minute later, with Maddox's strong arms committed to the unearthing, the box was fully exposed. Maddox stepped back, putting Marianna behind him, and aimed his pistol at the heavy chains encircling the box. His bullet winged the padlock, which jumped off the box and left the chains sagging.

Maddox flipped the top of the box open. It was crammed with papers. Frowning, he plunged his hand into the box and drew out a thick handful of papers. Marianna did the same. Each separate sheet was printed and sealed with the bold red wax stamp of the *Banque Royale*. At a glance, Marianna grasped the fact that she was holding French stock actions, but the full implication of what she held in her hands would still take a minute or two to sink in.

In wordless wonder, Maddox and Marianna paged through sheet after sheet: *Actions des Indes, 500 livres d'or. Billet d'emprunt, 1000 livres d'or. Loteries royales, 10,000 francs. Les emprunts, 100 louis, 500 louis, 1000 louis. Les lots viagers, 100, 10,000, 100,000 louis. Les Caisses d'escompte. Les Eaux de Paris*. The variety of actions and their denominations seemed endless; and they were all signed by the Royal Minister of Finance, Banque Royale, Hôtel de Soisson, Paris, and fully insured in the name of His Majesty Louis XVI des Bourbons, King of France.

At last Maddox lifted his eyes from the papers and looked across at Marianna. The moment had a terrifying alchemy.

"It could have been disaster," Maddox said harshly, perceiving the enormity of what they were holding. "A disaster."

"These papers," she said, gesturing with her hand, "these stocks and bonds. Do I assume correctly that Chaumonot intended to sell them to Mr. Vaughan? So that Vaughan could flood 'Change with them?"

"You do," Maddox replied, his voice still harsh.

"My God, there must be thousands of pounds' worth of trade involved here."

"Hundreds of thousands of pounds," Maddox corrected.

"I'm not sure I understand. Are they forgeries? Counterfeit?" Marianna asked, laboring through the implications of this extraordinary discovery.

"No, I've seen enough of them to know that they're real enough," Maddox said. "But they're not worth a French *sou* if the Banque Royale has no funds to honor them."

"You mean, if Louis is unable to hold on to his throne,"

Marianna said to this. She paused, then enlightenment came. "So that's what Mersenne meant! All those rumors flying about Louis regaining some of his lost power were simply that—rumors! Rumors for the consumption of the English buying public intended to promote a belief in the stability of the French government. But I doubt now whether Louis's position is as good as the rumors have portrayed it!"

"I am now convinced, by what I hold in my hand," Maddox said, "that Louis is doomed. This plan of flooding 'Change with worthless stock must have been predicated on Louis's demise."

Marianna thought this through. "Chaumonot was going to finance the French Revolution with English money. Not bad. It was a clever plan."

"A brilliant plan," Maddox conceded, "since it included the destruction of the English economy as well—or at least the end of Continental confidence in English banks, which would surely have had to finance a mountain of bad debt."

"But foiled, thank God," Marianna replied.

"Yes," Maddox said, his accents very harsh indeed now. "A true disaster has been averted. This may well be the turning point."

Thoughts of the potential ruin of the English economy crowded in on Marianna. Then, suddenly, "You can't think that I was in any way involved with Vaughan in this scheme!" she cried, aghast when it dawned on her what he might infer from the discovery of these papers, her involvement with Vaughan a mere three days previous, and her unlikely presence here at the cemetery in Stanthorpe.

"I don't," he answered, his harsh tones somewhat softened but still angry. She could not guess that his anger was focused inward, toward himself, toward their estrangement that might well have led to her death.

He wanted to say more, for there was still so much to resolve between them, but several government agents had heard the shot Maddox had fired to release the padlock, and they had come running to the cemetery in some alarm. They burst out from behind the thornbushes, brandishing their pistols.

"Lord Westleigh! Your lordship!" they exclaimed in unison, panting with exertion, half surprised, half relieved to see his lordship squatting on the ground with papers in his hand.

"We heard gunfire!" one said, "We thought that Chaumonot might have brought others!"

Maddox quickly reassured them that all was well. Then, the terse question, "Chaumonot?"

"Dead."

"And Lady Marsh?" Marianna asked, anxiously.

One man looked down at his boots. Another paled visibly at the memory of the embarrassing scene. "Adams took her ladyship to Maddox Hall," the first one said. "We were accompanying them there, in fact, and she was saying how she knew this Chaumonot fellow and that his name wasn't Chaumonot at all, but something else, and she also said ... Well! It was very strange! And then, on the way to the Hall, she was rambling a little, I think, and crying, too, and Adams told her not to talk, which I think was a very good idea, and then we heard the shot from the cemetery and came running! But just before we left them, I remember Lady Marsh saying how very tired she was. Very tired."

Marianna rose from the ground and gingerly placed the hateful papers back into the box. She shook out her skirts and said, anxiously, "I hope that Reynauld has had the presence of mind to give her a sedative. I think that I should go to her."

Maddox rose, as well, and would have accompanied Marianna, but he was prevented from doing so by the arrival of still more agents, who had been combing the forest and had fanned out over the coastline and into the village. Now was not the moment for Maddox to attempt a reconciliation with his wife.

Marianna quit the cemetery on the arm of one of the agents. Over her shoulder she glanced back momentarily at Maddox, who was answering myriad questions, at the gaping hole next to the grave, at the men milling about disturbing Lord Edward's slumber, all exclaiming and bending down over the heavy box lying open and exposed and as harmless as a defused bomb.

Marianna regained the Hall, where she spoke quickly and quietly with Reynauld. Oh, yes, her ladyship had been given a sleeping draft. Marianna knew the old house well and made her way to the room where Susannah had been installed. Marianna entered and moved softly, washing her hands, attempting to redress her hair. It was a futile attempt.

In the large bed Susannah was lying very still. An upstairs maid had unbound her hair and combed it, a little ineffectually, and had stripped Susannah of her tattered finery before tucking her safely into bed.

The shutters had been half closed against the sun, which had now risen to burn off the swirling mists. The window was open and the light breeze blew through the slats, warm and scented. Marianna pulled up a chair to the edge of Susannah's bed. There was a soft, light blanket at the foot. Marianna divested herself of her own ruined evening frock and wrapped herself in the blanket.

Susannah stirred and opened her eyes. "Jean left me, you know."

"Don't speak, my dear."

Nestled in the blanket, her head against the back of the chair, Marianna let the morning hours stretch into the afternoon. She was exhausted, but did not sleep. She kept her eyes on Susannah's sleeping and vulnerable face. She imagined the two figures side by side: Susannah and the man Chaumonot. The two did not fall into place. Marianna thought back on all the times she had been with the cool, golden woman, had admired her poise, her composure, her equanimity, her tireless energy, how she had hardly suspected that Susannah's face wore an easy mask hiding a dark, passionate, restless nature, a nature now spent. Marianna tried again to reconcile Susannah with Chaumonot, but failed. She did not know the secrets of Susannah's youth, what it was to have loved such a man and lost him, or, worse, what it was to have loved and lost, twice. Those secrets lay behind the closed eyes of Susannah, who was, for the next few hours, mercifully beyond their painful reach.

Two deaths, Eliza and Chaumonot. Not Chaumonot— Jean Desmoulins. Two deaths in two days. If only...

Marianna thought, If only I had not forgotten about the man who buried the box in the cemetery all those months ago, if I had not been so absorbed in my own altered life, if I had not so readily dismissed the fact that I saw the man again near Finch Lane all those weeks ago, if only I had told Maddox three nights ago why I had gone again to Finch Lane...

There was no end to it. If only I had seen the pattern in the carpet earlier, the beast in the jungle, I could have prevented these tragedies. But, no, Marianna decided, the pattern had been too big. Bigger than her own individual life, bigger than Susannah's life, bigger than Eliza's, bigger, even, than Chaumonot's. Susannah loved. Eliza gambled. Chaumonot blighted.

And Marianna...?

The sun rose higher. Marianna dozed. Later, Maddox entered the room. His entry was soundless, but Marianna awoke at his presence. She looked up at him and immediately brought to her cheek the strong hand he held out to her. He glanced down at Susannah. Marianna gave her head a tiny shake, as if to say that Susannah was for the moment—but only for the moment—beyond her grief.

Maddox drew her to the antechamber. He closed the door behind them. Her blanket had slipped from her shoulders to expose her underdress. He drew her into his arms.

"My God, Marianna, there is so much to—"

He was not given a chance to say it. Marianna murmured, "Not now," then reached up and kissed him.

He did not resist. Their instinct had to obey a signal, their passion took fire one from the other, and they returned kiss for searching kiss. When he made as if to release her, she drew his head down again and would not let him go. He abandoned himself to her kisses, but he retained enough of his senses to know that they could not stand in the antechamber to Susannah's room and finish what they had begun.

Maddox replaced the blanket around Marianna's shoulders. He nodded, wordlessly, to the hall door. In return, Marianna nodded her consent, then mouthed the words that she would not leave Susannah alone and would therefore have to find the chambermaid to attend her. Maddox accomplished this easily enough and then, his arms around Marianna, he led her down the hall and to an adjoining wing, to his personal chambers. Maddox still wanted a full explanation of Marianna's activities during the past four days, beginning with the reason for her return trip to Finch Lane.

Marianna would have none of it. She did not permit any conversation, but merely kissed him, and kissed him again. After their last, angry exchange of words, she would never have thought that she would have wanted to communicate with her husband so boldly, so bodily. She would never have thought that she would capitulate to him so easily, without first having an apology from him for the cruel words he had poured over her, or wish only that he hold and kiss and fix his body to hers. But it was not, in truth, a capitulation, and Marianna did not need to be told in so many words that Maddox bitterly regretted how he had treated her in their fight over the terms of Lord Edward's will. Marianna wished only to drown herself in her passion for her husband. She was, in fact, helpless to stem the dark, engulfing tide of her passion for him, her one will being, in those brief, precious hours, to submerge herself, to escape, if only briefly, from the demands of the precarious world that pressed ever relentlessly from without.

The sun had reached its zenith in the height of the afternoon. The demands of that precarious world had never been more real than that morning, but Maddox and Marianna were both willing, and most eager, to put those demands aside. They were not unfeeling, they were not cruel, they were merely in love. A few hours ago, a man had died by violence and a few more hours before that, a young woman. Susannah Marsh lay mercifully asleep in a chamber down the hall. Marianna herself had brushed up against death. She had not forgotten her encounter or Susannah's loss or the other tragedies, but just for the moment, happiness shook her, and she was deaf and blind to that perilous outside world, alive only to her husband in a world made for two.

Marianna discovered that happiness was a strange thing, and at times as uncontrollable as grief. She experienced a wordless joy, commensurate with Susannah's ineffable grief, and when their passion ebbed at last, and her tears of joy had dried on her cheeks, and their need had quieted, she slept, in Maddox's arms, deeply and peacefully.

XXV

Lord Edward's Library

Marianna awoke, hours later, replete and very happy. Midnight had come. She could see the black, starless stain of the sky behind the shutters. She shifted, the better to snuggle into Maddox, but found him gone.

She sat up and looked about her. The room was empty as well. She sensed immediately that something was wrong, that something amiss had drawn Maddox from her side. She pushed a heavy fall of hair from her face and stretched across the mattress to light the taper at the bedside. The sudden glow snuffed the black, but not her worry, and so she rose and, having no clothes of her own at hand, found a dressing gown of Maddox's to pull around her; and given her choice of dress, she decided that her hair could go unbound as well. She slid her feet into her ruined evening slippers of the day and night before, and if the whole of her attire was a little unconventional, at least she was in her own home now. Whoever might be up and abroad at this hour of the night could well accept the mistress of the house on her own terms.

She knew Maddox Hall well and made her way, first, to

Susannah's chambers. She knocked softly before entering, and was reassured, after penetrating the antechamber, to find that a maid was seated at Susannah's side, and that Susannah was still deeply asleep. She was assured that no turn for the worse in Susannah's condition had occurred.

Marianna glided down the stairs, across the entry and proceeded to a room at the end of the west wing, where she saw a glow of light squeezing from below a door. As she approached, she heard low, masculine voices. The door was ajar. She peeked around, unperceived by the occupants of the room. Several men whom she vaguely recognized as government agents were seated around a table, drinking, talking quietly, apparently discussing the day's events. Maddox was not among them. She drew back into the hallway.

Marianna had a sudden intuition where Maddox would be. She hastened in the opposite direction, down to the end of the east wing, to Lord Edward's library; and sure enough, when she had turned the corner that opened onto the wing, she saw candlelight spilling from the open door of her most favorite, familiar room in all of Maddox Hall. It was the library where she had spent so many hours with Lord Edward, in company with the books and the leather and the wood and the old brass, with tea and conversation and the incomparable, companionable friendship of Lord Edward. A serene room, the library, a room of magic tranquillity and contentment, where the world came to order on sheets of paper pressed between marbelized covers, where the sun could cast a soothing spell through wide, trefoil windows, or where the rain outside would leave the room wrapped in romantic ambience.

Lord Edward's room. Lord Edward. A man, once her friend, who, in recent days, had become her enemy. She would soon make her peace with him.

Marianna arrived at the open door and paused a moment before entering. Across the room stood Maddox, dressed but without his coat, staring down into the wide stone fireplace, now cold, with one hand resting on the mantelshelf, and one booted foot on the fender. He held a crisp vellum, crossed and recrossed, absently in his hand. She saw instantly that it was the delivery of this letter that had drawn Maddox from her side. She knew that its contents could not be good.

It had been her intuition, upon rising from the bed, to resolve, at last, the thick knot of problems that still lay between them; but seeing her husband standing there, understanding that some larger matter now troubled him, she felt her personal concerns recede and settle like dust upon a summer's road.

She remembered how it was for her, all those months ago, a young woman in her brother's household, to desire so desperately a taste of the life she had read about but never thought to live. In her girlish naïveté, she had never once considered the cost of such a life. She knew now the heavy price of purpose and mystery and passion. This knowledge would help her build a bridge across to her husband.

The moment she stepped into the room, her unspoken love for Maddox arched the abyss of miscommunication between them, and when Maddox lifted his head at the rustle of her entrance, she came toward him, hand outstretched, her face open and anxious and full of concern.

He acknowledged her with a slight nod, and accepted her hand in his, briefly, then let it drop. He turned his regard back to the fireplace.

"What is in the letter, Maddox?" she asked.

For an answer, he handed her the single sheet. She ran her eye quickly down the cramped scrawl. It was dated two days before and signed from Paris. Apparently a messenger had ridden the night and day through to deliver it to Maddox's hands.

Reading it a second time, she said, with horror, "Ten English agents dead? Ten?"

"Ten," he affirmed grimly. "I knew every one of them. Every one."

"And the reports predict that the king will be imprisoned?"

"So it seems."

"But *imprisoned*? It's unheard of . . . it's . . . it's unthinkable. It's *impossible*."

He shifted his gaze back to her. "It is all those things. And it is also inevitable. The impossible will come to pass."

"But what of the constitutional monarchy?" she argued, rereading the message a third time. "France is still a monarchy, no? and a vote won't be taken until—what does it say?—September. The king's fate will not be decided until September. He is still on the throne."

"A strange throne he sits," Maddox commented. "A house arrest, more like, after his flight."

"It still remains to be decided. There is still, perhaps, something more to be done to prevent his downfall."

"Read again," Maddox recommended. "Notice how the Legislative Assembly is now composed. That is the information which those agents were dispatched to Paris to discover! That is what our government needed to know. We got the information at the price of ten men. Twenty sent. Ten return. My God! It wasn't worth it! But now we know!" he said, a little savagely. "Now we know that it's the Cordeliers who hold sway in the Assembly. It's Danton and Marat. Hungry men. Bloodthirsty men. It could not be worse."

"But with Chaumonot gone . . . ?" Marianna ventured. "Is not some of their sting gone? Is there not some hope? You were inclined to think so this morning, at the cemetery, when we discovered Chaumonot's ruse with the stocks."

"That was before I received this," he said, shaking the paper rather vehemently in his hand. He spoke to the fireplace. "No, the France we used to know is finished. Her wound is too wide, too deep, too putrid. Much blood will have to be let, and because of it, the body will die. Oh, the English are safe enough, I suppose. Our economy is safe —for the moment, and I do not predict that England will become infected with the same disease as France. At least, I have been working for some years to prevent such an eventuality!" He paused. "Yes, Chaumonot is gone, but before he died he had done enough damage for many lifetimes."

"I must be somewhat to blame for that," Marianna said anxiously.

"You, my dear?" he asked. "How so?"

"I came rather late forward with my knowledge of this man Chaumonot," she confessed. "He could have been stopped far sooner, if you and I had not been at such odds."

"All of us have come too late forward with ways to help. All of Europe saw France's needs too late, not just you. No. A few days, a few weeks would have made little difference in Chaumonot's case."

Marianna made a clean breast of it. "But I knew he buried that box next to Lord Edward's grave, oh, months ago it was! Last February in fact . . . the very day after you proposed . . . that is, the day after you were constrained to propose marriage to me."

Maddox looked up and over at her then, his expression lightening, slightly, for the first time since she had entered the library. "Ah?" he said.

"Yes! I've known about him since then! But I never had an occasion to tell you about it!"

Maddox considered this. "I wonder why it is I suddenly think," he mused aloud, "that your knowledge of Chaumonot's activities is *not* the real topic of conversation?"

"I wouldn't know," Marianna said a little coldly. "You and I have a history of speaking on different topics whenever we are together. As far as I am concerned, the topic here and now is Chaumonot, and not—as you might be thinking!—to thrash out the conditions of Lord Edward's will!" When Maddox did not immediately respond to this but merely regarded her steadily, Marianna continued, with aplomb, "I came just now as your . . . well, seeing you with the letter in your hand, knowing it to be bad news, I came to talk with you as your friend."

Maddox's expression lightened further. He let his eyes roam Marianna's very beautiful unbound hair, his too-large dressing gown, which fell in provocative folds around her curves. Then, after a leisurely scrutiny, he shook his head slightly and said, "Not friends. Never friends."

Marianna was not going to be undone by his appraisal, nor would she be diverted from her purpose. "Be that as it may for you, *I* at least came as *your* friend," she insisted, "and want to help you. To talk with you! And what I think I hear you telling me about my complicity or your complicity—or anyone else's—in the magnificent tragedy that is happening in France, is that no one individual is responsible, that the problems in France . . . or anywhere else! . . . are bigger than the individual."

Maddox reflected. "That is right," he said.

"I came to a similar conclusion myself this afternoon," she said, taking heart from his answer. "And so I would hope that you cannot be too burdened personally by your failure to stem the tide of the Revolution in France or its bloody consequences."

He looked at his wife, as if seeing her for the first time. "You are right again," he said, slowly. He looked back into the fireplace. He seemed to be hesitating, as if turning over some weighty matter in his mind. Marianna waited, expectant, hoping he would reveal himself to her. At Marlborough Park he had chosen not to talk to her. She hoped that things would be different now. That he would confide in her. Be her friend.

When he began speaking, she very slowly let out the breath she had been holding. "Do you know how the Revolution in France—or any other war or trouble that has arisen in the last hundred years!—is spoken of in the Foreign Office?" he asked. Marianna shook her head. "It is called The Game. This one is The French Game. What amounts to the most violent revolution Europe has ever seen is spoken of as The French Game, as though it were a cricket match. The officers pore over maps, sticking in pins here and there. Different colored pins, of course, meaning a variety of different things. They pore over maps devising strategies."

Now launched, Maddox turned from the fireplace and faced Marianna fully. He shook his head. "It's not a game. None of it is a game. It is not a cricket match, and it never has been a cricket match. The object of a game is to win. The object of politics—internal or external—is simply survival. Survival, and nothing more. One side need not necessarily lose—although if one side is to lose, needless to say, I prefer it to be the other! I was hoping—foolishly! —that the blood that will now surely flow through French streets could have been stopped. But I . . . we . . . all of us . . . were too late! At least I have the satisfaction of knowing that 'Change will not be ruined and that English banks will not fold overnight, bringing the English government to its knees, as the French government has been prostrated. It is a puny satisfaction—I can assure you—but I shall take it, and be happy with it!" He paused again. "No, I do not see winners and losers. I see only survivors. Any bill I introduce, any measure I advance has but one goal: survival, survival of the economy, survival of stability. To let people live. That is all. The way I see it, it is just politics and economy and stability. Keeping stable the English economy is my narrowest goal, the international economy my broadest."

Marianna had been listening closely. "And the stability of your personal economy?" she asked.

Maddox's gravity vanished at the question. "Well, now, what about my personal economy?" he countered.

She was happy to answer that. "Surely your policies do

not begin at the national level. Your economic policies begin at the personal level, do they not?"

"Now that you mention it, I must suppose that they do," he affirmed. "And I am, furthermore, confirmed in my impression that Chaumonot and the French Revolution are not the real topics of this discussion!"

"Let us just say that the personal and the political are hopelessly intertwined!" she conceded. "And, the very example of that is the fact that when I began to think about your objections to my investments on 'Change," she said, "it seemed, at first and on the surface, that they were based on the fact that I was making an inordinate amount of money from companies heavily invested in the slave trade —which, of course, is very noble of you."

"That is correct."

He smiled the smile that she found irresistible, but resist him she would. She raised a brow and asked, "But the more I thought about it, the more other objections you may have had—less noble ones!—occurred to me."

"For instance . . . ?"

"That you did not care for your wife to be making money on her own," she answered, "to be so independent of you and your power."

"We'll come back to that, but for the moment, suffice it to say that, no, I had no objection in principle to my wife making money on her own. Satisfied?"

"Not quite! I have yet to understand the whole of your economic policies."

"Does your understanding of them make a difference to you?"

"A very big difference," she said, gravely.

"Then what is it you want to know?" he asked.

"It is this: I understand how it is that you are against the slave trade," she said. "It is simply and plainly immoral. But what I do not understand are your half-measures."

"My half-measures?"

"Yes! Your basic premise, as I take it, is that you want

to restructure one part of the economy—the slave trade—
so as to avoid doing another person harm, so that we may
all survive. But does it not occur to you that we could
easily restructure a larger part of the economy, and spread
the wealth around a little better? Slaves are not the only
people suffering in this world, only the most obvious ones!
Some have so much, while others—not just slaves!—have
so little. Is there not a better way of equably sharing the
wealth?"

"Ah! A revolutionary in my very household!" Maddox
commented. "Of course, such a scheme is possible. The
unequal distribution of wealth is precisely what the blood-
shed in France is about."

"Let us forget about France for the moment," she said.
"It's your *personal* economics that I am interested in. You
are wealthy. Others are not. Should not your wealth be
better distributed?"

"You mean for me to give my property away?" he
asked. "To whom?"

"I don't know!—the needy!" she replied.

"What's mine is mine," he answered.

"Is that not a paradox?"

"Not quite," he said. "We still need rulers. Informed
rulers and committed rulers. I could not do what I do if I
did not have the wealth behind me."

"That sounds very much like that old play on the golden
rule: those with the gold rule!" Marianna exclaimed.

"We have to have rulers, Marianna. Let us hope that
they have a measure of humanity," he said. Then he
laughed, a laugh directed inward at himself. "I have my
share, I suppose, but my humanity is not so great as to
wish to give my wealth away. I stand behind economic
reform. Not revolution." His eyes were warm as they
rested on his wife. "I'll grant you this, though: you have
easily found the holes in the very basis of my arguments!"

"Then you agree with my point, then, that your policies,

as right-thinking as they are, are bolstered by self-serving motives designed to keep your personal wealth?"

"Yes," he answered.

"So in the final analysis, are you first and foremost concerned with your own personal survival," she asked, "with keeping what is yours, what is your property?"

"Yes."

"And am I a part of your property?" she asked.

Maddox smiled. "I am against the slave trade, remember? I hold that people cannot own other people as their property," he answered. "But I hope that, in some sense, you do belong to me."

"Well, then, does that mean I am free to invest on 'Change," she asked directly, "as long as I respect your policies for economic reform?"

"You may invest your entire allowance, every quarter, and make—or lose—a fortune, as long as you respect my policies," he conceded magnanimously. "Do you still wish to invest?"

She laughed, a little. "I don't know! It seems that my motives for investing—which, in the end, were as ignoble as yours for stopping me!—don't exist anymore! I shall have to determine how independent I wish to be of your purse strings!"

"Ah, yes, our marriage of independence," he said, reminiscently. "*That* seems a long time ago . . . and firmly over, I should think."

"Yes, it does seem a long time ago," Marianna agreed, looking up at him, "but not, I hope, *entirely* over!"

"No?"

"No, I mean that I . . . I actually *learned* something from Susannah . . . by negative example, if you will! She had a marriage of complete dependence. She was so completely dependent on her husband, so completely, *unhealthily* dependent on him, that it has made me see that I . . . I can't risk putting my entire happiness into your hands."

"And I couldn't accept that responsibility."

"I'm not asking you to! It's rather my own responsibility, really. My own! Mine, and not yours! And that is precisely my point! It . . . it's so hard to say, but I do *want* to stay independent of you! I don't want to lose myself!"

He was looking down at her, a smile in his eyes. "Perhaps greater harmony is possible when two people maintain a certain independence one from the other. If a relationship is based on independence, then there's no danger of one or the other getting lost." He paused. On an inspired note, he uncharacteristically aphorized: "The osmosis of independence is really the secret of love."

Marianna's smile was in her eyes, too. "Are you saying you love me?"

Maddox nodded. "Independence has its limits." He drew her to him. "We are, after all, alone in this world. And the greatest luxury two human beings can have is to be alone together."

"When you say things like that, I must admit that I do not have the least wish to stay independent of you—despite all that I have just said!"

"I am glad."

"Can we cry friends, then, at last?" she asked, pulling away from him and holding out her hand in this gesture of friendship.

Maddox shook his head. "I repeat: not friends. Never friends."

Instead of taking her hand, he kissed her, once, and certainly not as a friend. After the kiss, Marianna relaxed against his chest and let his words and actions sink in. Then she smiled. It was a smile of wry self-knowledge. Lifting her hands to take her love's unhandsome and very dear face in her long white fingers, she looked straight into his eyes.

"*Bella figura*," she said.

He raised his brows. "My dear?"

"Beautiful face," she translated. "The opposite of *brutta figura*—which epithet I had occasion to apply to myself just recently! But when I look at you, I am not looking in a mirror. I do not see myself. I see you: a *bella figura*." She paused, her smile broadening. "And all I can say at this moment—to quote yourself on an interesting occasion—is that 'Uncle Edward had his moments.'"

"I said that?"

"In the gardens, at Marlborough Park," she reminded him. "You've forgotten it? Evidently your thoughts were elsewhere. Yes, I see that you remember now!"

"I do. And about Uncle Edward. . . ." Maddox began.

"Yes?"

"Your final assessment?"

Marianna placed her hands on Maddox's broad shoulders. "He was my friend," she said. "He gave me a choice, and I made it. He gave you one, too, and you made it. Our task was to live with the consequences of our choices. It's difficult to say in all honesty that Lord Edward *constrained* us, but perhaps you feel differently . . . ?"

"A long-headed gentleman, my uncle," was what Maddox said.

"Very long-headed," Marianna acknowledged, "but I am not sure that even he knew how the end would be."

Marianna looked into Maddox's face, which had gone quiet while a light shone in his eyes that were able to read her own. Marianna returned his gaze. Her love for Maddox was not the wrenching, suffocating love that Susannah had for Jean, nor the violent, destructive love of Jean for Susannah. Neither was it the wonderful friendship that Marianna had known for Lord Edward. Maddox might never come to know Marianna in the way that Lord Edward had known her, nor was that important to her anymore. Maddox knew her differently from any other human being on earth, just as her knowledge of him set her apart from all else.

No, the end was not predictable from the beginning. In the rapt silence of the library could be heard the throb and pulse of the crickets in the lush green surrounding Maddox

Hall. When Marianna reached her face up to receive Maddox's kiss, somewhere in the back of her mind hovered the unresolved questions on the fate of King Louis of France. Where would Louis of France be when the thick, green leaves on the walnut trees had burnished and fallen as summer surrendered to autumn? Would he be in prison when the damp, earthy scent of October was strong after the fresh fullness of July? Would he still be alive when the morning frost gave way to the sun as it glowed palely over the hedgerows, making polished beads of the rosehips and spotting the rowan trees with berries like lime lights on a filigreed backdrop?

She did not ask these questions, for she knew that neither Maddox, nor anyone else, had the answers. Instead, she accepted the unanswerable, the unpredictable as a part of her life. Her love, now complete, embraced the whole of existence. The unknowns that awaited Louis and his country; the understanding of Susannah's darkness, the winter of her love, her anguish; the vivid scene in the misty morning in the cemetery when Marianna had looked down a barrel of cold steel into the face of certain death; the image of the mossed and crumbling tombstones around her that should have been grim reminders of the fate that awaits all mortals, even ones as lively and voluble as Eliza Parrish; the acknowledgment of Maddox's deep sense of failure and regret that he was unable to halt the destructive forces of chaos on shores that lay uncomfortably close to home: these memories and more, Marianna would always associate with summer and her happiness.

The End